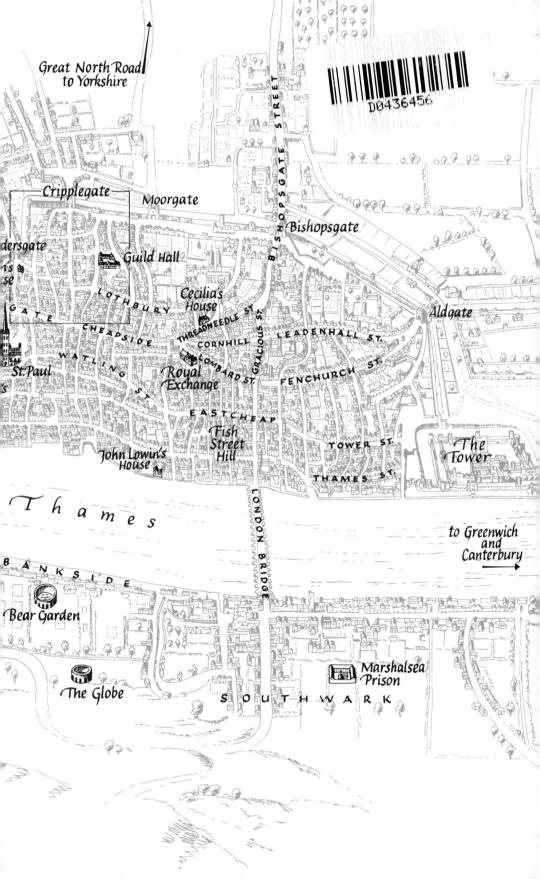

Great North Road
to Yorkshire

D0436456

Cripplegate — Moorgate

...dersgate

...se

GATE

Guild Hall

Bishopsgate

Aldgate

LOTHBURY

Cecilia's House

CHEAPSIDE

THREADNEEDLE ST.

CORNHILL

LEADENHALL ST.

BISHOPSGATE STREET

GRACIOUS ST.

St. Paul

WATLING ST.

Royal Exchange

LOMBARD ST.

FENCHURCH ST.

EASTCHEAP

Fish Street Hill

John Lowin's House

TOWER ST.

The Tower

THAMES ST.

Thames

to Greenwich and Canterbury

BANKSIDE

Bear Garden

The Globe

Marshalsea Prison

SOUTHWARK

THE
PHYSICIAN
OF
LONDON

ALSO BY STEPHANIE COWELL

Nicholas Cooke

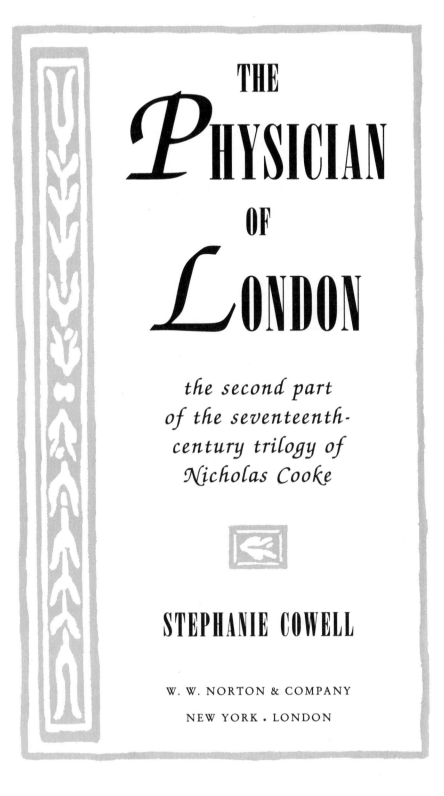

THE
PHYSICIAN
OF
LONDON

*the second part
of the seventeenth-
century trilogy of
Nicholas Cooke*

STEPHANIE COWELL

W. W. NORTON & COMPANY

NEW YORK · LONDON

First Edition

The text of this book is composed in Garamond Stemple,
with the display set in Onyx and Zapf Chancery.
Composition and manufacturing by the Haddon Craftsmen, Inc.

Library of Congress Cataloging-in-Publication Data
Cowell, Stephanie.
The physician of London : the second part of the seventeenth-century trilogy of Nicholas Cooke / by
Stephanie Cowell.
p. cm.
1. Great Britain—History—Early Stuarts, 1603–1649—Fiction.
2. London (England)—History—17th century—Fiction.   I. Title.
PS3553.0898P48   1995
813'.54—dc20   95-5597
ISBN 0-393-03873-4

W.W. Norton & Company, Inc., 500 Fifth Avenue, New York, N.Y. 10110
W.W. Norton & Company Ltd., 10 Coptic Street, London WC1A 1PU

1 2 3 4 5 6 7 8 9 0

*to my writers' group
and Russell
with love*

Also I heard the voice of the Lord, saying,
Whom shall I send, and who will go for us?
Then said I, Here am I; send me.

—*Isaiah 6:8*

THE
PHYSICIAN
OF
LONDON

Prologue
1641

H E WAS TO DIE THAT DAY.

All the spring night the physician could hear the sound of people walking through the cobbled streets towards the Tower. They had not woken him, for he never slept at all, but watched the flicker of their torches through the closed shutters of his house near the city gate, and heard the muttering and laughing through his wall. At five in the morn he could wait no longer, but dressed rapidly, buckled on his sword, and threw open his doors.

Still came the shadows of men in Sunday clothes and women in best lace caps, hurrying arm in arm towards the direction of river and Tower through the overhanging half-timbered houses down Aldermanbury Street. They moved as if fearing to be late for a long-made appointment, clutching baskets of bottled ale and meat. Their faces were greedy.

Drawing up his hood, he fell in beside them.

The streets were ever yet more crowded, the sudden laughter as troubling. Strangely warm was the end of the night with all the torches burning, and the closeness of strangers beside him, and as far ahead and to the west as he could see. Above them the stars were beginning to fade, and as they came closer to Tower Hill he noticed the faint rosy light of day rising beyond the ancient buildings as it had each morning since the beginning of time. More and more did the crowd jostle, though lanterns were slowly extinguished.

Then they'll really kill him at last? someone asked.

Yes, King signed the papers.

They said he'd never sign.

He was sworn against it, but he did.

They did not know; they could not. This thing, of course, at the last moment would not be done. Surely his Majesty would forbid it no matter what his agreement; surely friends would come with fifty horse to burst through the crowd and rescue him. What of the ships his faithful secretary had anchored at Tower Wharf? What of his wealthy tenants? These thoughts rushed through the physician's mind with such intensity that he hardly knew which streets they went or how well each was known to him.

Thus they came to Tower Hill.

All last evening and through the night the workmen had hammered nails to erect the wooden stands on which the more fortunate of the people would find a place and a good view. He looked about. A hundred thousand men had come to see Tom Wentworth die. They had walked from every ward in the city and many of the surrounding villages, carrying their dinners wrapped in cloth; they pressed against each other until the women cried out and the men threatened and the children began to weep. Bakers had left their shops in charge of their apprentices, and those young men in turn abandoned their ovens and came too with hats shoved down on their foreheads, hoping not to be recognized. Taverns around the city would empty that day and the booksellers at St. Paul's doze with folded arms from behind their stalls. Only the printers would be working, pulling ballad sheet after ballad sheet wet with ink and hanging them to dry, making a moral warning in fifteen small printed verses of the death of the black traitor. "O mortal man, beware, if so ye fall in sin. . . ."

What were these crowds, as far down the hill as one could see, chattering and blaming and spitting and scratching? What had this squire of West Riding who had served the King, and risen in that service, done to them? He had never done the common man a wrong: he had protected them from those who would drain their fens, or rob their land. Then why did they hate him? Ah, but men must hate something, as his friend Harvey once said. They have no name to put to their ills, their aching teeth or business failures or wives who no longer love them, or babes who sicken pitifully. They scratch against inflation, and when the ordinary thief is whipped at the cart's tail, they lick their lips and rejoice, for thus is represented all that ails them. The same with Tom Wentworth. To point fingers greasy with dinner eaten while standing discussing the merits of his life, they can feel the heart beat, hear the drum sound, hear (if they are lucky) the last words of the condemned above the shivering crowd: one bloodied back, one head struck off, and something has been punished. Does it matter what? Do they know its name?

And why had he the sensibility to know this, to despise, with curled upper lip, their witlessness, to have cuffed any number of them to their knees had he allowed his fury to show, and yet, in his work as priest and physician, to make them tonics for bad stomachs and, holding their newborn babes in his arms, baptize them? Tom Wentworth would not hold his babes again. And here was this vast panorama of man to man in a world ever expanding from a small, bluff, rough, rich country of wheat, woods, and hills, of cathedral, university, and palace, sweeping towards a future that no one could comprehend. Cut off one dark head and buy for a penny a ballad about it, to sing it by rushwick and go to bed contented that justice had been done.

His eyes burned with tears, nor did he know it until he saw a small child in her father's arms look curiously at him. Hours passed. He had found a spot on stands wedged against one of the walls. Before and about him stood thousands, yet so tightly pressed was he that he could not break away, even if he had wished it. The sun had risen almost to over the heads of the crowd when they brought Tom Wentworth from the Tower.

They said the imprisoned Archbishop of Canterbury, his close-fitting cap covering the grey hair, had looked out from the window above the path which the prisoner was made to walk. Wentworth stopped to kneel on the stones for the blessing, and the Archbishop had reached out both trembling hands towards him. Then the old man fainted. This he was told, for he was not near when his friend marched more, as they said, like a general at the head of an army than a man to his death. It was far away over the heads of the crowds when the physician Nicholas saw him at last, but knew his step as he mounted up to the scaffold.

Near him, one wood stand collapsed, the children fell under it, and the women were sobbing. They heard nothing of his words, which commended his love to the King. Nicholas saw him place his hands in those of his chaplain. "My body is theirs," he had written, "but my soul is God's."

And still Nicholas turned his face one more time towards the west and the palace of Whitehall, and the emissaries from Parliament which must surely come by boat with the recantation, and the joyful news that the Yorkshireman would live.

THE

FIRST
PART
1617–1619

ONE

The Young Priest

SLIGHTLY ABOVE ST. PAUL'S NEAR THE STONE ENTRANCE OF THE CITY called Cripplegate, in the year of Our Lord 1617, was a half-timbered house. It lay below the fields and farmlands which encircled the city in the parish of St. Mary Aldermanbury, whose streets wound down to the river Thames.

London at that time was already an ancient, crowded town of one hundred and fifty thousand people. Daily from the country came men in search of work: they found dwellings in the twisting lanes hung with washing, scattered with flowers, and threaded with leaking sewage until the very city walls, which had first been raised by the Romans, seemed to want to thrust into the fields and pastures beyond for want of space. In this particular fragment of the city and in this house lived a physician called Nicholas Cooke. He was also priest, but that so recent that if anyone called him parson he could not help but look about to see if it were addressed to anyone other than himself.

Upon waking at six that January day, he did not rise at once but lay still half in dreams in the crooked three-story dwelling whose walls smelled of wood smoke, listening to the bells die away, and the banging of the washtub as the housekeeper, Joan, began her work in the kitchen below. He could hear his sexton's boots crunch across the hard earth of the graveyard and the door creak as he opened it; the old man would be half unbuttoned, bandy-kneed, rubbing his horny hands and looking for his morning beer.

Still, the physician was not inclined to rise, for cold had seeped down the chimney and under the leading of windows, and he suspected the water in the washbasin had turned to ice. Dark green bed curtains half obscured the room, allowing him to glimpse the plain furnishings which stood upon the warping floorboards, and the wooden pegs from which hung his two cassocks, and one worn dress suit of breeches and doublet. He could see the edge of the great clothespress which had belonged to the priests who had lived here for hundreds of years before he had come.

Some bells still rang out from other parishes, but they were dull, as if unable to shake the damp from their aged ropes. Over them came the sound of a horse's hooves on the cobbles of the lane. Nicholas reached for his dressing gown. He made his way down the stair to his dispensary, where brown bottles and earthen clay jars lined the walls, and when he looked through the window, he saw that the water carriers had already splashed frosty silver drops between the cobbles.

In the kitchen, sexton John had warmed a mug of ale for him in the ashes. "Cold morn, master!" the old fellow muttered, touching his cap. "Bess of the almshouse by the wall was here yet before to see ye. There'll be some pestilence or other about. I can tell it from the way the cat cried last night round Aldermanbury."

Nicholas gazed about at the barrels of pickled eels, flour, and small beer and at the herbs which hung drying from the smoke-blackened rafters as he took the mug and felt with pleasure both the warmth of the drink and the fire's heat creeping under his gown. As he was breaking bread, his housekeeper came in with her purchases from the market in her apron. She was a fleshy woman of middle years who wore her heavy hair chastely pinned under a white cap, and her upper lip was raised perpetually as if she mistrusted the world. "God's grace, parson!" she muttered stingily. "God's grace, and I bought cracked eggs to save the farthing!"

In his chamber again, Nicholas dressed in his lesser black doublet and breeches, and stood by the wardrobe for a time to dip his pen into the inkwell and make lists of both the herbs he needed to buy that day on Gracious Street and the medicines he had promised to deliver. Then he hurried down again through kitchen and churchyard. The church door was unlocked, and he closed it behind him.

In this moment he was alone with God. Behind the pulpit, about the altar, in the very air, he felt that presence. Without moving, he began the words with which he always opened his service of morning prayer: "O send out thy light and thy truth, that they may lead me, and bring me unto thy holy hill, and to thy dwelling." Then he knelt.

St. Mary Aldermanbury, which rose above him and around him in its old rounded Roman way, had been founded some three hundred years before. He knew its every corner and crack. Stained-glass windows intersected the stone walls, depicting Christ fishing with His apostles and an unkempt, bearded Abraham hesitating over the sacrifice of his son, Isaac. Memorial slabs paved the nave under which slept the dead from the reigns of former kings, and the altar was placed before a fading fresco of the Resurrection. He knew these as well; he knew water leaks, and the worn letters of the stones.

To this holy building he had come as priest but the year before, having walked unsteadily towards that vocation all his life. Since that time he had struggled through first his sermons and breaking of the bread and the repetitive leaving of his bed three or four times a night to hurry through kitchen and graveyard to make certain the church had not melted into the dream that once it had been. For one year now he had been baptizer of infants, joiner of young couples in matrimony, teacher of psalms and creeds to the young, and peacemaker and negotiator for the small parish boundaries from Cheapside to the wall.

After he read the psalms for the day, he remained on his knees for some time with his hands covering his face, allowing his prayers to fall away into no particular matter and his thoughts to drift. His attempts to bring his small parish of some five hundred souls to God and keep them there perplexed him. Last night a young man had come past midnight and wept, "I have spent my wages on cockfighting and have nothing to give my children!" The young man cried, and Nicholas consoled him. Then he demanded money, and Nicholas had none, and the supplicant went away angry and muttering. But was that not human nature? With a sigh, Nicholas rose from his knees and went towards his patients and his work.

It was at eleven o'clock when he was returning down the wide medieval market street of Cheapside from the last of his morning visits that he heard his name shouted above the cartwheels. His churchwarden, John Heminges, a bluff, broadly built old theater man of some five and sixty years, was emerging from the carpenter's shop across the way. Carriages and carts of beef rumbled between them, followed by the twice-weekly coach from York.

"Nick," said the old man when he had reached him. "Wilt come and dine? I have something to ask of thee."

John Heminges, recently widowed, lived as he had always done on the corner of Wood Street with several of his children and an apprentice or two. He was a founding member of the King's Men and one of the original shareholders of the Globe Theater. Still the director of that theater troupe, he was known throughout London as the much-beloved dean of the actors, for there was not a dispute he could not solve: a difference between playwright and actor, costume maker and stage-keeper, or the company and the Office of the Revels which licensed their work.

A few actors were folding costumes in Heminges's kitchen as the old man and the physician came through the door. Toys were scattered beneath the benches, and piles of petticoats and musical instruments lay about the corners nears the barrels of flour and herring. Tacked here and there on the walls were playbills and costume sheets. Upon the trestle table lay several leather portfolios and a small pile of unbound sixpence quartos of the plays of the late William Shagspere.

John Heminges laid his broad hand on the physician's shoulder. He said, "As we discussed last year, dear Nick, I want to gather Will's plays, and here are all I've found to this moment! If we don't do this soon, many will be lost, for some weren't printed at all, and most that were are fraught with errors. Every actor in London must be asked to search his old chests for his parts, and letters must be sent round the country to those retired. I hope to print the plays in one great book, if we can afford the price. Wilt stop at the Globe this day if goest that way, Nick, and look into the boxes in the high shelves of the tiring room and mayhap in the trunks?"

Then, squeezing the younger man's arm, he added thoughtfully, "Dost miss his company as I do?"

Nicholas nodded. The quiet, enigmatic Shagspere, whose death had occurred the year before, had been his oldest friend since the days when the actors were just forming into a troupe. The writer had been known about the town in those years as a provincial fellow of some originality who reworked the old tragedies, a stiff but reliable actor, and a most stout friend.

Ship's flags from the great boats to the Indies glittered near the twenty arches of squared stone of London Bridge. On the south side, Nicholas passed the Bridgehouse, which stored timber and stone for repairing the aged structure, as well as breweries, bake ovens for the poor, and many shops supplying the industry of small boats which ferried the Thames at a penny a crossing.

Turning west, he walked over the blowing leaves in the lane past St. Mary Overy towards the weather-stained polygonal theater called the Globe, which was the second of its name, the first having burned down some years before when the thatch roof broke into flames at the careless firing of a cannon during a performance of *Harry Eighth*. Several players were staging a fight scene from one of the old histories. Nicholas mounted to the second gallery to watch the rehearsal, gathering from the floor orange peel and nutshells which yesterday's audience had discarded.

After a time, he climbed down to look for the playscripts behind the stage amid the dust of boxes of wigs needing curling, blunted swords, and prop crowns. There he found several packets of paper, and put them under his arm to study later. As he left he looked back once more at the banner flying in the wind. Most of the audience for the two-o'clock play had arrived; he heard the trumpets sound and the laughter which always greeted the clowns.

The theater had first been built in the last great years of Elizabeth the Queen. She had lain within her tomb now these fourteen years, yet her golden age lingered like the sun through the trees and across the Thames on late summer afternoons. Years before his own birth, she had ridden to her coronation, a young lass with red hair loose to her waist. From this she had evolved into the wise, crafty counselor who spoke several languages, played the virginals, danced, sang, and was the wittiest statesman in the Christian world. A virgin she stayed until it withered her, yet bore her crumpled breasts proudly and accepted homages to her beauty until at last she grew old, a lady surprised by time.

He paused on the bridge once more in going home, packet under his arm and the satchel of medicines on his shoulder. This city was much as Elizabeth had left it, and should never change: steeples, marketplaces, ancient river, bishops gently bickering in convocation, the houses blackened from coal smoke, cesspits and fountains, and riverboats.

And in the midst of this, himself, a curious, gentle physician who loved it all in a way that he sometimes felt he could not bear, so intensely did it come. He remembered the days of 1592 when, as a boy of thirteen years, he had first approached the city, nearly dead from hunger and fear and unwanted adventure, to tumble into the arms of the little theater troupe as an apprentice under Heminges. He had left only because he knew he must. He would never have done it otherwise. With these thoughts, he walked home more reflectively through the cold day with the packet of his friend Shagspere's incomplete playscripts under his arm.

TWO

By the Thames in Winter

NICHOLAS COOKE WAS AT THAT TIME IN HIS THIRTY-SEVENTH YEAR, A well-built, fine-looking, and tender man somewhere above six feet who moved lightly, shoulders slightly rounded, and with a sense of fierce shyness, as if he would cover his face with his arm if looked at too deeply. He wore a short beard, which he trimmed occasionally, and his thick brown hair, which curled slightly some inches below his ears, was tinged with grey. His eyes were large and brown. He was regarded by the older physicians of the city as rash and presumptuous, for though he was but three years a doctor, he would not keep his peculiar ideas to himself. Still, they could not help but admit he was strangely wise.

It was not odd that a man should be both physician and priest, for both professions had, since the earliest times, been closely related, but that this particular man should now take holy orders bewildered many who had known his wild youth. They shook their heads and said it would not last. Nicholas had, as one of the beloved old actors of his childhood used to say, no sense of moderation.

On a winter's day some weeks after he had begun to compile Shagspere's plays, a boy brought a letter to the dispensary from his close friend the bookbinder Tim Keyes. An eclipse of the moon had been predicted that night, and the bookbinder asked if Nicholas would take a bachelor's supper with him, and the actors John Lowin and Andrew Heminges, and then walk to Long Acre to watch it. And so when his patients had departed for the day, Nicholas set off towards the City of Westminster, where Keyes had his shop. He brought also with him a packet of medicine for one of the barristers whom he expected to find in Westminster Hall.

Behind him the spires of the churches of Cripplegate Ward disappeared into the thick, dirty air, as did the houses which lined the streets. Hoping to ferry towards Westminster, he made his way to the river, covering his mouth with one arm and holding the lantern aloft with the other. Nothing could he see from the wharf: not the great London Bridge, nor the shapes of shops and chapels which stood upon it, nor more than the closest of the masts of the many ships at anchor. Strangers, muffled to the hair, passed him with their yellow lantern light, and from the east he could hear the icy, deep, white water slamming against the bridge's foundations and the sound of a drum from the south side, guiding boats to safety. He should have to walk.

Yet even as he turned west, the wind began to rise. Mounting the hill and crossing the river by Fleet Bridge out of Ludgate, he bent his head into it. Temple Inn he left behind, then the palaces and mansions of the city set behind vast walls, gardens, and orchards: the sumptuous dwellings of the earls Essex, Southampton, Arundel, and Somerset, great lords of the land. Far northwest lay St. Giles in the Fields, where he often found herbs in the spring and summer.

Dry leaves whipped about the base of Charing Cross as he rushed past the park towards the river and then down the back streets to Westminster Hall. The afternoon session of court had just ended; the great doors were thrown open and the last of the participants were hurrying through them. About them rushed papers wrested from postings, and pages from old books. Plaintiffs, defendants, stewards, barristers, and clerks, tips of swords glittering, blew around the corners of Westminster Hall, to what lodgings and carriages they owned. The hall, when he looked within, was empty but for the stewards banging their brooms against the benches and the shoulder-high temporary wood partitions which made so many smaller courts in which cases could be argued.

This ancient place, the abbey, and the two other great halls where the Lords and Commons met when in session were almost all that remained of the once sprawling Westminster Palace. Parliament, however, had not met for three years. Now two stewards moved about the hall to douse the torches, while a thin, hungry-looking lad put out the smaller candles in the little carrels.

Nicholas turned from the river towards Whitehall Palace. A man could lose himself easily in this rabbit warren of streets, chapels, shops, washerwomen, courtiers, bakers, scribes, foreigners, priests, supplicants, and ragmen which surrounded the two-thousand-room royal residence. It all lay in shadows, for the last of the afternoon light was almost gone. Driven by the wind, he turned to the alley where hung the sign of the bookbinder Timothy Keyes.

Keyes was such a great fellow that it seemed he must have been stretched by two angels. For all that, he weighed little, and was said by his friends to be composed of bones not thick enough to make a hearty winter soup. Married with innumerable children, he was a bookbinder because he would not live without the feel of paper and leather in his large hands. Nicholas had been no more than a boy himself when they had met, both apprentices. They had been fast friends since.

"Pah, this foul air!" cried Keyes in his hoarse, loud voice, feeling for the tools in his apron pockets and pushing back the spectacles on his large nose. "The law forbids burning cheap coal, but who heeds it? God's greetings, thou louse of a parson. Say nothing holy, for I love this life too much to concern myself with the next! Supper shall be laid on my shop table as soon as I have cleared away, and 'tis the best pork pie and great cheese the ordinary hath to send us." With that he threw more coal into the brazier, rolled up the leather, and began to clear his counters.

Nicholas picked up a few books. "What hast here?" he said. "Philosophy, astronomy, history? What hast to sell for eightpence, which is my fortune, having given my housekeeper the last of my purse for eggs, and those cracked? I have eightpence to buy me a library and a whole world of knowledge I must gain!"

The tavern boy had come with the supper in covered dishes and two large bottles of sack in his apron pockets. Nicholas cut bread at once, put up his feet on a crate, and began to read while Tim raised the shop shutters for the night. "I've pretty news of the court!" he called. "Living so close as I do, it seepeth through the privy walls. His Majesty hath poured more honors on his favorite, George Villiers, and hath this day made him Marquis of Buckingham!"

"All kings have favorites."

"He drowns him in riches and the court's in debt."

"And so am I, and thou as well, and all but for the gentry who go in fine silks and lace! Wilt scold me for my poverty again? Marry, I shall throw thee in the sewage heap back of this dwelling." Nicholas stretched forth his hand for the lute, which lacked the upper string, and as he brought it to tune, the palace momentarily returned to his mind. Somewhere within those two thousand rooms so close was the King, James Stuart, the portly Scotsman who had inherited the English throne some fourteen years before. Foolish ofttimes he was said to be, diversely sexual, trying to wear cloth that was not cut to fit his ample-stomached body, fond of masques and plays, a staunch believer in witches and as staunch an enemy of tobacco. He ruled over an untidy, affectionate, unspectacular court; Nicholas felt his best contribution to his kingdom had been the publication of an English version of the Bible translated by some of the greatest churchmen of the land. Though King, he was also a scholar, as was his son Charles said to be.

These thoughts passed with the first strains from the lute. "Something Pythagoras said about divine harmony," he murmured thoughtfully, "that the intervals in music must be regulated between pitches." He began to sing.

"Oh mistress mine, where are you roaming?
Oh stay and hear your true love's coming
That can sing both high and low!

Trip no further, pretty sweeting,
Journey's end in lovers' meeting
Every wise man's son doth know.

"But was it Pythagoras? Kepler is to this day trying to represent plane-
tary motion by musical octaves. Dost know he hath discovered that the
orbit of Mars departs eight degrees from a perfect circle, making it an
ellipse, Tim? Hast read of the determination of the eccentricity? No more
of that, by faith! Where the devil can John Lowin and young Andrew be
keeping? 'Tis almost dark and the sky will clear for the eclipse."

"It wants two hours until then, hast made the estimate thyself," was
the bookbinder's patient answer. "And the wind's bad, but the sky's a
dark muddle, Nick. I'll wager we'll not see the moon tonight."

"Halfpenny takes it."

"Go to, Nick!" he said. Again the physician began to sing in his low,
soft way until they heard voices down the alley and John Lowin, a great,
bulky, bluff-spoken player some years past forty who seemed to take up
much of the room, came in. At his heels was John Heminges's fifteen-
year-old son, Andrew, whose wild curly hair, freckles, and good nature
made him a favorite of the younger players. He was a slight, delicately
built boy and charming both as clowns and young girls, though just this
Christmastide his sweet singing voice had broken at last. Not weeks after
that, complaint had been brought of him before the sheriffs for his lewd
comments to a merchant's wife, and he had quarreled bitterly with his
father over it.

"Never were any more clumsy than the ladies who danced this night,"
he said critically as a man who knows his craft. With this they drew crates
to the table and sat to eat.

"A fart on it, but we could not come earlier!" said John Lowin between
mouthfuls. "Knowst we were hired for the masque tomorrow to be given

at Whitehall before their Majesties and richly paid for by the Tailors' Company. Lord Buckingham dances as Apollo! Best legs in the court, 'tis said, but for my wife's taste they're too thin. Shouldst have stayed a player, Nick! No one had thy legs!"

Keyes said, "Nick was called by God."

"Voice on the wind, mayhap."

"Plague take thee both!" murmured the physician sternly. "The moon shan't wait us. Take the sack and sugar in thy pack, Tim, and let's to Long Acre! Thou too, pisspot, lend thy hand!"

"An hour and a half yet remains by thy reckoning!" replied Lowin stoically. "And by my troth, 'tis too cold for the fields. Come to my house by the water, and my sweet wife will bring us hot ale, though we'll not see enough light of the moon as a maid could piss out."

It was decided then that they should go to the waterside house on the north bank, and so they threw the food in a sack and Nicholas took the lute over his shoulder, and they made their way to the Strand, the lantern light glittering on the cobbles before them. Through the gate they went, Nicholas thinking of the varying elliptical wedges which could be drawn between the sun and a planet at different points of its orbit. Yet by the time they felt their way down the wet cobbles of the alley towards Lowin's waterside house, he began to concede Tim Keyes was right and they would see no eclipse tonight.

The houses here were left from the crowded merchants' city of the fourteenth century when the guilds first were strong. Lowin's, which had come to him from his grandfather, had belonged to a convent before the closing of the monasteries and was dark, damp, and flooded when the water was high. Before it was a small dock with steps going down to the water, for which some fisherman paid him rent.

Voices were heard from the other houses, and from time to time Lowin's children came out to sit with them. His maidservant and apprentice brought hot bricks for their feet, and as the wind quieted they uncorked the sack and passed the bottle between them. The heavens did not clear, and they began pleasantly to be somewhat drunk.

"Give us a song, Nick!" young Andrew said affectionately. Nicholas took off his gloves, felt for the lute, and brought it to tune. The boy joined his voice to the melody.

"Singst love songs, young one?" barked Lowin. "Thou shalt have a beating for thy bad ways from thy dad before the month's out, mark my word! Ah, a fart upon it! We shall not a star see this night, much less a moon."

From the distance above the sound of the splashing of the water came the faint sound of other music. Nicholas stood and, balancing against the wall, walked to the edge of the steps before the dark, tumbling river. By the faint light of houses on the bridge and down the waterside he could but make out the shapes of boats anchored in the river, and the smaller ones clustered upon the shore. A barge was moving towards them, lanterns glistening, and through the night rose the sound of a small band.

Young Andrew leapt up, peering out over the Thames.

"By the Rood!" cried Lowin. " 'Tis the royal barge, and by Christ's nails if it does not carry the gentleman ushers from the masque! King's gone to sleep in his nightcap, and his courtiers, pisspot drunk, have taken his barge to make merry with this night! And here they will be, still dressed as gods and nymphs and satyrs, I warrant!"

Icy water lapped to the edges of the men's shoes as they watched the glittering vessel approach and listened to the sound of music and laughter rising to the night. Closer it came with its costumed passengers. The lords cavorted on the gilded, decorated barge deck, two or three seizing one of the young ladies and lifting her round so her skirts flew out about her. A few played recorders. Then over the waters came the voice of the captain, crying anxiously, "My lords, my lords, we are almost to the bridge, and we must turn the barge. It's wanted to bring the Parisian ambassador up from Gravesend in the morning, and I dare not risk the fall of the waters under the bridge!" The words echoed from the water to the stone of the little house and back again. "My lords . . . good my lords . . . list to me . . ."

The Queen's ladies laughed and ran to the railing to wave at the little houses, and then came the shout of the lords saying, "Turn the barge! Turn her, captain! Go towards Windsor or anywhere there. It doesn't matter, only let us have sugared wine and more music. Sing, Lucius!"

From across the rocking water came the first chords of the lute and the melody and words of the Tom Campion song which Nicholas knew so well:

> "Shall I come, sweet love, to thee
> When the evening beams are set?
> Shall I not excluded be,
> Will you find no feigned let?
> Let me not for pity more
> Tell the long, long hours,
> Tell the long hours at your door!"

Slowly the great barge turned, and a cheer rose into the night. "God save the King!" came the cry, and impulsively throwing back his head, Nicholas cupped his mouth with his hands and cried as well, "God save thee, Majesty!" The words flung themselves out into the cold night.

"Nick, he's never there but long abed," said John Lowin.

Flushed with sudden emotion, Nicholas answered, "Nevertheless ... I have a right to say, *God save him!*"

"Amen then, good parson!" The men stood together at the wharf's edge listening to the creaking of boats and the song and the laughter as they faded away. Nicholas yawned and, stretching his head back, saw the night was perfectly clear, and that Our Lord had thrown handfuls of stars across the sky. There was the moon, uncovered, no longer eclipsed. And yet it did not matter.

Tim Keyes picked up the empty bottles. "Would we could meet often in such sweet fellowship! What's man made for but the fellowship of others? There's little sweeter in the earth but love of women, and that's much of the same. Would thou didst not go home alone, parson."

"Leave off."

"Thy pardon, I am drunk. Good night, sweet parson."

"And you, my friends. Art to Westminster, Tim?"

"Aye, as the wind bloweth us."

"Thee, Lowin?"

"To bed within: wife calls me: thou knowst Nell."

"I wish thee joy of her."

"And thee, Nick?"

"I shall sit here a time and then deliver this lad to his house."

"Good night, parson doctor."

"And thee, and anon."

For what seemed like a long time, Nicholas and the boy actor re-mained listening to the quiet sound of the water, and from the rooms above the rough whispers, and then silence there too. Christ's wounds, how cold had come the hour, though the wind had died away! It crept under his wool vest and hose and seemed to turn him to stone as was this wharf. With a sudden gesture he threw away the bottle in the river, where it clanked once against the steps and was gone, and mounted the winding streets towards his house, Andrew following unsteadily and singing under his breath.

Snow came the next day.

It began late in the afternoon when the evensong bells had begun to ring out across the tile and thatch roofs of the city. It fell on steeple and stall and gathered about the bottoms of horseposts and the house tim-bers. Hurrying home from his visit to some fishermen's children, Nicho-las stopped several times to raise his face to sky. He found the house empty, for housekeeper Joan was yet at market and the sexton gone he knew not where. In all the rooms from cellar to attic there was no one but himself.

For a time he searched through a cupboard for the part sheets from Shagspere's plays, finding bits of Hotspur and Orlando, and an early version of Jaques's "All the world's a stage." He found letters from friends, old journals, and lists on how to be a better man. One letter he unfolded and discovered a record of wool and cloth needed: "Of linen dyed pink second quality, six yards. Of white wool, two skeins. . . ." The spelling was poor, and he bit his lip hard, crumpled it, and walked to the brazier. Still he hesitated, the paper dangling from his fingers. In the end he put it between the pages of a random book, not knowing what else to do with it.

The snow now covered the empty branches of the quince tree.

Thrusting the papers into the cupboard, he shoveled more coal in the brazier and began to polish the new lenses of the microscope by the lantern. Dusk was gathering, and outside in slanting heaps the snow piled on the edge of the windows while the light shone on the medical books and at the back of the table the lenses for magnifying and the greater, longer tube for viewing the stars. The wheels of carts and voices of children were muffled. He did not know how long he worked, but when he looked up that peculiar light which lingers before the dark had come.

Of linen dyed pink second quality, six yards. . . .

Linen brought home in a basket, and under it women's satin shoes, and he mounting the steps with these things, but they were other steps and it seemed as old as something which had happened in a ballad. He lit his pipe and walked up and down for a time, the old confusion mingled with sensuality until it pushed away other thoughts. He fought it, closing his eyes, and sat by his table stunned, the polishing tools in his hands and the glass before him which it was now too dark to see. He did not at first hear the cries and shouting from Aldermanbury and within moments, the harsh jangling of the dispensary bell.

Joan hurried through the door. "Never 'tis quiet in this parish!" she announced. "Some poor lad's fallen from his horse and they call for thee. And he'll have no money as the rest have not had any, parson!"

Nicholas rose and went out. At the end of Love Lane he saw a small gathering of schoolboys, apprentices, and shopkeepers, one holding a horse, and when he came through them, knelt at once on the snowy cobbles. There lay a dark-haired youth in good, plain clothing. As the neighbors stood about offering advice, Nicholas felt the head for wounds and body for broken bones. The lad's head and face were flushed with fever; he had not been thrown, Nicholas gathered, but had slipped from his mare in a faint.

His knees were cold from kneeling in the snow; he stood and asked for help. A few of the men carried the sick youth to the physician's guest chamber, whose bed Joan hastily warmed with a brick wrapped in flannel, while a boy helped to bring up coals for the little brazier and began a fire. Nicholas removed the youth's wet clothing, and covered him well. When he groaned and opened his eyes, startled for a moment, the physician said, "I'm doctor here, my friend, and have taken thee up. Where dost ride in a fever?"

"I must go at once," was the hoarse reply. He struggled up on his elbow and looked about in a puzzled, haughty way. His lips were cracked slightly.

" 'Tis no weather to ride about so weary and ill! Stay and go in the morning." The lad studied him for a moment, and then, murmuring, "An hour, no more," closed his eyes. At once he seemed to have fallen into the deep sleep which comes from absolute exhaustion.

Down the lane, the bells from Cheapside rang out the hour of six, when apprentices may lay down their tools and cease work. As Nicholas walked down to his parlor again he suddenly realized that the youth had no papers about him; all men carried identification of their work or parentage, their parish or university. By the plainness of his clothing (though he wore no gown), he supposed his guest to be a student. With some surprise he looked at the purse which he had found in the wet doublet, the contents of which seemed to be more than he himself earned in many months. He locked it carefully within a drawer.

The housekeeper pursed her lips as she laid the table for supper. "Mind thy plate, master, for we don't know who he is or from whence he may come!"

Nicholas could only nod. The young man within his walls had not been the first he had sheltered in his first year as priest. There had been a family of actors, a foul beggar who had left lice in the bedclothes, and once a girl so pretty and so swollen with child who came weeping to him at midnight that the whole parish whispered of it until he found another place for her to go. There had been a thief, and with him had gone what little silver he had; he preferred not to remember that. He should perhaps not have taken in the youth who had fallen in the snow.

Taking a cup of potion against fever of blackberry, meadowsweet, and other herbs and flowers, he mounted up again. The boy woke from his sleep to drink with some reluctance, and then, pushing the cup away, burrowed his face in the pillow. No thief, Nicholas thought as he put up his shutters, covered the fire, and barred the door. A good family, and the arrogance of the gentry. Yet to ride like that, what has he to escape from? What is he riding away from or towards?

He had slept for a matter of hours when he was wakened by the creaking of a door. For a moment he thought to reach for his stick, and then shrugged. In the hall, he made out his guest standing some feet away, his hand balancing on the doorframe. "Idiocy!" the youth murmured. "That I should be taken ill when I must be on my way!" It was a low voice, with the slightly guttural overtones of the north country. He came stumbling forward, and Nicholas at once caught him by the arm. The youth was tall and lank, as if he had grown so fast he had had no time to fill out.

"Art hungry, lad?" Nicholas said wryly.

"That I am."

"There's broth left from supper, and it's warm near the hearth. Come and let me know a few words of who you are." He spoke firmly as he did when giving penance or absolution, and the youth, subdued by the tone, nodded and let himself be helped down the steps.

As they sat next the kitchen hearth, Nicholas leaned forward to study his guest as he drank the broth. It was a pale face which might have been perfectly handsome were it not so stubborn. The hands, however, were long and beautiful as a scholar's, though there was something practical about him, as if he would take what he learned in books and stride into the world with it. He was unbearded, perhaps a few years above twenty, and likely from good family.

The youth said, "We'd had a hard case in the courts, and I had not seen my pillow for three nights and was feverish also. Then news came just now from Yorkshire that my father died suddenly, God rest his soul!"

"I'm sorry for thy grief."

"You can't know who I am, for I left my papers at my rooms in Inner Temple in the second-story-front chamber of the house above the stationer's where I'm barrister. I'm Thomas Wentworth from West Riding, with nine siblings home, and an estate which must be managed, for it's now mine to do. I can't tarry here." The black hair fell over the pale forehead, and he pushed it impatiently away and began to talk of the beauty of his home and his love for the land.

He was a strange, dark, brilliant, and emotional boy, and he spoke as if he had kept much within for a long time. Twice when he remembered his father, his voice broke. He spoke rapidly and without concealment as a man does to another in a tavern corner even when they have just become acquainted. His talk touched on books, law, and science, and his voice filled the empty crevices of the room. All the while the snow fell down the lane.

Wentworth said stoutly, "As soon as I can I must be on my way! There's so much for me to do at home. . . ." His voice suddenly grew shy. "You are a priest."

"I am."

"I am myself a man of deep belief who wrestles . . . but I'm too weary to say it. Wilt give me thy blessing?"

Nicholas laid his hands on the bowed head. "Christ keep and guard thee, Tom Wentworth, in all thy journeys," he said. He felt suddenly a strange, startled affection for the still feverish youth.

He woke to bells again, for Sabbath had come.

Nicholas dressed in his clean cassock and surplice, hearing below him the chattering of the boy choristers who had come into the kitchen for warm ale before service. From the window he could see men and women of the parish coming down the streets, leaving footprints in the snow as they crossed to the church under the white branches of the trees. Birds pecked about the graveyard, hopping between the stones. His guest was still sleeping. Before he went to the church, Nicholas laid the dry clothes on the chest of the guest chamber and within them the bag of coins. The floor creaked as he left.

Downstairs he knelt on the polished brick of the now empty kitchen with his hands over his face, praying to be made worthy to go to the altar of God. As he came into the church through the graveyard, the people rose respectfully with a rustle of skirt and lace. He did not see their faces, for he saw only the communion table before him, and the cruets, chalice, and crusty loaf of new bread which lay waiting.

He saw nothing but that; he knew nothing of himself.

Throughout the service as the boys trudged through the metrical singing of the rhymed versions of the psalms accompanied by some actors and old John on sackbut, recorders, and viol, other aspects of his life passed before him like vaguely intrusive dreams: there were those he had loved, and all that had happened to him, and much he would not recall. By God's mercy, he would never recall it. Then the dreams left, and there was nothing but the chalice and paten before him, the deep red glistening wine, the good bread, and the fair cloth of the table.

He raised his hands in invocation:

"Almighty God, unto whom all hearts are open, all desires known, and from whom no secrets are hid; Cleanse the thoughts of our hearts by the inspiration of thy Holy Spirit, that we may perfectly love thee, and worthily magnify thy holy Name; through Christ our Lord. Amen."

Turning to the congregation, he said, *"Lift up your hearts."* And they replied, *"We lift them up unto the Lord."* His voice returned, *"Let us give thanks unto our Lord God."*

There would be among those who came to receive communion the man who had spent his wages on cockfighting, the sick, the lonely, and the joyful. They came to him with their troubles and perplexities: they wept, and laughed, and swore to do better. He knew them, and yet they did not know him. With few exceptions, no one knew him; he preferred it that way. Yet there was this, and with it he came joyfully into the center of his own soul.

Light floated through the glass windows and onto the memorial slabs of the floor. The congregation came forward to receive the consecrated bread and wine. They gave thanks, and at the end he lifted his hands once more in blessing and said, *"The Peace of God, which passeth all under-standing, keep your hearts and minds in the knowledge and love of God, and of his Son Jesu Christ our Lord: And the Blessing of God Almighty, the Father, the Son, and the Holy Ghost, be amongst you, and remain with you always."*

Children crowded about him when the service was done, and many men wished to speak to him. He stood at the door of his church in his cassock and surplice in the still January day to greet them. When he returned, Tom Wentworth had gone. On his desk, wrapped in the discarded paper of the draft of some minor lawsuit, he found several gold sovereigns. He stood holding them in his hand and listening to the boys playing in the churchyard below.

THREE

The Dance in the Kitchen

SIX WEEKS PASSED.

Nicholas was much engrossed in compiling the plays. He found the actors' parts from *Much Ado About Nothing* in Robert Taylor's storage chest. The prompt copy of *As You Like It* turned up under a box of long-disused wigs on a top shelf of the wardrobe room in the Globe, and the next morning the aged player Henry Condell brought one of the histories, which he had recognized in a box of scrap paper as he was about to light his kitchen fire with the beginning of Act Three. Several letters to the widow Anne Shagspere in Stratford by the Avon brought a curt reply at last that neither she nor her late husband would have kept such stuff but put it out for the rag and bone man. She underlined the words that Will Shagspere had died a good Christian and had forgot the theater. The men shrugged to remember his sorry marriage and gave up on that quarter for help. The sonnets at least had been published, though Nicholas vaguely remembered several which had not been included. He had also given up trying to find the two ballads about poaching which Shagspere had written to cheer him when he was ill as a boy. They had yet to find a printer for the folio.

Through all this the winter continued, bitter and blowing and seeking out places to worry beneath the cuff of coat and under the lacing of breeches. Nicholas's housekeeper left to visit her sick mother, and the rooms of the rectory were empty.

The wind came straight at him as he turned up Aldermanbury from his errands one evening. It was the time of night when families have closed their shutters and gathered about the hearth. In the doorway of a school a beggar slept. Around the churchyard and down the crooked alleys the houses leaned towards each other as if they would tumble to the street. The wind clanked against the fire hooks and swung them against the broad beams of the dwellings. It rushed across roofs, stirring the thatch and rattling the tile. With his face stinging, he thrust open his door and tumbled inside to the sound of laughter and dancing.

His kitchen was not empty. The actor Andrew Heminges and two young women were leaping over a burning candle set on the stone floor. It was an old game and Nicholas had played it himself many times.

The older girl was a stranger to him. Her face was round, pretty, and serious, and he made her years to be somewhere about eighteen; she had a perfect, plump body, though she was quite small. So startled was he to find them there that at first he had no words. Then he unfastened his cloak and said gruffly, "What do you, children?"

They had all ceased to move, and only the candle flame flickered in the dim room. "Why, Nick!" Andrew said comfortably. "The girls came to see thee for medicine and we danced to be warm while we waited. Here's Anne Jaggard from Aldersgate and her cousin from the country! Dancing will warm thee as well! Join us, do!"

Little Anne lisped, "Come, master! Join us!"

Nicholas shook his head, but she and the small cousin seized his hands to rub them. "Ah, art chilled!" they chattered about him. "Can thee not dance as in Whitsun? Young Master Heminges will fetch the broom for a hobby horse and wear a cap, upon my soul, and we shall have a tune!"

"What, thinkst that I dance?"

"We do."

"Come, parson!" continued Anne confidently. "We know thou canst dance fairly and are no Puritan! Do, and I'll play 'John Come Kiss Me Now' on the lute and my cousin who's come new to the city will see how well we do."

"Aye, parson!" echoed Andrew, and he snatched the ruffled cap from the table and pulled it down over his eyes. They had got Nicholas's cloak and hat from him, and, laughing and teasing, they directed him to the center of the room. The lute was slightly from tune, but young Anne played very well and the cousin curtseyed, then took both his hands in hers and turned him about. Round they went, careful of the candle on the floor, and the red-haired young actor clapped his hands and rode about on the broom neighing and stomping the floor in time. Around they went with the physician's arm now about the girl's waist: and she frowned, slightly cross-eyed, and bit her lip.

The tune was changed to "Sellenger's Round" as they pranced and the room whirled about them: the blackened beams seemed to tilt, the iron kettle swung, the ropes of onions, dried herring, and herbs swung above their heads. Each time they came close to the fire he lifted the girl so that her skirts danced above the flame. She did not look away from his face as faster he swung her.

"Mind!" cried the boy.

The flame had nicked her hem: it curled and glistened in the threads for one second, and Nicholas dropped to his knees and, seizing the cloth, folded it between his palms to extinguish the sparks. The lute strings grew silent, and the lovely, panting girl looked down at him. "Marry, what do we here?" he murmured with a sudden sense of bewilderment. "Is it not time you were home, maids?"

His dancing partner said, "We came only for the medicine against the cough."

"Ah, for that." Leaving the brightly lit kitchen and the girl, who stood suddenly flushed as if she had been scolded, he mounted the steep curved stairs to the upper rooms. When he came down with the powder, she was waiting in the shadow of the rounded turn of the steps. He caught her against him impulsively and, stooping, kissed her cheek several times. He did not kiss her mouth, but she kissed his in the sudden flurry of rough passion of the very young. His heart pounded; he would have liked to carry her up to bed then and with great difficulty put a little space between them.

Ruffled and shiny-eyed, she looked at him. "Ah!" she murmured with her throat quivering. Then, seizing his hand, she rubbed it against her cheek. Thus they came clumsily into the kitchen, where Andrew and the younger maid stood at once.

"We ate of the apples and cakes, but not all," the other girl said. "Didn't we, Katherine? Shall mother send more tomorrow?"

"Nay, my lass."

"The cake with nutmeg: a fair piece is in the covered dish."

"My thanks, but I have dined."

Andrew was tucking his shirt into his breeches. "Nick," he said with sudden anxiety, "thou shalt not tell my father of this?"

"I shall say nothing."

After they had gone, Nicholas gazed about at the microscope and books, the pages of notes, the unwrapped parcels of drying herbs, the lute thrust in the corner. He stirred the fire and then stood with the poker in his hand for some time. Then he went outside to the bricked, walled garden, which was arranged behind the house in square beds with narrow paths between; in the summer grapevines clambered up the walls and cherries hung from the crooked tree. Now only a few dried leaves of ivy shivered against the brick. He brought his fingers repeatedly to his lips where the girl had kissed him and after a time went up to bed.

At ten o'clock of the next morning when he had set beer to brew against scurvy, he dressed as quickly as he could in the cassock and broad, four-cornered hat which was the proper garb of the priest under canon law and set out over Fleet Bridge and outside the city walls to visit the elderly bishop, William Sydenham, who had ordained him the year before.

Long retired from the diocese of Winchester and now approaching his eightieth year, William Sydenham dwelt in a small stone house in the ancient precinct of Covent Garden, where monks had once grown herbs and fruits. There he shared his dark rooms with two sisters recently come to the city. The minute Nicholas turned down the lane, the bishop rushed from his door in slippers and gown, barking, "Pricklouse, what dost?" His two sisters, creatures even smaller and more fragile than he, fluttered about and then rushed away to prepare a meal.

When the two men were left to themselves in the parlor with its vases of dried flowers and one quite beautiful crucifix upon the wall, William Sydenham sat back with his knobby hands entwined on his stomach and studied the young physician. They spoke of trivial matters for a time, Sydenham of his acquaintances, whom he found either stupid or none too constant, and Nicholas of his work. After a time the younger man began to pour out much of what was in his heart. It was the usual matter of doubt about the efficacy of his vocation and his recurring angers with himself; he was, however, this morning much moved, and several times his voice trembled.

Sydenham turned his sharp, intelligent profile to the small window to listen and nodded now and then. "Well, well," he muttered. "The old matters, but men are tedious and tread the same weary road ever. Dear fellow, I have one task to set thee which to you will be a penance."

"And that is?" Nicholas murmured, letting his hand idly trail in the floor rushes and wishing the old bishop would take his advice in cleanliness and cease to use them.

"To love thyself."

"That old matter! 'Tis most difficult to do."

"Yes, that is why I have set it. I see much goodness in thee as a man,

Nicholas, but thou seest only thy faults. I hope you will grow from it."
He laid his hands on Nicholas's head in absolution and mumbled the
words, then added, "Wouldst say more? I see it in thy mouth! There
comes the price of letting people know thee!"

"How can I help others when I am myself so imperfect? Why do I
trust others when they so often fail me? Yet perpetually . . ."

"My dear Nick, one cannot live and not fall into error now and then!
If a man is determined to believe in the ultimate goodness of his fellows, he will occasionally be bitterly disappointed, yet if he cannot believe this to some degree, he can in no way see God. And we are none of
us perfect, for the very world maketh it so. There are good and bad in all
things."

Feeling for his stick, he stood clumsily, waving Nicholas away when
he sprang forward to give a hand. "Come, come, to dinner! I am an old
man and must eat!" He caressed the younger man's cheek and then
changed it into a light cuff as the door opened and his sisters came in
with candles, an elderly servant following with a heavy platter of meats
and fowls.

"Dost ever think, Nick," he said, as they sat together, "of the com-
mandments laid upon us? Love one another! Live in harmony and peace!
So beatific and simple when alone in one's closet, so impossible when
some whoremonger kicks gutter dirt upon thee, or takes thy sister lewdly,
or even disagrees . . . yes, God hath created us a litigious, hotheaded, and
self-concerned people. Would He had made us better! However, in His
wisdom! I ought not question His ways, but yet, when I lay this knotty,
painful body upon my familiar bed, I so presume. And to be a priest is to
turn people from their natural selves, which were ever truculent and
selfish since the apple was eaten and the garden lost.

"The mind of man is peculiar! By this very insouciant questioning, like
a boy who will not be still, we find the strength to build and to grow.
Were not for this quality of man's mind, would yonder great Cathedral
have sprung from rude stone and sand? Ah Nick! I know thee, for thy
heart's much like mine was when I was first ordained. Thou wouldst love

every man and yet are so afraid to come close to one of them for fear of them, of thyself."

He waited until more wine was poured and then continued, " 'Tis a tendency of the old to try to order the lives of younger men. I never listened to a particle of advice, and sometimes I was the worse for it and sometimes the better. Still, there are words on something of greater consequence that I will say if I might, for you are as hotheaded and rash a piece of manhood as ever I was myself. When I was yet Bishop of Winchester, I was privy to the conferences and councils of bishops and theologians in which specifics of belief and worship are worried as a dog does a bone until the magnificence of creation is lost in the paltry scuffle. Hast studied the history of our church as well as I! Think of the bitter disputes in the third and fourth centuries in Alexandria! Think of the division of religious sects time and again, from rival primates of the Roman Church in the thirteenth century in Avignon and Rome, to our own wretched persecutions of the past century. And what did they concern? Matters of interpretation of scripture, best left to the private conscience. I caution thee, Nicholas! God willing, hast many years as Our Lord's priest. Serve Him, and let others have their notions of how to worship Him. Serve God quietly in your heart as He cometh to thee, and do not waste time on small matters. More, beware of those who would drag thee into them, my friend."

"I have no troubles of this sort."

"Nor do I expect thou wilt. Still, heed my words shouldst ever need them, dear boy." More wine came and the excellent joint of mutton, and when they were full enough to want nothing more than to be in this pleasant room with the sun glistening on the floorboards, the bishop sat back sternly and folded his hands across his belly, drumming them and staring at the younger man from under his heavy eyebrows. One wisp of grey hair emerged from the skullcap; no more, for he was almost bald. "What wilt do now, pisspot?" he barked.

"What canst mean by that, my father?" was the shy reply.

"With thy life, with thy life, fool! What shalt do now with thy life?

So much of it before thee. But art still stunned with what thou hast been made, is it not so, friend? Time shall come when feeling Christ's breath in thine ear will not be so new. I ask too many questions, for you are still to my eyes a mere boy and cannot know these things. And when thou hast come to know them, I shall be dust and unable to be told directly."

"You confuse me, sir."

"I have never done less." Then he said, "And do not live so solitary. Dost mean to remain alone always?"

The bishop made the sign of the cross on the younger man's forehead, scratching him slightly with his jaggedly cut thumbnail, and spoke no more of personal matters. Later when the visit was done, he stood at his door to watch him turn towards Fleet Bridge.

The smell of ale and old straw and some scant warmth from the fire met Nicholas as he pushed open the doors of the Mitre Tavern on Wood Street a few hours later. With a nod he edged his way through the craftsmen and apprentices who stood about the bar reading the English-language newspapers from Holland.

"What news, lads?" he murmured, putting down his medicine satchel. He found a place at one of the benches and wiped the crumbs away from the cracked table before him. Well did he know this tavern, for here his friend often came for a mug of warm ale and called for a dish of buttered eggs or beef to be sent over from the ordinary. You did not have to wait for the monthly ward meetings to find out the local gossip. Notices were posted above the bar of men wanting work and plays to be given.

"Here's news of the East India Company, Nick!" a friend called. "I put down twenty-five pounds and so did my wife's cousin, and it looks fair to sure that shall be doubled." There was much discussion for a time about the new merchant company, which had been chartered only in 1600 by the old Queen and was already quite prosperous.

"Nay, here's writ a matter even more amusing!" another cried. "More knights have been made this week. 'Tis said anyone can be one, if the cash is pleasing to the King. Soon the fellow who scours the cesspools may join the peerage if he has saved the gold to do it."

Nicholas moved his back to the light of the small, dingy glass panes which overlooked the shops and horsecarts down Wood Street and began to read an older paper about travels to the Indies and what was found there, all the time cutting slivers from the great yellow tavern cheese on the board beside him. After an hour, the small bell above the door rang, and a carrier in stained leather breeches hurried in with packages and letters. The ale drawer looked at them briefly and then, edging his heavy stomach around the corner of the bar, bawled, "Here's a letter for thee, parson doctor, if you've time from the saving of souls and the healing of bodies to read it. 'Tis come this minute on the York coach and there's two pennies owing."

Wiping his fat hands on his apron, he gave it to the physician, and stood breathing heavily as Nicholas turned it over. He looked puzzled at the crest pressed into the imprinted rosy sealing wax; only when he unfolded the paper did he understand from whom it had come.

to Nicholas Cooke, parson and physician, Mary Aldermanbury in Cripplegate, from Wentworth, Yorkshire

Doctor,

The delay in writing has been from much work since I have returned to my estates. Nine siblings are much a handful and my wife was most happy to see me. Moreover, I have had a bit of the gout or other ranking pains in limbs remaining yet from my ride. So accept these belated thanks for what thou hast done for me, and recall I am thy debtor.

I miss London with a terrible aching and am determined to be returned to Commons if ever his Majesty convenes Parliament again, for I sat once as hardly more than a boy and never opened my lips to speak for awe. Now I shall prick him like a gadfly, for I do believe kings desire too much power these days and more should come to the landowners. I am a lover of the independent thinking man. These are modern times.

So you will cure the world of its spiritual and physical ailments, and I will manage the political ones, and after we are done, there will be naught left needs doing. I shall come and drink a glass with thee, and meanwhile God keep thee, gracious parson!

Adieu! I have toured the continent and am a linguist as you shall see, but there is more of me than that. There is a great deal of me, as men shall by and by know.

> Thomas Wentworth (not baronet, or any title, for I am not favored with one these present days but am only plain Tom as friends call me)

By that time someone had borrowed the Dutch newspaper, and another man taken away the tavern cheese. Nicholas called for ink, paper, and sand, wiped clean the table, and, closing his mind to the noise, began a reply.

Dear country squire, plain Tom,

Good news it is that you have arrived home safely as it was in my prayer thou shouldst do. Yet I must scold thee well for the long ride in the snow and the ensuing pains and will send shortly some remedies against rheumatism and gout which I have concocted myself out of old herbals.

I see no signs of Parliament being called, and hence of thy return. Be well, dear fellow, and at ease with thy life. Art young and still have much time to live it.

> Nicholas Cooke (sometimes parson, dullard doctor, who is much oppressed this month by the endless cold)

His pen lingered above the page, wondering if he should say more. And yet what should he say? It had been a brief encounter, and he and the boy from Yorkshire should not likely see each other again, for he now concluded Wentworth a dreamer who would soon be weighed down with estates, wife, and children in the north. And in the end they were very different. He was a scientist who might never find what he was seeking, a man alone with a hope of salvation and one presentable suit of clothes; the young Yorkshireman came blessed with good family, wealth, and a wife who loved him. In the end Nicholas closed the letter with candle dripping and a knife's blunt edge for the seal, and left it to be called for in three days when the next mail coach should leave for the north.

FOUR

The Science Fellows of
Blackfriars

S

PRING CAME SUDDENLY THAT YEAR AS WHEN YOU OPEN A DOOR AND find someone you love standing on the other side, far too early to be expected. It crept into every corner of the house and drew him to the garden. He sometimes thought of the girl with whom he had danced that cold winter night. He had learned she was but eighteen years old and the niece of the respected printer Isaac Jaggard, who had been approached to produce the folio of Shagspere's plays. She had come briefly on a visit, and was now gone home to Kent. Each time he walked over to Jaggard's shop near Aldersgate she came to his mind.

The printer stroked his thick, trimmed beard as he listened to the early specifications for the folio, which he declared an enormous undertaking and likely to lose hundreds of pounds. Plays were ephemeral and Shagspere's better left in fragile, unbound quartos, for in twenty years, who might yet know his name?

Behind him and above him as they spoke, the presses banged and

Isaac's father, William, interjected comments. The old man had been blind for some years, yet still managed the shop. Nicholas walked home slowly under the cherry blossoms down Wood Street, reflecting on the mortality of man. He was both relieved and sorry the lass was gone.

In June he received a letter from the College of Physicians.

That worthy organization had been chartered in the early years of the last century by King Henry VIII and had recently moved to Amen Corner in a handsome building leased from St. Paul's. The fellows of the College were among the most respected physicians in the city, and were charged with ensuring the competence of medical practitioners within seven miles of London. They had licensed Nicholas when he first returned three years before with his Cambridge degree. Now the letter informed him that he had been nominated as a fellow and that they would be willing to examine his qualifications in the month of June.

He could not imagine who had nominated him, for his stand against excessive bloodletting had been much ridiculed. In addition, his attempts to grind a better lens for the microscope were held in contempt by men who had been at their trade half a century or more; no physician in his proper mind could conceive that a microscopic world, if ever able to be seen, would be worth anything to the ancient study of medicine.

The oral examinations in physiology, pathology, and therapeutics, conducted in Latin, took place within one week. Following these were visits to the home of fellows so that they could ascertain his character, and finally on the day after the feast of St. John's Nativity in June, the College met to vote upon his admission. A bench and some chairs were placed in the vestibule of their hall, and there he awaited the decision under the portrait of craggy Dr. Caius, who had healed the sick of the city fifty years before. When called inside, Nicholas found the fellows at long tables, each wearing the broad-brimmed velvet hat of the trade. The faces were poorly lit by tallow candles, though he made out some he had seen about the town. In a shadowy corner of the room hung a portrait of the King. Nicholas had been elected a fellow and a place was created for him on the bench.

"Let me tell you, friend," said the portly physician to his right, turning back the sleeves of his black embroidered coat, "for I can read thy face! I was also a dreamer when young. I went into many a hovel and tried to aid a wife half beaten to death, I tried to persuade a drover not to drink away his earnings but feed his little ones. The wealthy also need physicking. The time will come when thy energy's not so prodigious, when you will not wish to be awakened thrice from a sound sleep on a bitter cold night to leave your warm bed because some fool carpenter has cut off half his thumb and not salved it well and it has infected the whole arm. Then you will be happy to have gold in a box under the hearthstones and stay behind your draperies with your feet on the footstool. Sacrifice is not thanked by the world, though perhaps, being in holy orders, that has some appeal for thee."

Nicholas then spoke in return. He spoke passionately of what he wanted to do, what he knew between all of them united they could accomplish. He spoke until the men about him grew silent, some in interest and some in amusement. What did they know? What could they begin to understand? He spoke of the Egyptians and their lost wisdom, of the medical books of the Arabs, of Fracastorius, of Roger Bacon, of Paracelsus and metals. He spoke of the theory of germs, of the danger of old floor rushes in which fleas bred. He spoke and spoke until a greater part of the men had left and a crooked usher stared resentfully at him as he put out the tapers. He then apologized for speaking so much, and found there was almost no one left to hear the regret.

Shaking hands with the secretary and house steward, Nicholas hurried from the hall. As he was turning past the Cathedral, still wondering who had put his name forward for membership and if the man now regretted it, he saw a small fellow with long, loose black hair waiting by the water carts near the churchyard wall. He knew the man at once, knew of his education at Padua and his service as doctor to many of the great men of the city, and not least of his theory of the circulation of the blood, which was spoken of with some disparagement by many older physicians.

William Harvey did not move, but stood with his wiry arms crossed over his dark doublet, and his eyes fixed on Nicholas with a frown as if the newly elected fellow were late for an appointment. The corner of his thin mouth twitched, and for a moment he almost smiled. "I have now one man at the College who understandeth my work," he said abruptly. "None other does but the Holy Ghost. Wilt walk with me to my lodging? I have been this whole day without imbibing a drop of coffee and am near to mental debility."

Murmuring his thanks, Nicholas turned with his new friend towards the water and the select, gated neighborhood of Blackfriars. There they came to a squat, crooked dwelling set in an alley to the right of the old priory gate where men still took lodgings under the shadow of a pointed steeple. The rooms were cluttered with piles of loosely stacked papers, books, alembics, and surgical instruments. Stuck into the edges of smoke-darkened paintings were sketches of amphibians and small mammals. In the last chamber, which had once been a storage room, the corpse of an old man with a neat flap of abdomen rolled back lay on a table. "My landlord," Harvey said with a sweep of his hand. "My former landlord, I should say. Nowhere in his carcass can I discover what made him so stingy. Remove my cat from the chair if you would sit and tell me of thy studies!"

Picking up the cat in his arms, Nicholas answered with some shyness. "I am much drawn to the microscope and hope to find the smallest particles of matter, not only for my amusement, for that's plentiful, but to find what causeth disease. Amid these atoms, as Democritus called them, I hope to find it. And as 'tis my way, when I see what's right and true, I cannot mitigate my words for fools." The last words were spoken with some sternness; he thought of death, which seemed always the enemy, and then continued passionately to explain other areas of his work.

Harvey had already ground dark beans and now brewed them into the drink he called coffee. Sipping the scalding, bitter liquid, he sank back on an unsteady chair with his feet on an empty herring barrel and said, "I nominated you, Cooke, for selfish reasons. I've need of thee. I've a fancy to form a society for scientific thought and want you within it."

Nicholas cried, "A fellowship for science! Marry, I would fancy that!"

"Wouldst come regularly and bring friends?"

"Aye, by my troth!"

"Good! All knowledge is the province of mankind. What we do not understand or have the wisdom to question singly, we may consider together. What is man if he cannot reason and think?" He leaned back and squinted at Nicholas; the sharp dark eyes followed him.

Nicholas had begun to walk about the cluttered room. "There thou hast said it!" he said impulsively. "What shall be our boundaries? Nay, why should we have them? By all that's holy, I would learn about magnetism, astronomy and the earth, wind, heat, weights, metals, alchemy, and the properties of light. If not these things in whole, then in part. . . ." Picking up the skeleton of a squirrel, he studied it as if he would memorize its structure at once.

Harvey shook the canister of coffee beans. "I have friends as well," he answered quickly. "A few lords, a few doctors, and a grocer or two. Bringst thine and we shall meet every second Tuesday as we live. And by Our Lord, we shall learn and study all until men shall say that of all ages 'twas not Athens but that of the Stuart kings which was the wisest!" His eyes burned with pleasure, and he cracked his knuckles and passed the back of his lean hand over his mouth as if to conceal his smile. They lingered until two of the morning, and then Nicholas walked out into the lane under the old priory gate and home.

Thomas Wentworth had said he would return to the city in his last letters, but autumn had come and the feast of St. Michael and All Angels, and there was no sign of him.

Unexpectedly, they had begun to write each other. The young landowner was loquacious and ambitious, and though he loved his shire, he felt much apart from things there. Nicholas found himself wanting company. He never recognized these things until they were full upon him, and then he bowed his head in resentment before them and hid them the best he could. Harvey was called away, and the projected science meeting did not occur. He would have gone to see Sydenham, but knew the old bishop would repeat his last admonishment, *Do not be so much alone,* and not gently this time. It was no state of mind in which to go to a court masque, but Sydenham had presented him with a ticket and he felt he must go to oblige him.

Presentation of these extravagant court entertainments had increased since the ascension of James some fifteen years before. For many seasons Inigo Jones had created costumes and scenery while his colleague gruff Ben Jonson provided the poetry. The old banqueting hall had been made of wood and canvas, boasted three hundred windows, and was roofed by a ceiling painted with suns, clouds, and stars. This new one was a heavier structure of brick and stone. Benches in tiers were erected around the platform.

The King entered, and all rose or knelt as they could. Nicholas from the side saw but the edge of his robe and heard his convivial grunt of greeting to those about him as he mounted the dais. With a creak, his Majesty settled his spindly legs on the footstool before his great chair, and with a swish of skirt and clank of sword, the court and guests seated themselves as well and turned happy faces towards the end of the room.

Trumpets sounded, and some of the actors tumbled in for the prelude; they were masked and wearing elaborate headdresses meant to personify satyrs, but Nicholas recognized the deft tumbling of young Andrew. Hours passed. The huge hall was hot, women perspired, the dancers' shoes clicked against the platform. Boys sang, and the King drank too much and laughed loudly. During the principal dance the ladies in yellow, blowsy chiffon descended from the platform to dance with the spectators. Proscenium arches parted to reveal another scene behind them. A globe revolved with eight dancers inside, and toward the end came the King's favorite, the Marquis of Buckingham, cast as a benevolent pagan god, and set the harried plot to rights. And then it was over, and, much relieved, Nicholas rose to depart. Instead of raising his spirits, the evening had left him with an expected melancholy and sense of loss, and he could not wait to withdraw from the crowds.

About lay the paraphernalia of a play now done: curtains half open, lutes and krumhorns thrown about the platform. Nicholas edged about the musicians' stands through the stiff farthingales of several women, and by a groom who had come in with a candle snuffer to begin to douse the lights. Then as he glanced across the crowded hall, he recognized the Yorkshireman Tom Wentworth standing with some men near the great doors, and began to make his way towards him.

As he came closer, he saw with some disappointment that Wentworth was no longer the grieving boy who had blurted the news of the loss of his father and then asked for his host's blessing. This was merely another haughty young member of the gentry, the sort who can bring a physician to his door and send him away again with no thanks and a curt nod. Nicholas remembered the gold coins, which he had spent he knew not where (an actor perhaps who needed charity, a book, an astrolabe?), and bit his lip. The coins stood between them like an unsteady bridge over deep water. He wished he had not spent them.

Yet looking closer, he could see that Wentworth's mouth under the trimmed dark mustache was constricted with uneasiness, and that the youthful squire stood in this great place among the glittering courtiers like a man who wants with all his soul to belong and does not. Nicholas felt himself soften to him, ashamed of his brief, profound resentment.

Wentworth, however, barely returned his smile. "I did not know if wert still about the city, parson, for I wrote some weeks ago and no word was replied," he said critically.

"No letters came to me but for the ones I answered."

"Not one concerning Margaret, my wife?"

"Nay," answered Nicholas simply, "not of thy wife. Is she ill, prithee?" To this the squire shook his head angrily, and taking the physician's arm, urged him through the doors.

The yard was thickly packed with grooms and horseboys rushing about, and dark restless horses wanting to be away. Another heavy carriage thrust off, splattering them with dirt to their knees, while behind them Whitehall Palace seemed to fade into the darkness. In the cleaner air of the night, Wentworth breathed more easily.

He said with more consideration, "And thou? How dost fare, parson?"

"I am heavy with my own company."

"Ah!" was the blurted answer. "I am the very same!"

"Where dost lodge this night?"

"With friends, but I cannot find them."

"Then come home with me," said Nicholas impulsively. "Give me thy fellowship, as mine's not to my liking. There's no one in my house but my housekeeper, Joan, who disapproves of everything I do, and I, poor wretch that I am, have not the courage to send her off!" Another carriage groaned its way too close to their feet, the coachman shouting at them to make way.

Wentworth flicked the dirt from his coat. "I will come," he said. "Art kind, Cooke! For Christ's mercy, let's be gone from this place, for I have not done well here this night!"

Departing their ferry at Queenshyde Wharf, they began to mount the steep streets together towards Cripplegate. From Basinghall Street they could hear the banging of the cesspit cleaners. Nicholas talked freely, and they laughed over much of the play. Arriving at his house, he swiftly unlocked his door, lit candles, and hurried to the cupboard for cheese.

Wentworth stripped off his coat and walked about the room with his hands clasped behind his back. Indeed he had lost the peculiar, lingering innocence of his first visit, when he had been near tears over his father's loss, and now appeared as any other handsome, impatient, somewhat vain young fellow who has some great importance in his own shire and is surprised to find himself of little interest to anyone when near the court.

Nicholas hesitated at the keg of ale and said, "I can offer you little but plain fare."

"I want nothing more; at home I'm happiest eating with my bailiff and his friends. I don't use a fork as they do in Italy when I have my own good hands," answered Tom bluntly. "I come to you hungry! Have you bread?"

As they sat down and began to eat and drink, both untied their collars and rolled up their sleeves. "Word about my shire is his Majesty is wanting to raise more money," he said between mouthfuls, "and willing to sell a handful of titles. Hundreds of men bought theirs in such a way early in the reign, and the College of Arms could hardly keep track of them. Though whether he's not selling or unwilling to sell to me, I can't say. I've only come two days ago and cannot get a sense of it."

"Why should he not sell to thee?" Nicholas asked, reaching for the bowl of apples.

"God knoweth whom he favors—it turneth on a feather. This city's a brutal place when a man wants to climb, and there's no influence in court without friends. The King knows not my name: Wentworth of no place in particular, someone called me. Hardly that! I am descended directly from John of Gaunt, one of the great peacemakers of our history! I have mayhap his strong will. I intend to take a house within the city so that men can know me. If I were prettier it would be easier. Buckingham did it with his legs, but it's not my legs I have to offer him. It is my mind."

Nicholas gazed at the eager, hungry, dark-haired youth, who now held the bread like a farm boy against his chest to cut. "I know almost no one," Wentworth continued, "and of those I do, half are too busy knowing someone else to know me. Truth is, nothing fancies me more than hunting at home, yet there's this part of me that drives me here. . . . We are composed of diverse parts, are we not? Diverse parts we are, and thrown together in one body and soul like so many different matters of books together on one shelf."

Even as he spoke, the Yorkshireman's anxiety over what he had not yet discussed was as palpable as something you bump into the dark, and feel the corners of it with your hands and understand it will be moved but with difficulty. Nicholas listened to the sounds of the words, and waited for a pause. "And thy wife," he said quietly. "What of her? Is she ill?"

"No, thanks be to God!"

"Then what can it be?"

"Parson, thinkst if a man's wife doth not conceive that it may be from some sin of their making?"

"I think not so."

Wentworth pushed away his plate and allowed the words to spill out.

"Margaret and I wedded several years ago when I was a boy, and still she doesn't conceive. Men about my shire have said the fault's mine," he added, flushing with resentment, "though God knoweth it cannot be! I've not spoken on this matter to anyone, for I don't trust the physicians at home! What remedy hast?"

"Do her courses flow?"

"Aye, monthly and in profusion."

Nicholas thought for a moment. " 'Twas a lass about these streets who didn't conceive for two years. I gave her seeds of wild carrot boiled in wine, and her womb swelled, but whether from that or another reason I can't say. I found some carrots at the edge of a field by the Old Kent Road this past week. Come." Taking a candle, he eagerly led the way into the dispensary and pulled open the little drawers. The seeds were soon simmering on the hearth. Stirring the brew, Nicholas asked, "Wilt thy wife come to the city as well?"

"Yes, week next, as God wills it."

"I would like so much to greet her."

"And she you."

More wine was heated, which they drank hot and plain, and they talked of various matters while the watch called the hour and the faint coolness of night crept at the door. Nicholas sat back and felt the sadness coming upon him again. He said carefully in a slightly drunken voice, "I would thou hadst not left the coins for me."

"I wanted to give thee something in return for thy care," was the surprised answer.

"The care was freely given."

"Hast anger with me for this?" was the astonished, shy question, and Nicholas suddenly felt shame and murmured, "Nay . . . 'tis naught. What you wish, let it be. As you wish, young Wentworth. It cannot matter. . . ." He felt his throat swell, and, falling silent, drank more from his cup.

From over the roofs and church spires came the tolling of the bells. When they had ceased, Wentworth leaned forward and said openly, "I have on this visit and the last said much of my life, and you little of yours."

" 'Tis of no particular matter."

"I feel you have much to say."

"Mayhap."

"Assuredly you can trust me!" was the passionate answer. "Tell me, hast not wed? No children, pray?"

Nicholas caught his breath. "I was wed once," he said.

"Wouldst not speak upon it?"

"Not this eve. Look here, I have this letter of a meeting of men who love science: come if thou art about the city. The hour's late, my friend. Sleep upstairs where you were that time before, and in the morrow the potion will be done."

Nicholas had intended to go up with his candle as well but did not. Instead he listened to the mounting footsteps and the creaking of the bed, and at last the sigh. He put up the shutters and drank the last of the warm wine. Then he sat down in the coffer chair, and thought of his own marriage.

He had been an actor then and she daughter of his old master Heminges. He was so young when he first took the vows, and though he did not love Susan, he tried in his serious way to make her happy when it did not go too sorely against his own inclinations towards freedom. But it had all gone wrong, tumbled down, splintered apart: the soft voice complaining in the darkness of her loneliness, the hiccuped sobs into the pillow, the final wrenching apart and her rushing home to her father, who had saved him from himself as a boy, cuddled and disciplined him into a profession and an uncertain desire to live, and then given him his daughter.

Heminges's reproachful muttering, thick hands clasped behind his back. *Thou knowst, Nick!* And then the bitterness. Oh the bitterness. And the lies told to the ecclesiastical authorities that Nicholas was her unknowing kin when wed. Then, through the ban on consanguinity, the marriage was dissolved and he was set adrift on the miserable sea of himself, in which he nearly drowned, aye, many a time. It had gone wrong, and she wanted not him but his best friend from the Irish wars. He let them go and traveled to Cambridge for his doctorate in medicine and was made priest. Six years passed; Heminges and he had forgiven each other. His former wife and her new husband had gone to Heidelberg, where he found work as a musician. Nicholas had never seen her or the children since.

Six years: and sometimes in odd moments when he found himself too weary, it seemed of a sudden centuries, and that there was a division between himself and others that had not healed, that would never heal. One thing he knew: he could never risk the love of a woman again.

Covering the fire, he mounted to his sleeping chamber, undressed to his shirt, and said his prayers. Still, when the psalms were done, he was drawn to the clothespress, and, kneeling, pulled out the lowest drawer. From under many tattered shirts and books needing binding, he felt for a certain cloth, and taking it on his lap, unfolded a child's gown, slippers, and cap. He began to weep then until his sobs tore at his ribs as if trying to get out, and reached for the edge of the chair to rise, and toppled it. He did not know how he got back to his bed.

When such a grief is released, others sense it. Men saw him as he went about the parish with his lips compressed, and face slightly puffy from tears. He wept more in those three days than he had since he was a lad, and when it was done he felt in some strange way he had changed.

He also knew, from the puzzled, tender looks his guest had given him the next morning, that Tom Wentworth had heard his grief as well. Wentworth did not leave the city, but rented a house in St. Martin's Lane within Aldersgate and from there, a few days later, sent over a letter.

My friend—

I do believe in destiny, not the sort the poor souls do in Geneva which has infiltrated some of our small Puritan sects here of damnation or salvation before birth. The God I know is merciful and saves us with His grace. This grace is at times given through the meeting of people, and thus I am somehow certain that our lives will be intertwined. Therefore may I say that I know thou wouldst fill thy arms with others as I do, and yet holdst back from fear—of what? Of loss? Loss will come, finding us even in a small room. Yet it doth not matter. I know this alone: that what we want as much as our lives we will surely, surely be granted the grace to obtain!

But by Christ I trust thee, and let us be true friends unto death, for the world is sometimes a cruel place and I have had men laugh at my pain, and truly it must have been for thee. Is it fitting for a man to say to another, I know thy grief? By Christ's love I believe in friendship as one thing most divinely given. Pray for me each day of thy life and I will for thee, and thy happiness.

Promise me in all thy life whatever comes thou wilt not cease to do what's fitting for thee: thy research, thy studies. And I shall go forward always to do my best, which is my vow, wherever it leadeth me.

Margaret comes this week and hath in her letters sent her love to thee. We both embrace thee and look with joy to thy company.

Wentworth

Nicholas folded the letter carefully. In the next few weeks as he continued to work and gather the plays, he felt his heart opening. It was a strange physical sensation, as if a window lattice were unlatched; he felt it with wonder.

Margaret Wentworth did not come to the city, though the house on St. Martin's Lane was being made ready. Nicholas sent wormwood flowers steeped in brandy against Wentworth's gout and compiled what he could find of remedies for barrenness from his old books of Galen and others. Wentworth in turn wrote letters thanking him profusely and telling him that he had dined with the elderly Archbishop Abbot at Lambeth Palace across the river and several other influential men, and felt he was beginning to make friends.

A few days later word was sent round that the first meeting of the society for natural science would take place in the rooms of the physician William Harvey in Blackfriars. Tim Keyes came with a large cheese under his arm, speckled with gold dust from his work, and John Lowin arrived with some skepticism, for he did not trust physicians other than Nicholas. His was a scant interest in science, but he could not bear to be left out.

Harvey brought two physicians. Henry Bartlett, also a fellow of the College, was a bulky young man not many years above thirty, who wore rings on his thick fingers, carried a silver walking stick, and was courting a wealthy widow. How the courtship of his widow progressed, they later came to understand, determined his disposition. Bartlett's Latin was impeccable, his humor wry, and there was, Harvey said, no better diagnostician in the city of London nor one who knew better the wisdom of the Arab doctors. He made no secret that he wished to rise in his practice high enough to serve the King himself, and thought he could do it better than those who did. He flattered the women he attended, and yet was known for extreme kindness in unexpected ways. The deaths of children brought him to tears.

The physician Lawrence Avery, who seemed to walk always three steps behind Bartlett, was a delicately built, small man with the narrow chest of a consumptive and stooped shoulders. He lived in poverty, it was rumored, somewhere along Thames Street and had two great passions. The first was the study of madness; he walked over every morning to visit the incarcerated souls in Bedlam outside the gate, arguing with the guards to treat them gently, sometimes reading to them or bringing in a hired lad with a lute to sing them songs. Music, he insisted, could cure much. The second passion was for the history and topography of the city, which he was in his spare time compiling into a lengthy book. Outside of these matters he seemed to doubt his own opinions, or hesitate to express them. His face was sweet, and he loved jokes, which he recited in a grave way. He seldom said anything without looking for approval to the stout Bartlett, with whom he seemed inexplicably bound.

Some time into the meeting Harvey stood. "To knowledge and friendship!" he said, raising his mug. "Tonight we are come together to uncover the mysteries of all the world. We will speak of navigation, longitude, astrolabes, and all that is within and without this universe. We will speak of heaven and earth, for there are no secrets that we are not meant to discover!"

"Sayst well, bones!" replied Bartlett from his chair.

Nicholas murmured, "Amen!" By this time he had made up his mind that Wentworth was not coming, but soon after they heard a horse in the lane and in a moment the dark, quiet, almost scornful young landowner stood at the door.

It was a small dusky room with its skeletons and alembics, and jars of metallic substances, and surgical tools, and hundreds of books. The men who were supping sat by several candles, and the newcomer was yet in the shadows. At last at their welcome he came forward, smiling in a brilliant, boyish way, and shook their hands. After a time they all rushed out to see a shower of meteors over the spires and bridge of the city, falling ever towards the north.

Later Harvey said, "Another lad who wants to sit for Commons! Well, Parliament's not called, and God knoweth when it will be. Still, there is something honest about him." They hoped to have Wentworth come again, but he had gone home to the north.

FIVE

The Printer's Niece

SUMMER CAME, AND WITH IT HIS LOVE FOR THE PRINTER'S NIECE.

With Heminges and the other actors, he had consulted printers for the best price and time to print such a massive folio as Shagspere's work would require, and at last settled as they expected on Isaac Jaggard. Jaggard gave them an estimate of four years to print and proof the sheets, resolving to do one play at a time, in the order in which they were received. It was when Nicholas returned with the first act of one of the histories on a warm day in June that he saw Katherine had come back to the city, and his heart leapt.

She was seated on a stool under the shop sign making a list upon the blank side of a discarded folio page pinned to a board on her knee while behind her through the open door apprentices set type and hung newly printed sheets to dry. At the sight of him she fell to tucking in loose strands of her hair under her embroidered cap.

Raising his voice over the banging of the presses, Nicholas said, "Is Master Isaac within, lass?"

"Nay, gone to deliver some work for binding."

"I did not expect to find thee here. Hast come to stay?"

"Aye, for a time."

Nicholas remembered the kiss on the stairs which had passed between them. He sat down near her, glancing at her round face with its freckles across the nose, and her hands roughened slightly from housework and stained with ink. One may look as long as one likes at a flower but not a person. He only wanted to remain there talking of small matters, and gazing at the freckles which were scattered across her neck and down her bodice.

In the next few days he was so possessed with thoughts of her that once he did not raise his pen from the page he was writing, and found it had leaked a round spot of ink through to the table. He recalled her round little figure and the shimmering hair which was like the sun on wheat fields. He made a pretense of walking that way and then going inside to ask for this or that, hoping to find her behind a desk where she might be writing out the bills. Other times she would be before the door sorting through boxes of type to discard those worn and chipped. Then he would sit beside her and talk.

She was the youngest child in a household of brothers, who all had contributed to educate her. For a country girl she had read much, and was eager to talk of it; she also spoke to him of God, and when she did this, she wrung her fingers together and became suddenly shy. He talked to her sometimes of the love of man for his brother, and when he raised his eyes would find her smiling radiantly at him with the loose pieces of type spilled to her apron. They would look at each other as long they dared. He would run home warm and sweaty, and bathe in the tub before the fire for a long time.

She was betrothed to a farmer in Kent.

Still, he remembered the round, soft flesh of her arm where she had pushed up her sleeve. He felt terribly young then and retreated protectively behind his books. He spoke in words too complex for her to understand, and then repented it. Still, to be her teacher suited.

Many a morning that summer he woke to the singing of the birds in the quince tree, the good smell of wet leaves and the fragrance of herbs rising from the garden below. Those were sweet days when he would come down the street to Aldersgate hearing the clanging of the presses and the laughter of the apprentices. On warm lingering evenings, not quite gone five of the clock, half of London sought to be upon the water, windows were thrown open, and the fragrance of flowers drifted down the winding streets above the other scents of mews and muckheap. Young girls, just come by boat from Southwark and the theaters there, glanced at him.

Then the local alderman forced the cesspit men to cart away muck of all description to the ditches beyond the city wall, and a gentle wind blew up from the river. That was the first time he took her and her cousin to the play at Blackfriars. The theater, originally a school and then a boys' theater run by unscrupulous men in the 1590s who were not above kidnapping country lads with pretty voices, had been bought some twenty or more years before by the King's Men and made into the most successful enclosed theater in London. He did not remember what play was given, for he was too absorbed in watching Kate's alert face as the men danced. They walked home in the darkness through the narrow streets, reciting bits of Chaucer's *Tales,* which she knew well, or singing part songs as they remembered them. They sang "Three Merry Men" and "Come o'er the Bourne, Bessie!" The girls' linen underskirts moved against the slender iron frames of their farthingales. She kissed him casually good night, and he burned like a boy.

Sometimes she came alone. Then they wandered to Finsbury Fields for fresh milk, and other times to the brick kilns. The windows of the city were thrown open, flowers bloomed in pots before the doors of houses, and streets were shady with heavy trees. Once the Lord Mayor rode past in his carriage towards Smithfield for the opening of Bartholomew Fair, his retinue marching before, staffs in hand; there were alderman in scarlet gowns, clerks of office, and several companies of militia: men of middle years, muskets over shoulder or pikes borne before. Before and after came the trumpets and flutes.

Sometimes they rode upon the water with the gulls shrieking above, and the boatmen's harsh cries and the sound of the rapid current under the bridge. Or they went up Cheapside between the stalls of silks and custards, or to the Royal Exchange where the double rows of shops contained linen from Holland, and Irish wool, civet perfume, farthingale pins, sugar cakes, and fruit from Portugal. Now and then Katherine turned to say something to him and he felt a warm, stupid blur of happiness.

They went to the Tower to see the lions caged there, and he related the story of the elephant who had died on shipboard during the voyage to England. They gazed at the place where Lord Essex had been beheaded, and his fingers touched hers as he told her how he had followed Essex to the Irish wars when a boy and how that lord's death had grieved him. To the wharfs then they went to see the ships, and back up to Finsbury, where a small military company was drilling on the green under the lines of washing strung from trees. They went to the Globe Theater across the water to see *The Knight of the Burning Pestle,* buying nuts from the attendant. They wandered in the antique church of Middle Temple, where the stone effigies of knights lay about the floor in full armor as if fallen in battle with no one come these hundreds of years to claim them. And in all those long days the sensual lay like an unopened box between this betrothed girl and himself, and neither spoke of it.

She came to his house one day because it had begun to rain.

The skies were darkening as they hurried down Wood Street, past tailor and tallow-chandler shops. In his parlor the light was dull upon the frayed chair cushions and unpolished brick of the floor, and dust particles hung about the air. He took her hand and led her up the stairs to the garret, where they looked through the dingy window over the tiled and thatched roofs to the city wall. "In such a room but down this street I came as a boy," he said. "Dost fancy it?"

"Oh, aye."

On the second story she stood at the door of his chamber gazing curiously at the narrow, worn brown-curtained bed and the clothing on pegs. Some dirty hose he kicked with the back of his boot under the legs of the standing wardrobe and hoped she had not seen how dusty were the lattice panes and how he had writ the altitude of Venus in its closest phase therein one idle night last spring.

She said seriously, "Show me thy work."

So he took her to the dispensary, where he opened brown glass bottles, displayed drying herbs and the contents of the small drawers of powders, opium, laudanum, mercury, and rose oils. And all the time he was aware of her small, soft figure and intelligent face which noticed everything.

The rain was falling heavily. They shut the windows, gazing at each other in the sudden grey shadows of the day. From Cheapside the bells tolled the hour of six. He said, "I did not think it would rain."

"Nor I."

"Let us wait until it ceases."

They pushed aside bowls of onions and turnips on the kitchen table and sat down together, his hand near hers. To have her so close and yet not to touch her confused him. She became a blur of yellow embroidery, and his throat was parched with longing.

Katherine took mending from her bag and quietly began to repair worn places in a sock, which he presumed to be her uncle's. Still before he could make up his mind to comment upon it, she put down her needle and said, "I must go now."

"Rain's still falling."

"Not so much."

"Then I shall make thee a map to this house that you may come back again as thou wilt, sweet Kate."

Rapidly taking pen and ink from the shelf, he began to draw the streets. "Here we have great Cheapside and its cross and water conduits and shops!" he said stoutly. "Down away from the river toward the London Wall runneth Wood Street, where I lived as a young apprentice. Here, before the holding prison and down from the tavern. Goeth this way and cometh to Love Lane, called for the harlots who worked there

some centuries back. Here under the overhanging second and third stories which almost touch and come ye to my house, which hath outside it
painted in the wood the sign of three sparrows, why no one can remember, and where we at present sit. From my kitchen door it is three steps to
the graveyard of my church, and among others there lieth . . ."

"There lieth . . ."

He ceased to draw. "My son . . . my first from the time I was married.
The others I granted my wife when the marriage was annulled and she
took them with her. They live far off and don't know my name." The
words had come suddenly and so shocked him that his mouth dried and
he could say nothing else. Grief clawed under his ribs to find a place to go.

She turned and drew him against her in a soft, womanly way so that
her fair hair brushed his face and he could feel the beating of her heart
under the blouse. "Oh what sadness!" she said.

"Aye, life hath much of that," was his gruff reply.

"Wilt tell me more?"

Uneasily he folded his arms across his chest. "I have no family nor
have not since I was very young," he said roughly. "I was five years old
when they hung my father for stealing. A shiftless fellow he was, full of
too many excuses, yet I loved to ride on his back when he went out
walking with my mother by the hand of a Sunday afternoon. He wept to
say goodbye to me."

Then he didn't know what he didn't tell her: his heart spilled open as it
had not in years. He told her the story of his youth, not in the amusing
way he often did but of terror and blood and that he had almost killed a
man when thirteen years old to save his own life. He told her about his
marriage, and how he had often heard Susan's weeping in the darkness
because he had withdrawn from her, and how for a time he could not love
his children nor anyone else. He told her he was afraid to love again.
Then, exhausted, he murmured, "The rest thou knowst. Let me take thee
away now."

But she said, "Dance with me as thou didst before."

The neighbor's son, young Mark, who played in one of the guild bands, had begun a tune on his sackbut which floated over the roofs and down the chimney. It was one of those stately court dances, and Nicholas pushed back the table, and humming along with the melody, took her left hand in his right, and began to show her the steps. The rain dripped down the upper stories of houses to the cobbles, and somewhere a child fretted, but Mark played on.

Her cap had come off, and her hair fallen loose.

"If thou wert here and mine own lass," he said, " 'twoud be a pretty place."

"Aye, I would make it so!"

"Wouldst wake when I came late at night, for in my work I ofttimes do? Wouldst wake?"

"I would not sleep until you came," she said solemnly. "Oh master, I like thee so! Art all gentleness."

Someone called, and the music ceased. He looked down at her and brushed her hair back. "I must take thee home, Kate. I don't wish it, but it must be," he said.

"Wilt come for me tomorrow?"

"Aye."

The rain had lessened but for the water which yet ran down the gutters to the path. He took a lantern, and walked out to the lane with her. The city smelled richly, as it always did after rain, of old stone and ancient earth and wooden doors as they walked west towards the old fortress hill and barbican.

It was before the portico of a church that he began to stroke her face. Her hair fell loose once more, her cap tumbled, and he caught it, holding it behind him. She cried out, "Oh I like thee so! Canst not like me as well, mayhap forever?" She kissed him now, whispering in a hot, flushed, childish way, "I'd have thee above all others, this I swear."

He whispered in awe, "Kate." Then he kissed her, feeling the line of her farthingale against his groin, and the soft heat of her breasts. He was incoherent with longing and barely could walk on.

At the sign of the printer's shop she turned. "Tomorrow!" she said. He waited as she ran up the steps, stumbled home, and did not sleep at all. It was just past dawn when the printer's youngest apprentice knocked upon his door with a note from Katherine tucked in his sleeve. Word had come of her mother's illness, and she was leaving for Kent at once. Hardly dressed, he ran out towards Tower Wharf where the ferry departed for Gravesend and saw it disappearing into the misty morning down the long river which led to Kent and the sea.

We are beggars without love, and fools with it, as his bishop, William Sydenham, had sometimes told him. Write me, she had implored him. He bent his head and hurried home to do so.

He knew, of course, that he must have her back at any cost, and would find himself sleepless in the middle of nights, lighting his candle and writing at great length, much of which he tore up. He was uncertain what he wished to say, and the truth was he wanted her at once as one desires something of a sudden, and was in a frenzy of uncertainty. He fancied her daily within his rooms and then turned from the thought.

In his garden the yellow quinces had ripened at last, and Andrew helped him boil some seeds to make the milky substance that was so excellent for treating sore throats. The year turned to late autumn. Scents of slaughter from the Shambles hung in the cooler air. He threw water in the gutters before the doors to cleanse them and hung rosemary before the windows. He brewed purgatives and prepared his paper on the properties of light for his friends. As a priest he grew in gravity and solemnity, as if he were again reaching for a deeper aspect of his soul.

He wrote Katherine often, and as often he would find upon his dispensary table replies from her in the now familiar hasty, small handwriting; he could almost see, as he broke the seal, her nibbled nails, sturdy fingers, and large brown eyes. And yet how much did he know her, or rather, what was there to know but that she was very young, and soft, and wanted him? She had called him as "all gentleness." That she believed in part of him which he had, upon the dissolution of his marriage, ceased to believe in himself was most potent. He would have liked to think her right, and his experience wrong. So the letters grew. They filled the crannies of his life, and wedged between apothecary jars, and under the orations of Cicero near the broken candleholder on top of his bedchamber wardrobe, where they glistened faintly when the moon came through the window on sleepless nights.

Sometimes he wrote with distance; another time, after officiating at a wedding, he wrote a letter of such emotional rashness that he could not bear to forward it and ended scribbling an analysis of a patient with swollen belly on the back, and then, with severe editing, recopying the missive to send off at last. Again and again he drafted a letter asking her hand in marriage, and put the papers in the fire.

to Nicholas Cooke, physician and priest, The Rectory of St. Mary Aldermanbury within Cripplegate, The City of London

Sweet parson!

Thy letter came this morn, the third this week, and I have read it now once again. I often think of what we began to speak of that evening, of how it would be between us. You could teach me to brew purgatives and beer against scurvy, and I would come every Sunday and sit in the first pew to hear thee preach. I would like six children; wouldst more? And at night I would wait up for thee, and make a warm place under the quilt when thou camst late from thy work.

So thy words puzzle me, or rather the lack of them, for thou hast writ of every matter from catechism classes to the birth of twins and never on the one of which we spoke. What shall I do? Knowst my mother and father have chosen a husband for me, and he is good though not like thee. Still he cometh twice weekly with presents and sits on the courting bench, and it's expected I'll have him. And I would have, had I not seen thee.

But thou art silent, and weeks pass and dost write of every matter but this one. Yet thou hast writ again and again, and sent thy love once more, and what can it mean? I must make answer to the boy, so dearest parson, if truly thou shouldst want me as wife, board the ferry at Tower Wharf and make fair for Gravesend and Kent and speak for me. I kiss thy hands and sweet face, as I have done thy letter this and many more times.

Kate

He wrote several answers, discarded them all, and then wrote one which told her much but not that which she wished to know.

Sweet girl,

Kate, I am here sending thee a beer I have brewed against scurvy from watercress, brooklime, and scurvy grass, flavored with cinnamon and juniper berries. I am giving it to all the children in the parish who come to me lest they suffer from the symptoms before spring cometh.

On other matters, I think how to form the words. I shall come presently, presently. You shall hear my plans very soon.

A thousand kisses, sweet Kate.

My dear pastor,

We had last night our first real frost. I ran out in my shawl and saw the field glittering in the grey dawn.

Dearest parson, when may presently be, and when may be soon? Send me news of thee.

Sweet girl,

The news of me is thus: I have a worried countenance, and I walk with my hands behind my back, studying the cobbles.

I shall come I think by All Souls' Day to speak to thy honest mother and father. I shall by that time do it, dear Kate.

Dear Master Cooke:

All Souls came and I waited by the house until dark, and no sign of thee, and then cometh a letter saying nothing of the matter. They press me to have the banns called, and what can I say?

73

The pile of her letters grew under his broken candleholder on his dresser; he could not think of prayers at night for the pages which whispered to him. Sometimes he took the latest to bed and found bits of green sealing wax crumbled to the sheets in the morn. He was haunted with old memories, and said bitterly, aye! Aye she loves me now, but when we have satisfied the first lusts and the newness of it, when the shutters are put up and the fire damped and the watch calls, what then? Would she expect me to bide with her, and there will be no sound but the cradle rocking? Then will love fall away as it did before? And if any drover or baker's lad can make a satisfactory home, why not I?

Christmas came, and the white rose.

Tom had returned to settle for a time in the small stone house in St. Martin's Lane within Aldersgate behind a garden of trees, and when Nicholas came around the corner of the church, he looked to see the candles in the upper windows. In the vestibule hung a new portrait of James Stuart, and the voice which called to him sweetly from up the stairs was that of the mistress of the house, with whom Nicholas had at once fallen a little in love.

Margaret Wentworth was a tall, fragile, and soft-spoken girl who seemed bewildered by the growing number of people surrounding her vigorous husband. Now and then Nicholas took her wrist in his hand, concerned for the rapidity of the pulse beneath the delicate flesh. It seemed to murmur, I cannot conceive, I cannot bear a child! Her blue eyes begged him to help her as she leaned slightly towards him in her marital chamber rich with tapestries and statuary and every beautiful thing which Tom Wentworth had bought for her in his love. Nicholas suffered for her, now and then wondering if the fault might lie with the husband rather than the wife. These words he did not speak, grimacing to think of Wentworth's astonished, hurt denial. He merely murmured consolation to Margaret and continued to bring her tonics and tell her stories to amuse her. Then, when they heard the carriages and horses of supper guests, she would go downstairs on Nicholas's arm, suddenly gay and wanting to welcome everyone in her husband's name. She adored him.

Nicholas met many people in the house that winter, including the President of St. John's, Cambridge, William Laud, a small man with a pointed greying beard, plainly dressed, who hurried about on little feet. He was one of the King's chaplains, reputed to be a great educator, for he had reformed much of Eton and vastly improved the instruction and library of his Cambridge college. He did not, however, come often to court, not being in favor with his Majesty.

There was a young lord, Michael Dobson, who stopped by now and then, his beard perfumed, his nails manicured, talking much of art, women, and the court. He knew Harvey, he said, having been bled by him once, and was eager to join the society for natural science. There was an older lord, John Harrington, who also strongly applied for membership on his interest in the earth's crust, mountains, and seas. A bluff, huge, and gross-spoken barrister with flowing grey hair to his shoulders in the manner of former days, he had been at war with Sir Walter Raleigh in his youth and was now approaching his sixtieth year. These and many others came and went in the stone house that year.

Thomas Wentworth welcomed them all. The house was also full of his close friends: George Radclyffe, who had been at school with him, and Christopher Wandesford, who was his secretary and traveled at his side. On a table in the corner of the parlor some legal books often lay open, generally Fitzherbert and Rastell's *Terms of the Law;* when he was in the city he would often read them late at night after Margaret had mounted to bed.

Now that Nicholas began to know him somewhat better, he saw at times a strange brooding about Wentworth. Still, he knew the young landowner would have given his cloak on a cold day to a friend, or the last coins in his pocket. His energy was prodigious: it was nothing to him to race back and forth from Yorkshire, where he had acquired more land and a little more influence in the politics of his shire. He left Margaret in the physician's care when away, and Nicholas would walk over several evenings a week to see her. She liked to tell his fortune with tarot cards, and in turn he told her something of his heart, including a few words of the printer's niece in Kent. And placing her soft hand on his and looking into his eyes, she said, "Go and marry! Do, Nick, and shalt be happy."

Then Wentworth would return, and there would be the small dinners again and music up the stairs. Everyone knew that he wanted a peerage as a hungry man wants bread, and the King would not sell him one. That troubled Nicholas, who felt even then the desire to protect him. So came the approach of spring and Lent, and the removal of the science meetings to the house of the new member, Michael Lord Dobson, in the Strand.

Dobson was a young man of striking beauty who wore his long hair curled to his shoulders in the new fashion of the younger men of court. He came from an old northern family whose men had served under Henry at Agincourt two hundred years before and had inherited a title from his father, but little else; he was twenty-five years old and had just returned from a tour of the Continent to take up residence in his family's damp, aged house halfway to Westminster. He was by this time a close friend to Lord Buckingham, the handsome favorite of the King, and hoped with this influence to be rewarded revenues on the importation of sweet wines. Nothing delighted him more than the physical world, and there was not another member who brought so much curiosity.

It was on Tuesday of Holy Week that Nicholas first came down the Strand towards the lord Dobson's house, with the air cool and the streets threaded here and there with children begging for pennies. Andrew Heminges trotted by his side. The lad had once more quarreled so badly with his father that the shouts could be heard to the wall, and he had run with his few belongings to stay with Nicholas for a time.

Entering through the side of the house to the stone kitchens, they discovered two barefoot young women frying pancakes. Upstairs the other men awaited in a parlor hung with threadbare tapestries, the one above the chimneypiece darkened from a century of fire smoke. The heavy physician Henry Bartlett was jubilant, for his wealthy widow had consented to their marriage and he could leave his small dispensary and set up an elegant large one. Greeting each other with the usual shouts and disparaging remarks, the men hurried off with Dobson at their head to tour the house and Wentworth at his side.

Paper peeled from the walls. The furnishings were old, and they found books and maps in the attic which had belonged to Dobson's father, all faintly mildewed and spotted. They also explored the lower cellars, where they remarked on the foundations of what the fascinated Avery declared to be the remains of a Roman temple, and he took out paper and a lead pencil to write down its measurements. With a quiet smile, Dobson told his friends how convenient it was to be on the river, for girls from the Southwark brothels could come across at his pleasure. One girl who had come by night had dropped a cheap paste necklace between the wet stones of the cellar. He did not recall him which she was, he said, holding it between his fingers.

Returning to the parlor, they gathered about a table and began to speak of Agricola's great study of the earth's crust published some sixty years before in Basel. Nicholas talked of his new work on the study of light. Hours had passed and the disinterested Andrew gone to look for the girls in the kitchen when the double doors burst open, and one of the young creatures herself rushed into the room.

Dobson drew her to him, but she pushed him away with both hands and blurted her news. A small boat had just landed at the wharf from across the water bearing one of her friends who could scarce walk, so badly did she bleed between her thighs. The men leapt up at once, following the lord down the steps towards the kitchens.

On a low stool sat the girl, shivering in spasms under her shawl, leaning against an older, pockmarked woman who was stroking her arm. The girl's terrified eyes met them as she rose to attempt a curtsey. Beneath her flimsy skirts the blood dripped to her yellow satin slippers.

Dobson whispered, "Sally!"

Pushing between them, Nicholas lifted the girl in his arms and carried her up the stairs. The guest sleeping chambers had not been warmed, so they laid her on Dobson's great ancestral bed, whose posters were as thick as a man's waist. Harvey, stroking his beard as he did when agitated, barked instructions.

As the girl whimpered, "Christ, have mercy!" the story was babbled by her older friend. The lass's flosses had stopped two months before, and now she bled and bled. Then the woman confessed she had stuck a slender rod into the girl's womb to abort the child; she fell to her knees before them, grasping at the men's hands and begging she not be tried before the ecclesiastical courts as a bawd.

Dobson pulled away from her in fastidious horror. Seizing the lace of his cuff so that it ripped in her hand, she cried in an accusing voice, "The child was yours, good my lord, for she was a maid when you took her and she never since that time had a one but you. She did it from fear of thy displeasure, good my lord."

Nicholas had by this time torn a clean shirt from the press and stuffed the strips into the entrance to the girl's womb. Against the extravagant satin bed rugs and embroidered pillows, she lay panting and whimpering, her thighs trembling. Young Andrew stood beside them, his eyes opened wide. They fed her beef broth, and prepared infusions against infection. All this the weary girl knew but little, and closing her eyes at last, she fell asleep, the blood flow lessening and after a time dwindling to a seepage. Nicholas also closed his eyes for a moment, for his legs were trembling. He wondered if this girl had been the one who dropped the paste necklace and who had come softly on pretty feet on the little boat from across the river to this mansion's wet steps. Laying his hand on her sleeping forehead with a prayer, he turned from the bed.

Dobson had remained apart, his arms clasping his chest and with a dark frown on his face. Now he spat into the fire, walked to the door, and opened it. The men followed.

Tom Wentworth had remained silent while he tore the sheeting: the lithe body had compressed itself and bowed as he ripped the linen, and when the crisis was passed, he had thrown back his head and compressed his mouth so hard that his face took on a sternness that was patriarchal in its warning. He had left the room where the girl slept without a word, and as they all walked down the steps, he turned to his host and said coldly, "Dobson, dost bed a lass and allow thy child to be murdered? Art a whoremaster to have done such a thing?"

"What sayst?" was the stunned reply. "Sally's dear to me! I would have fed the bastard. Did I ask her bawdkeeper to stick in the rod?"

Wentworth answered, "Were I judge in the north as I shall be and thou called before my bench, wouldst have shortly of thy deserving." He began to pull off his doublet. "I won't honor thee by a challenge, but will beat thee with my fists."

Nicholas shouted, "Tom, stay!" but Wentworth had taken Dobson by the shirt, while the young lord, cursing, struggled to pull out his dagger. They were parted with difficulty; the men were all shouting and the old woman had run out of the room above.

Then Dobson turned his head and began to weep. The sound stunned the group into silence, and Nicholas murmured, "God-a-mercy, Tom, enough harm's been done! Wouldst add more?"

Tom pushed him off; he stood, hatless, thrusting back his thick hair. " 'Twas only," he stammered, "for what I want more than all the world was given this whoremaster so easily and thrown away. . . ." His throat quivered. With his hat still in his hands, he ran down the steps and out the door, his boots echoing in the empty hall. Andrew and a few of the other men ran after him, but he was gone.

The next day Harvey found a small clean cottage south of the city, and sent the girl there to recover her strength. She did not stay long, and they could not find what had become of her. Dobson fell into a high fever, and Nicholas borrowed a horse so he could ride quickly between his other obligations to see him. The young lord lay in a little sleeping chamber, sweat glistening above his mustache, hair uncurled and tangled. In the yard of the house, servants had slit open the ruined mattress of the great chamber to clean the feathers for use in another bed. Nicholas threw wide the chamber windows, and the cold wet air of early spring blew in from the river.

Andrew reconciled with his father and left the physician's house, a pile of a dozen books of poetry he had been reading remaining on the small chamber windowsill with leaves as bookmarks and his dirty hose on the floor. Then Tom came shamefaced to the dispensary some days later to ask for more physic to help his wife conceive.

Nicholas, who had been up all night with a sick old woman, took him by both arms. "Tom, Tom," he murmured sternly. "There's sadness enough in life! Nothing must come between us, for we are sworn fellows. Make it up with Dobson, as you love me."

"I shall," said Wentworth. "For none of you shall dislike me . . . others may. But not these and thine." He rode solemnly to the house on the Strand and drank with Dobson all night and came away friends, as if there were no differences between them and could never be again. Between these two then was a sudden, extravagant, flowery love. They had a crafty understanding of each other's determination to make their way through the thorny briars of the court to stand at last before James Stuart the King. Dobson wished to flatter him, Wentworth to hold up his hand wisely so that his Majesty would know how far he could go and no further and yet, somehow, be grateful for it.

Even so, they were for that season, and sometime further, as close as men could be. Dobson wrote even to Tom's wife, "Beloved chosen of my own beloved!" Once they fought playfully with dull rapiers the length of the hall of the old house on the Strand, empty as it was of almost everything but pictures in warping frames. The clanking of the swords, and their shouts, rose up the stairs and out the window to the Thames.

SIX

Eastertide

ASTER CAME WITH ITS ANCIENT CRY FROM HOUSE TO HOUSE:

"Christ is risen."

"The Lord is risen indeed."

In the wet early-spring morning, Nicholas walked to the fountain to fill his bucket. Already the neighbor's son was practicing his krumhorn to accompany the psalms during the service with his father playing bass viol. Sun rose and day broke dully over the tiled roofs and the gargoyles of the steeple.

A procession was made to the altar, with the boys singing and the actors playing their instruments. Nicholas consecrated the bread and wine as he had done weekly in the two years of his priesthood. Then early the next morning he left the city with his horse by the ferry towards Gravesend, the water grey before him all the way to the sea. He had seen the nearness of death and the precariousness of love sharply and had made up his mind to hesitate no longer but to make the printer's niece his wife.

Katherine Jaggard's family house was a stone manor house with root cellar, brewery, bakery, and stable, and some barns for grain storage in the midst of soft brown fields. Nicholas, who had worn his cassock and broad-brimmed clergyman's hat, dismounted and, finding the doors open, descended to the kitchen, where several men were standing about.

Wild birds lay bloodied, slack-feathered and newly killed, upon the table. Removing his hat, he asked to speak to Kate, and the oldest brother escorted him to a small, dark parlor. Her drawings were about, as well as some musical instruments and many old books. Thick matted rushes from last fall lay on the floor, though someone had sprinkled them with dried roses. He wanted to take up the embroidered cap on the shelf and hold it against his heart, which beat so violently under his black coat. He touched everything with the tips of his fingers, for she had touched these things as well.

He was yet standing by the window overlooking the fields when he heard her steps. She wore the yellow dress embroidered down the front with flowers, and he knew he wanted nothing more in the world than he wanted her. Shutting the parlor door firmly, she stood before him, her lips parted and the freckles across her nose darkened with emotion.

He said, "Oh my sweet!"

"Master, art come at last?"

There was faint scorn in her voice, and he replied, "Didst not think I would? Didst think I could forget? Kate!" He moved to touch her arm but instead passed his hand over his mouth. "Kate," he said. "I want to make thee mine. Whatever thou wouldst want, I would provide it. However to change myself or my life for thy happiness, gladly, gladly I would give all."

She bit her lip and said nothing.

"Kate," he continued. "Knowst me well, for there's little I have not told thee. I have not until this moment trusted myself to make a woman content, but by Christ's blood, I think I could thee." He said very much more, then concluded with "Sayst thou, Katie," and fell silent.

There was no sound at all for some moments, but for the birds outside, and the whining of the bitch from the kitchen, and far off, her brothers calling from the field.

She whispered petulantly, "I was married last week and am only home to see my mother. Why didst wait? What hast done, parson, all the while I stayed for thee?" Raising her chin, she looked at him through defiant tears which glittered and did not fall. He was too stunned to say much more but made his way blindly to his horse, barely mounting, and felt the gaze of her father and brothers from across the fields as he rode off. He locked himself in his house when he returned and became as drunk as he could ever remember.

Spring passed into summer, and he moved through the days between a small outbreak of pox and some furious debate about whether further burials should be allowed within the city, and some poor wretch being whipped down Cheapside, his cries echoing to the wall. He fell into the sacraments of his church, preached sometimes haltingly and other times with a hope of heaven which seemed irrelevant to his mildly prosperous, somewhat unimaginative parish.

In those warm months he often woke and walked out on London Bridge to look over the city. Surely other men had stood much grieved on this very spot since saintly kings in pointed shoes had lodged in the Tower. Even he had come here other times (it seemed another life) choked with feeling for some cause he had now forgotten: he had been beaten mayhap, or wrongfully accused of something, or could not fit the jagged shape of himself in the too solid shapes of his world.

In this confused state when past and present grievances mingled, when the most recent love lost became all loves, he would stand and listen to the sounds of the city, which somehow comforted him. Beyond him in the darkness lay the great sloppy labyrinth of Whitehall Palace, extending chamber by chamber to the surrounding streets. Above, around, and beyond it were church steeples and the tiled roofs of houses, each holding individual lives with their own private disappointments which might find nearness to his. (Still he did not quite believe it.) Under garret roofs, boys must lie as he once did, reading of the greater world of opportunity that is the world of men, not knowing that one man, full-grown, stood upon London Bridge and found himself yet in a small room, and that of his own making, and unable to get from it.

A few taverns would still be open. In one mayhap young Andrew Heminges might sit at the feet of the corpulent, aging playwright Ben Jonson, to hear the silver verse:

> "I now think Love is rather deaf than blind,
> For else it could not be,
> That she
> Whom I adore so much, should so slight me.
> And cast my love behind."

And then half sodden with port (for Jonson thought it a sin to drink water) creep home and climbing up the beams of his father's house, drop softly to the floor.

Nicholas listened those warm summer nights to the creaking of boats as they pulled against their ropes, and the lapping of water against the bridge starlings. Crows and gulls fluttered to the wharfs beyond, and in all the houses on both sides of the Thames, lovers turned with a sigh and drew each other close. What dreams he indulged in upon stumbling home at last were too intimate to remember. They were gone with the dawn.

In the morning bruised young women would come to his dispensary who swore their husbands did not strike them, journeymen coughing sputum and blood, visitors in need of absolution, friends in need of conversation, messages from friends or Bishop William Sydenham, who was not well. Young Andrew would arrive. He consoled the poor, and regularly brought to Nicholas pregnant girls, beaten wives, a felon whose back was torn open by the whip, and once a leper. He brought them with trustful eyes, saying, "Heal them, Nick!"

And Nicholas would answer, "Come, lad! Asketh of me more than ever I can give!"

In those days he prayed very much for wisdom and strength, and the gift of healing others. Word came from Tom: "Do not forget our promise to each other!" He thought, what promise 'tis? And he remembered and returned to his work. There were the suppers, the meetings, the letters of the friends: the young chaplain of the President of St. John's had joined them, and a grocer. And strangely enough, after a time he himself began to heal.

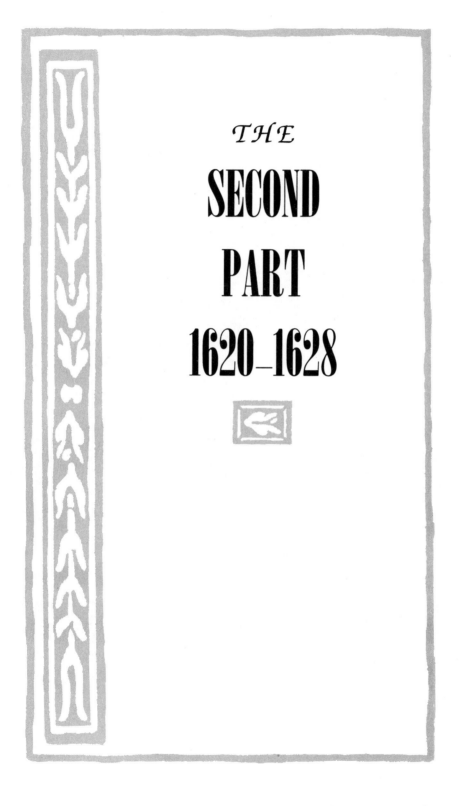

THE

SECOND
PART
1620–1628

ONE

Parliament

Y
ELLOW LEAVES LITTERED THE ALLEYS OF THE CITY ON A NOVEMBER
morning of the year 1620 as Nicholas walked over to the house
in St. Martin's Lane. He found Wentworth kneeling on the floor
of his library with law books and accounting ledgers from his estate
spread across the polished boards, and his secretary, a cheerful dark-
haired boy in his early twenties, cross-legged beside him. Leaping to his
feet, the lanky Yorkshireman embraced the physician with one arm.
"Parliament's called!" he shouted. "First in seven years! End January
'twill be: I am sent for West Riding by a pitiful margin, but the chiefest
thing is I'm sent, and will thumb my nose at them who'd stop me. Nay,
go upstairs, for my Margaret's asking for thy company!"

When Nicholas returned towards his own house later that afternoon,
he discovered that much of London had already heard the news. Even the
scrawny baker hurried from his shop wiping his floury hands on his
apron, saying, "Parliament's called! Grievances shall be addressed, on my
soul!"

Christmastide approached. Cold crept into the city, and chimneys flung out grey coal smoke, which dusted stone, cobble, and cloth. Carols drifted from church doors and the lips of housewives on their way to market, and here and there snippets of holly and ivy, customs left from the earlier pagan land, hung in parlors and over doors. And in January of the year of Our Lord 1621, members of both Lords and Commons began to arrive from every county of the realm. They rented small stone houses or opened their own long-unoccupied city dwellings, engaging a perfumer to sweeten the rooms.

Down the streets of Cripplegate and in the booths of the Mitre Tavern, tradesmen gathered to speak of wars and corruption, the two principal topics to be laid before the assemblies. The lord Buckingham held too many monopolies, and greatly was it resented, nor did they like his foreign campaigns, which must be paid for with English money and lives.

The physician William Harvey at the next science meeting burst out with his own particular dislike of the unprecedented number of men who had paid for knighthoods and peerages since the reign began. The corner of his mouth twitched as it did when he was profoundly irritated, which gave him a spastic look for a man just in his middle years.

"Oh, there's naught in that but it spreads power too freely!" was Dobson's reply. Then he added with an angelic smile, "And debases pure noble blood, such as mine."

Nicholas had spent much time with books of the annals of the country, studying the history of the government since the early kings when John Lackland had been forced by his nobles some four hundred years before to sign Magna Carta, giving them some constitutional restraints on royal power. Wentworth talked of little else but Parliamentary procedure, and Nicholas felt as if he peered into the inner mechanism of some complex timepiece, and touched the cogwheels and springs with the greatest interest. His old love of things mechanical filled him, and he cried, "Come, Harvey! Shall we see the procession which openeth the day?"

"Nay, not I!" barked his lean, reclusive friend, but in the end he was waiting on Nicholas's lane at five in the morning with bottled ale and bread in a satchel and a certain amount of disapproval on his long somber face. Together they set out, the lanes lit by many lanterns of men also going that way. At Milk Street they were joined by Avery, who rushed down from his new lodgings, hatless with his wild fair hair askew. He was dressed as usual in the same dark brown suit, worn thin at the doublet cuffs and seat of the breeches. As they hurried along, he proceeded to give the genealogy of city processions from the days of the crusades, frowning when an exact date eluded him.

Halfway down the Strand they came across Henry Bartlett's ostentatious new carriage. The jovial physician, now a lawfully wedded man, leaned out with his wife and shouted for his friends to come up. They shook their heads, knowing full well that the streets towards Westminster would soon be too congested for such a large conveyance to pass along. Also, to their consternation, they were unable to like the new Mistress Bartlett for her sharp tongue and shrewish treatment of her husband. Wishing them well, they once more continued to push their way towards Westminster.

Tens of thousands of people hung from windows or lined the streets waving torn bits of cloth, and Old Palace Yard could scarce hold a soul more. Representatives who had come late were emerging from their carriages or hurrying with their secretaries from the wharfs. Red-robed bishops floated past, chaplains and clerks hurrying behind them. Above the cries of ballad sellers and costers came the rich cursing of ostlers and the wild neighing of a rebellious horse.

The procession began. Up past the church steeples rose the music of the bands and the chaste singing of the choristers from St. Paul's praising heaven and earth. The breaths of the vicars choral who provided the lower registers were white in the cold air. Aldermen came, their scarlet gowns dusting the cobbles; then the sheriffs and the Lord Mayor, followed by members of both houses. "Ah, there's Tom with the Commons!" cried Avery, his chest expanding. "And Harrington and Dobson for the Lords!"

There followed bishops and the King's counsel, more drums and horns, and great wheeled barges decorated with gilded plaster and silk banners, and the volunteer military bands with musket and pike. Robes and horse coverings, still smelling of camphor against the moth, had been taken from their long storage: wafts of dust lingered in the cold air as the marchers passed. Lastly came the King himself, his heavy face smiling now and then in a begrudging way, extending his ringed hand to the crowd as if to say, "Ye have all my love. . . ." Emotionally the men of the city returned, "God bless ye . . . God save you, Majesty!"

The three friends struggled across the yard. On ordinary days the Commons would come to St. Stephen's Chapel and the Lords to the Painted Chamber, which had long ago been a presence chamber. Today both houses would meet in Westminster Hall, once a tennis court.

Doors were flung open and the crowd stumbled in.

Partitions had been carted away and long benches rose to the upper windows on both sides, while at the end of the hall a dais for the throne of the King had been erected. The Lords, each man a great personage in his own shire and now here among his equals, fussed about with quills and candles. The friends found places in the upper benches and looked about in fascination at the torch-lit, crammed chamber.

At the sound of the silver trumpet, men whipped off their caps and standing, bowed. From his chair of red velvet, erect in his ermine robes, James Stuart addressed his Parliament. His voice, still thick with the guttural brogue of the Scots, rolled to the rafters and over the much-trampled rushes of the floor. He spoke of the responsibilities of every man under the roof to uphold the country and his reign. He reminded them of the bitterness of foreign wars and policies, and asked for their help. The trumpet blew again.

He spoke then of his beloved daughter Elizabeth, who had some years previous married Frederick, the Elector Palatine of the Rhine. This past winter Frederick had accepted the throne of Bohemia, and the Catholics had declared war against him. He spoke of the marriage he hoped to contract between his son Charles and the Spanish Infanta, and also hoped by this that Spain would help restore his daughter's throne. Once more the trumpet blew.

Nicholas looked about at the Lords and Commons, who sat on opposite sides of the hall. A bishop sermonized, evoking God's help upon the proceedings. Near the King sat the beautiful George Villiers, Lord Buckingham. There were ballads about his rise in court: first to Gentleman of the Bedchamber, then Master of the Horse, and now Master of the Wardrobe. When he spoke briefly his golden voice was lost amid the shuffling of the attendants. The Lord Chancellor, Francis Bacon, the finest scholar in England, came forward with his silver walking stick, preceded by the Chief Usher bearing the Black Rod.

Pigeons flew indifferently about the rafters.

Voices rose, were lost, and appeared again. There should be an army sent to Bohemia, there should not: how many ships, how much provision, what arms. At eleven, Parliament was dismissed with a great shout from the Chief Usher. Nicholas and his friends forced their ways to the yard, where they found Dobson and Harrington waiting impatiently for them. "A man could die to take a piss for that the King spoke long!" said Dobson wryly.

"But not a fart: enough were laid freely about," rejoined Harrington in his gruff, loud soldier's voice: he always seemed ready to command the storming of a foreign city wall. He smiled broadly, showing poor teeth, and brushing back his long, dirty grey hair. "By Christ's wounds, lads! Let's proceed."

To a tavern in the back streets near the bookbinder's shop they went, passing the thin boys who rushed in and out of the doors carrying covered plates of food steaming hot from the ordinary some doors down. Capons, beef pie, smoked eel, turnips were whisked by them to be enclosed in private booths. The friends tumbled into a booth of their own, banging mugs on the rough planks of the table, demanding service, while the lethargic drawer rubbed his heavy hands and said, "Anon, anon, good sirs!"

Dobson threw back his head. "Where's Tom? Where hath the pricklouse gone? Where's Bartlett?"

"Still captive in his carriage, I warrant, being scolded by his wife. . . .

Nay, here he cometh, and I hear Wentworth's voice as well! The lads had wit to find us!"

The door of the booth was flung open, and Wentworth stood before them in his black doublet and simple collar of fine lawn, papers under his arm and his secretary by his side. His face, which was shining and grave, brought them to silence for a moment.

"By the Rood!" Dobson exclaimed in astonishment. "The lad's like a virgin come from his first time with a whore! 'Tis the countenance of an undefiled saint! I saw thee meek and eager on the Commons side, Wentworth! Uncapped before the Lords as is the old custom: is it not so that ye must sit uncapped before the Lords, thy betters?"

"I uncapped as was the custom," was the vague reply.

"What say ye, men! The lad's speechless from emotion! Didst not hear the lord Bacon say the lads of Commons must carry themselves with all duty and reverence befitting towards his most excellent Majesty? So doth this one. Wilt make thy maiden speech to us?"

Wentworth sat slowly beside them. He took a deep breath and replied, "I say I will love my King but will not ever let him take o'er his due."

"Whoreson, must stand for everything which I abhor?"

"And for what dost stand, Dobson?" was the grave answer.

"Myself . . . and therefore I abhor all that is not myself, and therefore do not stand for anything but myself." Dobson threw back his head and laughed. "All men feel the same; 'tis a mere guise that they appear otherwise! Thou wouldst have the best of lands and rents, and stand against the King, and in truth, 'tis not out of ideology, but interest, cleverly conceived."

"Now fellow!" said Harrington bluntly. "Let the lad speak."

The men grew silent once more, though the noise of laughter and singing from other booths and from the streets continued, and there was the sound of a recorder which squeaked and piped some country tune.

Tom looked about at them. " 'Tis this, friends. Under the good Queen Elizabeth there was perfect balance of harmony between court and country, between sovereign and Parliament. I speak not of one's prerogative

nor the other's and feel 'tis on this balance that all depends. And if the balance must upend, 'tis better the larger half be with the country, not the King. Therefore I shall prick him for his loose, unauthorized spending on wars and favorites. I would be a servant, an adviser. And I would tell him with all my heart that I believe there must never be an irrevocable division between Parliament and King."

Henry Bartlett snorted. "He chooses servants who would not admonish him like a schoolmaster with a switch, Wentworth! Mayhap 'tis the way among the ruder folk in Yorkshire, but not here in the very center of Christendom!" He looked about, greedy for approval, and then, nodding to himself, drummed his heavy, ringed fingers on the table.

Nicholas pushed the large round cheese from him. For some moments he studied the intense face of his friend, and the high chest, which moved steadily with emotion. Well did he remember that one of the most powerful men in Yorkshire was even now trying to discredit Wentworth's election. The young representative had already made enemies. The truth was, of course, as Nicholas understood it, that if a man as much as ventured an opinion, much less was elected to a post, he would achieve someone's enmity. That was the world. And there was Tom with his vast energy, rapid mind, and pure idealism plunging in like one of the prophets, the youthful Isaiah perhaps. *Then flew one of the seraphims unto me, having a live coal in his hand, which he had taken with the tongs from off the altar: And he laid it upon my mouth . . .*

"Eat, my friend," he said.

"Nay, I am filled to the stomach's top with this day." Wentworth pushed the bread away and, sticking out his lower lip, became so silent and sullen that they were glad when he excused himself with his secretary and went away.

TWO

Travels and Margaret

IKE MANY DEEP-THINKING MEN OF GOD, NICHOLAS FOUND IT DIFFI-cult to reconcile the sadness of the human state with the ultimate power and goodness of the eternal. He was often angry about injustice, and yet could not look outside his window without seeing it in many ways. Vagrants were whipped bloody, the old poor forced to beg their bread, and the unwed mother mocked as a whore. He balanced himself with his books, in which he could assemble, in his mind, a more perfect world, and then walked out, impelled to bring what he felt so strongly could be achieved to his fellows. Sometimes he did and some-times he did not.

He thought of Katherine now and then, but it brought sullen pain until it seemed no kindness could touch him well enough to heal him. There were many young women about the parish who glanced at him as he strode about his work, but he received such glances skeptically, and went home alone, thinking it would end the same, and if he did not betray or weary of her, then she would do it of him. Inside he felt strangely vulnerable, as if he did not want to risk a great deal. He believed in God's goodness, and tried to cut the world to that same cloth, and when it failed, closed the shutters and returned to his reading and studies.

From these he again was made aware as in his boyhood that the ancient Greeks and Romans had known periods of civic harmony with a benevolent emperor or chief consul, a democracy in the wise advice of senate, a clean, marble-faced world of poets and thinkers and statesmen. It had been much the same, Wentworth often exclaimed in their many walks in the fields outside the city walls, in the days of Elizabeth the Queen, and what she had begun would and must now go forward. James Stuart was a benevolent statesmen and a good man, though at times he played the fool. Thus Nicholas balanced in himself, and in the vision of his country, both good and evil. He tried to balance his longing for the spiritual with the aching of his flesh.

One day when walking to Lambeth, he passed some young women splashing in the muddy, half-stagnant pools before the Archbishop's palace, linen shifts clinging to their uplifted breasts. "God give you good day, sir priest!" they called like chattering birds, then covering their mouths to hide their shrieking.

"Oh do look but once, sir priest! 'Twill not send thee to hell!"

"Come and see us, then, master!"

Throwing back their heads, long loose hair trailing the dirty water, they wrapped arms about each other. "Marry, art a bonny fellow! Canst not smile at us?" One splashed hard, and water wet his doublet. She touched her palm to her lips and wafted the kiss to him. He went off to their laughter, his handsome mouth set hard. As poorly as he had managed love to this moment in his life, he knew that what he wanted was not simply a hasty embrace, whether freely given or paid for, but a sympathy of minds. He wanted to love and be loved wholly, and if he could not have this, he would have nothing.

Plague returned to the city in the summer of 1621.

Bartlett and several friends at the College of Physicians had mentioned there were signs of it in the slums outside of Westminster, and the bookbinder Tim Keyes reported his upstairs neighbor felt poorly. Two women of the parish were feverish, and though Nicholas did not think much would come of it, he wanted to search his medical books to once more read the pages on contagious diseases. The dispensary bell did not ring, though the post brought a letter from a friend of Galileo in Florence saying that great man was rethinking his recently published work on comets.

Harvey knocked on the door at the end of the afternoon, shoulders hunched and mouth grim. "Come look at one of the women in our ward," he barked. "Tell me what thou thinkst."

" 'Tis returning?"

"I am half sick to name it," was the answer.

The evening was warm, and the scent of gardens and the cool June winds permeated everything else. Near the gate of Blackfriars they passed under an arch, down an alley, and up some steps above a bakery. A plump woman sat there with embroidery on her knee, and when she saw them, bit her lip in a confused, anguished way as if they were come for the rent and she did not have it. They sat down next to her on stools, murmuring to calm her. "Now show thy breast, mistress, for Christ's good mercy," said Harvey in a far less brusque way than was his normal manner.

"Dare not."

"My friend shall not startle thee, mistress: cannot see he is in holy orders and a good man who payeth his yearly tax and tithe! An honest man! Now showst the lesion, mistress, by our lady. We mean thee but well."

"And if 'tis a dark sickness?"

"Well then, 'tis, and we must manage."

She clenched her hand so that the embroidery hoop clattered to her feet and began to wail. "I have three babes and my sister's ill!"

Nicholas was much moved, though impatient, and murmured, "Dear mistress." Then, her chest heaving, she undid her blouse with fingers roughened and pricked by the needle, and there were the dark spots and another half hidden by the brown hair under her fleshy arm. She sat with her bodice unlaced and her heavy breasts sagging as if ashamed, and wept, wiping her eyes with the heel of her hand. " 'Tis the sickness, is it not?" she whispered. "My granddad had it in the first year of the King! Must I burn herbs gathered under a gallows against it?"

"Nay, mistress."

"Then what shall I do?" Her voice rose in an angry, accusing wail. "What shall I do?" She gathered her bodice and laced it, and wiped her nose on the back of her hand. "I'll work until I sicken," she cried, "but I'll not sicken. I have a splinter from St. Paul's staff, 'twas my great-grandam's! I shall put it in a pillow of sweet sachet. . . ." With much compassion, Nicholas took her hands and told her she must go to bed, and drink hot ale, and if the black spots increased, to send a boy to his house. As the men hurried away down the alley, she threw open her shutters. "Charlatans! Pisspot pickpockets!" she shrieked.

They stopped in two or three more houses, and found a man who had the same spots, purged him, set rosemary leaves burning, and got him to bed. By that time night had come. As they passed the Tyburn gallows, they noticed two men and a woman beneath it on their knees cutting plants with a knife. They stared at the physicians defiantly, and one spat, but the woman began to cry.

From another neighborhood they could hear the faint sounds of wailing. "We are called to the fight once more, and yet once more we've not the forces," Harvey said. "From whence doth it come? What have we done that it returns?"

"I do not expect it to be great."

"That Our Lord agreeth to thy expectations, my friend!"

It was not yet midnight when Nicholas ran downstairs to find a little girl crying in the street for him to come. Her father on Addle Lane had broken out in dark splotches on his groin.

So went the summer. It was the worst pestilence he remembered since his little son had died in the year 1604 before he had his medical training. Many of his friends left the city, as did a few of the doctors, as it was permitted to do under the ethical code lest they be uselessly struck down. Many, however, remained, and some fellow physicians about the west part of the wall from Aldersgate through Moorgate met to discuss the isolation of the sick and how best ward constables could be persuaded to enforce the laws against muckpiles by doors or emptying of chamber pots into street gutters. Theaters were closed and public gatherings forbidden.

Dobson moved to his country house and took Bartlett and his wife with him; the portly doctor, bright-eyed as a boy who tells tales, stumbling and ashamed, made loquacious excuses of his poor wife's health as they clambered into the springless carriage and were jolted away. Avery swore solemnly to remain. Harrington and his wife packed neatly as they always did and philosophically went north.

He sent notes over to the Wentworths in St. Martin's Lane, not willing to go himself and expose them to possible contagion.

Tom,

You would grieve could you see what I have seen these weeks! The worst is in the hovels down alleys near Aldgate and behind Westminster. In my parish the ward constable has cleaned the cesspits daily and washed the streets down, but two darling little girls who had always waited behind corners to surprise me when I walked about the streets have been taken as well. I still expect them to leap into my arms at odd moments.

If ever hast power, wilt help the poor! Why do I say this? For what's debated is bribes and foreign wars, while disease and poverty are undefeated within our streets.

Most heartily do I miss our walks.

Nick

from Wentworth, St. Martin's Lane, writ before dawn

Nick,

Our household is well, though I am in trouble in my own county again, having now offended the Lord President of the North. Meanwhile there is a rumor that I may be made Comptroller of the Royal Household. I need sell some of my land, for my expenses are great living here and maintaining my siblings at home with schooling and dowries. Still I am reluctant to leave London for fear I will then never obtain influence at court. Parliament will sit again in the fall, I do believe.

If any man shall defeat such plagues, my friend, it will be thee. I say this with all my heart. Margaret sendeth love.

Wentworth

Nicholas wrote back copiously late each night. Extensively he poured out his regret that there were no hospitals for the stricken; those existing were for homeless, infirm, orphans, felons, and loose women. Hospitals had at first been a place where guests were received, an asylum for travelers and victims of disaster. It was less than this now and not much more. There were the very ancient St. Thomas on the south side, and St. Bartholomew on the north, where Harvey served as physician. Nicholas had gone with him once or twice and noted the scant supply of poorly washed bedlinens, and the matted, odorous rushes upon the floor. Flies gathered about the mugs and trenchers. Before the monasteries and nunneries had been dissolved in the last century, men and women in religious orders had cared for the ill. Now these were gone. There were a warden and matron at Bartholomew's, but she was often drunk and he surly. One time during the pestilence Nicholas walked home with Harvey wondering if it were possible to staff an excellent hospital for the sick, and teach young doctors their trade on the premises.

Harvey shook his head. "The College will not stand behind thee," he said. "Art but one of the newest members, and they'll not give thee power. Then, it taketh a wealthy man to endow a privy, much less a hospital, and that if I am not mistook is not thee. To whom hast given thy crowns away to now, Cooke? Never mind: do not tell me. Wilt die a pauper. Return to the grinding of lenses."

Fall came.

Cooler air cleared the dirt and infectious matter from the cracking wood of houses, and the deeper ruts of lanes. Stalls overflowed with apples and pears from the country, and streets around Smithfield resounded with the lowing of cattle driven to market. Court and King returned, and Londoners became accustomed to seeing the royal carriage again. Cripplegate Ward began to take on its old comfortable shape once more. Nicholas slid into it with a sigh, threw clean water before his door, and gave heartfelt thanksgiving for the return of health to the city. Dobson reappeared, as did Bartlett, somewhat ashamed of having left, fiddling with his doublet buttons until he wore the fabric from them, and biting the edge of his fingers. Harrington came last in the nearly packed carriage with his practical wife; they threw open the windows of their house and scrubbed the floors. The science society began to meet again, and the letters betwixt the men were brought by hurrying little boys in stained leather jerkins for a farthing.

writ gladly 4:00 A.M. of the clock, 11 September, on the kitchen table 'twixt crumb and butter by Our Lord's grace!

Harvey,

I have been torn from my sleep by my great mental engagement with the study of light, which is capable of being propagated into illimitable space and requires no time to do so, for, as it is without material substance, it offers no resistance to the moving force and henceforth hath infinite velocity. I find a mind unfettered to be the best of all, so here I remain, scant allegiance beyond decency to king and country, greatest to those holy spirits of intellect. No, I protest too much, for scarce cometh a day when some matter doth not torment me like a flea, like my lady louse in unclean inn.

Didst mark Venus last night, but a sliver in the sky? I have had the chimneys cleaned for winter and soot drifts about this room. I cannot sleep for my mind which shakes me awake and whispers, "Come on, come forward!" Ofttimes I wake and the words of one of the psalms come to my lips; another time it is as if I am not priest at all, but some ancient citizen of the world who *must know*. I think always of God, and then again very little of Him. My passion turneth to indifference. People talk of their sins, and I think of their bodies as well as their souls until soul and flesh go round about in me, like some pagan's dance about a tree.

I have worked more upon the properties of light and have concluded that it must be particles, moving infinitely quickly, but particles are substance, and therefore it must be otherwise. Oil reflects light better than does water. We must go through Kepler's works on optics page by page when thou hast time, arguing and reasoning it through. No, we are not meant for marriage, thou and I, for sooner or later I would want to talk of these things, and she would not be able to do so. And would I want her to? And why are we so limited, friend?

Nick

to Margaret Wentworth, St. Martin's Lane within Aldersgate

How kind that you send me cakes once more and hath knitted me a jerkin, badly needed. My old one was in holes, for moths favor bachelors. As I hold thee dear, I would make thy best dreams true, sweet Margaret.

I have followed thy louse of a husband's speeches in the present session of Parliament and am confused. "The greatness and power of his Majesty is our prop" and "The King and his people are to be considered jointly and not apart." Whence cometh this change? Doth he favor King or the houses? What doth he mean? What is this conciliator? Actually, I am pleased, as it is much to my mind even though conciliating seemeth not possible with neither side willing to move.

Kisses on both thy lovely hands!

Nick: parson, physician, and bachelor

He was in love with someone for a time, but she was married and he struggled bitterly with his vows, visited her twice, and in the end left her alone; still, he wondered what meant this burden of morality he had strapped to his back as a poor woodgatherer straps his ragged twigs to his shoulders and bends under the weight. There was always the desire to hurl it off and cry, Be damned! Still, he did not.

The first meeting of the College of Physicians since the plague had retreated from the city walls was held at Michaelmas with the fellows assembling once more under the portraits of King and medical predecessors. They greeted each other with shamefaced joking, drawing about themselves the dark robes of their profession. Contagious disease was the one thing they wished to avoid in their speech, and yet all thoughts turned round to it.

Arguments broke out. "Prayers and fasting are the only efficacious and sure method," cried one man. " 'Tis sin has brought this upon us!"

When Nicholas could be heard above the noise, he once more began to put forth his ideas of what they might seek under the microscope. Shouting answered him, and after a time the meeting drew to an untidy close. Some men were heard to say they were sorry they had admitted him. He was so angry he bid no one goodbye, but took Harvey's arm as they hurried away towards Paul's yard and the bookstalls.

"What did I tell thee?" Harvey said stiffly, opening a book on astrology, then pushing it away from him. "They wish to continue the methods they evolved when they were chartered in 1518." He stamped on the cobbles by the gate so that several pigeons squawked and waddled away. "There's nothing to be learned here, Nick!" he said, his mouth twitching and cheeks pale with anger. "We should go away to Paris, to Padua and Florence, like the wandering scholars of some centuries back. What do we in this dirty city?"

That evening a musician friend from Dieppe stopped by Nicholas's kitchen to tell them about his performances in the courts and noble houses in Holland, and what he had learned of lenses. He had brought back several wrapped in velvet and packed within straw in a locked box, and they were up late that night trying combinations of the convex and concave, altering the distance between them in the instrument shaft, to find the best resolution.

Harvey nudged his friend's arm. "Go abroad to study, Nick," he said. "We are seeking things we can't know we're seeking." When they left, Nicholas sat for some time looking into the glowing ashes of the fire, his mind greatly unsettled, the old questions rising slowly. What is the nature of God and of matter? How is this great world made? Why did he need the love of others?

from Wentworth, St. Martin's Lane, to the physician Cooke, Cripplegate within the Wall

My friend,

Harvey stopped by this morn to tell me that he hath proposed you to travel, and we also think thou shouldst go. I thought to for a time myself, for Parliament's concluded and I can see no prospect for advancement here for me. All possibilities to serve in the court have come to naught as are quickly my hopes for agreement between King and country. Still I feel I have been given much power, and it must be used for good ends. You have also, and we are both under divine guidance to use our gifts properly. I feel it as strongly as I do my breath.

Tom

Fall passed with its wet yellow leaves, which littered St. Paul's church-yard and caught about the edges of the booksellers' tables. He marked the seasons by the church festivals and his garden. Once more he harvested quinces. On the eve of Christmas Day, Dobson's man came on horseback with an invitation.

Old good soul,

There is to be a supper and merrymaking at my house at six tomorrow on the eve of St. Stephen's Day. Come to meet my wife, who is as rich as she is beautiful and just sixteen years old! Some men costume as they do in the masques: wilt wear strange garb and come as Neptune or Hercules?

Tom hath writ he shall drag thee if thou comst not, a fierce threat as we know our northern lad. As I love thee,

Dobson

Snow fell on the cobbles as Nicholas set off the next night down Wood Street, carrying under his cloak one Christmas rose which he had found in his garden for the pretty new wife. From several other houses he heard the bright warbling of wassail, wassail. Every church spire was covered with snow, and the bells when they rang sounded dull and comforting against the stone city walls. Three cloaked young men passed him, their faces concealed under gilded masks.

The house on the Strand glittered like a jewel at the end of the lane, and as he came towards it he could hear the sounds of recorders and viol. Inside, the rooms were decked with holly and ivy and someone had stuck a sprig of mistletoe above the parlor door.

Half of London and the courts seemed to be there already, and the other half arriving by carriage or horse down the lane. Hardly had he become accustomed to the many people when Dobson appeared on the steps, triumphantly clad as Apollo in a gilded tunic and cloak with a lyre in his arms. "Here cometh the god of music and beauty!" someone said. "Where is Diana?"

"Yet in the hands of her maids."

"Wilt play and sing?"

"Nay, nay! I cannot sing!" Dobson protested. Thrusting his bare, muscular arm about Nicholas, he began to take the physician about the room. "Hast not costumed?" he chided.

"Aye, canst not see it? I am disguised as myself."

"Pisspot parson! Come, speak with my friends! My lords and ladies, here's my friend who will tell you of the elliptic plane!" And Nicholas, thrust onto a couch, found himself expostulating on the orbit of Jupiter's satellites, until some pretty woman seized his hand and made him dance the gavotte, and afterwards kissed his mouth under the mistletoe.

Music sounded and everyone turned towards the stair.

Dobson's new wife was descending stiffly for her heavy gilded skirts, bow and arrow across her back, and an embarrassed smile on her pretty full mouth. Her husband at once lifted her, kissing her brow and turning her about like an object of art. Then handing her to friends, he whispered to Nicholas, "I've not had time to tell thee! My older sister's come from France! Now I shall be impoverished, for there's none but me to maintain her!"

Wentworth had just arrived with several men from court. He also wore only his plain, good dark clothing, and his wife, Margaret, tall and fragile with her golden hair in curls, stayed at his side and gazed shyly about her. Nicholas made his way to them at once, saying with a wry smile, "See, I have obeyed and come, and now I entreat thee to release me early, for my books most plaintively call me!"

The room had grown quiet, and when he turned he saw that a slender lady in an ivory-white embroidered kirtle and bodice had sat down to the virginals to sing. In profile her nose was slightly hooked, and the neck long and slender; her lips were chafed and her hands bare of rings. She wore no cap on her dark hair, but a locket was hung about her neck on a velvet ribbon. Her voice was hoarse and boyish, and the song was an old melody from France, "L'Amour de Robin et Jeanne."

Turning to Harrington, who stood near, Nicholas murmured under his breath, "Would this be Dobson's sister?"

The old soldier stared at him with his very blue eyes and answered indignantly, "Aye, the lady Cecilia Lawes, who arrived of a sudden some days ago! She parted from her husband, who's ambassador to Paris, a year since, and lived in a poor quarter there amid writers and actresses and priests! Now she's fled with crates of furnishings and Dobson hath installed her in a small house he owns."

Nicholas gazed across the room with a slight frown as the song ceased. He saw the lady Cecilia Lawes in a blur of ivory-white bodice, and heard the rustle of her skirt and creak of iron-stiffened petticoats as she stood. She had been speaking French to a friend and broke off in her sentence.

She was very slender and tall. Dobson called him then, and he went with some reluctance.

Taking his hand formally, she said, "My brother hath reported you are the cleverest man in London, Master Cooke."

"He is too kind. When have you come, madam?"

"A few days ago. I had forgot how I loved this city! I only want to be out looking at it all! What makes us love certain things and not others? You must know this!"

"Nay, madam," he replied clumsily. "I hardly know in myself what hath drawn me to one thing and not another." She was too witty, and with the noise he could not hear all her words, so he kissed her hand and left her. Harrington, pleasantly drunk, had seated himself with his stout legs clad in old-fashioned wool hose outstretched towards the fire, and was expostulating in a serious blustering voice, "I saw his blessed Majesty touch for scrofula once! The men stood in lines all the way across the garden, poor souls! Kings are holy."

Then Harvey, who reclined in an upholstered chair near, replied dryly, "Mayhap 'tis so. Still, I've examined the royal piss, and marry, it stinketh like any other man's."

With a joyful shout, the doors to the hall burst open and holiday mummers, dressed as the Three Kings, fell into the parlor. Nicholas recognized a few of the servants in their royal disguises, and that the page was the cook who had made the fine pig. Wentworth was now standing at the other side of the room with some friends. Nicholas attempted to make his way to him again, but several other men from the court had come with their ladies and the mummers were taking their gleeful bows; by the time he reached where Tom had been, the Yorkshireman and his wife had gone.

Furniture was pushed aside, and there was dancing, and in the midst Harrington, his great chest swelling under the half-buttoned black doublet, made an ebullient toast to the old Queen.

At eleven Nicholas found his cloak and bade his host goodbye. Outside in the street the snow now covered the cobbles, and in the darkness horses pawed, carriages creaked, and coachmen came forward seeking their masters and mistresses. The church spires seemed to rise up into the night.

Without turning his head, he felt the lady Cecilia standing beside him, and for the moment he had the strange sensation that she had come with the snow, which would soon claim her again. "Little hath changed within these rooms," she said almost to herself. "I came to this house with my father as a child and hid in a wardrobe once in an empty chamber, and when they ran about crying my name and wringing their hands, I held my peace. I was angry concerning some matter, long forgotten."

Amused, he replied, "Is the wardrobe there yet?"

"Nay! 'Twas musty and worm-eaten; Michael had chopped it to firewood! Sometime after I hid there we were sent home to the north, Michael to school and I to our house. Now I've returned with much ended. How odd life comes to be!" She turned her face.

Several women had rushed shrieking into the snow, twirling around, and a barrister, slightly drunk, played the soprano recorder to their dance. Cecilia gazed at them curiously for a moment. "My friend," she said in her low, slightly hoarse voice, "word's sent my maid's little girl's worse of her cough and feverish; if you'd see her this night, I'd send you home in this coach which Michael hath lent me."

"I would not refuse, but will not morning suffice?"

"Aye, but not as well."

"Then to please you, my lady," he said with a sigh.

Outside the carriage window the snow fell on the gravestones of a churchyard, and by the light of the moving lanterns he saw a beggar huddled against the wall, his cloak covering his face and snow on the edges of his begging cup. The carriage moved from this, and the scene was plunged in darkness. Wheels and hooves on cobbles lulled him. He began to think again that she had come with the snow, and glanced curiously at her.

It was a small stone house in Threadneedle Street which had recently belonged to one of the city livery companies. Within, furniture was stacked upon itself and crates and trunks, and dozens of pictures leaned against the walls. A tight-lipped Frenchwoman past her youth came in her nightgown to greet her mistress. Words were passed and he was left alone. He stood at the window looking out through the glass at the blur of houses down the street, one a bishop's and another belonging to an alderman, until the maid came back and motioned him up the steps.

In a room on a white cot lay a little girl, breathing in a raspy way. He gave orders for hot water and wet rags in a basin, warmed them again by the fire, and held them to her throat, chest, and mouth. When he had promised to send medicines in the morning, Cecilia bent for a few moments over the child. She murmured softly, "Hast a true kindness, Master Cooke, a rare quality in men."

"I think 'tis not so rare."

"Then you've not known the men I've known."

A rug had been laid over half the table in the parlor and set with goblets. Two candles in a silver holder shaped like a griffin, its tail curled about itself, cast flickering light on the decanter. Though he would have preferred to go at once, he drank wine from politeness, and gradually she seemed less sharp. Yet try as he could, he could begin no conversation with her: it was as if he found himself in a long corridor with many doors, and though he saw men go through some, when he himself tried, they were locked.

He said, "Wilt return to Paris?"

"Nay. No more on that! My brother's spoken of thy studies. Tell me, an thou wilt, something of light. There is nothing that touches me so, for instance, the wet greyness of it on rainy summer days! What maketh it come?"

Nicholas drew in his breath in surprise: he had heard the midnight chimes ring across Cheapside, and had not expected to attend to a patient at this hour who was not in danger, still less when his tongue was groggy with sleep to talk about his work to an eager, dark-eyed, strange lady. He began several times, and felt he had failed.

When she bade him good night almost indifferently, he had the strange sensation that she was going to a lover, or that one was waiting for her, and then the touch of her hand burned his palm. Days later he could feel that touch, and began in his own slow way (for he was conscious of little but his work those days) to long for her. Then she became a rustle of dress, a warmth of hand, a way of leaning forward to listen, a gesture, and all these things began to form an image inside of him which for some time did not go away.

A sudden loss pushed it aside.

He was hurrying out some nights later when William Sydenham's servant ran over to beg him come at once. The elderly bishop had gone out to his rainy garden with his cane looking for a stray dog, and was found there under the trees, his gown soaked, his eyes open. Within the half hour Nicholas had come to Covent Garden, and was by the bed calling the old man's name. He knew nothing could be done, and wept.

For three days they kept the vigil, sitting all the night by the coffin in the small chapel of the house. Friends and churchmen came to pray and when they left, squeezed Nicholas's shoulder. He remained on his knees much of the time, hands covering his face, thinking of this difficult old man who had known him better than he knew himself, and had made him priest. A strange dark emptiness settled upon him in those hours. He believed in heaven and did not doubt his old friend was now there troubling angels and saints, but heaven was remote: these rooms full of books and creaking furniture, the clink of wine decanter against glass, the dust on an Italian crucifix which hung on the parlor wall, seemed themselves a closer paradise and all his heart could want. Yet walk as he could through the low, dusky rooms and call as cunningly as he would, the old man would not in this life come forward again, gown rustling, to greet him.

Lord, let me know mine end, and the number of my days; that I may be certified how long I have to live.

*Behold, thou hast made my days as it were a span long: and mine age is
even as nothing in respect of thee. . . .*

William Sydenham was a practical man and a loving one; he left to the
physician, whom he had often called his son, some money for travel and
study; he also left him the house in Covent Garden, and Nicholas found
himself a man of small means for the first time in his life.

In the winter after the plague, he had continued to rise in reputation.
His friends had recommended him and he was subsequently made associ-
ate physician to Harvey at St. Bartholomew's Hospital. In addition, he
had given his first lecture on perspective lenses to the College of Physicians, to which the fellows listened with good manners and some skepticism.

Now one colleague gave him referrals to physicians and glassblowers
in Florence and Holland. Another unfolded a letter in Latin from the
great Florentine mathematician Galileo Galilei. "Go and meet him!" he
urged. Nicholas considered and did not see why he should not go. Tom
Wentworth had returned north for a time, saddened at the loss of yet
another opportunity. The Yorkshireman was now thirty years old, and
felt he had done nothing with his life.

Avery and Bartlett had agreed to take his practice on themselves, and
he found an older priest to say the services, marry, and baptize. Friends
also gave him phrase books for the languages of Italian and Dutch, and
Tom from his northern estate sent raucous stories of his own travels
among the French. He took letters of credit and introduction, some herbs
and tonics carefully wrapped in cloth and packed in straw, and small
coins given him by his musician friend from Dieppe. He was bound for
the Netherlands, then south to Padua to visit the medical school, then to
Florence to see if the astronomer Galileo would receive him.

The ravens above the Tower croaked and the Thames slammed
roughly into the piles of the old bridge the morning he was to embark.
Harvey, who had come to say goodbye, roughly kissed him on both
cheeks. "God's blessings on thee in all thy journeys," he said sharply, for

he did not like farewells. The ropes of the ferry were let loose and soon it made its way towards Dover and the sea.

It was a strange and wondrous experience to be set free of ordinary circumstance and, having money in the pocket, to journey out alone to see the world. Other travelers nodded to him, polite but guarded: he exchanged perhaps a word or two, no more. They kept their privacy, and he guarded his own.

Still he learned that among the others on that rocking boat to Calais were merchants, men on some minor ambassadorship with secretaries hovering close, and lads with their tutors set out to study fencing, dance, and Latin in one of the Paris academies and already preparing to live a wild and dissolute year. Nicholas wore the blue laced doublet and breeches of an ordinary gentleman. With the salt wind of the channel on his face and the white cliffs receding, he felt a cry of joy rising from his throat; then he was like a boy leaning on the rails, nodding at passing boats, sea-sprayed and soaked with privacy.

Whither goest?

Amsterdam.

Murmured conversation rose above the creaking of the ship, the heavy flapping windy sails, the wind that knocked and bumped crate and trunk and barrel; disinterested seamen, their hair short and grizzled, carried coils of rope; and the sunlight shimmered on the waters, and the occasional silver fish flashed in the channel.

Whither goest?

I'm at my leisure to study lenses in the Netherlands.

But the violent flapping of the proud sails drowned his answer, and the gentleman who had asked had left him. Thus they came into the port of Calais, and above the grinding of wood against wood and the dragging of heavy trunks and the pulling down of those sails and throwing of rope, they heard the shouts in French. "Garde! Ici, ici!" And he was propelled to another world, not knowing at this moment where to go, at last finding himself in a tavern of a sort where they gave him grilled fish blackened by firewood, sweet wine, and crusty bread.

Où allez-vous?

A slender fellow in wool jerkin and cap rushed in and shouted for the men who wished the Amsterdam boat. As he came up the plank, Nicholas saw his trunk and tipped the sailor, and the fellow bowed and wished him a good voyage. Not far from sight of the coast, they sailed northward, the spring air cold and wet. In the Netherlands he fell asleep in a clean chamber in a bed of many pillows and quilts and woke to a world of inexplicable neatness he had seen through paintings in the house of friends. For a day or two he wandered about, watching the boats come into harbor. Then his mind turned once more to lenses.

There was by Old Fish Street Hill in London a glassworks with a furnace of three compartments to which he had first gone many years before to watch the molten glass poured. They did not do the fine Venetian work of white lacy fiber, but two of the craftsmen from Antwerp specialized in spectacle-making. In halting English, they had explained to Nicholas what tools he should need, from the rotating thin iron blade for cutting the glass to the cast-iron dishes for roughing and trueing to curve, smoothing, and polishing, and finally the lathe for edging. They had showed him the uses of pitch and emery mud. It was more complicated than he had imagined, and it took him many visits to understand the simplest part of it.

The ancient Greeks had studied geometrical optics, but it was not until the Islamic teacher Alhazen and, two centuries later, Roger Bacon at Oxford that the study of lenses began. Galileo currently used a refracting telescope of two lenses, though it produced aberration of the object, rather than a reflecting telescope, which employed mirrors.

The best craftsman Nicholas knew was Jannsen, who lived in Middelburg. When he arrived in that town, he found that lensmaker no longer living, but the present owner of the shop had trained under him as a boy and knew much of his methods. So for three months until early summer, Nicholas stayed with the family and learned more of this trade. He would have stayed longer, but a party of travelers were bound for Italy, and he went with them.

They were led in a group by a guide across the lowest part of the mountains, stopping here and there for meals and to sleep. Once a monastery sheltered them. In one village church of the region which led from France towards Padua and Verona he had the strange and beautiful experience of hearing the mass sung without accompaniment. There was also, in a city nestled in a valley, a nunnery with a little hospital, all very clean. He admired the white linen sheets and scrubbed tile floors for a long time, and how the sunlight came through the clean windows.

Thus he came to Padua on the Bacchiglione River with its brown walls and its reputation throughout the world for medical teaching. There were arcaded streets and bridges, palaces with their loggias and the church of Il Santo, dedicated to Saint Anthony, which yet held his bones in a chapel. Dante had lived here, and it was here that Galileo, Vesalius, Fracastorius, and Fabricius had taught.

The second day he was able to obtain a ticket by bribery to the dissection theater with its perpendicular, rising balconies and stand among students from several countries. Later, men who knew Galileo showed him a telescope which the master had constructed with his own hand and with it had made out that the Milky Way was a collection of small stars. Nicholas sent a letter by royal courier to the great teacher in Florence and within six days had an answer that he might come.

When he had arrived and found his lodgings, he was directed to the house called Bellosguardo in the middle of a street of arches and a fountain in a little square. It was a warm, sticky day with many flies and other insects whisking about. Removing his hat, he knocked upon the low door, and after some moments it was opened to him by a tall nun in her middle years.

She said, "Art the bailiff? We have no money at present till the stipend's sent! Waste not thy breath, I recollect me who you are! My father's expected you: why do you come so late and keep him from his drink?"

With some awe he followed her up the stairs. Ever since the work of Copernicus, that great astronomer who declared that the sun was central to the universe and the earth traveled about it, Europe had trembled with the desire to understand the heavens. In Denmark, Tycho Brahe had charted a thousand stars, and his assistant Kepler had calculated from the observations the motions of the planets. Still, of these the Italian master commanded a rare respect. Nicholas felt his breath shorten in anticipation as they reached the third story.

With a sharp gesture, the nun threw open a small door, and he found himself in a light room. A tall man of perhaps sixty years with full lips and wide forehead at once leapt up from the desk and rushed at him, waving his large hands and speaking in rapid, passionate Italian.

Nicholas entreated the use of Latin.

"What!" said the old man, appalled. "Art not the wine merchant? Hast brought me no samples of the grape? May the inferno keep itself warm for thee! There's naught to drink but well water, and that's the pestilence, and this last bottle, which is ass's piss. Sent a letter, sayst? Too many letters come! They all want to visit, young beardless boys, priests sneaking from their seminaries, the stupid and the bad-mannered. I cannot help but wish thou hadst been the merchant! What a plague my life is! I had once a sweet concubine, and among the presents she gave me was my most holy daughter, whom you've seen. Never mind: speak, speak if you will."

Nicholas bowed, and walking to the window to gather his thoughts, he gazed out at the church basilicas, the bridges over the river, and the washing hung between the stone houses. From below came the rapid high chatter of children in the dialect of the city. Turning, then, he explained that he had come to hear the master's advice on the magnification of the infinitesimally small.

"My advice is short," barked the old man. "Think nothing on it. The microscopic world we shall never see, for the clarity of magnification cannot be improved. The glass quality is too uneven. Hast wasted thy journey."

A fly buzzed about a plate of hard, odorous cheese, and Galileo flicked it away with his long, untrimmed fingernails. "Dost seek wisdom in Italy?" he said. "The country's a pestilence from sea to sea. I'm surrounded by fools and eunuchs! They value my thoughts when it brings a

profit to their cities; otherwise I am a suspected heretic, and again and
again they murmur to have me investigated by the ecclesiastical authorities. I have been accused before the Congregation of the Holy Office in
Rome for declaring Copernicus's vision to be truth, not supposition.
Why not? I do not believe that the same God who has endowed us with
sense, reason, and intellect has intended us to forgo their use. But they
make so much of this small part of my work that they forget the rest.
Such are inferior minds, cowering before a God they suppose shall strike
them for audacity. He smiles at their foolishness; mayhap He weeps."

Angrily he began to sweep about the room in great strides, his voice
surely carrying out the window and to the streets beyond. "I have tried to
convince the Jesuits of my views, and intend to travel to Rome to convince the most holy father himself! I am not afraid of anything but the
darkness of not knowing. Still, I do recall that but some thirty years ago
the philosopher Giordano Bruno was fastened naked to an iron stake, his
tongue tied, and thus burned to death. They killed him, the devils, may
they rot in hell, the elephants, the fools! They burned the flesh from his
bones for saying there were many universes, not just this one. How doth
any man know there is but one? He, however, the darling who understood so much . . ." His stride was now so rapid that it seemed he would
rush into the street at once.

At this his daughter hurried into the room with a sweep of black cloth
and berated him in raucous Italian. Their quarrels rose to a shout, and the
mathematician took the cup of bad wine from the table and hurled it
across the room. The horrified woman dropped to her knees and began to
gather the broken fragments. "Madre Dio!" she muttered between her
teeth again and again.

With a peaceful smile, the master turned back to his guest, his breath
quite calm again. "As we said, amico mio, Giordano Bruno was burned
and his soul's with Christ. Why do I not bring flowers there more often?
Because perhaps I have lied, perhaps I am a little wary. And they make
such fusses of these few small lines of declaration, and forget about the
rest. I have, for example, this morning, as the sun rose over the river,

begun thinking of the indestructibility of all matter." Turning, he barked at his daughter, who seized the tray and took it away, banging the door behind her and stomping down the steps.

Then his face softened again and he clasped his thick hands on the stomach of his scholar's gown. "We shall have music!" he said happily. "When the Jesuits and I quarrel, we soothe ourselves with music. Come!" He hurried on stiffened legs to a little portable organ; his great knees moving beneath the instrument and his large hands hurrying delicately over the keys, he began to play and sing some songs of his city. Nicholas found a lute in the corner, and in turn sang back an English melody concerning how England had wooed the old Queen.

> "Come o'er the bourne, Bessie,
> Sweet Bessie, come over to me!
> And I shall thee take and my
> dear lady make . . ."

"Music's sweeter than all," said the teacher. Hearing the sound of a cart on the step, he rushed to the window and cried out joyfully, "Wine's come! A most holy cardinal will shortly follow, a sensible man with a good stomach, but he cannot abide my students and visitors, so thou must return another day!"

Nicholas left as the sedan chair of some great personage was indeed coming down the street, and a ragged lad was furtively unpacking wine bottles to bring into the cellar, slipping one under his shirt. He hurried back to his lodging to avoid the street ruffians of which he had been told. There he wrote of the day to Wentworth, who had returned to London, and Harvey, underlining much, laughing aloud, and covering page after page. Below his window some soldiers made merry, and sang some of the same songs that the master had played to him that day. A procession of monks passed. When he returned the next morning, the master was too busy to see him, and the daughter in holy orders screwed up her mouth in a bitter way and slammed the door.

In Paris, thick packets of letters from friends awaited at the ambassador's mansion. The recollection of London, the houses bending close towards each other, the city gardens, and the ringing of ancient bells, would not leave him. There was nothing in the packet from Wentworth, nor had there been news of him for some time.

He reached Calais by carriage some two days later and boarded the boat to Dover. In three days more he rode through the gates of his city, shouting like a boy with his satchel over his shoulder.

Many letters lay on his table, and when he had looked at the half of them he found the message from Wentworth for which he had hoped. It was sent from the house within Aldersgate, dated two days before, and said only, "I've need of thee." Jumping up so quickly that the other papers fell to the floor, Nicholas ran out down the lane towards St. Martin's Lane, opened the door with his own key, and hurried up the stairs.

The hot, wasting summer had left its stale odors and bad air in the curtains and about the little sculptures which Wentworth's wife collected. He thought the house to be deserted, until from far below he heard a maid weeping from the kitchen. He pushed open the master bedchamber. The quilt was neatly laid, as were the basin and pitcher. Then the door creaked, and with it, Wentworth came towards him.

"Art just arrived?" he said dully.

"Aye, but these few hours, and ran as soon as I came across thy message! What is it, Tom?"

"Margaret's dead: a fever came upon her."

They sat down on the bed's edge, and Nicholas took up one of the pillows which she had embroidered, and wept. There they remained until the small hours of the morning, Tom relating the week of illness, and how Margaret had fallen deeper into the fever, and how they had read scripture and recited psalms as she could. The men knelt together by the bed's edge and prayed for her soul. Nicholas embraced his stunned friend and did not let him go.

The next day he ordered silver candlesticks with her name engraved upon them that the angels might remember her and placed them on the altar of his church.

THREE

Cecilia and the Folio

T
HE FRIENDS WALKED ALMOST EVERY AFTERNOON THAT FALL OUT TO the fields, Wentworth always wearing a heavy black band of mourning on his arm. They made a solemn coterie as they proceeded with heads lowered and hands behind their backs, over the grass and past the windmills and flocks of sheep.

When Wentworth had recovered enough to speak of anything, he recalled the Parliament which had concluded the previous winter. "It came to naught," he repeated, trailing a switch through the high drying grasses. "James Stuart needeth money and Commons was reluctant to give it for fear it would be used for my lord of Buckingham's foreign wars."

"There's yet the problem of the Spanish Infanta," barked Harrington, thrusting forth his stomach as if in argument. "His Majesty still wishes to marry the Prince to the girl. *Catholic Spain!* God save us, gentlemen, from papacy. Any good Englishman hates a Catholic like the plague!

Surely surely our Prince cannot marry such a lass."

Wentworth felt for the top button of his doublet as if cold, and found it already fastened. He gazed over the field towards some boys playing football beyond the brook, though from the look in his eyes his companions knew he did not see them. "Poor Francis Bacon, Lord Chancellor as he was!" he said softly. "To remove him from his office for taking bribes. 'Twas more than for bribery, in truth. The matter is they disliked him: the power of dislike is strong, gentlemen, and finds its own reason to validate it."

"By Christ's wounds!" Harvey muttered furiously. "The bastards! To bring down the greatest man of science of our country, who has taught us experimentation! Why, marry, were all men in office who took bribes to be put down, our governing body must needs be composed of pigeons; men bribe each other, and have for the five thousand years of this world's existence. And what did Francis Bacon gain by it? Knowst his essay on power? 'Men in great places are thrice servants—servants of the sovereign or state, servants of fame, and servants of business. So as they have no freedom, neither in their persons, nor in their actions, nor in their times. It is a strange desire to seek power and lose liberty. . . .' "

The side of his mouth twitched, and his dark eyes flashed. "Hath he lost liberty now if they send him away with naught but his curiosity, or hath he gained it?" Then he laid his hand on Wentworth's shoulder. "Art thyself thrice a servant, Tom? Aye, it thinks me. First to thy ambitions, second to the country, and third to thy grief."

The blood rushed to Wentworth's cheeks and he said nothing.

Harvey thrust his arm through his. "Shall we watch the military bands drill, gentlemen?" he said casually. "Marry, 'tis a day most fair!" Kicking the leaves and walking so close that one man seemed to step on a leaf just as his friend's boot had left it, they continued together through the fall afternoon.

Wentworth was ill on and off through Christmas, though Nicholas could find no cause but his loss. When they were with others they spoke of King and country, but alone they talked more intimately of their desire for happiness, sometimes praying together in St. Mary Aldermanbury when the light slowly withdrew from the windows and the worn names on the memorial slabs were obscured. "You're God's priest," Wentworth said. "That makes all the difference to me."

In the early cold days of January, he returned to his estates in the north with little position but appointment to a minor council or two. He seemed so weary that they did not know if he would come back.

February evenings found Nicholas in his parlor again, presses of books, microscopes, portfolios of notes, and sturdy boxes of letters on the shelves about him. With the candle illuminating the faint edges of the spiral stair and the Christmas holly, which had now dried hard and brittle, he dipped his pen and wrote. The fire crackled within the brazier and the stray cat he had found by the walls curled at his feet. The clock ticked, the house creaked. His housekeeper was abed.

He was writing a treatise on light, and some shorter papers on the indestructibility of matter and the properties of the air. He was now corresponding with Kepler and had became a frequent visitor once more to the glassblower's shop on old Fish Street Hill. Slivers of glass littered his parlor floor, glittering on the bricks. And in all of this he sometimes ceased to work and sat with pen in his hand, listening to the crackling of the warm brazier and something inside himself, like footsteps coming ever closer. And on the margin of Kepler's book which lay open before him, he wrote carefully the name of Dobson's sister, Cecilia.

He had met her again at a private supper party in Blackfriars that winter.

"You were away for some time," she said.

"I've been back for some months."

"Yes, my brother mentioned it."

"And you've decided to remain in London?"

"I'm reading law. Do not ask me what I shall do with it, being a woman. I am immensely interested in justice."

"So must we all be."

"Indeed," she said.

They bowed their heads together to speak above the noise of the dinner table, where all the talk was of the workings of the last Parliament and the impeachment of Francis Bacon. "Ah," he murmured, breaking his bread into very small pieces and gazing ruefully at the crumbs on the cloth, "that was a crime."

"I think not if he took bribes."

"There we disagree."

"Then so be it, dear parson! But what dost think of the riots of men left unemployed by the cloth trade?"

"I do not believe rioting can mend such grievances, but I am heartily sorry for them! There are two within my parish, and I have given them . . ." He bit his lip and fell silent, unwilling to say more of that.

"There we agree," said Cecilia, looking at him quietly.

Later they quarreled and moved to opposite sides of the room, both a little angry and ashamed. He was sorry he had sought her out, for men said that the beautiful and brilliant young Lord Kenelm Digby was her lover. Nicholas burned in a hot, uncomfortable way.

Still he found himself unable to concentrate as he would, and sometimes threw down his pen, hurried upstairs for what clean clothing he could find, and came late to some supper he had previously refused, trying not to look for the one face he wished to see. By this time he had a reputation among the men of the city of being truly mad with his passion for lenses.

At times she would be there indeed, glittering as she always seemed to do, somewhat carelessly dressed and the locket about her neck. Mayhap it had been the falling snow that one evening they had spent, or the wine, or the unfinished rooms, but they had come too close in those few hours and were perhaps both wary about it. So they stayed at different ends of the chambers to which they were invited. Hers was an angular face, appearing different from every way one looked; tall and black-haired, she left men murmuring her name after she had gone. Once across a table he heard her say that she would have liked to be a barrister.

He had no idea what he wanted from her, or how to approach her, but when she was in the room he listened only for her voice. It became so that his heart beat faster when he came near her street, but he never saw her there, only the maid shaking the quilting out the window.

On a windy March evening a request was sent for him to give spiritual consolation to an old woman who was unable to leave her house on the Strand. As he descended solemnly from his visit he looked down the hall and saw Lady Cecilia in the window seat, gazing out towards the river. From below rose the sounds of a quiet supper party, and from outside the glass windows he could hear the wind and the knocking of boats in the night.

His heart beat faster as he began to walk towards her. "My lady," he said, "dost sit by thyself?"

"Aye, though they're waiting for me below. The servants before called that a ship's blown over on the Thames, but I can see nothing in the darkness, though I've been looking through the glass because the window won't open."

"I heard them speak of it as I came in! Let me help thee!" He knelt on the cushions and forced the window wide. "There!" he said, starting back as the cold wind flung itself against him. "Look to thy left, past those masts! It lieth even now in the water with the sails white. Canst hear the cry of the boatmen?"

She leaned forward over the stone walk below, and he reached out to steady her. "I'd go gladly down to see it!"

" 'Tis bitter cold! I should close it now."

"Presently!"

"Nay, my lady, 'twill rush through every crevice of the hall and stair. Then my elderly dame up the steps will be too chilled to read the scriptures I have set her, though I doubt she remembers what they are!" With a thrust of his arm inward, he brought the lattice closed again and secured it. Then, laying the satchel of medicines on the ground, he sat down beside her and rubbed for a moment at the small panes between the leading to clear the frost.

"The glass is so imperfect," she said with a sigh. "Now I can only see the lights of the houses on the bridge."

His hand, which lay on his knee, was near hers, and for a moment he wished to take it. "What dost alone," he said gently, "when they are laughing so much below?"

"To be with my thoughts! At times other people oppress me, for I've the need to be witty whether I want it or not. I don't know why I'm here within this city; I have no particular work yet, and still I could never return to Paris. I am neither this nor that. I love so many things and don't know quite where I am. My brother feels I will come to some trouble: then we quarrel, and it sickens me. Dost know, parson, that when I was a child and my stepfather made to strike me, Michael would throw himself between us? He was such a little boy, and felt it his duty all his life to protect me! He does yet."

She rubbed her hands in a practical way, and then clasped her arms about her narrow chest. "Oh parson, we grew up strangely in long cold halls with no one but the servants with whom to speak. Perhaps because of this we can't love, not in the ordinary way. He's already a torment to his little bride with his restlessness. He'll have children, at least; mine died at birth. And yet it's perhaps for the best, for the Lord knoweth I've little patience. Tell me of thyself, for thou dost seldom."

Then he did take her hand, and they spoke for a long time. He told her a little concerning his marriage, and the death of his first son in the plague, and lastly his foolishness with young Kate. That brought the blood to his face and he wished he could tear the words up, or find himself back in a time that he had never said them. Through the blur of his feelings he realized she was speaking again, but he could only make out the sound of her voice, not the words. His hand lay on hers, and he could feel her pulse.

He said with a smile, "I have made a family of my friends. Tell me of thine, lady."

She answered with a shrug, "My family? On our father's side we fought at Agincourt. My mother is French. I had great-uncles who died in that fight of the Huguenots against the Catholics in France some eighty years ago. The other half of her lineage was Catholic: I am like the place where two great rivers have met, and within me swirl about. I married at sixteen, and it ended in sadness. I am terribly afraid of the world sometimes, parson. I am frightened of growing old, of sickness, of loss, of failure, of many things. Surely you're not."

"I cannot say," he answered thoughtfully. "I wrap God about me like a cloak and it protects me."

"Suppose it were not possible to do so?"

"But of all things, this one is always possible."

She leapt up. "I must see the ship upon the waters!" she cried with sudden impatience. "Wilt come?"

Passing the room full of guests and musicians, he found his lantern, which he'd left in the hall. They wrapped their cloaks tightly and walked out to the gardens before the house. The wharf was soaked, and the air wet. Immediately the wind thrust them back so hard that he stumbled, then caught her arm and held her about the shoulders.

Before them in the darkness of the Thames they could see the great white tangled sails upon the water and the broken mast. "Have a care, dear," he said.

"Wilt have a care of me?"

" 'Tis my custom to care for my fellows."

"Dost truly believe that all men should love each other?"

"We are instructed to try."

"But knowst, 'tis impossible, men being what they are. . . ."

"Still, my lady."

They looked up. The window by which they had sat had come loose and was slamming back and forth against the house. Suddenly some panes shattered and fell down with a crash on the stone walkway which led to the wharf. The shards had fallen near, and one of the housemen came rushing around from the kitchens.

When Nicholas hurried up the stairs he found that two small glass panels were broken and reported it to the house steward, saying he was certain he had fastened the latch. Upon leaving he looked through the doors of the dining hall and saw Cecilia laughing with friends. He had thought to bid her good night but was struck with such a sudden fierce shyness that he had no words.

Three days passed. He awoke in the middle of the night to the rustling of old dry leaves in the wind; he stretched, his body safe under the feather quilting. Sensuality crept in the bedcovers and wound itself in the hangings. He lay there comfortable as when one has come at last to a difficult decision, and felt his soul leave the chamber and walk up the steps of her house, turn into her door, and cross the room where she lay sleeping. On its wooden peg across the chamber, his cassock trembled in the draft from under the window.

He had made up his mind to court her.

Yet he was some days about it, though the throb of it grew within his body, for he wanted the words to be right. Then again he was not certain, and hungrily returned to his work, but the thoughts faded from his mind as the ink dried on the uplifted tip of the quill. His soul arched and preceded him, each night, towards her street and up the steps. In those days he did not see her, and no one spoke her name, yet he felt that she knew. Though he had not approached her, he felt her hand in his.

For a time she had not existed: indeed, for most of his life. He would have walked the very same street, and not known her. Then she had been a woman in a room of many women in a too boisterous, masked gathering, attracting him by something he did not understand. Then she was one among the others in his memories, all his failed loves and some which had been for a time blissfully happy. And then she was alone of all, and he saw nothing but her, and was astonished that there could be anyone else. He gave her, without asking, his heart.

He was not sure she wanted him: she was one moment emotional, almost sensual, and the next diffident. Still he went. It was early evening on a spring day as he walked to Threadneedle to knock upon her door. A little French boy with large ears answered and at once stood aside that he might walk within.

More than one year had passed since she had first come to London, and in that time she had made this place her home. Embroidered table rugs and chair cushions lay about, curtains of antique French design hung from the windows, and an old blue-enameled Venetian glass bowl with an allegory of love traced upon it rested on the mantel. A book of French poetry lay open on the table. He saw all this at once as when one takes in much in a state of heightened sensation.

She was reading by the fire with feet in worn satin house slippers on a stool, in a loose garment of dark red velvet with her hair in looped braids bound in some ribbon. She looked as if she expected him. Could her sleeping form have somehow known these past nights how his soul had come to her, crossed the creaking floor, and slid between her sheets to seek warmth, companionship, and comfort? He felt she knew, and yet it did not embarrass him. He stood for what seemed minutes gazing at her hands on the book.

She said with a smile, "Master physician, art come!"

"What dost read?"

"Spencer's book on the Irish wars. Thou wert a soldier there, I'm told. I have asked my brother much of thee."

"Wherefore, madam?"

"I wished to know thee, and you did not come. To speak practically, 'twas no other way to know."

She rang the bell, and the little boy, who obviously adored her, rushed in and after a time returned with a plate of meat tarts and a large jug of ale. Nicholas had folded his cloak neatly over a chair, then refolded it. She said with some amusement, "Dost care so much for thy garments?" and he flushed and answered roughly, "Not a whit, enough to make them find their pegs at night and not the floor."

Then she laughed and said, "Nor I. . . ." Still she gazed at his cassock and neck ruffs, as if she did not approve of them. "Comst as priest," she said sternly.

"As myself, madam."

She sat back, gazing at him like a schoolmistress. "So one cannot divide man from priest! Still, art rare among churchmen. They do the world little good! I could trust thee, I think, and I seldom do that. But what hath God to do with us and we with Him? Tell me, Master Cooke! Heaven is very far off, and the present world so vital and so needing our attention!"

His heart beat because he felt suddenly close to her and he wished them both back on the wet, windy bankside so that he could hold her arm. She bent her head forward to listen, now and then raising her hand to play with the ribbons of her bound hair. He said, "Thou must see with the heart."

"I see many things with my heart, but not that."

"Why, prithee?"

She threw back her head, and the firelight caught the hollow of her white neck. "I'm not interested in heaven, but the potential of men to do good. Nay, I do not mock thee or what's dear! My tongue's sharp and I can't say what's in my heart, so I speak of other matters. Oh parson! Thou canst not like me or approve of me! I know thee and men like thee and what you find endearing in a woman . . . softness, by Our Lady, and deference and curtseying. Now you have frowned. And yet my friends all know how much I hope to see you, and go to suppers where I know or hope you'll be found."

"Marry, in truth?" he whispered.

"Aye, 'tis so. No words?"

"Aye, many. The first are that I cannot understand thee! One moment remote, the next teasing. In God's sweet name, if canst not say the manner of woman thou art, how can I touch thee even with words? How can I do aught if wilt not say?" It came with a cry of his heart, and she seemed chastened. For a moment she turned her head.

He murmured, "Now I have offended and wanted only to know thee."

"Hast not offended."

"Speakst truly?"

"Aye."

They began to talk of so many things that their sentences sometimes were but half finished: they talked of poetry, and the quiet of the night when wild cats could be heard on the wall, and her childhood in the north, and the sadness of her marriage, and how she had read everything to escape it. She told him that she had a fancy to draw, and it was the deep qualities of men's faces which made her take up her pen. She despised all that was shallow and reductionary in mankind, and would give everything for brilliance and honesty. Sometime in the middle of this he dropped to one knee beside her, began to stroke her cheek; even then there was something quiet about her, as if she were listening to him. He moved his fingers across her lips and then kissed them, thinking, yes, now, of course.

"I've not played well at courtship," he said clumsily. "I don't do well to say some words when I mean others. I want to know thee with all my heart, but it shall be unlike anything else . . . Cecilia, an thou wouldst. I do not know what love is, truly, anymore, or how to begin it . . . only surely it must be more than 'twas my ability before, I being somewhat wiser . . ."

"Sweet, come! The little boy will stumble in here and find us!"

They stood so quickly that one of the blue wine goblets toppled: it did not shatter, but the red wine ran between the plates and dripped to the floor. After a time they mounted the steps to her chamber and in the darkness moved towards each other. Surprisingly, she wept, and he said, "Oh thou!" and came into her. It was that simple and whole. He had already made love to her so many times in his mind that this seemed not quite the first time. Already he could not imagine that he had ever lived without her, or that there might be anytime on this earth in all his years to come that he would cease to do so.

Somewhere between that night and the next few, they fell in love. It astounded him, for it was nothing as he had expected it to be. She was sometimes sharp as broken pottery: her words, an elbow in his side in the middle of the night. He felt part of him had become dusty and dull: she was too quick. She was strict, and then playful, and then sensual; she was the most sensual woman he had ever known. In some ways she worshiped him, in other ways challenged him. He felt alive in places he did not know were within him to live at all. He ran down streets, and leapt at the branches of trees. His friends, delighted, teased him unmercifully. The day began and ended with her body and spirit, the taste of warm ale on her lips in the morning and the rustle of her sheets at night, and the nasal calling of the constable outside her lane as his large feet crunched over the dirt. He put her tattered ribbons in his pocket and took them away to touch now and then.

Spring had come once more, slowly with its cool breezes; he was as impatient as a boy. Strangely this love, unlike all the others he had known, was not apart from all that was dearest to him, but in the very center of it. If he had not loved her, he would have wanted her friendship. There was nothing she did not wish to know; she had read voraciously. Absolutely she gave herself to him and took him in return. She was slender, with small, dark-nippled breasts and long graceful legs. He sometimes slept with his arm about her so as not to lose her, but when he awoke found her looking down at him. He did not ask anything of her marriage, which he had heard from Dobson had been bitter and rift with her husband's flaunted infidelities, nor did he ask of the beautiful young men of court who in her short time in London were linked in name to her. He closed his mind to his own knowledge that to bed her without marriage was for him in particular a sin; in his mind he remade the tenets of his church. He shut out these things, and loved her.

Salvation, in the Greek, implies wholeness which must be attained, and Nicholas did attain it to some degree in those last years of the reign of James Stuart in the house in Threadneedle Street. She told him much of the world outside England, which she had traveled far more extensively than he. Her house was full of Huguenots, of Dutch, of Flemish, of Germans, and bitterly she grieved for the ills of foreign wars. She was an exquisite musician and linguist. It was a glittering, sometimes cold mind, and yet warm when she loved. She had never loved anyone in her life as she loved him, that she said many times, and later he came to understand it was true, though neither she nor he comprehended her complexity.

She saw him from the first as a man who could do anything, who was on the very edge of his greatest strengths and yet had not the courage to plunge fully within them. He was then a few years past forty, graver if possible than he had been before, and compassionate, walking rapidly and softly, often deep within his thoughts. She saw him as simple at first, and found within him a love of God so complex that it could not be disentangled from the rest: his intellect was the same. He was proud, and loved to laugh, and knew the men he loved as one knows the palm of the hand, or the creak of one's own straw mattress on the rope supports. She was moved unexpectedly when he showed her his prayer book, which he had had since a child and whose margins bore the supplications of a lifetime etched with a fine-tipped quill pen.

His need for children she did not approach; she would dissolve in sudden furious tears and he not know how to comfort her, for she had lost two at birth. She was also wary of marriage and love fading after the vows, and he was as well, so of that they also did not speak.

She loved him absolutely and would lie in her bed with the faint light coming through the small windows, tracing the line of muscles down his bare back, until at last he woke and looked at her with great gentleness. She was then in awe of him. By breakfast they were teasing and kissing, as puppies do, and then talking of deep things as they broke bread. If he was needed early, the aged sexton, John, who with a certain number of trusted friends kept their secret, would come bandy-legged up the lane seeking him. In her house they spoke of courts, kings, and science; when staying in his small rooms, which they did less often, he told her of his childhood. In the evenings there were supper parties with her friends and his, and talk of all the world.

It was a good time in those years of 1622 and 1623, when they had all reconciled themselves to Buckingham and the wars and inflation because they were but a bothersome background to the true world of science and thought, and the ringing of bells to call people to service, and the dirty, sweet streets of London smelling of flowers and muckheaps, every lane and alley shaded with trees, and swans on the river and wine in the taverns and plays in the theaters. And she there to hold his hand, sometimes coming into his house at night when he wrote his sermons and quietly taking out her embroidery so as not to disturb him. After a time she began to come to the science meetings.

Wentworth remained in the north. Nicholas wrote him frequently, and was saddened to feel that his friend had lost some of his ambitions in his grief. He missed Tom achingly, and sometimes read his long letters to Cecilia as they lay in bed. "There's no finer man in England," he said, "nor, in the deepest sense, a kinder one."

"Sayst? I've seen him here and there and find him arrogant. He needs not seek the good opinion of others, for he holds a higher one of himself than any other man could hope to do!"

"Nay, 'tisn't so! He needs affection and lets few see it."

"Lovst him, Nick?"

"Aye, with all that I am."

Dropping her voice, she said gently, "Wherefore, cony?"

And he answered, bewildered, "I know not, sweet. He's like a brother to me—whatever fault she has, his tenderness maketh up for them."

Cecilia's political understanding was both complicated and simple. The workings of law and Parliament fascinated her; she was drawn to the little formality the harum-scarum court contained, and though she venerated the idea of the monarch, she found the grossness of James Stuart's personal ways distasteful. Her affection was already for the fastidious young Prince Charles. Talk for a while was all of how he and Lord Buckingham had gone in disguise to Spain to win the hand of the Infanta and returned unsuccessful, and ripe for war with that insouciant country. Sometimes her parlor was full of Huguenots and Flemish painters and barristers discussing these things. Then when they were all gone, Nicholas would run up her steps two at a time to hurl his coat across her room and pull her into his arms. She bought him books of theology, and listened graciously if somewhat bewildered to his stories of frustrated meetings with his church vestry, who never seemed to be able to collect enough coal for the poor, of his affection for his boy choristers, whom he took to plays and helped with their lessons, of his unhappiness when a parishioner whom he cared for deeply left his church for another sect. He always felt any failing was due to his own insufficiency of faith.

They walked over London much in those years, sometimes with friends and sometimes alone. Sometimes they walked far south through the villages and farmlands, and coming back on the crooked wood bridges which forded the streets saw the windmills behind Lambeth and the great palace of the Archbishop of Canterbury. They picked herbs and flowers by the edges of the stone walls which marked the division of his gardens from the common land. He found wild burnet and roses, and she held up her skirts for them or carried them on the crooks of her arms.

They debated endlessly if man was poor because he was ignorant or ignorant because he was poor. Nicholas had found the progressive growth of slums towards the back of Westminster and those about Aldgate distressing, for he could not forget that the pestilence had struck hardest there. Yet when they walked through the high grass of the fields with the sweet scent of ground wheat coming on the wind, the dirt and sewage of London's back streets seemed far away. And as to the question whether man was poor because of ignorance or ignorant because of being poor, neither Nicholas nor Cecilia could answer it.

Then they argued what maketh a righteous and good king, and discussed King James's books on kingship, which he had published many years before. "The state of monarchy is the supremest thing upon earth," and the words returned by the Commons, "Our privileges and our liberties are our rights and due inheritance, no less than our very lands and goods."

They remembered with some awe the words the stern Dean of St. Paul's circulated among his friends and fellow clergymen: "Any man's death diminishes me, because I am involved in mankind; and therefore never send to know for whom the bell tolls; it tolls for thee." The world was littered with the falling yellow leaves which floated under the bridge and clung to the hem of her dress, and both felt in those moments involved in all mankind. They walked arm in arm under the apple trees which still hung with fruit.

On a cool fall day in the year 1623, the works of Will Shagspere were at last published in folio. Over the six years from its inception, Nicholas had often walked over with his former master, John Heminges, to Aldgate to review each set of printed pages before they were bound. Before the plays were inserted tributes to the writer by Ben Jonson and several others. He never blotted a line, said Jonson. There was a frontispiece portrait of poor quality; Nicholas could not help but laugh to look at it.

A celebration was to be held at the Globe. Cries of the beasts from the nearby Bear Garden drifted in the wind, the mills were cranking, and the afternoon's performance at that theater was just ended as Nicholas came with Cecilia up the planks which covered the marshy paths. Many of the writer's colleagues, now retired, had journeyed to toast his memory, including Condell and Heminges, who arrived with a cart with a full keg of ale. Earlier in the day the apprentices and the actor John Lowin had put a sheep to roast, and the rich scent rose in the air. Many had brought instruments.

As the men played tabor and recorder, young Andrew Heminges began a jig. He started where the groundlings stood during performance, and soon pulled himself to the first gallery, continuing there whilst many children ran up the steps to follow him. Over the benches he danced, and on the ledges, swinging to the second gallery, turning and walking on his hands, and cartwheeling.

Below, his father, John Heminges, walked stiffly to the center of the stage, some papers held against his heart. The boys ceased their play and perched on the gallery rails, legs in wool hose dangling, and the men laid down instruments. Quietly the old theater man looked about him. Around the stage were gathered the thirty-odd present members of the company with their wives and children, as well as playwrights and actors from the Swan and Drury Lane.

"We have celebrated the great printing," he said. "Yet I must further beg your patience for a more personal matter. My son Andrew, who sitteth so high above us, is this month one and twenty years. By the tearing of the papers of his apprenticeship, he is hereby this night released from his indentures and become a sharer in the King's Men."

"Ah, marry!" shouted out the men.

Heminges said, "Jackanapes, come!"

Andrew quietly climbed down. "A theater man, my son!" John Heminges said stoutly. "That thou hast been bred and will be always. 'Twas before thy birth we tore down the old playhouse outside Moorgate in the bitter cold winter of '99 and carted the lumber across the ice when the river froze and built here this Globe. I am an old man, born to a rougher age: thine is one finer-spun. May this theater stand until the world is ended. Lad, say amen."

"Amen, good father."

"Aye, lad, then kiss me."

Some men came forward with a kite they had made from disused prompt sheets, and John Heminges cut the apprenticeship papers into bits and tied them onto the tail. Andrew and the boys ran outside the theater to the fields so that it should catch the wind, and soon it did, and rose wobbling at first and then broke free above the firesmoke and above the weather-worn slats of the Globe into the sky.

As the evening wore on, Heminges repeatedly climbed to the stage to recite speeches from his great parts of Falstaff and Titus and Polonius, chiding his old friends when they could not remember them their own lines, calling for a blunted rapier to see if he could manage the duels. After a time he was drunk, and, wiping his face, he said, "No more, 'tis time my bones were abed," and climbed into the cart with his younger children and daughter-in-law. He held out his hands to Nicholas, and the physician felt his old master's warm, salt tears. Then the cart began to rumble away through the high grass, and even as it did, young Andrew leapt across the planks and onto the slats by the wheels to throw his arms around his father and climb beside him.

It was quite dark when Nicholas and Cecilia went home.

Much they shared in the next two years, until their emotions became inseparable. Tom Wentworth wrote weekly, though he did not return from the north, and the small prelate of St. John's, William Laud, was made a minor bishop and came to London. Harvey continued his work on the circulation of the blood, and on writing the book which would explain it. Andrew married for love, and the great philosopher and former Lord Chancellor Francis Bacon retired to his estate in Gorhambury to devote himself to science and research, conveying his regret at having wasted himself in worldly service.

It was while walking home from Cecilia's house one early evening at the end of March 1625 that Nicholas first heard the bells. They began with the tolling of the great ones of Westminster Abbey until every parish chime took up the answer in the dullness of that winter day: even his own. What means this noise, he thought, lifting his head as if in a dream.

From the bell towers thousands of birds rose, startled, into the last grey light of the sky. His Majesty King James was dead.

FOUR

Coronation and a Child

THE MORTAL REMAINS OF THE UNKEMPT, INDIVIDUALISTIC JAMES STUART lay at Westminster Abbey under a hexagonal catafalque of plaster, wood, canvas, and wax. At his funeral procession the College of Arms carried his achievements of tabard and shield, and hundreds of men, among them the actors, followed the coffin in mourning clothes, black feathers in their hats. And then with a shout, the city broke into joy to welcome young Charles Stuart.

On a mild day in late April, Nicholas was coming from visiting a patient in the back streets of Westminster when he found himself in the midst of a crowd forming along King Street. A cry of pure happiness rose suddenly as a great carriage turned up towards Charing Cross from the yards of Whitehall, raising the dust as it went. Like the roar of the wind came the joyful voice of the people until they rang like bells on a holy day. Nicholas understood at once. The new young sovereign was coming towards them.

For a moment only, the physician saw him: a small youthful man, with delicate wrists and fine pointed beard. His reddish curled hair fell down the wide lace collar, and he lifted his hand in its embroidered, scented glove to the crowd, though his eyes were wary. Then he was gone, and a sigh of satisfaction passed like a shudder through the closely gathered people. "Ah, the sweet!" said one woman, laughing and wiping her eyes. She clasped her bundles of wash and went off with the others.

That night Nicholas wrote effusively to Wentworth. He said he felt Charles Stuart was a good man and that now he had come to the throne, Wentworth would at last begin to rise in the country as he deserved. London, he continued in his rapid, flowing hand, was full of more life than he had ever seen it. He could never remember it like this before.

From the taverns to the courts to the prisons, men talked of little else but the new King and his sixteen-year-old bride, the French princess Henrietta Maria, who had arrived from Paris with a retinue of hundreds, including twenty priests of her Catholic faith. A few men bristled at that (Harrington snorted, "Papacy!"), for they remembered how England had wrested itself from the Roman Church less than a century before. Still, most were tolerant of the tiny, timid princess; they wished the King the joy of his wedding night, and a large family to come.

It was a time of growing prosperity in London. Every day the streets spilled with more of the goods and languages of the world. Slippers were imported from Portugal, spices and silks from India, glass from the Italian states, and many craftsmen and fine goods from Sweden, that small, insular, shipbuilding civilization. Printer's shops doubled. Bookbinder Keyes was so much in call for his work that he hired two journeymen to help him.

In the window of a painter's studio, Nicholas saw a portrait of the new ruler: youthful, narrow-chested, long hair curled at the shoulder. He thought to buy it as a present for Cecilia, and found to his amusement the paint was not quite dry. So many men wanted them, the artist said with an embarrassed shrug, that he could not copy them fast enough. In the area of Old Palace Yard, ballad sellers set words to some old melody on the goodness and benevolence of the Stuart kings, and each time he passed Whitehall he always found some shy boys lurking about the gates, hoping to catch a glance of Charles. The new sovereign, everyone understood, spoke several languages, loved art, and was deeply reverent in his faith. He was no warrior king, but one who would want peace.

It was not only the first Parliament of the new reign that June which drew Thomas Wentworth to London, nor did its repetitive frustrations occupy his entire mind. He had come to seek a wife. There had been a rumor that the childlessness of his long marriage was due to his impotence, and a few men refused him their daughters. He suffered this in his dark, sullen, angry way. Then he met Lady Arabella Holles.

The daughter of the Earl of Clare, a landowner from Nottinghamshire, she was sixteen years old, beautiful, and hardly taller than a child. Those who knew her called her educated, modest, and sparkling, and bragged that she made a friend of all about her. Wentworth kept her oval miniature in his pockets. In the science meetings he would interrupt a discussion of magnetism to rhapsodize on Arabella's rich, plenteous dark hair.

He arrived impulsively one morning at the rectory in Love Lane and found Nicholas in his shirtsleeves with beard untrimmed writing the order of next Sunday's service on the back of a sheet of music. "Put on thy clerical things, parson!" he cried. "Make me look presentable with such a friend as thee!"

"Why, where are we going, Tom?"

"Where thinkst thou, dolt! We are going courting, or rather I am going and you are coming with me to vouch for my character and strength as a lover."

The sun glistened on the stone buildings all through the city, and deep green trees overhung them as they rode through the streets in Wentworth's new carriage. "Ought I have worn musk?" he asked anxiously.

"Thy barber's cut thee sore."

"A plague on him! But Nicholas, we've no flowers!"

"There was a maid a-selling them by the Fleet."

Wentworth leapt up and banged upon the roof of the carriage with his cane. "Turn back, sirrah! Turn back to the Fleet!" He had risen so quickly that he struck his head and sat back rubbing it ruefully, flushed and biting his soft lips above his small, dark beard.

After they had ridden about for some time they realized they were lost, and had to go around again. Descending at last before a medium-sized stone house on the Strand, they were admitted to a sunny parlor where they found Arabella Holles reading a book of French poetry with her little dog at her feet.

They kissed her hand, and she in turn curtseyed. After a time Nicholas excused himself, for he had a patient awaiting him, yet came back, having forgotten his satchel. The two lovers were sitting close; Wentworth had taken her hands and was gazing at them as if they contained all his future. They were married in the fall, and in the winter when the second session of Parliament was prorogued Wentworth returned to the north.

The joyful news of the lady Arabella's pregnancy arrived but two months after the marriage. Exuberant letters from Wentworth followed weekly as the birth approached, heavily underlined and filled with expressions of joy, saying, "If ever you loved me, parson, come to see my son born, for surely it must be a boy in answer to my prayers!" Not that he did not trust the family midwife who had birthed all his brothers and sisters, but he was concerned that some matter might go wrong ("Women are made so delicately, Nick!"), and there was a faith he had in his friend from Aldermanbury which far outweighed tradition. With some wryness he concluded, "Harvey writes you are too busy to sleep these days! Bring that most peculiar lady whom thou hast so fancied, and you shall both have a holiday, on my soul!"

That evening after prayers Nicholas walked reflectively over to Cecilia's house in Threadneedle. He found her in the parlor, and when he had told her his proposal, she looked up from her embroidery with some strictness, and then said, "Can Wentworth really wish me to come? He seems so stern and forbidding at times! Dost know what Dobson says some men have begun to call him? Black Tom."

He sat down next to her and took up the embroidery to study its pale brown floral pattern. "Cannot you like him, Cecily?"

"For thy sake, aye."

"Not otherwise?"

"Oh, we have discussed this! I do not dislike him terribly, nor do I like him particularly."

"Well then, do not come."

"Nay," she said, retrieving her work and kissing him. "Thou wouldst wish me to, and I shall, for I want to be with thee always. And we do not see each other much these days with thy work, and such friends who have need of me."

"Those who love and live under one roof have not these difficulties," was his quiet answer.

They rented a carriage, coachman, and four horses, though Nicholas was somewhat scandalized at the cost of it. Over the ancient roads of the country they traveled, some laid by the Romans some sixteen hundred years before, past farmhouses and inns and low villages surrounded by fields quivering with wheat. The words which he had spoken in her house left a slight disquiet between them. He was uncomfortable in the inns, and slept badly, wanting his own bed.

As they traveled on the second day, she leaned forward shrewdly and said, "What dost?"

"Naught."

" 'Tis some matter, I warrant."

He opened his prayer book and began to read the psalms for the day, his hand covering his lips as he did when trying to restrain himself. Then she retreated to the corner of the carriage with her thin arms about her body, sticking out her lower lip. "I am civil to him," she said at last in a choked voice. "I would not be otherwise and have always been. But he is to me far more ambitious than gifted, and he never calleth but that you rush to be at his side. Seest not thine own gifts for his, Nicholas! Thy humility sometimes irks me!" She placed her fingertips on the edge of his prayer book and moved it up so that he had to cease to read. "I do not know," she said quietly, "if I am pleased or no to love a man of God."

"Lovst me as I am, and such am I," he muttered.

"But dost not love me."

"Sayst, Cecily!"

"Wantest more than I can give! Wantest what I cannot give . . . marriage . . . a child, that indeed . . . and yet I have never loved anyone as I love thee, Nicholas." She turned her face to the window, and the tears ran down her cheeks. He thrust aside his book and took her in his arms. "In love people always disappoint each other!" she whispered. "And I despise that I weep, and yet can't help it with thee. With thee I can't shut myself away, though I try and try. Oh will life be over for me one day, and that the tale of it will be only that it was an ordinary, simple thing?" He continued to rock her and hush her, yet could not admit, even as they made love that night in another inn, how much of the truth she had spoken.

Nicholas's vague discontent did not leave him as they came to the counties surrounding the city of York, and saw the minster spires rising to the blue sky. It puzzled him, for God knew he was joyful for his friend. If the babe had been his, he would scarce have been happier, and he remembered the carrot seeds in wine, and kneeling to hold Margaret's hand as she wept for the shame of her barrenness, and how she had died. He felt stripped naked with emotion, and hardly fit to walk out among men.

The carriage turned towards West Riding and the ancestral manor of the Wentworths. Even as they came into the yard, Tom came running across the dirt, leapt to the runners of the carriage before it had completely stopped, and almost flung himself in the window. "The babe came two days ago!" he shouted. "I have a son! Do not think of the bags but come at once!"

The windows of the bedchamber had been thrown open to the countryside, and the smell of fresh grass blew in with the soft wind. Arabella had been nursing the child, and flushing shyly when she saw them, tried to extract her nipple from the babe's mouth. The child broke into a hollow fuss, and hushing it, still reddened with joy and the delight of seeing them, she allowed it to continue to suckle.

Nicholas had come to the mother's knees, and dropping to the floor, touched the back of the head of the nursing child. The fine dark hair, the same color as his father's, clung to the skull and showed its shape. Where the bones had not yet hardened, the pulse moved. He was so overwhelmed with the beauty of this new life that he could not speak. It was Tom's son whose hair he touched, the seed of his body. And yet in some inexplicable way, he felt it was his also. He remembered the carrot seeds in wine again, and his friend's shame.

"I will baptize your son," he said when he found his voice.

Many of the wealthy families from the county came to the sacrament the next day, as well as hundreds of tenants from the lands who crowded to the yard outside the chapel in their brown smocks and gowns. The babe had been swathed in yards of ancient yellowing linen and lace; still Nicholas could feel how the legs kicked out and the small chest arched as if considering a protest. He held the boy in the crook of his arm, and before dropping water over his forehead thrice, said the words which had been spoken for sixteen hundred years: *"Dearly beloved, forasmuch as all men be conceived and born in sin, and as our Saviour Christ saith, None can enter into the kingdom of God, except he be regenerate and born anew of water and of the Holy Ghost . . ."*

"Give him here, parson!" said the new father, holding out his arms when the sacrament was done and all had prayed.

Nicholas felt the lengths of old lacing drift slowly over his arm as he surrendered the child. For a moment Wentworth rocked the infant, swaying back and forth and murmuring some song under his breath. Then he looked up at them all bewildered, as if he had forgotten he was not alone. "I have an heir," he said in awe. "My name shall not die. I shall create a dynasty for him, and what he shall inherit is my work."

When the hundreds of guests had departed the celebrations and night had fallen over the countryside, a few good friends gathered in the library, a musty room fitted with wall hangings, tapestries, and portraits of ancestors between the book presses. Wentworth twice excused himself to go upstairs to see how mother and babe did. Each time he returned with his face so joyful that he passed his hand over it in embarrassment, and then shrugged, as if to say, I cannot help it. . . .

"I stand as sheriff here now," he said reflectively when pressed by his friends concerning his life in the north, "and having been at least appointed to this, do what I can to put down greed and wrongdoing. I gain some enmity, but there is no gentle way to put down villains. I despise those who trample on the rights of common men. I hope when my son is grown he will know that I have tried to be a righteous man."

Cecilia had withdrawn to a corner of the room with a slight frown on her long face; she looked at these times much like a portrait of a stern medieval Florentine woman which Sydenham had hung in his bedroom, a still-youthful matriarch with a delicate hooked nose, pale and judgmental. There was about her mouth the dismay and difficulties she had discussed in the coach, and she felt this house and county oppressive. The other women had gone upstairs, and twice she thought to do so, and each time did not. To Nicholas the place was rich: to her a reminder that she had somehow failed. Taking her sewing, she silently began to embroider flowers on a cap.

Wentworth had looked across to her several times, biting his lip, and uncomfortable, and resentful perhaps of that. His joyful boasting seemed to dry away, and after a time he made as if to pour more wine, and then turned to approach her with more clumsiness than Nicholas had seen before. "Madam," he said, "we've seldom spoken, yet I feel uncertain what to say to you."

"Why, must say only what would to anyone else."

"I understand you study the law."

"I do: 'tis a great passion for me. I have faith in our judicial system and feel 'tis what maketh us great," was the short reply.

He murmured a few words, and then they spoke some sentences of politeness, and she looked up and smiled. He kissed her hand, and seemed most glad when he turned his face to get away. In those moments Nicholas felt the accumulated sadness which he had fought since leaving the city settle upon him with its dreaded weight. She was right. He loved her so much, and yet . . . each year he was more bound in her, and yet she was not his. His feelings arose with such violence that he felt he could not trust himself, and making some excuse, he hurried out the door to the chapel across the yard.

A dog barked. The evening was clear and full of stars. It was a very old chapel with some saints' statues from the time when the country was still under the Church of Rome. He sat down in one of the creaking chairs and covered his face with his hands.

Sometime after he heard the door move and did not need to look up to know who stood there. "Why dost leave thy guests, Tom?" he murmured.

Wentworth scraped a chair to sit close so that his knee almost touched that of his friend. "Nicholas," he said with an attempt at sympathy. " 'Tis a most peculiar lady! I find her sharp as nettles, and she maketh me feel untutored when I come near, and God knoweth . . . nay, I like that not at all, not at all."

"She feeleth much the same of thee."

"Oh doth she indeed!" said Wentworth, throwing back his head the way he did when challenged. "By Christ's wounds, what matter's this! Her husband's yet living and thou art longing to have a child! Why dost torment thyself? Dobson told me the man's aged and ill from his whores, but he may live long. What madness to love a lady who cannot wed thee! What a sharp, perverse wench to so inveigle thee when thou couldst have half the wenches in London. Arabella hath a cousin . . ."

"Cease: I want this one only."

"Oh dost, stubborn? I do not know that women should meddle with the law. There was much talk of her also when she first came to London concerning one or two noblemen who came and went."

Nicholas stood up. "I don't wish to hear this, Wentworth," he said sharply. "Don't speak of her in that way. I love her, and I will always love her. And when her husband dies, she'll be mine. Go back if thou wouldst to thy guests. God knoweth I am happy for thee, Tom! Ask our King to appoint thee Lord Deputy of the North, as you deserve. I hold thee to my heart, but do not speak of her like that to me or I will be angry." His voice trembled, and he touched his friend's shoulders and walked clumsily from the chapel, knocking into the chairs as he went.

The wind blew outside the house that night as he lay sleepless in the great bed of his chamber. He thought he heard the newborn infant wail, and then the delighted, laughing voice of the new father consoling him. His own desire for a child returned with a dark cry and much envy, and he buried his face in his Cecilia's long, loose hair.

They had spoken, of course, from time to time the words "When the French ambassador dies . . ." He could not bear to say "thy husband," nor could she, for it seemed to defame them. Then they hastened to speak of it no more, for it seemed sinful to wish him dead even though he was then past seventy and had been ill a long time. They did not make plans past that possibility. Divorce was extremely difficult; she did not ever suggest it, and he supposed it was because the man she had run impulsively away to be with at the age of sixteen would not allow it.

And then he did die: news came by messenger from Dobson, saying at the end (and underlined), "God knoweth what my sister will do now, for she flees always to her own perdition! If anything good cometh her way, she will certain rush from it."

Nicholas put the note in his pocket and walked over to Threadneedle with a large bunch of dried flowers and herbs. Entering with his key, he mounted slowly up the steps. Cecilia was folding dresses on her knees. "Hast heard," he murmured, "Cecily?"

"Aye, yesterday."

"Said naught to me?"

She did not raise her head but continued her work, and after a time spoke in such a low voice that he could scarce hear her above the delivery of the coal from a wagon on the lane below. "What shall we do now?" she murmured. "What wilt expect? Nay, I know it well. Rings and vows and such matters. I think we should not do it."

"Not marry . . . Cecilia!" he cried, striding to her and wanting to lift her, and somehow reluctant to touch her. "Not marry thee! By Christ's wounds, there hath been no day since first I kissed thee that I did not wish it, nor any time I performed the wedding ceremony between a man and a maid when 'twas not you and I who stood there!"

Looking away from him with some impatience, she murmured, "Oh well, parson, but I know how it would be. Didst weary of thy last wife, hast said it thyself."

"She was not thee!"

"And then wouldst change? Those wedded words hath a kind of spell to them that maketh a drover who loved a maid feel inclined of a Wednesday evening when the soup's cold to beat her. Wilt be to me as my husband was? Wilt woo me and then abandon me for others, speak scathingly? For when I was but sixteen he came with flowers, dropping to his knees before me. . . . 'Twere not for my brother I should have never got from this marriage! Now shall I have another? Wouldst wish it?"

"But Cecily!" he cried. "I am myself and not this man . . . and as for soup and drovers and such, I do not give the damn what's cold if thou art warm to me."

"It can't bring happiness but 'twill spoil what we already have, and I have been happier than ever in my life. Would that he had not died that now you come like any other to make me thine own!" Her voice rolled into a tight, small place, and she turned her shoulders. He wanted to take her against him, and felt somehow that his hands were covered with coal dust or some other matter, and he dared not presume to touch her. And yet this was she who had sighed in his arms, and called him every lovely name behind the bed hangings and sometimes wept in her love.

"Cecily."

"Nay."

They remained for hours, during which time his voice broke and she stared at him with haughty tears in her eyes. When he had used up all his words and found not one left, he walked out stunned and wandered around the shops of the Exchange gazing absently at lengths of silk and embroidered caps she might like. In the end he walked to Paul's yard and bought her a book of sonnets by some new writer. Many people greeted him, and a matron of his parish even pinned him by the churchyard wall and told him the troubles of her feckless man for a long time without so much as a breath. He came home to offended letters from patients who had tired of waiting for him, and another from Harvey for a supper to which he had no inclination to go.

Nicholas was a stubborn man, and once he had set his heart on a thing and conceived it to be good, was reluctant to turn away from it. Even as the days passed and Cecilia made love to him in a penitent way and he felt his monastic withdrawal lessening, he clung to what he felt should occur. He did not suppose that a marriage between true minds could bring anything but happiness. He knew she loved him.

Their quarrel rushed back and forth through the crooked streets from his house to hers, and broke forth yet again when his housekeeper called him from the church one late afternoon when he had been singing through parts of an old mass by Byrd with his music master and choristers. They had been at end of it and he had promised to take the boys to Cheapside to buy plum cakes. Telling them to wait in the churchyard, he hurried to his house to find Cecilia in the parlor.

She had come on some excuse or other, but really to once more tear open the dispute which by this time had utterly wearied him. "Give reasons why it should be better!" she demanded.

"How could it not be?" he muttered. "Firstly, the clumsiness of the secrecy of our love! I must come in the silence of the night to thee!" He moodily clutched the latch of the cupboard which was under the stair, and opened and closed it with a creak of wood. "And then there's my work, lady! I'm priest here and it's wondered why I've not married! Goodmen think I must, and thrust their childish daughters at me all beribboned and tearful with hope . . . and when I do not fall panting to the courting bench, they mutter I'm unmanly. Do I not love thee enough? Dost want another? I'm weary of dewy maids gazing at me during the sermons with their bodices laced low!"

His voice had risen, and he realized his words had likely permeated through the kitchen door and fallen upon the ears of the young boys who awaited him amid the churchyard stones. They expected calmness: he was after all both parson and doctor. He should be as unperturbed as his blue glass bottle of camomile flowers which had sat always on the upper right-hand shelf of his dispensary, the ink of the first two letters obliterated by a bit of water, so that it now read "momile flowers." And himself, reasonably and respectably greying of beard, with his priestly demeanor now graven into the very way he opened his hands, and kindliness ruthlessly imbedded. He did not feel kind now.

She twisted her hands before her, disturbed to suspect that she could not answer the argument as successfully as he had put it. "Marriage always . . ."

". . . is different when the fellows are. 'All men do, all men must!' I am not so much of men but of myself. If canst not see it after all this time, need better spectacles, my lady." Catching her against him, he spoke to her hair, saying, "I love thee as my life, and would have wished children . . . thou knowst! The endless use of the linen sheath which by now should have failed us . . ."

"I cannot bear children: for that 'tis not failed. Wouldst have me try again to see it die?"

"Trustest not my skill?"

"Mayhap, and then again, no."

"Well, and even that's not the matter," he cried, now angry. "We are too different. Mayhap I should have sought another."

" 'Tis not too late for that."

"Speakst fairly?"

She stuck out her lower lip and her eyes flashed. "Aye, I do! We would be unhappy. . . ."

"We are not so now, but for this matter," he replied. Still he continued, sinking into his low voice of clerical reason, which maddened her. Now and then she accused him of taking refuge in his faith, whereby he replied so the scriptures instructed him to do. Then she cried he was as small-minded as any farmer for all his learning.

Placing her hands on the table, she demanded, "Who's wed in perfect happiness?"

"Only the angels enjoy perfect happiness, my lady, yet I warrant with our love we could fair approach them. If thou lovst me," was the last comment before he turned on his heel and went dark-faced and sullen to his now quiet choristers, who were waiting for him swinging thoughtfully, as he suspected, on the churchyard gate.

He wanted to tell her he was sorry, but she was gone. He could not believe when he walked over the next day that the house was shut up with only the man to guard it.

One of those heavy, sweltering city summer days it was. From the direction of Smithfield came the stench of slaughter. Beggars crouched in doorways and the half-witted man from the parish next his ran after him shouting gibberish. Papers stuck to sides of shops and church doors advertised cockpit matches, a performance of *A Woman Killed with Kindness* at the Phoenix, and the public health report; they announced a hanging and a deportation and a ship sailing week next from Plymouth sponsored by the Tailors' Company. At the lutemaker's stall, two gentlemen were trying the instruments, and the crooked water carrier from Cheapside, his two buckets suspended by a heavy pole across his shoulders, left small puddles between the cobbles as he passed. A little boy sat in a doorway of a house of seamstresses and wept with grimy hands over his face. Now and then down some lanes there were flowers, and the sudden heavy scent of roses and fresh-cut hedges.

He despised all of it, and sent scribbled notes to Harvey and Avery to come for supper.

They trudged respectfully into the rooms as if to a house of mourning, bringing a bag of coffee beans instead of funeral meats. Harvey bore the latest newsletter from the Netherlands under his arm. "Cecily and I have parted," Nicholas said abruptly. "She's gone off, the saints themselves know not where. Dobson knows, the whoreson, but won't say.... Nay, I speak unfairly. He knoweth naught of her but that she will be free and hell to pay."

Harvey shook out his coffee beans into the mortar which he had borrowed from the dispensary. " 'Tis the way," he growled. "Englishmen know not how to control their women. My wife lived under my roof one week before the skeletons frightened her and she went home to her mother. I have never regretted it. A man of intelligence hath no business to marry! Wife and children are impediments to all mighty deeds, whether good or ill . . . he who hath them hath given hostages to fortune. 'Tis writ in Lord Bacon's essays."

"Aye," cried Avery. "I have the exact words of it about me somewhere," and he began to pull papers from his pockets.

They blew upon the coffee and drank it, bitter and dark, from wood mugs. Harvey pushed off his shoes, put his feet on the fender, and opening the newspaper, began to report on the great monies earned by the newest ship returned from India. Upstairs the housekeeper muttered to herself, and the conversation wound round about, closer and closer, to the subject of the dark-haired lady who had swept away with her trunks, they did not know where.

Avery said, "Mayhap she'll return, Nick, like a homing pigeon."

"Nay, she'll fall in love elsewhere," Nicholas muttered. "That will happen, and she'll not return. She's most peculiar, yet I love her." Much saddened, he rose in an aching way sometime later and took a candle to light himself to bed. The two other men remained talking softly by the fire and then departed in the sultry night, the air heavy with aged dust.

It was three weeks before he heard from her.

Written from Bath, 25 July, St. James Day.

from the lady Cecilia Lawes to the physician and gentleman Nicholas Cooke of Cripplegate Ward

My own Nicholas,

Parting from you, my eyes suddenly filled with tears. The truth is I had to come this far away to grieve for thee. I love thee so much I dare not tell it even to myself when close, when even within a mile. Now, some fifty or more away, I think again of lying in thy arms. Should I come closer, the thought might rush away like a bird that's frighted.

Shall I be alone? Will I prefer it?

I have seen friends of Thomas Wentworth and my lady Arabella and they are incredulous that we have parted. What, should the very river divert from its ancient banks, should the bridge not cross the water? Where thou hast been have I been also, too much I think thy shade. So I wished to go off, but where should I go? I who was once at home in all places am at home in no place without thee.

Thus I find myself in the ancient city of Bath where they come to take the cure for the French disease and sit naked in the old baths but for their caps, men and women both. Strangers gather about the top to see them. I went with my maid Suzanne and we sat as God made us and splashed each other like children. I cannot help but be moved of the very antiquity of where we sat and of this our country, or as thy old dear friend Shagspere once called it, "This blessed plot, this earth, this realm, this England!"

Would I be unhappy as thy wife? Wouldst be so with me? Or would it be just the same, with the blessing of the church which thou so lovst! And what if I cannot bear a child! Do I not see how lovingly you look upon your choristers and every child we pass? Do I not know how much you want this? Wouldst bind thyself to me with this uncertainty?

I have not minded to return nor to stay. Thus I can say nothing, nor give any promises, nor say any truths, but that I love thee and miss thee most achingly, and long for the quarrel to be made up in the sweetest way, as we do, behind the hangings of my bed on Threadneedle. It is almost worth the quarrel to make up so delightfully with thee . . . but enough of that.

He stroked his beard, and sat alone many nights, then rushed out to find company in the Mitre, where John Lowin and Andrew Heminges often stopped in for a glass. Or he walked over to Blackfriars and drank coffee with Harvey. She was traveling about the south, staying with friends here and there.

He wrote,

My own dearest love, not in my shade, but by my side! Strange what thinkst? That ever thou couldst be in my shade!

Sweet, I am drowned with the many things occurring in the city. Avery is preparing his work for publication. Thy brother's wife's with child yet once more: she barely deflates but that she swells again. All manner of men in the parish wish to pour out their hearts to me while I sit, hands folded on stomach, nodding wisely as if I were by my four-cornered hat made beyond my own pain.

Oh mouse! The river hath not returned to its banks, and the very trees along the shore wither.

They wrote much during that month, and it was as if they were coming to know each other all over again. She returned in late August when the first soft breeze came from the fields and from the river. The sweetness of the harvest and of long voyages came with it, blowing away the heat of the city from the stones of Chancery Lane and the old mill house. She came late at night when he had already put up the shutters. He was seated in the inglenook chair with several books at his feet and the cat in his lap when she opened the door with her key. They went up to bed, and were awakened by the dawn. "I will marry thee with all my heart," she said, "and love thee all my life."

He ran barefoot with his shirt unlaced across the graveyard to Mary Aldermanbury and rang out the morning bells so that they pealed back from the city walls.

Thrice he called the banns from his own pulpit: the wedding of Nicholas Cooke, bachelor, of the parish of St. Mary Aldermanbury, and the lady Cecilia Lawes, widow, of St. Anthony's, Threadneedle. If any man knew reason that they should not be joined, he did not come forth.

He had requested Bartlett to walk with him to Lothbury, the old street of goldsmiths which had first come to prosperity in the thirteenth century and now was raucous with people shouting in half a dozen languages. They made their way from one shop to another, each replete with scales, weights, and boxes of necklaces and rings. It was three hours before he found the ring he wanted, and carefully gave them a bit of string the size of Cecilia's finger so they could adjust it.

They stood for a time talking by the great Cheapside Cross, and then Nicholas said offhandedly, "Our friend Avery must come to the wedding! Hast seen him?"

"Nay."

"He lodgeth I believe me on Silver Street above a ragman's. Shall we walk over and leave him some word?"

They hurried through the warm late afternoon towards the wall and up the streets above a shop where clothes too worn to be repaired, greasy rags, and piles of old bones were heaped before the door. There they found the good-natured small scholar in a fever, without so much as a blanket to cover him. Everything had been pawned. The press of books was empty, but for the Bible with its minute commentaries on the margin. Bartlett bit his lip. He began to pull off one of his rings, since he had not his purse about him.

By this time the landlady had heard them, and came huffing up the steps to complain of her tenant: he had lived six months on her charity and seemed soon likely to die at her expense as well. Angrily Nicholas took all the coins he had about him and laid them on the broken table. He threw into a bag what foul socks and neck linen lay about the floor. "Speak no word, Avery," he said abruptly, "for thou comst with me to bide from this day. Couldst thou stand, I would trounce thee for thy silence!" Cecilia, when he asked her later, did not mind at all.

Within a week they had furnished the garret with a draped bed, a wardrobe, a coal brazier, and a desk by the window, while Cecilia hurried to the pawnshops and booksellers to retrieve what she could of Avery's library. Dobson supplied several volumes and Keyes rebound them. On putting them away on the shelves, Nicholas noticed a small pile of Puritan tracts, would have asked his friend about them but forgot. Meanwhile they were closing the house in Threadneedle. The French maid returned to her own country, and they apprenticed the boy, who was now a great fellow, to a stationer.

At six on his wedding morn, Nicholas woke, bathed his hands and face, and dressed. The housekeeper hurried about, and Avery came down without his shoes and ineffectually poked a broom in corners. By nine of the clock the men had arrived in court clothes, raucously perfumed. Tom had sent twelve cups of silver from the north, and a wry private note wishing his friend all the best fortune.

The bride came walking from Threadneedle, holding her yellow-and-brown gown above the cobbles with her impatient brother by her side. A young priest from a nearby church was to perform the ceremony. Light filtered down through the windows to the memorial slabs in the floor as they took their places before the altar, and when Nicholas spoke the words *"With my body I thee worship; and with all my worldly goods I thee endow,"* Cecilia raised her eyes to him and smiled.

Scarves, ribbons, and banners had been hung from houses on the lane and down Aldermanbury. The party spilled from the rectory to the street and churchyard. Gradually the long day faded and friends took their leave. Sometime about nine he mounted the steps with Cecilia, she hardly able to untie her petticoats with fatigue. She snuffed the candles, and dropping her clothes to the floor, slid under the quilt. There he followed.

Several months later, to the astonishment of both, she found herself with child.

to Thomas Wentworth, West Riding, from his great friend Nicholas Cooke, parson of Mary Aldermanbury

Squire,

I thought to be the first to tell thee of my wife, but Dobson said last eve he had writ already the news. Altogether, she is such an astonishing woman that I feel I hardly know her from one day to the next. Still I cannot but be somewhat concerned, for she is above forty years.

News about the city is that our Bartlett hath been elected alderman of his ward. Written in haste and happiness.

Nick

Squire,

I must add some words also, the first being that you must not be concerned on my behalf, for I always do all well that I put my mind to and this I have truly decided I will do! You and I are both stubborn in this way.

The second is that I have resolved not to be a torment to thee any longer but to take my good husband's word that thou art not an altogether bad man and may amount to some small matter one day.

Hence I lay down my weapons such as I have and call thee brother. Let us hope you are indeed given work more worthy of you and that we shall all be with each other soon.

Cecily

Two months later she miscarried of the baby.

FIVE

Prison and Renewal

THOUGH NICHOLAS SAW HIS FRIEND SELDOM, HE THOUGHT OF HIM very much between his own troubles, mulling over Wentworth's problems as if to find a way to solve them. Wentworth badly wanted to find some court position and thus begin to rise under the new King, yet, as with the former sovereign, he could discover no small doors in the wall surrounding him through which he could enter. Other men rose easily; he went forward a few steps, stumbled, and was forced back.

Twice a week on the coach from York, Nicholas received long letters in which his friend poured out his heart, scribbling rapidly, underlining much, the words hardly contained on the paper for his yearning.

Your brother-in-law and our *esteemed* friend Dobson's rising in court life and growing wealthy, according to his letters; he knows painting and sculpture and the classical ruins now being venerated in Europe and that Italian architect, Palladio I believe he is called. He knows well how to please the proper men. He writes me and says he has two mistresses and I must make myself more pleasant to others if I wish to get on. I tell him he may be damned.

To my grief both King and country continue to circle around each other and go *nowhere.* That Parliament at the first session refused to grant the sovereign his tonnage and poundage, his guaranteed income for life as had always been the custom! Knowst I urged conciliation and was rebuffed. (Dobson laughed at me last time we were together on my seriousness in this matter, and God knoweth I came near to striking him!) But what has his blessed Majesty done to reward my efforts? I am appointed *sheriff* so that I cannot be returned to Parliament, cannot urge anything at all, and the fools in Commons who want only their own ways have all the power! Neither will he appoint me Lord of the North, which I am so well qualified to be. This is how it is with me, dear parson! I am now nearly five and thirty years of age and have achieved almost nothing.

Oh how precise we are to guard our divisions in religion and politics when the one thing that matters is we must not be divided! Something must bend, sweet parson, someone must concede. But my hands are tied.

One day shortly thereafter in the early summer, Nicholas looked up from the sermon he was writing to see the Yorkshireman's secretary, Wandesford, coming through the door, as cumbersome as a large dog who has just bounded in from the fields and threatens to shake his wetness over the parlor. "Parson, God's grace!" he blurted.

"God's grace! Why, Wandesford, what do you?" said Nicholas, making sure his hands were clean of ink before he gave them to the eager boy. "If you're about the city, Tom must be. When did he arrive? I spend a year's supply of quills returning his heavy letters, and now he's here and does not come."

"Sir," said the boy, rubbing his soft, short beard, "he cannot."

"Oh? And why cannot he, eh?"

"He's been called by the Privy Council."

"Indeed! He hath recently writ they do not so much as know his name, so little is his reputation! And what did they want of him?"

"Much, sir, that he wouldn't give, and he was determined to go."

"Go where, friend?"

"Marshalsea Prison with seventy-odd others."

Nicholas grasped the edge of the table so hard that the ink toppled and fell to the floor. "Christ's wounds, prison! What for?"

"With the others, for refusing the forced loan his Majesty placed on the gentry and landowners."

"What forced loan?" cried the physician. He swore aloud, shouted for his housekeeper, dashed a note quickly to Cecilia, seized his parcel of medicines, and threw on his cloak. Within minutes the sexton had fetched his horse, a wedding gift from Dobson, and with Wandesford seated behind, he made his way through the streets to the bridge. Halfway across they found a cart had broken down, and had to wait behind many irate tradesmen, mounted messengers, and gentry, none of whom could get by the narrow passage of the bridge road between the shops which lined the structure.

The prison, set in marshy grounds, was as ridden with plague, lice, and rats inside as any of the other infamous ones about the city where men were thrown for murder, thievery, heresy, or debt. Though Nicholas occasionally visited them in his work, his ribs always seemed to contract when he stepped past the warden's gate. Too many he had loved had entered these places and not come forth again living men.

Imprisoned for refusing a loan—how much was assessed? Tom, even with his brothers and sisters to provide for, could have somehow afforded it! Nicholas dismounted in the yard, which was full of carriages and carts unloading the rich belongings of the seventy or so other miscreants who had refused the King's demand for money. Tapestries were taken down, fur coverings, silver plate, maps, globes, leather slippers and embroidered dressing gowns, riding whips (he wondered why), bedlinens and goose-feather pillows, portraits of plump country matrons on wood, their hands modestly folded over rotund stomachs. He thought of the little dark-haired Arabella and wondered if she was within.

Wandesford led the way up the worn steps. Like any other prison, the

Marshalsea was a motley heap of filthy stone, dark corners, and the scent of old meals and bad sewage. No perfumer, no straw mixed with herbs, could hide that, nor could tapestries entirely camouflage the damp walls. Below in the common rooms, ordinary thieves lay with a bowl of gruel a day unless they could beg for more. Here was something different. It seemed like the parts of Whitehall which were given to court retainers in order of their eminence—thirty rooms to the house steward, two to a secretary—but that the ground was wretchedly damp and its foul odors hung about the walls. Though he knew some of the men who passed him with their servants carrying armfuls of quilting and upholstered chairs, he was not interested in them in the least. Wandesford held open a low door and stepped aside.

Wentworth with his sleeves rolled up was writing at his own desk, which had been removed from the house on St. Martin's Lane. His face when he looked up expressed disapproval. The boy knelt to unpack two large trunks, examining the books as he took them out and placing them in some order on another small table by the wall on which already stood Wentworth's heavy, well-thumbed Bible, which he had from his father. In the front, Nicholas remembered, Tom had inscribed the names of both of his wives. He strode across the room at once, took the empty chair opposite his friend, folded his hands on the table, and looked at him sternly.

"What forced loan?" he demanded. "And why couldn't you pay it?"

"I could but I didn't wish to, nor did these others."

"You have refused the King?"

"I have."

"Is this the best way to exert what you'd wish from him?"

Wentworth threw down his pen, leaned back, and began to bite darkly at the edge of his hand. "Charles Stuart's demanding a compulsory loan from gentry and landowners. Notice came to West Riding, and I refused it, was called by the Privy Council for my actions, and placed here. The matter's this: I'm through with him! I don't care what he does to me, for if he's not for me, he's against me, and I'll do nothing for him. I'll not give

Charles Stuart my money for Buckingham's wars!"

His fingers on the table trembled, and he closed them into a fist to hide them. Nicholas was silent for a moment. He understood that his friend was in a state where a man denies what he loves because he is so angry he cannot have it. He carefully laid his hand over Wentworth's fist, and felt the whole body stiffen.

"Tell me why I should do these things, parson!" Wentworth said. "With what favor doth he look upon me? What hath he done for me? What will he do?"

Nicholas glanced about the small prison room; he could not bear to think his friend here. His instinct was to reconcile, to have young Wandesford throw back the books and linens, cart them downstairs himself, and himself march to Whitehall and slap the money down upon the treasurer's desk. He said reasonably, "Dost oppose the man you wish to please?"

"I shall oppose him into his grave! It's over between us. . . ." Nicholas was fascinated and appalled at the depths of feeling his friend had for a man with whom surely he had not had more than a few hours' conversation in his life. Nor could he touch him again, for Tom moved back and forth in such hasty anger. "To give the Presidency of the North to Scope, who makes a muck of it! For what reason? How much further will I be humiliated and ignored when men of far lesser abilities are promoted to high office? Shall I be a beggar all my life?" He swung around to return to his copying, the injury he felt so deep it filled the room and seemed to push out through the wall hangings of scenes from the lives of the apostles.

Nicholas said gently, " 'Tis damp here, Tom! What of thy gout?"

"I have no sign of it."

"Ah, nor rheumatism? And where's Arabella?"

"She has lodgings nearby. Will you see her?" Anxiety came into Wentworth's voice for the first time. Nicholas nodded and before returning home stopped by the house where the young wife lodged with maid and nursemaid, greeted the small heir to the Wentworth estate, who was just beginning to walk, and noticed that Arabella was once again with child.

"Wilt care for Tom?" she murmured.

"I will do what I can."

"His gout is paining him, and there's rheumatism as well."

"Ah! He stoutly denied it."

"Parson, you know that's his way," she answered with a sigh.

Through the summer Nicholas rode daily to the Marshalsea with ointments against gout and rheumatism in his satchel. From time to time, members of the science group came as well. Avery, polite and observant, looked about the halls of men in their dressing gowns dictating to the secretaries, or playing chess. " 'Tis better than Bedlam," he said wistfully. "On the other hand, hath poor light!"

Dobson crossed his arms over his chest. "Too small," he pronounced wryly. "Are London accommodations so scarce, Wentworth, that must come here?"

The friends crowded about the narrow chamber, seizing bed pillows to sit on the floor. Bartlett stretched out on his back on Wandesford's lower trundle cot with his portly arms under his head and gazed at the ceiling. " 'Tis a damp spot that looketh like a fair naked wench," he said reflectively. "One such died under my care this week, Wentworth! They called me too late. 'Tis a pestilential summer."

"Tom didn't like St. Martin's Lane! Too many carters come from the fields, kept him awake."

"Sayth the south side's better, though unfashionable."

"Christ's blood, we shall all have to move here as well for fellowship's sake!" exclaimed Harvey.

Harrington strode about, poking his walking stick behind the wall hangings and testing the window bars as if looking for poor rations. "God's wounds!" he said stoutly. "Hast better devise a way to amuse thyself on thy estates hereafter, Wentworth, for shalt never find thy way to court and Commons again! Ha! Art finished, lad."

They ate meat pies and sat about discussing the possibility of a calculating box with wheels for mechanical multiplication and division. "I have sketched such a thing," said Bartlett. He sat up, clasping the knees of his breeches with his arms. When he left he shook his head, saying, "Repent, repent, Wentworth, for the meek shall inherit the earth!"

Then one day in the late fall when Nicholas arrived by ferry and foot, he found the yard was clustered with carriages and servants packing. Most men had been released. Wentworth had gone home at once, the warden said, the dust of his carriage wheels still lingering in the marshy air of the south side, taking no clean clothes and leaving all to be sent after him. Even his wife was not allowed to accompany him in his haste. He had rushed to West Riding, Nicholas later learned, to arrange for his return to Commons. Writs had been issued for the third Parliament in March 1628, and he was determined to be heard.

Elected he was and arrived in the last days of winter, this time leaving Arabella behind; he flung open the house in St. Martin's Lane but was seldom in it. About the courts and around, Nicholas began now and then to hear the name of Wentworth. Again Parliament met but could come to no agreement, and Wentworth most vocally urged the King's assent to the Petition of Right. "We must not imprison men without cause, must not make them serve in foreign wars, nor billet soldiers upon citizens, nor tax without Parliamentary approval." He did not blame the King, he said in his speeches, but the administration. If the King would guarantee these freedoms, Commons would vote his Majesty subsidies. Nicholas went twice to hear him. He spoke fluently, evocatively. He wanted the best for crown and country, he said, for both were inextricably bound together. Everyone in the court and houses began to attend to the tall, slender, yet vigorous member of Commons whose steady voice and sure manner were coming close to uniting both houses and throne. Nicholas watched quietly from his place on a bench with a sense of awe. All the friends were deeply disappointed when the session ended once more with no agreement between King and country. And then for some time, they heard no word from Tom Wentworth at all.

Cecilia was once again with child. Daily she pressed her fingers against her belly, hoping to feel a difference in its shape and firmness. Eagerly she counted the weeks . . . six, seven. Exhausted, she slept a great deal, sometimes half dressed across the bed. The warm rains of summer had come and beat against the house and the garden; she slept knowing nothing, while below the clock struck yet again and Nicholas sat with his lenses and perspective tubes, hunched by candlelight, reading his notes.

He did not hear the knocking at first in the rain, nor when he opened the door did he recognize the man who stood there with his hood drawn up. In the next moment he felt himself embraced so hard that it took his breath away. "Comst like a ghost, Tom," he cried, pushing his wet friend from him. "Pah, I am now soaked as well! They should send thee to haunt here and there, for there are people will do much to see a sprite. They say sprites can cure much!"

"What is o'clock?"

"Past one, but my watch ever runneth slow."

"Invite me within!"

"It needeth no invitation, my friend," said Nicholas. By the candlelight and with his hands he could make out how drenched was his friend; water even dripped down his rapier sheath, which he unbuckled and shook ruefully over the kitchen stones. "Dost always walk abroad this hour?" he asked, handing Tom a cloth to wipe his hair.

"I have walked the whole night! Nay, 'tis a warm eve, and what fire's left will do! I want no drink, I am too filled with happiness. I thought to come in the morn, but I was unable to stay abed! I walked to Westminster, Nick, and stood looking at it, great ghost of a place that it is in the rain . . . shadows, full of all the kings and ministers passed. My ancestors! I am descended from John of Gaunt. I called up to it that I had come, and it made no reply. No, I cannot sleep this night!"

"What wouldst have done had I been abed, eh?"

"Dragged thee from it, sluggard!" Wentworth wiped the water from his face, and then slowly began to strip off his shirt. The dark hairs of the narrow chest glistened in the faint candlelight. "Where's Cecily?"

"Asleep; she's with child again."

"God's blessings on you both!"

Wentworth reached up to swing the kettles, pots, ropes of onions, and dried meats which hung from the rafters as if he were a peculiar sort of bell ringer. "Knowst why I come to thee?" he said playfully.

"Aye, verily! Art mad, and Avery will come down presently and certify you to Bedlam."

"Aye, I'm mad! And that with happiness, and contentment, and overly long waiting for a thing that's come at last!" He took Nick's arms and looked into his face. "I can hardly say the words," he murmured, suddenly shy. "When I woke this morning my secretary brought me a message from Whitehall which said come at thy leisure, which meaneth, of course, come at once. Come, it said, and 'twas signed 'your assured friend, Charles Rex.' I cut my chin in haste to trim my beard. The King's ushers took me to the water, where his Majesty had sent his barge for me, and when I stepped in one of the stewards stood and called me . . . *my lord.* I thought him wrong, but said naught. By God's life, Nick! I shall never forget that ride! All along the Thames, from dock to warehouse to palace, elms hung over the water, and here and there wild flowers sprang between broken boats. Swans drifted near the shore."

He stopped to catch his breath. "And then I came to him. He was standing at the end of the hall in his dressing gown, for it was early; he had just come from his prayers and had that soft, otherworldly look which he hath then. He took me by the arm, and we walked up and down the hall for a time." He was trembling. "I'm raised to the peerage, Nicholas; I am now a lord and will no longer sit in Commons but with the Lords, for I am this day Baron Wentworth of Wentworth Woodhouse!"

"Tom!"

"Do I dream? Surely I dream! I have told my household, I have told the very stones of the city. Ah, Christ's love, Christ's love, Nicholas! It hath begun for me. I have waited until it wore me to a nub. But who's come?"

Avery was crossing the room with a childish, concerned smile; his short nightdress showed his thin, hairy legs, yet he gave the appearance of an urchin who had got up from his cot petulantly for company.

"What's this?" he muttered, rubbing his eyes. "Hath plague come?"

He opened his eyes wide when he heard the news and solemnly shook Wentworth's hand for some time. "God's grace on ye, Tom!" he said. "Wilt no more sit in Commons?"

"Nay! I truly believe that those who lead Commons now aren't capable to govern a country in one unity. And it must be so done: there cannot be any division between King and Parliament!"

They talked in low eager voices for some time until they heard the stair creak. Cecilia was coming dreamily down, barefoot in her dressing gown, a candleholder in her hand, crookedly held for her weariness. Her dark hair hung loose to her waist, and she gazed at the three of them with a slight frown.

Wentworth stood with a sudden sense of shyness, looked for his shirt, and not knowing where he had put it, took up an old quilt from the window seat, which he pulled over his shoulders. It gave him the air of an old supplicant seeking alms.

Cecilia said, "Comst here seldom, and now unexpectedly, my friend."

Nicholas took her arm in his and, turning her face, whispered the news. She drew in her breath with surprise. "Then Tom, much joy!" she said. "Or must I call you 'my lord'?"

He shook his head and clumsily began to speak again. He spoke drunkenly as a man so wanting sleep he cannot put ideas properly together, so excited that he is between violence and tears. He spoke of the country from the estuaries to the fishing villages of Cornwall, from the Welsh hills through the rough north shires to the edge of coarse Scotland, from whence the late King James had come, and back down the east to the channel which led to France and the islands thereby. He spoke of the history of kings and landed gentry, of bishops and monks in the days before the Reformation, of taxes, tariffs, shipping, mining, and the fishing and wool industries. He spoke like a man ravished by love. Then he seemed to huddle inside the quilt, and ended with a brusque mumble as if he wished to dismiss it all. "His Majesty would rather have me by his side than against him—mayhap this is why he did this. He felt my power." He stood still then, stunned.

Cecily had remained with her arm in Nicholas's, leaning slightly against him. "There are some who will think badly of thee for this change from Commons, my lord," she said simply.

"Damned if they do," was the violent answer.

She put her hand on Wentworth's, and thoughtfully kissed his cheek. "God keep thee!" she said, and then turned and went up the stairs again.

The chimes struck the hour of two, and the rain had begun to lessen. The men talked for a time more, and Avery made toasted cheese on a long fork which he dropped now and then on the hearthstones. Wentworth ate ravenously, and then sank and closed his eyes. Nicholas took him up the steps to the room which he had been in some times before, and his friend fell asleep without pulling back the quilting.

Some weeks after, the lord Wentworth, as he was now known, was appointed Lord of the North and sent back to Yorkshire. There he would be responsible for protecting the King's interests in lands and taxes and law and order. This administrative post, Harrington speculated expansively, was but an interim one to test the mettle of the servant's worth before Charles Stuart brought him to London again. Still, Dobson said that though Wentworth might have come this far, he would go no further, for he was not the sort of man the sovereign liked.

Fall came gently: they woke each morning to the knowledge of the babe inside her womb. Nicholas would trace his hand over the hardened mound of belly and in wonder count the weeks. Each day he felt safer and more secure about it. He began to consider where they would put the cradle. He could not quite imagine his beloved Cecily as a mother, for she was studying both midwifery and law, and sometimes coming to bed late he would have to displace several heavy books which she had scattered on the quilt. He wondered where she would find patience or time for a child.

On the late afternoon of All Hallows' Eve when he was giving instructions to his sexton to watch the graveyard that night that mischievous apprentices might not disrupt its sanctity with their yearly pranks, a child of the parish came running into the dispensary, crying that the royal carriage had stopped at Aldermanbury by the church. In a moment William Harvey himself came through the door in his court clothing, shouting, "We are both called to attend the King this hour: dress, prithee."

Nicholas stood at once. "His Majesty to call me! How comes this?"

"I know not! Mayhap he hath heard thou art priest as well, and canst give him the last rites should my purging kill him. Forsooth, come!"

When Nicholas ran up to the bedchamber he found Cecilia sewing by the window overlooking the garden, the hoop balanced against her belly. Royal carriage and coachman were waiting, and as soon as the men had leapt within, the carriage turned towards the western gates of the city. Before them rode one usher on horseback, now and then blowing the horn to let people know that those within the vehicle were on the King's business. At the Holbein gate the sentry thrust open the doors of the carriage that they might descend to the yard. Past the guard, they were ushered into Whitehall Palace.

They proceeded through rooms with carpets upon tables and Italian marbles in corners. Down halls and in every chamber hung paintings from the Italian states; one depicted the ruins of Carthage. From far off they could hear the sound of a small chamber orchestra practicing. Some of the upholstery seemed threadbare, many walls wanted new papering, and one pair of fire irons Nicholas glanced upon was rusty.

Outside the wind rattled. Young boys began to light the candles in the wall sconces; one little fellow stifled a yawn. Occasional warmth from a well-stacked fire crept across the floor and curled about the men's ankles as they hurried on. Thus they came to the royal apartments and the first small waiting room within. A painting of Charles Stuart hung on one wall, and next it one of the Queen, her upper lip raised over her large teeth, and a single rose held in her hand. They were led down another hall and up some stairs, through a sitting room, and into a sleeping chamber. At the end were several gentlemen, and in the midst, seated upon a chair with shirt open at the neck and a handkerchief in his hand, sat the young King.

They pulled off their broad-brimmed hats and dropped to one knee. Motioning them to rise, the King murmured, "We welcome you." The slightly hoarse voice seemed to echo to the pargeted ceiling and the wood carved angels which decorated the large wardrobe door.

Harvey stepped forward and with great decorum began an examination of Charles Stuart: heart, pulse, much more, and the urine sample within the pot. He then bowed and said, "Sire, here is the gentleman and physician Nicholas Cooke of Cripplegate Ward, whose attendance was commanded in the letter sent to me. Will you now lend this scholar your wrist that he also may examine your person?"

"He may approach us," said the King.

Crossing the room and dropping to his knees again, Nicholas took the slender hand beneath the lace cuff. For a moment all the chamber seemed to blur: there was naught but the soft, masculine hand in his and the tickle of the excellent lace against his skin. He could see the silk lacing of the shirt, and the slight amount of fair chest hair. A smell of musk was over everything, mingled with that of the fire. Then it all fell away, and he was a physician again, and the man before him but a gentle youth with a congestion and hoarse voice. Lemon balm, he thought quickly. A mild purge. Hot broths, a good fire to the chamber, warmed sheets, and untroubled leisure. I would prescribe the same for any fellow of the parish. Christ's mercy.

As that moment a knock came at the door, and some pages came in. Harvey beckoned Nicholas into a corner near the bed, where they discussed the proper physic. Both dropped to one knee again before being given leave to go. As Nicholas looked back, he saw the handsome figure of George Villiers, Earl of Buckingham, emerge through an antechamber door. The Earl touched his full lips to the King's wrist and said with familiar chiding, "What, unwell, sweet Charlie? Shall not ride this day?" The double doors were closed.

The physicians made their bows to the gentlemen who awaited them

and soon were outside the privy chambers. Then Harvey muttered, astonished, "Fool, what is it with thee? Dost laugh?"

" 'Tis thou! No gravedigger could have been more solemn! And then
when last I knelt I thought of a sudden . . . how thou hast said . . . the
urine of the King smelleth as any man's . . . there being by the pot, I . . .
And yet by all the saints, I was moved to near the most damnable tears, I
know not why."

"I must confess, 'twas Wentworth's doing you were asked."

"Christ's blood, I knew it! But come now, for I think Cecilia's not
well. It hangs on me now, her looks."

Arm and arm they passed rooms and rooms, and after a time someone
ran after them with gold wrapped in a cloth. The wind was colder yet as
they came from the door. When he came home he found that Cecilia had
once again miscarried a child.

Tom, I cannot say what I feel. First my eyes are swollen with tears, for
Cecily is ill and can eat almost nothing. I think sometimes between the
three of us I am forced into the role of the one who is calm, which, God
knoweth, was never the way Our Lord created me! And then I am bewildered by my visit to the King and why it moved me so. What is this man to
me? I have always drunk the health of our sovereigns and shouted, "God
save your Majesty!" when their carriage splattered my good hose with
mud, even when they did not deserve it. Yet this one somehow does.
Harvey and I again discuss: is the King sacred? He was marked with holy
oil on hands, head, and breast at his coronation, he was ordained. Well, I
know not. The office is sacred, of course, but the man is only a probability,
and yet in my heart (would you believe that I am trembling?) I would say if
any sovereign is sacred, this one must be. There's a goodness about him. I
write by instinct and hearsay: the brief words spoken in my visit compose
the entire sum of all I have ever said to him or he to me.

He trusts so easily that he could trust the weak rather than the strong.
By God's sweet breath, may he come to trust thee! But my thoughts are
scattered, and Cecilia is calling from above. Her voice is so weak! What
have I done? I am as selfish as those I despise in even allowing her to try to

conceive a child! And I cannot bring her contentment truly; I fail at that and it wearies me.

I must go now. My deepest love to you and your family.

West Riding, Yorkshire

Dear parson!

No thanks are due to me, for you are my friend and I am determined to do what I can for thy advancement. I intend to be a very great man in this country and have you one as well. I will do all I can to bring it about, and may God grant you and your wife a child!

I am here an exile from the center of my heart and ambitions, but by my faith, if it is Charles Stuart's will to have my service be in this more barren place, then bow I my uncovered head. He knoweth full well that I am a man in love with kingship and would polish his walking stick humbly rather than be absolutely apart from his knowledge. I am full of such love and ambition these days that I cannot say which hath precedence.

Sometimes I walk out early mornings and feel the country rushing forward beneath my feet as a river when the spring comes, swollen and joyful and pushing ever on. So as thy mind calleth to thee, doth the country whisper to me. Yet more and more my beliefs have crystallized. The authority of a king is the keystone which closeth up the arch of order and government, and which once shaken, all the frame falls together in a confused heap of foundation and battlement, of strength and beauty. To uphold this will be my life's work.

I have writ my friend William Laud, the Bishop of Bath and Wells, to be aware of thee, make thee his physician, and mayhap see to thy promotion in the church. He is a most dear fellow, for all his fussy ways, and one of much faith. In the meantime I am ever thy friend as thou art mine, and hold thee to my heart.

Tom

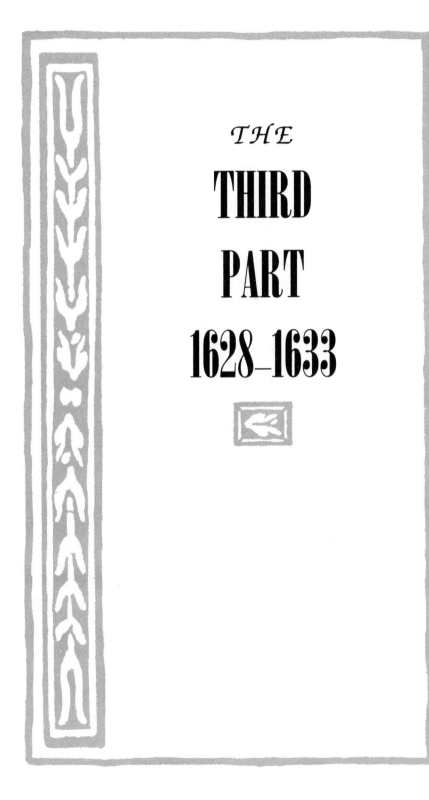

THE

THIRD
PART
1628–1633

ONE

The Bishop of London

A SOFT WIND WAS BLOWING BOTH THE DRYING LEAVES AND THE WASH ON the line that fall morning when the sound of shouting made Nicholas hurry from his church. He stood with his hand on the gate as a girl in a red dress ran sobbing down the lane, one arm covering her face. Some lads threw a handful of filth after her. He was about to shout at them when more people rushed past, obscuring them from his sight. "What news?" he cried.

"Hast not heard, parson? Lord Buckingham's been killed!"

In the Mitre men were banging on the tables and talking so passionately that their voices rattled. "Knifed to death in the middle of his men in the town of Dover," one cried. " 'Twas a vagrant soldier out of work, simpleminded they say . . . came in for an audience with the Earl, concealed the weapon under his cloak."

Nicholas looked from one face to the other. "Why?" he said.

"Why, parson? No particular reason, man was crazed . . . but the Earl's dead and the King's in grief. Locked himself in his chambers when he heard and won't come out."

"Even with this," muttered another, "he's better off without him. The country's sick of Buckingham's foreign wars and monopolies."

Nicholas gazed about at his neighbors and fellows. The Mitre was much the same as always, with its smell of ale and unwashed clothing, its large chalkboard with the debts of its patrons scribbled on it, its collection of wooden, pewter, and earthenware mugs, some too smashed or cracked to be of use anymore. By the dirty window were piles of fragile newspapers. Two lanky apprentices trembled with interest. He had heard them shouting as fervently over autumn football.

Yet a man's life had been lost: it was to him that simple. A man had walked through his admirers who'd come on petition or with well-wishes, and been stabbed to death in the heart. Refusing any drink, the physician walked slowly down Love Lane under the hanging laundry.

Later that night he rode with Cecilia to Westminster. The palace of Whitehall was quiet, the windows shuttered. Even the carts seemed to think better of it and go more softly for the grief of the King. Nicholas felt his throat swell with compassion. He had been no admirer of Buckingham; his rise had been more from the fanatical favoritism of the old King and the solemn, boyish devotion of the new one than from his own merits. Still, he remembered how he had felt the solitary beating of Charles Stuart's heart when he had examined him, and thought how much more heavily that heart must sound tonight.

They walked back quietly hand in hand, leading the horse, hearing singing from some taverns and the name shouted. "Buckingham! Damn tyrant . . ." And then again, "Ah, poor fellow! Poor fellow! What will his widow do? 'Tis always the women left alone to grieve. . . ."

to the physician, gentleman, and priest Cooke of Cripplegate Ward, London, from the Lord of the North, Thomas Wentworth

Nick,

There's no news in the north but Buckingham's death. I don't know what this will mean in the King's love to me, for I do believe Buckingham stood between his Majesty and my advancement. Nonetheless, I grieve for him. In what direction will the country go now?

Feelings are high all over the land. Dobson wrote his houseboy fought other lads over it, and was badly hurt. London apprentices, ready with any excuse as always for cudgels and bonfires!

We hear that Charles Stuart hath drawn closer to his little Queen in his grief, sent her French retinue home, and means to make her with child. He trusts Laud, I know, and that's well, for the new Bishop of London, as you will find, is a truly good man.

On a warm drizzly fall afternoon some days later, a deferential cleric in a cassock with worn buttons knocked on the door of the house on Love Lane bearing within his satchel an invitation for the priest Nicholas Cooke to drink a cup of wine with William Laud. Shortly thereafter, Nicholas hailed a ferry west, his mind filled with thoughts of the new Bishop of London, whom he had met three or four times but briefly over the past few years.

"Laud's rising quickly," Wentworth had said on one of their last walks in the fields outside the walls. "Buckingham made sure he was granted a minor bishopric, and he gave the sermon at the first Parliament—remember how sourly some took it, being on the divine right of kings! Charles Stuart's most pleased with the small fellow and will one day make him Bishop of London. Dost wager a copper penny against it, Nick?" He had whistled, and held out his palm.

The great brick house of Fulham lay behind a flower garden. A youthful steward hurried to the door on the third knock; he murmured apologetically for his sawdust-covered boots, saying they had all been unpacking since dawn and everything was in disorder. He left Nicholas in a sitting room hung with many large portraits of former bishops and archbishops until the double doors flew open, and William Laud himself hurried towards him on little round feet with both elegant hands extended.

The new Bishop of London was now somewhere about the age of fifty.

There was, however, little sign of the importance of his position, for he wore only a simple black robe and a close-fitting black knit cap from which escaped some soft grey hair. His eyes were beautiful and sharp and the brows were thick; the beard was trimmed to a point. The delicate nostrils alone, held stiffly, gave him an air of vague disdain.

"My good friend Tom Wentworth hath writ of thy learning!" he said cheerfully. "Words which made me listen well, for naught's dearer to me than studies!" He gazed about him with a sigh at all the pictures of his grave predecessors and the clock which ticked the seconds noisily. "Mayhap I will have time within these walls to continue my own translation of scripture from the Hebrew, if so Our Lord wills! But come to the library!"

Nicholas caught his breath at the sight of the great room with its thousands of books in heavy presses reaching far above their heads; books were also piled about the floor and on chairs, the leather upholstery of which had been well scratched by a cat's paws. He took a chair as bidden, and found that the small bishop, who had seated himself opposite with his hands folded pensively over his stomach, had grown quiet studying him.

"Hast done much!" he exclaimed, when Nicholas had told him something of his life and work. "I myself have never married; my household's my family. Good souls that they are, they've not ceased from working! I believe that's Nell from the kitchen below hanging the pots and scolding the lads! Ha ha, poor sweetings! Even the stable lad bids me good day in Latin as I've taught him, for without learning, what are we?

"This house is large," he continued. "From these windows I can see the river and all the ships traveling on their business. I was born a poor tailor's son, and I recall me that as a boy my window had waxed paper only to let in light, and looked upon a broken priory. We live in an age and a country when honest men of ability may rise freely under their sovereign! A most gracious prince, a most kindly one, and of deep faith."

An old woman hurried in with wine and apples, and when she was gone, the bishop shook his head and continued, "So much must be done that I scarce know where to begin! I have traveled about the country, dear parson, and what I've seen saddens me. Many churches are in disgraceful disrepair: roofs falling in, sacristies used for pigs, dogs running about . . . why, it's the fashion now for a man to come into a church with no more respect than a tinker into an alehouse! On this matter there's something in particular I would show you, for I'm told you have some interest in architecture. Look at the papers on the desk."

"My lord, are these renovations for the Cathedral of St. Paul?" Leaning over the desk, Nicholas began with some excitement to unroll each one under the light from the high windows. He knew the great, squalid Cathedral as well as he knew his own kitchen. There was not a shabbier place in all London. It had been that way since he had arrived as a boy in the city and hidden himself in its chapels. The ensuing years had not made it better, for the citizens of the city had long used the crypt for dumping garbage, the spire was unrestored since it had burnt in a fire some eighty years since, and a coterie of whores, lawyers, pamphleteers, and cutpurses had long made the nave their meeting spot, nor could anything urge them away for more than a few days.

Looking up dreamily after a time, the papers still smoothed under his hands, he murmured, "My lord, 'twill be a great undertaking and one which I never in my life thought to see. This of all places must be made sacred again! Any assistance I can give to you, I would most humbly!" Sinking back in his chair once more, he gazed with wonder and a certain shyness at the small man before him. Some men did not care for history or preserving what had been, yet the past had always seemed to Nicholas the very thing which permitted the present: he was who he was and where he was for what had gone before him.

The Church of England had belonged to Rome until the last century, when bluff King Harry declared it independent. It was into this church Nicholas had been born, and many years later, ordained priest. As William Laud spoke quietly in a modest voice, playing with the folds of his cassock, Nicholas saw his own faith reflected in him. He felt for one moment that he could reach out and touch it. They spent the next hour talking of the beautiful ways and customs of the old church which had been laid aside when the new church was formed and which Laud wished to restore. Eventually he said he hoped to return vestments to the priest and incense to the sanctuary in every parish of the land.

The trees of the garden appeared to glitter about Nicholas as he left some hours later, and the air itself seemed luminescent. The day had stirred him, and he felt bound securely in something far greater than himself. Standing by the wharf with the sun sinking beneath the water, he experienced yet again the joy which he had felt when God had first called him as priest and he had answered humbly, Here am I.

Winter came again. Water in the basins froze overnight, and they shook woolens out of camphor and lavender where the housekeeper had put them last spring against the moth. Barrels of coal were delivered. Men had gradually ceased to speak of Buckingham, and Nicholas also sometimes forgot him and much else in the joy of his marriage.

In November he had been elected both as secretary of the College of Physicians and to their committee which examined the practices of unlicensed doctors within seven miles of the city gates. Some men still hung out a shingle of medicine though their training may have consisted of little more than passing the house of a physician and staring for a time through the window. They confiscated rose water which some old fellow sold as medicine against consumption; they also discovered a girl of seven who was rented out to families as a healing spirit. It was bewildering work, never effectual for long, and he was always happy to leave it and come home again.

Cecilia's lute leaned against a corner by the stair; her books were piled upon the table next to his microscopes, under the bed, and on the stair. Lace bodices and embroidered caps lay in lavender leaves in the wardrobe drawer. He would reach to the shelf whereon he had by custom these many years lain his spring watch each night, and encounter a bowl of hair combs and another of pins and fastenings. He loved to watch her tie the laces of her hose. Again he contemplated her with all tenderness: she would begin to study something, fling herself deeply in it, and then abandon it.

Only law held her in the end, and one day she sat down and wrote a letter to Wentworth, asking his help in allowing her to enter at Middle Temple as a barrister's apprentice.

The reply was quizzical.

> I will do what I can, my lady, but I doubt I can do much. There are some things even the King cannot do! I beseech you if this can never come to pass to find other ways of employing your excellent mind. I do not know what else to tell you. I cannot wish indeed for my friend's sake that Our Lord had made you other than female; nor could I wish it for my own, for now that my initial alarm at you has passed (and now that it is gone I do confess it!) I find you charming as you are, and of great depth and wisdom.

He continued in the formal, slightly playful way he had devised to write to her, and she returned in kind, sighed, and found an elderly barrister to tutor her nearby. Still, she would not put from her mind what she wanted most: to enter Middle Temple as apprentice, and to bear a child. Each seemed beyond her. She was in the end too interested in life to remain long unhappy and assisted in the delivery of her first babe from a woman of the parish. Still she felt this was not in the end her proper work. To find it! She spoke of it now and then and continued to study.

Everyone came to their house in those days: those seeking healing or a renewal with God, and those wanting friendship, actors, neighbors, doctors from the German states and glassmakers from the Netherlands, his friends from Padua and hers from Paris, apprentices hoping to change their work to physicking, his closest fellows, and messengers from the Bishop of London or his chaplain. Avery continued to help in the dispensary, and was soon taking over much of the work.

An uneasy Parliament sat in Westminster in the winter of 1629, discussing taxation yet again and what money should be allocated to the

King. There were also murmurs in opposition to the new Bishop of London's proposed increase of religious ritual. Charles Stuart, who also favored church beautification and a formal service of prayer book and candles, would not give in when Commons demanded he modify his stand before they granted his subsidy. Wentworth, once more in the city and taking his place in the Lords, stood solidly behind the unification of church and state, which surprised Nicholas, for he knew his friend from the north preferred plainer, shorter church services to the more elaborate ones of the King. ("Candles or not, 'tis the very same Savior," Wentworth said with a shrug. "But if it's candles and vestments his Majesty wishes, it will be my wish as well. Damn the Puritans if they oppose him!") Everyone spoke of these things from tavern to guildhall.

On a late winter day Nicholas walked over towards Blackfriars to secure tickets for the new comedy. The lovely hall, with its balconies rising up and its elegant candle sconces, was filled with the high sweet sound of a single soprano recorder. The actor John Lowin, grown stouter and greyer of beard, lumbered forward to shake his hand. They talked awhile before they heard someone calling them, and turned to see Bartlett, with his silver-handled walking stick, entering the hall.

Henry Bartlett had been alderman for Basinghall Ward next to theirs for a year now. All things he did well, but for his marriage, and he was so popular both in his ward and in his work that it sometimes seemed there was not a soul in London whom he did not know. Still, he seemed like a man who had rushed passionately to his fortieth year, and when he reached it, looked about trying to remember what he had hoped to find when he arrived there.

He was flushed and perspiring slightly, and taking out a large handkerchief, he wiped his forehead. "Hast heard of Parliament?" he panted. "Nothing is more obscene, more outrageous!"

"Nay, I've heard nothing," replied Nicholas.

"You soon will! The King ordered the session prorogued, but some members of Commons wouldn't let the Speaker dismiss them until they'd passed certain bills against his Majesty's rights, so they locked the door and held the Speaker in his chair. His Majesty hath imprisoned the rebels and swears he'll never call another Parliament."

Lowin frowned. "May they see the inner walls of the Tower until they are weary of them!" he cried. "To flout his Majesty, the sweetest sovereign ever come to the throne! Doth he keep mistresses, put wretches to the rack, curse like a swine? Nay, good masters! And yet the country hath granted him no money to pay his baker and cobbler as any honest man must do. Must he go and find a trade and join a guild to earn his bread? Must he become a bricklayer, by Our Lord's death? 'Tis bad to treat our anointed sovereign so!"

Several actors now hurried down into the theater to talk about the adjourning of Parliament. The King was their patron and served them well, and most felt he had been right. Bartlett narrowed his eyes and mouth. He listened but briefly before contradicting them.

"Dost not see the country's changing?" he said stoutly. "Men are far less willing to give up their money to the King for wars they abhor and other matters! They don't trust his spending habits, or what unholy alliances his Catholic Queen will put him to, for she's all his favorite now that Buckingham's dead. We are no longer in the age of the Tudor kings!"

Then he added, "My lord of Wentworth will disagree with this, of course. Oh, since he's raised to the peerage, he feels very differently about things! He takes the King's side now."

The two physicians walked out into the cold March day and towards one of the gates of Blackfriars. Bartlett was thoughtful, and clasped his hands behind his back. "I shall one day put myself forward for the city for Commons," he said. "The northern lad's not the only who will have his say in these matters." At once his face softened under the thick pale brown mustache, and he began to whistle.

Charles Stuart remained true to his word, for he did not call another Parliament. Harrington, who knew the finances of the royal household well, said the King raised ship money to pay some creditors; there were also loans, and gifts and interests here and there, which somehow sustained him.

The court continued as elegant as ever. Between the palaces there was a full complement of ushers, gentlemen, maidservants, cooks, pastrymakers, scullery girls, musicians, gentlemen of the wardrobe and of the privy chamber, cupbearers, and pages. Seventeen hundred servants there were, and the King dined to his own band. The Queen lived in Somerset House, but also had suites of rooms in Whitehall. No longer did she have a retinue of twenty Catholic priests and a bishop to see to her spiritual needs, but made her confession to a Scottish clergyman, and seemed satisfied to do it. Their first babe, miscarried in the eighth month, had lived only long enough to be baptized by William Laud, who hurried in sympathetically with tears in his eyes. Still, the diminutive Queen had become close to her royal husband since the death of Buckingham. It was said to be the happiest marriage in Christendom, though Nicholas did not think it could match his own.

Thomas Wentworth had at last been appointed a member of his Majesty's Privy Council, though he wrote wryly that with the work he had been set in the north, he doubted he would be much about to advise the King. "What I feel about this matter with those fools who presently surround Charles Stuart and know little more than horses and art, I shall not say, but knowst it well, friend," he wrote. Two or three times a week he wrote expansively of government and how with a perfect balance of power it could serve the well-being of both sovereign and subject. Nicholas sometimes tried to puzzle from the letters Wentworth's deepest feelings for his sovereign: they were resentment, criticism, hope, and unwavering, almost religious love. Whether Wentworth loved the holy office of kingship or the delicate, fastidious man who held it, Nicholas could not say. He doubted Wentworth knew himself. Cecilia read the letters as well, leaning her cheek on her hand, her other arm encircling her full belly, for she was now once more with child.

For her Wentworth wrote,

Tell the lovely Cecily that to no avail I have attempted to obtain admittance to one of the law temples for her to study and that most certainly her present state makes it less likely yet that I shall succeed. I have not forgotten, though.

I have enclosed some thoughts on strengthening the government, and if you will let me have your response on them, I would be grateful. If Cecily will use her goodly wisdom this way as well, I shall take it as a great kindness.

That made her smile.

Months passed, and her belly continued to grow. For the first time since he had known her, Nicholas found his wife to be almost perfectly peaceful. She never left his thoughts, and if he had to be away for a whole day, he would send a little boy to ask after her and give him a whole penny for taking the message.

He was often in those months with William Laud. Two or three times a week he would ferry westward and walk up the path from the river to Fulham House. Each week wall hangings, Italian paintings, or freshly rebound volumes of the life of some saint were added, gifts from those who admired him. The small bishop scarcely noticed them. He now and then sent over an odd or beautiful book to Nicholas's house, a note scribbled in his large, generous hand. When his capacious orchards were harvested in the fall, he sent baskets of fruit to the rectory in Cripplegate. Nicholas was sometimes invited for supper and twice brought Cecilia, whom the bishop found witty. He loved nothing more than to laugh.

A year had passed since their conversation in the library, and during that time William Laud had continued to rise in the government. Often present about the house were a dozen or more deacons, laymen, and nobility. He was now Treasury Chancellor, and Chancellor of Oxford and Cambridge, and in and about the Privy Chambers. Sometimes when Nicholas called to see him, the freckled page would humbly entreat him to wait: the lord bishop was at counsel with the Star Chamber, please your worship, or with delegates from Oxford concerning the expansion of the library, or with the King, who sought his advice about religious dissidents or political preference. Nicholas made himself comfortable until he heard carriage wheels and the little man himself rushed in on small, hasty feet, swaying slightly.

Once on an autumn evening when the hour had gone late, the carriages had rolled away, and the servants had replaced the rugs on the dining table and taken up the scraps for the poor, the bishop asked him to stay for Compline, the ancient last prayer service of the day. Instead of turning to the chapel, the men mounted the stairs into a sleeping chamber. It was plain to austerity, containing only an undraped, narrow bed, a small desk, some chairs, and a prayer desk.

When they had closed the door, Laud said wistfully, "Art a man of science, parson! Dost put stock in dreams? I have such strange ones. I think sometimes dreams are not in the power of him that hath them but in the imagination, which wanders any way it pleases. Still, I believe that some dreams are impressed upon us by some superior influence. What thinkst thou?"

"It may be, my lord," answered Nicholas. "Of what did you dream?"

"That I came to a high place, and all turned their faces from me and wished for my destruction. It frightened me! What will God require of us, my friend? Shall it be more than we are able to give? And how do we know we are worthy or able to do what He hath requested?"

They lit the candles on the prayer desk and said the office together. Afterwards Laud wished him a good night. As he went down the hall, Nicholas remembered some further thoughts he had on dreams and turned back, but when he looked through the open door he saw William Laud had knelt once more, his hands covering his face. Quietly Nicholas went down the steps, bid the stableboy a good night in Latin, and was ferried down the river towards the dark bridge.

TWO

The Child

J OHN HEMINGES, THE OLD STAGE MANAGER, STOOD UP SUDDENLY FROM his chair by the hearth one day that fall and, clutching his chest, cried out in a hoarse voice; the accounting books slipped from his lap as he crumpled to the floor. Nicholas reached him while he was yet warm and sat for some minutes, stroking the thick, stiff grey hair. Heminges's cap lay where it had fallen on the polished bricks of the floor.

They laid him upon his bed and washed his ample body, clothing it again in a well-mended shirt down to his round knees, for he would have abhorred the waste to bury a man in good clothes. One by one the family members came to give their goodbyes: his seven living children, the oldest to the youngest, and their wives and husbands and children. Nicholas covered his face and, kneeling, said the prayers for the dead. Heminges had once bade him to watch over the actors. Now silently he answered, Old man, I will.

Many friends crowded the house in Wood Street. The vestry of the church came, and many of the parishioners, for he had been senior warden for nearly thirty years. They buried him near the wall of Mary Aldermanbury next to the body of his wife. Cool was the November day, and the wind rustled the pages of Nicholas's prayer book and played with the hem of his cassock as they took Heminges from his coffin and laid him to earth in his shirt. Nicholas threw the first handful of dirt, and the old man's sons and daughters followed likewise. Rest eternal, they said, and let light perpetual shine upon him.

Andrew covered his face and gave himself over to grief. Boys from the parish rang the six bells until it seemed the very city walls sang back the cadence. Nicholas raised his face and looked across the churchyard to his wife, who stood reflectively with her hands folded over her now much swollen belly. There had been no difficulties at all this time, and he felt for certain there would be a child in midwinter.

It came unexpected on Twelfth Night.

Hundreds of wax candles illuminated the new banqueting hall when Nicholas entered it, holding Cecilia's hand. The early January winds had blown them from Aldermanbury Street down to the wharfs, and her narrow fingers were still icy cold from their ferry ride up the Thames. She had been listless, and when Dobson had unexpectedly sent over the tickets to the Queen's masque, they decided at the last moment to go.

They made their way with some clumsiness past the court favorites to an upper row of the benches which were ranged in tiers on either side of the room, and then sat down to look about. Gone were the flimsy wood and canvas, homely brick, and spangles of earlier halls. This building was faced in Portland stone and had a gallery from which the people could watch their King at dinner. The wall panels depicting the joyous reign of James Stuart were even now being painted on commission in the Netherlands. Dobson, who had had a part in arranging it, had told him about it. Nicholas rested his hands somewhat grimly on the knees of his good brown velvet breeches. He had quarreled slightly with his wife before leaving, for he had some misgivings about coming at all.

"But the babe's not expected for two weeks yet," she had said as she had sought among her few dresses for the best one which would fit her.

Now turning, he gazed down at her face: the pale mouth, dark hair pulled back under a cap embroidered with silver by the brilliant candlelight. "Art concerned?" he had said, and she had shaken her head impatiently.

"I am not one to fret!" she had exclaimed, and he knew from the tilt of her chin not to question her further.

Nicholas knew masques and was not particularly impressed by them, save for the mechanics of the scenery. Of the ones performed by court members, some were given by the King and his gentlemen, and others by the Queen and her ladies. This was the Queen's, and she was of all ladies in the world most valued by her sovereign, for she had presented him some months before with a healthy fat child who was now heir to the throne. Still, the actor Lowin had told him, she had taken the time to memorize much of her role in English to further please her husband and the court.

Several times Nicholas noted with some old professional interest how the actors rushed out to bring a prop, or once more check the placement of the instruments. At last a hush fell over the hall, the small door at the end opened, and the King entered. All leapt to their feet, whipping off their hats, while pages, courtiers, and others in the first rows who were able to do so dropped to one knee. Several bishops and ministers followed. With a gentle gesture the small King seated himself and motioned for the masque to begin.

There came music and the first dancers.

The first row of scenery parted, revealing from the side view a forest through which court ladies costumed as nymphs stood amid perfumed cloth flowers. The piece was called *Chloridia* and narrated how a nymph was transformed into the goddess of flowers by the love of the West Wind. The Queen and her ladies danced together in green cloth embroidered with gold. Many times the young King leapt to his feet and clapped heartily at some pretty song or speech by his Queen, and then the whole room would rise with a violent rustle of silk to clap and cheer.

A cloud had descended with young treble singers from the Chapel Royal serenading the nymphs in a madrigal when Nicholas noticed his wife was not only holding his hand but pressing it very hard now and then. Each time she seemed to clutch tighter, and finally she leaned closer and whispered above the singing, "Nicholas."

"Cony, what dost?"

"My pains have begun."

"Christ's wounds!" he muttered. "How close?"

"To say truth, close."

"Said naught to me?"

"The waters broke before we left, but there was no pain. And I couldn't stay to think on it, and fret. I couldn't do this thing again, dost understand? After . . ." Her voice trembled.

Had it been another time and place, he would have sworn aloud. He looked down the rows of courtiers before them, the well-stuffed sleeves and breeches and the wide heavily petticoated dresses of the women, and grasping her cold hand, whispered, "I must think what to do, Cecily!"

"Don't fret! As soon as the masque's done, my brother will take us home. The pains are hardly much at all! The child can't come until the morn." Some courtiers seated before them turned around at their voices, and she fell silent.

With a frown he began to study the plan of the hall as a general does the battleground. To leave at present they would have to make their way to the doors behind the throne, hurrying past the King, court, and ambassadors. Or they could try to wriggle through the actors, stagehands, propmasters, and scenery to depart as they had come. She hath sadly mistook this time, he thought grimly, feeling her sudden gasps through his own body. The hall was hot, and sweat had gathered down his back. By his pocket watch he found her pains were but three minutes apart.

The last dance had come, and the goddess of flowers left her lover, the West Wind, to step down and give her hands to the King. At once the several hundred people in the lower rows hurried to the center of the room to embrace each other. Nicholas seized his wife's arm and guided her through the crowd to the yard. "Art frighted, sweet?" he murmured, and in a voice so low he could scarcely hear it, she said, "Aye."

He thought he saw Dobson pushing across the yard with one of his mistresses, but so many carriages had clustered about the door with their grooms and servants that he could not reach him. With Cecilia's arm in his, stopping every few minutes for her to breathe deeply, he hurried about to find someone he knew with a carriage to request a ride. Each time he was about to approach it seemed the carriage drove off with a splat of mud from the wheels.

The actors' cart was slowly moving down the cobbles from Whitehall towards the water. "Christ's mercy, men!" he shouted. "Cecily's time's come early!"

They made place for her amid the trunks of cloaks, swords, wigs, and lutes, and rolled to the wharf to find the Revels ferry which was to meet them for the journey downriver. It was nowhere to be seen. Lowin and Taylor sprinted ahead on the banks, waving and shouting at other smaller craft. One ferryman drew near, but shook his head doubtfully at the weight and size of the cart. Nicholas glanced at his wife, and understood that she was frightened indeed. He peered at his watch again, but it was too dark to see it.

Half the cart needed unloading before the ferryman would take it. With two of the sleepy apprentices appointed to wait behind, the other actors pushed over the familiar grey river. Clear and full of stars was the sky, though the moon had set already in the west. They whistled softly in the night. Up the cobbled, crooked streets from the river they mounted towards home.

Inside the doors of the Aldermanbury rectory, Nicholas swept Cecilia in his arms and carried her up the stairs, where they threw open the bed hangings and laid her on the sheets. A few minutes later he received his child into his open hands. Andrew's wife had run in her dressing gown from Wood Street and set water boiling below, and Lowin stoked a great fire in the chamber brazier as they cut and tied the cord and washed the newborn boy. The babe squirmed, feeling his way into the world with tiny hands, touching his father's wet shirt, thrusting his legs out, arching his back. Nicholas gave him to Cecilia to put to breast.

"The child hath not died," she murmured wearily.

"No, my sweet."

" 'Tis of good health."

"Aye, and a fair lad!"

Tears filled her eyes. "Praise God, I did it perfectly," she said.

"Hast indeed," was his exhausted answer.

They called the babe William after the playwright and friend whose picture hung covered by a red cloth in the hall. Harvey assumed it had been after himself, and they did not contradict him in fear to hurt his feelings.

THREE

The Lord of The North

OR A TIME AFTER THE BIRTH, CECILIA HAD FRETTED THE BABE MIGHT not live. The actors' wives lent baby linen, and Harrington offered his own antique christening gown as a loan. A cradle was ordered and sent by the lord and lady Wentworth. Nicholas hoped for another child, yet hardly dared impregnate his wife again, for she was three and forty. They left off the linen sheath, both despising it, and gave it into the hands of God. She did not conceive.

Cecilia endured the parish women's chatter of teething and weaning with some grace, and then shrugged and returned to her barristers, artists, and a French woman poet whom she had known in Paris and who was now living within the city walls. With one foot on the stool and the baby at her half-unlaced bodice, she discussed the ramifications of the Poor Laws, which had been passed early in the century. She translated some of Shagspere's sonnets into French and set them to the lute, and still urged Wentworth to do his best in admitting her as an apprentice, though now not as stubbornly. She did not like to be away from the baby too long, and had begun to resign herself that she could not do everything she wished at one time in her life. The books of law cluttered their bed, and sometimes one fell to the floor with a crash in the middle of the night, waking the irate housekeeper, Joan, who once more threatened to leave them.

Avery loved her. He now always answered the dispensary bell after darkness fell, that the weary new parents could take their rest, and the creak of the attic floor as he walked about it late at night was one of the small comforts which defined their lives. They sometimes wondered why he slept so little, and what could be on his mind.

A few years before, William Harvey had at last published his great work, *De Mortu Cordis,* containing all his discoveries on the circulation of the blood. No sooner did word go round that he claimed blood was not endlessly engendered by the liver than many of his patients left him. A fool he was called, a half-witted dreamer, and even some of his fellow physicians whispered behind his back. "This cometh when faith is naught but superstition," he spat when he had walked over to Love Lane, chafing from a further rejecting letter which he held in his hand. With a furious gesture, he hurled it into the fire.

Harvey was not a man easy to know: he presented to his friends his caustic wit, and to those who had a desire to look closer his burning need to understand the human body. Further few men went. That he had had parents whom he adored and who had died both in pain he had confided to Nicholas, and that he had once been married for a short time. He had woken each night, he said, unable to breathe for her presence in the bed. Whether she had left him or he had shown her the door was unclear, for the story changed each time he told it. He still sent much of his money to support her, but no one knew her name. Nicholas sometimes wondered if Harvey remembered it himself.

Now the angular physician spoke bitterly of his empty dispensary. "This cometh when men feel to question God's universe freely is heresy!" he cried. "Look at Bartlett! He learned well, and performs well, and hath no desire to do better. He placates, while I ..."

They made a hot brew from coffee beans, and sat drinking it by the kitchen fire. Upstairs Cecilia and the child slept, while in the attic room they could hear the soft creak of Avery walking about without his boots.

Harvey said, "I'm going away. His Majesty hath asked me to travel to Florence and Venice to acquire paintings of the great masters."

"Paintings, my friend!" said Nicholas. "What knowst of art?"

"Naught: I cannot tell wheat from chaff. Still, he pays me, and if it is in this way he wishes to employ me, I'll go. What doth it matter if my patients turn from me?" He bit his lip, and for a moment his dark eyes filled with tears. "Don't console me," he said. "Don't make me think kindly of anyone, even thee." He shut himself away and shortly thereafter left for Italy.

Before Harvey's departure, however, he had introduced Nicholas to the brightest of the Dutch painters who had now come to stay in the city. Painting was the rage of London, both what could be imported of the great European masters and the extensive craft of miniatures which had come up under the Tudor kings. Now the large portrait was in demand, and the year before the King had brought to London the handsome young Anthony Van Dyck from the Netherlands, and set him in a studio in Blackfriars near the river.

Languages flew across the easels there and behind the draperies, guttural Dutch, Flemish, and sometimes Parisian French, as the apprentices rushed about and yet another person was ushered to sit for his likeness. Men both wealthy and of moderate income had begun to come to be painted if not by the young master, then by the men who trained by his side. Andrew Heminges was portrayed with a single rose, the soft brown eyes looking dreamily from the canvas. Bartlett had his likeness made, the face brilliant and cold as if to say to the world, You see, once I believed in you, but now the truth's been revealed. . . . He had a copy created for the College of Physicians and kept the original himself. Dobson was drawn in Grecian drapery.

Courtiers came by barge to the Blackfriars landing. Ladies stood for their portraits in low-heeled shoes garlanded with rosettes and stiffened underskirts, dressed as shepherdesses and goddesses; men wore padded trousers, curls falling to flat lace collars, feathered wide-brimmed hats, or now and then armor. Long velvet cloaks swept down and were arranged in folds across the studio floor. All about were profiles of churchmen and ambassadors, and everywhere portraits of the royal family.

Nicholas's own family had been painted as well. The preliminary sketches were quickly done, and the depiction of the faces the debonair Sergeant Painter Van Dyck accomplished in a few sessions of two hours each. Folds of lace, gown, and jacket as well as the Arcadian background of terrace and meadow were completed by a fair, round-faced Dutch boy who assisted him.

The work now hung in their parlor, and Nicholas had looked at it often, astonished at the depth of the beauty of the woman he had married, and not entirely displeased with himself. He had in those days a certain dignity, and the painter caught the humor about his lips as if he were just about to break into a smile. He wore a flat lace collar, black breeches, and doublet padded with bombast; she wore blue silk. His arm was about her shoulder, her small breasts rose above her bodice lacing, and the bottom corner of the canvas bore the legend "Mr. Nicholas Cooke, Wife and Child, 1632." Little William's expression was demanding and bored, for he hated to be still.

The friends were fascinated by the studio and walked over there whenever they could. However, Nicholas had a particular reason to stop by that late winter day, for the lady Arabella Wentworth who was sitting for her portrait had sent a note for him to come.

During his four years as Lord President of the North, the now Viscount Wentworth had become one of the most influential men in England. He sat on innumerable councils, and his patronage was sought by hundreds of men. He also continued to take every opportunity to build his private fortune. There had been a corn shortage in the country some time ago and it was rumored he bought low to sell high, but it was also known he gave great thanksgiving when the threat of famine passed. There had been a plague about York, and long letters passed between him and Nicholas on sanitation. Wentworth opened pest houses for the sick, but did not remove himself or his family from the city. The steadfastness of the King's servant was noted by some with awe, by others with a shrug. He was blamed for the corn, and praised for the quarantine. He took it all with equanimity, attributing all his good fortune to the mercy of God and to the love of his young, beautiful wife. She had traveled to the city with him, and their house was full of people from dawn to dark.

When Nicholas came through the doors of the Blackfriars studio that cold afternoon he saw her standing on a low platform in blue satin posed as a shepherdess, crook in hand and lamb in arms. The creature was struggling and kicking, and one of the apprentices came forward to take it. Seeing Nicholas, she wrinkled her nose and cried, "They'll paint him in later. They're stronger than they look, parson!"

The lamb was now nuzzling behind the large equestrian portrait of the King, which had not quite dried, and the apprentice had gone after it with a broom handle.

"Tom wanted me painted that way," she said, as she patted the edge of the platform for Nicholas to sit beside her. "One day when the lamb's tough mutton and I'm an old woman we'll both look back on our youth." They talked of small matters for some moments: lambs, housewifery, court and theater fashions. Then, lowering her eyes, she studied the satin folds of her skirt in silence. "I wrote thee for my husband's sake," she said at last. "Oh parson, I fret for him when we're here! He was to come with me, but just as we hurried from our door the Lord Treasurer sent word and said, 'An hour, my lord! I need thee only for an hour!' That, of course, meant far more. Scarce do we have a moment when someone cometh from Whitehall or the Bishop of London! Why, we were abed this morning when Mr. Laud himself came. I had barely but time to lace me, and he did not know whither to turn his eyes!"

A shy painter's boy was approaching them with the lamb once more, and she looked at it disdainfully as if she were done with such things, shook her head, and motioned it away. Viscountess Wentworth, the boy murmured, as your ladyship wishes, please your ladyship.

The girl received the deference with equanimity. Raising her lovely face, she murmured, "They come and flatter him, Nicholas! They say what they don't mean, and they come so fast they seem as a blur to me. Whom do we trust? Whom do we not? My lord of Wentworth . . . good my lord . . . my lord viscount! He's so tired at times. He sleeps five hours here if that, and sometimes I wake and find him writing at his desk. He says he's sorry the pen scratched and woke me." She hesitated and then said, bewildered, "Why must he work so hard?"

" 'Tis his way, sweet. There are many reasons: he's not easy to know."

"Wilt you scold him for me?"

"I shall do my best."

"He trusts thee more than anyone; he says you'll keep him close to God if he ever is likely to fall away. Say thou wilt come north to visit us soon!"

Nicholas nodded slowly. There had been this visit no long walks with Wentworth outside the city walls. Strolling as they had done so many times, hands clasped behind their backs, kicking at a broken brick or stone, they always fell after a time into the old intimacy. Then they spoke of things they never thought to say otherwise: of ambition, love, power, fear. In those hours there was perfect trust between them. When they returned, dark was always falling over Cripplegate, and they both felt somewhat cleansed and enriched.

When he left he looked back to see the girl standing quietly. She had drawn a shawl over her pale shoulders as if she were cold.

On an early day in June they went to York. Dawn had just broken when the carriage of the Lord of the North bearing the Wentworth arms and drawn by four horses pulled up at the end of Love Lane. Their trunks had been loaded, and Nicholas carried by his side as too precious to put elsewhere a leather satchel of letters and papers from William Laud. Cecilia brought a box of rose petal tarts.

Henry Bartlett also climbed into the deep red, richly upholstered interior with his medical satchel and a papersworth of tobacco. He had unexpectedly asked to come, making some pretense of business in York to escape his wife, and Nicholas, who could not but feel sorry for his friend's relief when the doors were secured behind them, had agreed, though he knew the stout physician was less and less a favorite with Tom Wentworth.

As the heavy carriage heaved and turned down the street, Bartlett looked enviously about at the deep cushions and swinging brass lanterns. "Christ's wounds!" he whistled boyishly. "What wealth: a man could fain be envious!"

Then he smiled and began to sing in his low, melodious voice the old miller's song of Dee:

> "There was a jolly miller once
> Lived on the river Dee,
> He worked and sang from morn till night
> No lark more blithe than he!
>
> And this the burden of his song
> Forever used to be,
> I care for nobody, no, not I—
> And nobody cares for me!"

Holding Cecilia's hand, Nicholas turned to the window. The sewage dumps and brick kilns outside the city walls were long past, and he could see nothing but the fields and trees of midsummer. Now he turned to his wife, who gazed back, her eyes dark green beneath her reading spectacles. He wondered if she would fret to miss little William, who was now two years old, and had been left to the excellent care of Andrew Heminges and his wife. He did not know how he had ever persuaded her to do so; he did not know how he had persuaded himself.

As the journey was long, they planned to stop in three separate country mansions, the first owned by a good friend of Wentworth's and the next two by lords who were patrons of astronomy or the theater. There they slept in feather beds, and wandered through small libraries full of books on husbandry and farming and sermons, some hand-tinted and others written in some obscure monastery centuries before. All hosts were eager to speak of how things stood within the country. As they opened their windows each morning, they always saw Wentworth's carriage waiting for them, its brass lanterns polished. Nicholas wrote letters in those early hours, which he entrusted to the house servants to leave at the next large inn, whence they would be taken by the twice-weekly York coach towards London.

to William Harvey, physician, Casa d'Or, Florence, from his fellow in wisdom and foolishness, the physician N. Cooke

Sweet friend,

As I love thee when thou art whereabouts thou art in the land of the ancient Caesars, find me a better set of compasses; they do not need to be engraved, and I will give the money when you return. I have money these days, and there is always some left no matter how carelessly I spend. However, I have had no time to work further with lenses, to my grief.

Concerning the survival of children born too young: there is a good woman of our parish had a child in the sixth month but it was too tiny to breathe, though we washed it in wine and kept it warm. It could not suck. I must speak with thee concerning fetal development, particularly that of the lungs. We have also had two boy children joined at the chest born to a woman servant in the house in which we are staying. They lasted only a few hours. I would you had been there! I would have liked to perform an autopsy but have not done so without you, and as priest, I could not ask. My vocations conflict but seldom, but when they do it chafes me. Mine good hosts would not know what to think of the man who consecrated the bread and wine that morning and dissected two household members shortly thereafter. I merely baptized, anointed, and then buried them.

By my soul, I miss thy ugly face.

Devotedly,
Nick

Seven days had passed when the cumbersome carriage rolled through the streets of medieval York and approached the dwelling of the President of the North, which stood at its center. Sentries threw open the gates as they rumbled inside and came to rest in the yard. Before them rose the great house, its many windows glittering and boxes and tubs of flowers wavering gently in the last light. Above hung the new moon, and the sky was flung with stars as far as one could see.

They had barely dismounted when Lady Wentworth hurried towards them with her children, followed by torchbearers. "I greet you alone!" she murmured happily, embracing them in turn. "My Tom's at the council meeting and he swore he'd be done by ten. Come!"

Touching his knuckles lightly to the young woman's slightly swollen belly, Nicholas said mischievously, "He must be home then and anon to make this little mound, lady!"

"Oh, that he is!" she said, laughing. "Bartlett, how dost!"

"Well fair, mistress," said the portly doctor, kissing her hand extravagantly several times. She spoke to him for some moments before turning away and exclaiming, "Supper's kept hot: do come!" Then, clapping her hands for the trunks to follow, she hurried into the house and through the halls.

They dined in the great room lined with old portraits on wood and then were shown upstairs. Nicholas walked about the heavily furnished, perfumed bedchamber as Cecilia undressed for the night. Beneath his feet crinkled old, dry rushes. As he unfolded his clothing from the trunk, he saw a small brown rat rush from underneath the wardrobe, and shortly after heard the playful victory of the cat in the long hall.

As they had just climbed into bed, Arabella hurried in wearing a white sleeping gown and carrying a dish of stewed pears. She sat on the bed's edge with her feet tucked under the gown, for she had forgotten her slippers, and rocked back and forth. Her dark hair, down for the night, fell over her shoulders to the small stomach which she embraced happily with both hands.

"What new plays are given in the city?" she asked eagerly, and when they told her of Shirley's Florentine tragedy *The Traitor* and the rumor of a new tragic comedy by Will Davenant to be entitled *Love and Honour*, she shook her head with longing.

She asked what new songs were popular, and Cecilia whistled the ones she knew. "Wouldst return, lass?" she demanded affectionately.

"Yea . . . and then again, nay! I don't like the court."

"Wherefore, prithee?"

"He wants it so badly he'll have naught else. It's a dark place for him. Sometimes I wish . . . it would all . . . fade away. No, we will not go back. I'll tell him he must not do it." The words were so firm and somehow angry that they were all silent for a moment.

Then they turned to other matters and she chattered happily for a time in French with Cecilia and after took her candle and crept away down the hall. Sometime later they heard the carriage and the whistle of the Lord of the North as he came through his yard, and the household dogs which barked to welcome him.

The straw-filled mattress creaked on its rope supports, and faint particles of dust from the bed hangings rose to the dim, moonlit air. They slept deeply, and when the first light of dawn came and Nicholas opened his eyes, his first sight was flat pictures along the walls of ancient landowners and men in black armor; there were also witty dames in white wimples, their elongated fingertips touching in prayer. Rising softly from the bed, he dressed and left the chamber.

The halls were empty but for a few housemaids and pages, and one dirty-faced fellow with a chamber pot. After searching the empty library and some other rooms, Nicholas turned towards the baking kitchen, where he found Tom Wentworth, his shirt unlaced and unshaven, writing at the trestle table next to a large bowl of onions.

With a shout, the Lord President of the North leapt up to embrace him, and immediately began to explain his absence. There had been difficulties in the council meeting, and he had not come home until almost midnight. "I've read the papers from my lord the Bishop of London which you brought until the sun rose," he said gaily. "Have I slept?

Not at all . . . but it doesn't matter. Hast brought Harry Bartlett. I shall try to greet him with charity!"

Birds sang from the fruit trees of the kitchen gardens, and the sound of water buckets clanking and girls laughing came from outside the wall. Sunlight glittered through the small opaque windowpanes and danced upon the tile floor.

Wentworth cried, "To breakfast! They'll be hunting and a dance, and the whole old city to see. Where's Cecily? Half my brothers and sisters dine with us. Come, I'm famished!" They hurried to the large dining hall, where friends, relatives, and children were already gathered.

The day was spent visiting the sites of the ancient city, accompanied by Arabella and her friends, for the Lord of the North was again called away. The promised hunt came the next morn, with the horns sounding in the courtyard, and the scolding of the grooms, and the dogs barking exuberantly, impatient to be gone. As Nicholas hurried down the steps with the cool air of the north blowing through the opened windows, he recalled the old song of Harry Tudor which he had learned as a boy in the city.

> The hunt is up, the hunt is up
> And it is well-nigh day
> And Harry our King has gone a-hunting
> To bring his deer to bay!

Small white clouds blew across the sky, and from the gardens rose the smell of lemon balm and mint. He leapt to horse and Cecilia to hers. The children were rushing about to hail them off as they trotted through the gates of the house, then the winding city streets of merchants' houses and craftsmen's stalls, and finally out from the walls of York to the countryside.

Wentworth pointed out his lands to them. His dark eyes were clear, and the fine chest and shoulders took in the clean air easily. He held the reins lightly in his beautiful hands, and after a time Cecilia drew her horse beside his and they began to talk.

He said, "Didst live in these parts one time?"

"Aye, as a child. When I was a girl, I loved nothing so much as hedgehogs! I had one which used to come into the garden, and I made it a little house."

"A hedgehog, madam?" said the Yorkshireman with a smile, reining in his horse to stay close to her.

"Oh yes, indeed! I called him Harry Bolingbroke. I never knew where he went one day, but I was inconsolable. They're rough creatures outside and tender within, as with the best men. Harry had such soulful eyes. My lord, you laugh!"

"Oh Cecily!" he said, wiping the tears from his eyes, and then cried over his shoulder, "Nick, can she speak in truth? Hedgehogs, madam? Sayst, if 'twere hedgehogs today, wouldst hunt them?"

"Nay, I'd protect them on my life."

"Is any man in present company like unto these creatures?"

"Askst in truth, my lord?"

"Aye, lady, I do!"

"Ah, but I shall not tell thee!" She tugged on the reins and dug her heels into the horse, and with a laugh he watched her move ahead near Arabella's mare and waited until Nicholas came beside him.

Still smiling, he said, "What is discussed these days in the meetings?"

"Such as they are, Tom, with Harvey gone and Bartlett here and there. We hear dark things of Galileo's trial from Italy; they want him to recant his belief that the world moves about the sun, and if he doesn't they may torture him." Nicholas raised his face to the blue sky, and down across the expanse of field, as if to take it all to him.

"And thee, Tom?" he added. "What wrote my lord bishop?"

"We met several times at Fulham House when I was last there. We're devising a plan of government which will make secure the honor of our sovereign and the good of all his people. We've called it 'Thorough.' There must be one law, one church, and one united land. About the world, governments fall, people suffer, much is loss, but here . . . I can't wait to show it to you both."

The fox was sighted, and the horses sprinted ahead, and their voices were lost in the wind and dust. Before them the land was green, hilly, and soft.

All day carts came with things needed for the reception, while the Lord of the North sat closeted in his library, dictating to his secretary. Finally darkness fell, the full moon lighting the roads and carriages rolling easily into the courtyard bringing people from miles about for the dance. When Nicholas descended he saw the hall was ablaze with torches and already full of friends. Many of the people whom he had met at the christening years before were here, along with several of Tom's siblings, some of whom were employed by him in one capacity or another, and the children, who came down with their nurse dressed in lace and velvets and were allowed for a time to run about. The boy followed him about affectionately.

A band of horns and viols and recorders struck up a dance, and at once the Lord of the North gave his hands to his lady, bowed, and took her to the floor. He was as merry and free then as if he had rested the whole day and his leg had never troubled him. Up and down the rows in the ballroom he danced, stamping his feet, leaping and lifting Arabella time and again into the air. It was not the newer, more stately dances of the court but an older one of the generation or two before: "The Carman's Whistle" and "All in a Garden Green." People clapped and cheered on the side as the couples turned, bowed, and turned again. The horns played "Wolsey's Wold" and dances of John Dowland.

Nicholas danced a time with Arabella, whom he found so merry and small, and Wentworth took Cecilia about the floor, every now and then whispering in her ear with a burst of laughter, "Hedgehogs, madam! On my faith . . ."

Bartlett spent much of the night dancing with the plain daughter of a landowner, fetching her cool fruit and other sweets when she was weary, standing by her side with one foot on a stool, exuberantly extemporating on the life of the London man. Meeting Nicholas by the cider table, he confided, "There's one could make me happy! Could one begin again?" When the family realized he was not a bachelor, they withdrew their daughter as one folds ribbons in a box, and after a time he went despondently to bed.

"Poor Bartlett!" Cecilia said.

Nicholas was captured by a local apothecary, who engaged him in a discussion of ghosts. There were spirits of one of the old Roman legions in the minster undercroft, the apothecary said; he had seen them walking one night in formation, breastplates glimmering in the faint light. By this time Arabella had bid all a good night, for she was tired and Wentworth had found his own corner with two boyhood friends. People were leaving for their homes, and the musicians had begun to pack their instruments but for the recorder player, whose fluted tunes continued for the amusement of the plain little girl whom Bartlett had found so lovely.

Nicholas and Cecilia wished their host a good night as well, and mounted the steps; behind the bedcurtains they made love, while below they could hear the servants still clearing away, and the last dance sounded by the recorder player.

He did not know at first where he was, or what awakened him: he lay with his arm thrown across Cecilia's back behind the heavy, dusty bed hangings with the sunlight pouring through the room. Then he became aware of a strange cry which had carried through the opened windows, and yet lingered in the air.

She was awake as well.

He sat up, his body weary from the dancing and the slight ague which had made him seek his pocket handkerchief before sleeping. They looked at one another, and then Tom's voice rose from the garden in one word: "Nicholas!"

The physician leapt up, covering himself with his nightshirt, which had fall to the floor. He threw open the window as far as it would go and looked down into the garden, but he could see nothing for the heavy trees. Then when he looked again, he noticed something pink on the path like a cloak or banner. He blinked again and made out a woman's hand outstretched from it. Again came the cry, in a tone he had never heard before: "Nicholas! In God's name, parson!"

Leaning out, he shouted down past the beds of flowers and herbs, "Tom, what is it?"

"In Christ's name, come!"

He paused only to pull on his breeches, and then, barefoot, with shirt still unlaced over his chest, he threw open the chamber door and ran down the steps to the garden. Several servants were hurrying before him so that when he arrived on the path he had to push through. Tom was kneeling on the stone path, and by him, with her head to the side, lay the lady Arabella in her loose pink morning dress. Her eyes were closed, and through her parted lips came a soft intake of air. She was perfectly limp, and down the side of her mouth trickled a stream of vomit.

Nicholas felt a spasm of fear in his stomach.

Tom looked up. "She doesn't know me," he cried. "She was cutting flowers and I came towards her and then . . . I don't know what then . . . she gave such a cry as never I want to hear again, never . . ." His voice shook. "Never such . . . and grasped at her head with both hands and her stomach heaved . . . and fell. And a moment before she had been laughing. I tried my smelling salts, but she makes no response at all."

Nicholas dropped to his knees and patted the girl's cheek. He put his head against her breasts: the heart beat faintly but rapidly. His skilled hands felt down her back and about her head for bruises. Her neck was curiously stiff. All he had ever known rushed through his head in search of reason: breath good, pulse regular, and fallen into a deep faint. Taking her against him, he cleaned out her limp mouth with his handkerchief, then, asking for Tom's help, turned her to her face head down over his knees so that if vomit remained in her throat it would not choke her. He patted her back several hard times.

Tom cried out. "Marry, I don't hurt her, lad!" Nicholas said. He stretched on the grass beside the girl to push back her eyelids; the violet eyes, slightly rolled up, stared unseeingly back at him.

Wentworth had thrown himself down as well. "Nick, what is it?" Nicholas did not reply. He gazed about him at the garden full of every flower and tree, of holly and vines, of broom and violets and rose bushes, and worn wood benches beneath the trees, and here and there a birdbath, and the sun shining down through the trees, and then back to the insensate girl who lay before him. In these moments his training had taught him great calm. Gently he moved his fingers to the cluster of blood vessels at the base of the skull. Again, he felt the stiffness of the delicate neck, and he was removing the locket when he understood.

Something had occurred within the brain. He stared ahead of him, recalling his first study of Galen, blinking once. Christ have mercy, he thought to himself. Christ look down upon us: it cannot be what it seemeth! Bartlett knows, canny diagnostician that he is, and he stands with dry mouth, fumbling with his hands! Still, this must be a foul dream. This lass upon my knees cannot be the girl I danced with so merrily up and down the hall last night. Lord look down upon us in thy caring!

"Tom, take her up," he said.

With great gentleness Wentworth lifted his wife in his arms and carried her into the dark house and up the steps, pink gown catching at his knees. "Naught!" he whispered to her dark hair as he ran. "Naught, mouse . . . 'twill be well soon!" Laying her down on the quilting, he began to unlace her bodice.

Again Nicholas felt her torso and neck; his fingers searched the shape of the skull under the heavy, now tangled hair.

"Nick, surely 'tis but a faint from the fall."

"I fear something more. Harry, come here. The heart beats, but she's breathing unevenly. There's no injury anywhere on the body. She hath no consciousness." On her lips, which they had wiped, some small particles of foam appeared. Nicholas raised his eyes to Bartlett, whose face had grown red with his desire to weep. Then, closing his eyes for a moment, he turned to Wentworth. "I believe it to be an apoplexy to the brain, which is why she knows nothing," he said. "It hath cut off perception mayhap, or at least the ability to respond. She may be able to hear us, she may not."

"This manner of thing doth not happen with girls so young! It cannot be! *Art wrong, Nicholas!*" Dropping to the bedside, Wentworth took his wife's face in his hands and whispered persuasively, "Come, 'tis enough, awake, lady! Speak, thou wilt . . ."

Afternoon came and went; shadows moved through the small window-panes and across the floor to the quilting which hung askew to the floorboards from the great bed. The lady Wentworth remained with her head to one side, indifferent to the world: her eyes when they passed a candle before them saw nothing. The breathing was now erratic, and again the soft foam came between her lips.

Four times Nicholas had opened her veins, the blood gently splashing to the bowl, until he was afraid to bleed her more. If I only understood, he said to himself, gazing down at Tom's thick dark hair as he bent over whispering the edges of promises into his wife's ear. Once years ago, before he had had medical training, Nicholas's firstborn son had died in his arms of the plague. Since then he had stood in strange relationship to death, preaching the preferability of heaven while attempting to keep those to whom he ministered in this world, however shabby, however desperate their state in it might be. Some who died under his care were old and worn and might joy to find the many mansions promised to them; to the young, however, he could not but think that death was a thief.

And he knew as he stood watching his friend that the stricken girl was going to die. The bones of her face had grown sharper, the delicate nose a shadow, the lips pulling slowly up from the gums. A vast disgust for himself and the bitterness of it overwhelmed him. In his despair he ached for one thing, and that was to be alone with his prayer book, to put this situation before God in the silence of his chamber, and to receive consolation and counsel. Cecily knew it, for he saw her face. He stood.

Tom leapt up: he looked like a youth condemned to hang, whom Nicholas had known, who had wept all the way in the cart, reaching out to catch at the leaves of trees to hold the earth to himself as long as possible. At the end the boy had fallen to his knees, and seizing the edges of Nicholas's coat, had bitten it to fill his mouth with the taste.

Wentworth whispered, "Naught? Canst do naught? I have never believed in a man as I have in thee. Wert away when Margaret was taken, but *art here now and dost nothing.*" Falling on his knees, he covered his face with his hand. "Lord Jesus!" he cried. "Do not desert us here who have loved Thee! An You spare her, mayst take from me all I have. I will go in my shirt to live it matters not where, if she be at my side!"

Towards four in the morning, Arabella Wentworth breathed once more, and then ceased. Her soft hand with its many rings, which had lain at the bed's edge, dropped and swung back and forth. The sobbing of the children from the chamber's edge broke the silence.

The physician said with an exhausted voice, "Tom, she hath gone now to her Savior. Lord have mercy on her soul and give us now the living the strength to endure this loss."

Wentworth looked up at his words. Then, rising from his knees, he climbed into the bed, and taking the dead girl to him, buried his face against her hair. For more than an hour as the maids closed the draperies still tighter against the coming day, he rocked his wife in his arms.

Nicholas had gone to his chamber for his book, stole, and holy oil; with the girl still in her husband's arms, he leaned across the bed and anointed her, saying the prayers for the dead.

> "*Depart, O Christian soul, out of this world,*
> "*In the Name of God the Father Almighty who created thee.*
> "*In the Name of Jesus Christ, who redeemed thee.*
> "*In the Name of the Holy Ghost who sanctifieth thee....*
> "*Into thy hands, O merciful Saviour, we commend the soul of thy servant Arabella, now departed from the body....Receive her into the arms of thy mercy....*"

The women who were to prepare the girl for her burial now came forward. Tom gazed at them, slowly releasing the body of his wife, and began to back away towards the door. When Nicholas raised his face and closed his prayer book, his friend was gone.

Christopher Wandesford was at his side. "In Christ's name, parson!" he whispered. "My lord ran down the stairs so quickly I couldn't stop him, and he's now gone to the library and locked the door. His pistols are there, sir, and I don't trust him. I've never seen him like this. He'll answer to you if he answers to anyone. He loved her as he loved his life."

Several men and women joined them as they ran down steps and the dark corridors towards the library. Nicholas tried the knob, and then rattled the massive door. "Tom!" he shouted several times, but no answer came.

Someone cried, "Go about the street, through the windows." They would have gone that way, but the housekeeper hurried up the steps with her keys. The lock creaked, and the door opened to darkness.

Nicholas moved forward in the room. He could see nothing but again felt the fear, as thick as fog, the same as he had felt from the boy to be hanged who had held on to his coat until he ripped away the buttons. He lowered his voice as he had that terrible day, and said, "Tom."

There was no answer.

Nicholas listened sharply, making out the rustle of clothes. His eyes gradually made out a form in the great chair by the desk, and he said in an unsteady voice, "Dear heart, come. God's with thee. Forgive me that I failed you. I am not Christ but His humble servant. I can't raise the dead, but could it be done, God knoweth I would do it now. God knoweth for thee."

A flicker of candlelight shone from the door. He had reached his friend, and took him in his arms. The widower's sobs began: they rose violently through the beautiful speaking voice. He crumpled like a child, retching and gasping. " 'Tis well, 'tis well . . . she's with God," Nicholas said, his own voice breaking.

Wentworth pushed him away and covered his eyes with his arm. He staggered a few feet across the room and then sank to the floor. Cecilia ran across the carpet and gathered him against her. "Oh sweet!" she whispered. "Oh sweet!"

Quietly the servants walked about the halls. Already black banners were being hung from the window to announce to the city that the house of the Lord of the North was one of grief. Outside in the street, straw had been laid to muffle the sound of carriage wheels, and one little maid quietly covered the mirrors that the dead soul might not appear in them. The bells tolled from York Minster.

For two days Wentworth would not come from the room, nor touch food. After the funeral he returned to the library again and fell asleep for the first time in days on the floor. They slipped pillows under his head. So went the time: it seemed neither day nor night. Hours passed in minutes, or stretched into weeks. The heavy curtains and draperies kept out the light. Maids walked softly, wiping their eyes with their aprons.

Nicholas had not rested for more than a few hours at a time: he would wake thinking the dead girl was calling him, leap up to go to her to undo what had been done, and remember it was too late. Cecilia wept a great deal.

In that time, no one remembered Bartlett. He had at first been one of the many shadows who passed the hall, but when Nicholas woke on the fifth day the alderman came clearly to mind, and splashing his face with water, he went to look for him.

Bartlett was seated in the dining room sitting before a decanter of sack, which he was pouring resolutely into a glass. Nicholas realized that he was drunk, and had probably been drunk much of the time since the funeral. He squeezed Bartlett's shoulder and sat down beside him, holding out his own goblet for sack to wipe away the bad taste in his mouth.

Hoarsely Henry Bartlett muttered, "She was all loveliness."

"Aye, she was."

"I know not how he can live with himself."

"Who?"

"Viscount Wentworth."

"What sayst thou, friend?"

"There's rumors among her family. They say he struck her, which is why she fell, and that's why he weeps. They say he beat her often when angry. Else why should she suffer apoplexy and why should he ask for forgiveness?"

Nicholas stood up so fast that the decanter quivered. "What madness is this?" he cried. "What vile rumors? Struck her, thou pig's ass? He adored her! What of his tears?"

Bartlett had also stood. "I don't believe them . . . and I don't believe he loves aught in his heart but his ambition. . . . Nicholas, by Christ, look not at me like that. I have never been afraid of thee before, and this moment, by Our Lord, I . . ." Leaning against the marble tabletop with its generous vases of flowers, he began to weep, and wiped his nose with the back of his hand.

"Yes, madmen, both of you," he sobbed, his heavy chest heaving. "And I am a whoreson, and jealous mayhap . . . yes, I am a whoreson . . . but honest, Nicholas, more than he! No Judas . . . and I am loved, whilst he . . ."

At that moment a little boy ran in. "My lord Wentworth calls you, master parson," he whispered. "Wilt come?"

Tom Wentworth was sitting at the library desk, writing. The candle-light caught the few silver strands in the thick dark hair, and the sensual mouth was set so hard under the dark mustache as if to compress in all feeling forever. For a moment they looked at each other as if they had been apart for so long they could not remember speaking of anything, or laughing, or sharing any past or future.

Tom rubbed his palm over his forehead. "The carriage goeth towards London in three hours with urgent letters, and will take thee speedily home! William Laud's not well, and needeth thee."

"That and much more would I do," said Nicholas, his voice stumbling for feeling. "But Tom, how wilt do alone?"

"I shall go on with my work."

"Wilt come soon to London?"

"Aye, soon enough." Wentworth stood, leaning on the desk with both hands. "Forgive me if I do not embrace you, my friend," he said wearily. "I cannot bear another's touch. Write when you have the moments and take my love, which is ever thine."

Even as the carriage turned away, the three travelers saw the lord Wentworth standing motionless in the door, his hand raised in parting. Five days later they came through the city gates.

Cecilia was more quiet than she had been for a long time, and sometimes Nicholas found her at the window with her small son in her arms and tears in her eyes.

FOUR

London

WORD CAME THAT GALILEO HAD WITHDRAWN HIS ASSERTION THAT the earth revolved about the sun and was now sent to house arrest with his daughter the nun to care for him, and instructions to publish no more. Queen Henrietta Maria bore yet another child: bells rang out in the city. Nicholas remained somewhat indifferent to it all.

His consolation in those months was that William Harvey had arrived back in the city, thoroughly disgusted with foreign lands, hungry for beef pie. Of his old school in Padua alone he spoke warmly. "They welcomed my book!" he said, his eyes cast down to keep his pride to himself. He had been through such stages of anger and defiance at the challenge to his theory that he almost could not bear to think of it. The two men began to spend much time together again.

They were dissecting a pregnant doe one evening by the light of a single lantern in the back room of his dark house in Blackfriars. Harvey's apron was covered with dark blood, as were his fingernails. He had the absorbed, peaceful look which came to him at these times. Nicholas bent close beside him, their heads almost touching. Sometimes they murmured over the work, but mostly were silent.

They had just come from the College of Physicians, where they had heard Bartlett speak on disease. Now as they bent over the animal, Harvey muttered through his pipe, "What sayst to the lecture?"

"Henry wishes to please the greatest number of men."

"Exactly. How old dost make this fetus, Cooke?"

"Two to three weeks greater than the last."

Harvey adjusted the wick of the lantern, so that the doe's tawny skin glistened under the light. "His Majesty's kind in giving me these deer, God bless his royal head. Aye, Bartlett will be president of the College one day."

Nicholas nodded. He had said nothing of Bartlett's outburst in York, which he put down to the shock of his grief. Certainly that physician had tried to show his repentance in every way for his angry words.

His thoughts returned to the afternoon in the College and how solemnly the rolling Latin phrases of the lecture had been received as each physician thought his own thoughts of wife, or sweetheart, or increase in his estate. Theirs was not unlike the other halls of London, each rich with the dignity men could give each other. There were twelve great livery companies from the medieval days, and seventy or so smaller ones. These in turn left centuries of names inscribed on church stones, portraits in guildhalls, books, confessions, titles. Honor was all. It filtered from sovereign to merchant and moved back again.

He thought of his own brief speech on disease, with the men he knew so well about him; he thought of the dead girl in the arms of her sobbing husband in the house in York. He dreamed of her, and carrying her somewhere. Again and again it returned to him . . . why? But we are not all meant to know why; some secrets God keeps.

He had risen from the lecture and gone outside for a time to the physicians' herb garden, yet still he thought of Arabella and her arms about his neck as he had tried to lift her and how they had fallen limply away. Bones and dust.

Harvey straightened, rubbing his lower back with his hand. "Thinkst too much, Cooke!" he said. "Come, we shall have coffee and cheese by the fire. Death cometh, dear heart."

A faint burnt smell hung on the October wind the next day. In a sudden conflagration, several of the houses on London Bridge had burned the past month, and charred bits of timber floated yet down between the foundations. Now just past noon, the water glistened and glittered everywhere, in puddles on the docks, nudging the moss-encrusted wooden steps which descended deep towards the river bottom. The sky was alive with the cry and dipping of gulls.

As Nicholas stood by the river, he saw a barge moving downstream towards the bridge bearing the banners of William Laud, Bishop of London. Seated at the prow was his scholar and chaplain, Luke Malverne. The young cleric cupped his hand to the mouth and shouted, "Nicholas, hast heard?! . . . William Laud's been appointed . . . by his Majesty's favor . . . Archbishop . . . of Canterbury. . . ." And with that the chaplain's voice was lost under the pounding of the water by the bridge and the cries of boatmen and gulls. Nicholas turned the words over in his mind until he understood them. The small priest who so loved education, whom the old King did not want about the court, who worked unceasingly for the restoration of old customs, was now the highest churchman in the land.

The red brick ecclesiastical palace of Lambeth lay low on the southern bank of the Thames, which now and then flooded its stables and cellars. Years before it had been owned by monks who had farmed the marshy lands to the south in neat plots, until one archbishop, desiring to live closer to the court, had turned it into his London residence. There was manor house and chapel, and the usual stables, coal and wine cellars, butteries, drying house, ale shed, and gardens of a large self-sustaining domicile.

To here one week later, Nicholas and some friends from the church ferried for the ancient ceremony of elevation. The day before, one of the barges bearing Laud's books, furnishings, and plate, which had been poorly loaded, had sunk into the Thames. Even now he could hear the happy shouts of half-naked boys as they dived for the silver.

Lords and barristers, bishops and clergy were also mounting up from the wharf. Inside the gatehouse a London band played fife and drum, and several alderman attended the Lord Mayor. The new Archbishop's household servants were there as well, pressing themselves with much awe against the wall of the manor house near the fig trees. Then the chapel doors were thrown open and they moved inside to find places in pews, on stools, and against the baptismal font.

William Laud entered with four bishops. The high-arched grey eyebrows were raised under his close-fitting cap, and the face flushed with emotion as he gazed about him. With a shuffle of red gowns over long white linen rochets, the five men moved before the altar, to the right side of which had been singularly placed a blue velvet upholstered chair.

Then, as they waited, they heard voices from across the courtyard and his Majesty Charles Stuart hurried in with several court members, wearing white embroidered satin and feathered hat. Approaching William Laud, he kissed him on both cheeks. "My lord's grace of Canterbury, you are welcome," he said. Then, motioning the crowd to be seated, he took his place on the blue velvet chair and the ceremony commenced.

The service of communion began with Collect, Epistle, and Gospel, and after the Creed the four bishops presented William Laud. They questioned him in the old manner as to his true calling to the Ministration, according to the order of the church and the will of the Lord Jesus Christ; he put on his robes and knelt while the *Veni, Creator Spiritus* was sung over him. They prayed,

"Grant, we beseech thee, to this thy servant, such grace, that he may evermore be ready to spread abroad thy Gospel, the glad tidings of reconciliation with thee; and use the authority given to him, not to destruction,

but to salvation; not to hurt, but to help; so that ... in due season ... he may at last be removed into everlasting joy. ... "

The bishops then laid their hands upon the bowed head of William Laud and prayed that he receive the Holy Ghost for his work in the church. He, in turn, pledged loyalty to the country and at the end dropped to his knees before the King and placed his own delicate fingers within those of his young sovereign. The bells rang out, the organ played, and the choristers sang lustily as William Laud, or, as he would hereinafter sign himself, William Canterbury, was made Archbishop.

All fell to their knees for his blessing as he left the chapel to walk towards the stables. Following him was the King, who once more turned to whisper in his new Archbishop's ear. He then departed to his oared river launch.

Later in the hall, William Laud moved graciously and swiftly between his guests, greeting all by name under the hammerbeam roof. "Yes, yes!" he said happily. "My work can go forward now! I'll return the chapel of this palace to the splendor it once had, with tinted glass, silver candlesticks, and vestments for the priests, as soon as I can. We shall use the altar again for communion instead of a table!" When he came to Nicholas his face saddened and he murmured, "Poor Tom. . . . Hast seen the motherless babes? Ah, the lovely lass!"

From the gates people cheerfully bid their goodbyes as they stepped into ferries, the canons' broad-brimmed hats or cloaked hoods up against the cool weather. As the barges pushed off to the river, they turned to raise their hands in farewell to the small prelate in his close-fitting dark wool cap, who had come to the wharf steps to see them go.

Voices muttered, laughing. Slowly they lurched over the water, the boatmen pulling directly across the current, while above high on the bridge someone hung a lantern on a grocer's shop which had once been a chapel. Nicholas was lost in his own thoughts when a man behind him muttered, "So he'll restore vestments and candles to the church services!

And what will he do with the thousands of Englishmen who cannot bear such things, but want to worship plainly?"

Nicholas put up his cloak. He was not in the mood for controversy. One by one, the oars dipped through the silvery water. The moon had risen and the ancient red brick of the Archbishop's palace glistened in the distance so that every chimney and gate was perfectly clear.

He missed Wentworth greatly. Each time the courier came from the north he hoped for words of him, but letters came seldom and then spoke only of his work. The few letters he sent were angry at the stupidity of his fellow Yorkshiremen and the idiocy of the court. They left Nicholas wondering if he and Tom would ever have the times together which once they had. He wondered if Tom, in wishing to put away the pain of his grief, had found it prudent to put aside his closest friend, who had witnessed it. Nicholas could yet feel Wentworth's tears on his hands.

By the winter Nicholas received a brief word from Wandesford that his lordship was about the London court. Then a week later a note came in Tom's own hand saying, "I am building a new house and have employed thy ideas of sanitation: come and see it."

Since anyone could remember, London had been a city of crooked, half-timbered structures. It was a place of alehouses and dungheaps, thieves' dens and smoky brewhouses which filled the streets with smog; it was a heap of prisons squeezed in gatehouses, shanty stalls along Cheapside, and the slaughtering grounds of Smithfield. Cities had been built on cities: remains of corroded piers, sealed privy cesspits, or bits of Roman wall. Streets of foul tenements had grown up outside Westminster and around the area of the Tower. Thatched roofs dried dangerously, and a perpetual stench rose from the Fleet River as it crept through the ditches outside the wall. Houses were built out over the streets until not enough sunlight came down between them to dry a pair of wool hose on a washline. Since the Romans had first forded the river with a bridge of boats roughly lashed together, London had been the center of everything. No man could tire of it.

It was still the center, as any sensible citizen knew, yet it was changing. The architect Inigo Jones had been trained in the classical Italian style and had brought its sense of proportion to the court. There were even plans for tearing down all of Whitehall and building it anew, though how it would be paid for no one knew: Charles Stuart was yet scrambling for enough gold to keep his households together. Whitehall must remain for this time a scrappy thing of old timbers and stones with the new banqueting hall its sole beauty. His Majesty made up for the shabbiness by filling the rooms with great art, grace, and dignity.

Still, change went forward. Mansions of wealthy citizens sprang up with porticos and wainscoting along the Strand. There were marble halls, sweeping grand stairs, terraces overlooking the water with its swans and sewage. The old dwellings of Covent Garden, including that of the late beloved William Sydenham, had been pulled down and the whole of the area rebuilt as an elegant piazza with surrounding terraced houses and a Tuscan church. There Tom Wentworth was building another dwelling to suit his new estate.

He was balancing gracefully between tubs of cement by a stack of marble tiling as Nicholas and Cecilia came across the piazza, while at his feet his children picked wild grass and bits of wood, whispering together at the treasures. Wentworth gave a shout and came running towards them with his arms open. "Come and see!" he cried. "God's blessings, how do you both? How is the little one? Did he receive the toys I sent him? Naught's done but the foundation, but oh, what will be!"

Foremen, journeymen, and boys who stood shyly with their tools at their sides pulled off their caps as they passed. The house would be exquisite when done, the front Grecian with a portico in the new style and the greater body of brick. Tom's children, after greeting them, continued to climb among the foundation beams, the little girls holding up their skirts and looking back at their jubilant father.

"Here will be the entrance hall!" Wentworth shouted. "And here's the receiving room where we'll entertain. 'Good day, my lord bishop!' Ah, here's the Earl of so-and-so . . . what, art come to Tom Wentworth's house? He's no earl, but mayhap one day . . . mayhap one day his most sacred Majesty with naught else to amuse him will walk this way, God save him!"

He threw back his head and laughed. "Here's drainage pipes for sewage, Nick! High up where the rooms are full of light will be the children's chambers, for I want the sun to come through their windows and wake them each morning so they may look out and cry, London . . . and from the window looking across the square, they may see me come home! Ah, Papa's come . . . hath he brought cakes? Eh, my love . . ." He lifted the two small girls one at a time.

Then he said, breathlessly coming to rest, "Now let's go over to Paul's and see what Laud hath done to the cesspool of a cathedral while I've been away!"

The small party mounted into Wentworth's large carriage to make the journey down the Strand and into the city, Wentworth's children holding on to his fingers. Harvey and the lord Harrington had joined them: the eminent physician with a bag of coffee beans in his hand and Harrington expansively sprawled on the red cushions.

They could hardly see the entrance of the Cathedral for the scaffolding. At one end workmen were carting away broken furniture, rags, and a stinking mass of garbage from the crypt, where the citizens of London had dumped it those many years. All above them the sun glittered on the stones. They walked about the churchyard, which was filled with bookstalls and buyers, and under the scaffolding, where the marble columns of the portico would rise.

"Let's go inside," Tom said.

Entering from the back, they found themselves in a series of small rooms. The sacristy was a crowded chamber of racks and hooks filled with cassocks and surplices of the vergers and the boys, boxes of burnt candle ends, candle snuffers, and several long crooked shelves of books with their odd old leather scent. Wentworth took Nicholas's arm and pulled him towards a low door which opened to the Cathedral.

The place was a forest of still more scaffolding for the cleaning and restoration. They went down the great nave of thirteen enormous bays. From high above came the voices of the workmen as they washed the bosses above the chapels, and the water, filthy with ages of dirt, lay in puddles all about the floor. Between these walked a few whores with disheveled bodice lacing and much rouge; a crippled beggar approached them, and three or four boy choristers raced by. "God bless Laud!" Wentworth said. He turned and gazed with a moment's reverence towards the altar screen and the great altar behind it. "He hath said he will do it, and that he will!"

The children skipped and raced between the bays. Light filtered down from the clerestory windows, and the boy suffered a splinter in his palm from the wood. Wentworth brought the small hand to his lips to moisten it, and after a time Nicholas, squinting in the dusky air, extracted it with his deft fingers and the point of his pocket knife. "Must wash it well, Tom," the physician said. He had not been this close to his friend since they had parted in so much grief months before. There had come a division between them, this he knew, though he did not understand why. It was as palpable as the warmth of the child's hand as he took away the splinter. He raised his head and gazed at him.

Wentworth looked away.

Between the scaffolding and the boy, who had wandered behind a tomb for a time, they became separated. Nicholas emerged at last into the sunlit, crowded yard with the child. Of their party only Harrington stood by the booksellers' stalls, clenching the hands of Wentworth's now subdued daughters. " 'Tis a madness of Laud's to think he can clean this up!" he barked. "For if he scrubs the nave and extracts the dust from the nostrils of the effigies of dead kings, he'll not keep out the purse snatchers or the whores. Where the devil's everyone gone, Cooke? Wentworth delivered these babes to me and hurried away. Have I been reduced from captain to nursemaid in my later years?"

Blinking in the sun, they glanced about at the bookstalls, the ballad sellers, the foreign travelers come to gape at the Cathedral, the pretty women chattering in corners. Presently they saw the small figure of

Harvey rounding the edifice in his brisk, impatient way, the lank dark hair swinging against his collar. "Nick," he said, "Cecily bade me say she hath gone with a friend and will be home late. Here cometh Tom. Now that he hath the King's ear he says naught of consequence into any other."

The Lord President of the North was coming towards them, his rapier at his side. All three children at once rushed across the yard, and he dropped to his haunches to embrace them. Taking the two smallest in his arms, he called his farewells to his friends and went off listening intently to the chatter of his son. Harrington had gone with them and only Nicholas and William Harvey remained.

For a moment they were silent, gazing absently at the pigeons and sparrows which pecked about their boots. Then Harvey said with a yawn, "I'm perishing for ale and food. Wilt join me?"

"Nay, I'm to my work."

"Come for some moments! I've something to tell thee, Nicholas."

With a shrug, Nicholas followed him some streets away to a tavern in Lothbury, where they found places in an unenclosed booth. The room was noisy with the tales of someone who had just returned from the Americas, and they listened to the edges of the words for a few minutes until Harvey turned away. "East or west, home is best," he muttered. "Drink, my friend: they shall mark it on the board to me. I owe thee much, the least being thy goodwill for these many years. Not many others bear with my humors."

He turned his talk to small court matters and patients whom he saw and could not bear, and then after a time pushed away the eel pie he had been eating, and scratching the edge of the table methodically with the edge of his knife, he muttered, "I can't conceal the matter that's heavy on my heart, Nick, and which too many men have seen but thee. Wentworth liketh thy wife too greatly."

Nicholas broke into an astonished laugh. "Pricklouse, what madness!"

Harvey scowled at the wood residue on the blade. "Have I ever said aught untrue to thee? I do not joke on such matters. God knoweth I admire Wentworth, for I know the difficulties of working for something not easy to get—the disappointments, the weariness, the turning away of those you thought close! I believe there's no more brilliant man on the Privy Council, nor one whose great gifts are used so poorly. And still I love thee more, and I say, look to Cecily."

Nicholas replied nothing.

Harvey continued in a murmur, "I came upon them just before in one of the sacristy rooms behind the altar, and she was weeping and he pleading with her. When he saw me pass he gave me a look of such cold haughtiness that if he could have silenced me by any means I believe he would. He was asking her if all his letters meant naught, and was between fury and tears. Then he made to kiss her."

"No more."

"I am sorry to tell this news, my friend."

"Then don't say it—no more!" Nicholas did not know how he rose and pushed his way through the crowded tavern. Once in the streets he went around the carts and stalls of silks and vegetables and lace, not wanting to let so much as the edge of his hand touch them.

There had been letters and thick packets of paper, but he had thought little of them. Wentworth had written to her over the past few years, and she had always shared the letters, commented on the speeches and drafts for bills, and written back effusively, leaving the unfinished responses uncovered on the desk. Then he did recall coming across her once reading seriously through her glasses, and how she had flushed and thrust the paper away in her apron pocket.

He did not know precisely where he was heading until he understood that there must be more letters than the ones he had seen, that he must see these for himself and was going home to search for them. He could only remember again and again the sight of her dropping to her knees on the floor of the library in York and rocking Tom against her breast, and how distant and withdrawn she seemed sometimes to him.

The house was empty. He was ignoble perhaps to look, he thought as he slowly pulled open the drawers of her wardrobe. Lace cuffs, letters from her brother, notes on government, lists, dried flowers he had once given her, the poems he had written when they were first in love (they were not good poems). He knelt with all this on his knees, the fragile flowers crumbling on his dark breeches. Still he understood that even if these secret letters were not here now, they surely had existed. He felt their presence, ominous and dark, the wax sealing hardened, the words betraying. Again he shivered as if ill. He rose and vomited in the chamber pot, and went early to bed.

He slept in a kind of fever and woke in the center of the dark hours with the terrible knowledge that she had not come to bed. Sitting up, he lit the candle and looked about the room. Her day garment hung upon its hook, and her nightdress was gone. Then he gazed about and saw the drawers of her wardrobe which he had not closed, and all the contents on the floor where he had left them in his illness. Still, he felt the presence of the letters which were not there. He knew she had come in, understood, and left again.

Softly he opened the door and walked into the hall. From upstairs he could hear Avery's comfortable snore. In the smallest room William was asleep, his hand grasping the bit of blanket he was never without and some stickiness about his lips; she had put him hastily to bed. Nicholas knelt and moved his own mouth to the child's, tasting it. It was so pure.

He stood up, his stomach still queasy, and holding on to the banister, descended the stairs heavily and slowly. When he walked through the parlor he could see that she was sitting by the kitchen hearth in her white nightdress with her hair loose. He felt such grief and fear that he hardly dared cross to her, and knew again the feeling of his youthful soldiering, when he took his pike and went forward though he knew he might never come back again the man he had been.

In an aching, painful voice, he said, "Cony."

"Aye, sweet."

"Dost Tom love thee?"

"Don't ask me this, Nicholas."

"What hath he said to thee? Answer me!"

She shook her head, and he began to shout. In the end she muttered wearily, "He loves me, and hath told me so. What's done is done and I'm thine for my life, as once I said I should be and ever shall. I can't bear to say more and be torn twixt him and thee. Should be forgotten, Nicholas, I beg thee."

She slept as far apart from him that night as the bed would allow, her small shoulders a barrier he could not cross. More than the world he wished to hold her against him and would not allow himself to do it. Unable to sleep, he rose at last, took the child from his bed, and walked up and down with him in his arms.

FIVE

Portraits

T HE FIRST THING HE SAW WHEN DAWN CAME WAS THE PORTRAIT OF HIS family on the parlor wall which had been completed by Van Dyck. He had been very happy then, but he was not happy now, for his heart was dark with jealousy. He did not understand the complexity of his tenderness for Tom Wentworth, but lacking it, did not know himself. He felt himself inside to be a hollow man. He had set his life carefully, and expected it to remain as he had placed it. He knew from what he had wrested bitterly from her that there had been many letters, and that some intimacy had occurred in Yorkshire. For the first time in his life he mistrusted Cecilia, and he was sick to confront his friend. He thought as he stood there idly that he would kill him, and there would be the end of it. The lord Wentworth who took what he wanted! Mayhap Bartlett had been right, mayhap Dobson as well.

When the city was filled with the peculiar wet grey light which means rain may come, he buckled on his sword and left the house. Not even the schoolboys were from their beds, and one old man with twigs tied across his shoulders glanced furtively at him. Outside the walls of St. Paul's three vagrants slept, piled on each other like stray dogs against the damp morning. He hardly saw them, for he knew nothing but his steady, angry breath and the sound of his bootsteps on the cobbles, and the light weight of the rapier at his side and how his leg brushed the sheath.

Thus he came around the corner of St. Martin's Lane within Aldersgate, and saw the familiar house against the sky, set back behind the trees. When he was walking down the path, a young servant girl hurried out with a bucket of water and dropped to her knees to wash the steps. Hearing his tread, she looked up, confused, and then bobbed her head respectfully, saying with pleasure, "Oh master physician, 'tis thee! Why, I thought 'twere the milkboy come, for not even the messengers from court arrive so early!"

Wiping her hands, she thrust open the door. "My lord never came home last night," she said with a slight frown. "He's like that since our mistress died. But sir, he always bids you welcome! Will you come inside?"

"Where has he gone?"

"Marry, sir, neither Master Wandesford nor the other secretaries know, for he says little these days. He'll be about the courts, I should think, as he always is when in the city."

Nicholas only nodded, and turned his footsteps towards Westminster. He did not think to ferry, but walked all the way as the morning came, and the carts and carriages increased, and passing Middle Temple and Gray's Inn, he saw the young law students in their gowns walking somberly with books under their arms. They reminded him of his wife and all her impossible longings. Past tavern and church he walked until he saw Charing Cross in the distance, and then, turning, the buildings of Westminster and the palace beyond.

Here and there he went, asking in a low voice which he would not let betray his feelings for the lord Wentworth, and everywhere came the answer that no one had seen him. At eleven in the morning he walked back, searching the grounds of the new house in Covent Garden as the workers tipped their hats. At last he came home, and threw himself into a chair. His housekeeper informed him that both mistress and the boy had gone out, and that Avery had been all morning in the dispensary. There was stomach ache, a broken leg, and many other complaints. A man had come wishing to confess to him, and two priests had stopped by. Everyone had been asking for him and irritated that he was not about.

Avery raised mild eyes of reproach and said nothing.

Nicholas shut himself brooding in the parlor, crumbling bread and throwing it down to the floor. He opened his books and slammed them shut again, covered his eyes with his hands but was too angry to pray. Then towards midafternoon a soft knock came at the door, and the bookbinder Timothy Keyes's wife, Nan, came in with a portfolio of sketches under her arm. Harvey had obtained for her permission to study under the Dutch painter, as she was a talented artist.

Looking at him kindly, she said, "Parson, what dost? What troubles thee?"

"Naught."

"I think mayhap 'tis."

"Why hast come, Nan?"

"Why of no great matter. I only wished to say the lord Wentworth is this afternoon in Master Van Dyck's studio by the water for his portrait. He bid me say it if you should want him."

Nicholas waited for some time until she had gone, and then stood up slowly. Then he walked from his parlor and, telling no one where he was going, turned towards Blackfriars.

The artist's studio was as usual cluttered with painter's boys, courtiers, easels, and costumes. From a corner a lutenist played the melancholy strains of Dowland's "Tarenton's Lament." Tom Wentworth was standing in the center of the room in a full tight-fitting suit of black armor, helmet in his arms. An expanse of velvet drapery hung down and over the floors. He turned his head as Nicholas came in and saw the physician's expression, and a deep flush rose to his neck. Still he would not betray his dignity, and his voice was cool when he said without breaking his pose, "If hast leisure, we must speak, Nicholas."

Nicholas had come close enough to answer softly. Folding his arms, he replied, "Mayhap, my lord."

"Callst me such?"

"I do. 'Tis said about you take what you want, and mayhap what you wanted was mine."

"Did I pick up the very stones of the base of the bridge in these hands, they could not be heavier to me, my friend, than these words!"

"There may be more than words for thee."

Wentworth put down the helmet abruptly and signaled the painters to stop. "Enough for this day! Parson, I pray thee, come out with me to the waterside and we will talk there." When he walked from the dais, he limped.

The wharf in Blackfriars had been newly built for the King that he might come easily from Whitehall to sit for his portrait. The two men walked slowly towards it, away from the houses. There was a bench where those inclined could rest themselves while awaiting the royal barge. Fading light hung over the masts of boats and the water silvered by the descending sun. Wentworth gazed at it for some time before he began to speak.

"I betrayed you," he said, trying to keep his voice low. "Though 'tis a poor excuse, I say that I was blind with grief. Nay, I must say it . . . I must speak these words and have all laid open between us." The words grew louder, uncontained. "I lay on the floor in my house in York and she knelt beside me. I opened my arms and she came into them. I can't say I made her mine, for she's thine and hath never been elsewise. Still she gave herself to me. Poor coupling it was, both of us in tears. One time. I sent you both away then; I wanted you to stay, and could not bear it . . . that I wanted both thy love and hers." He bit his lip hard.

"Ah," said Nicholas without moving.

Wentworth had meant to say no more, but the words rose up from his chest and burst out, scrambled, too loud, tumbling over each other. "I sent you both away, and was left alone. Then the pain of my loss drove me from my bed and sent me wandering through the house; the one I had loved more than my life was gone, and the other woman to whom I had opened my heart was far away with my friend in Cripplegate Ward. So I wrote her letters, not meaning at first to send them . . . wild scratched things. And then they were sent: I lived but to write and send them. They begged her to come away from you for pity's sake and be mine. She wrote she loved me but she would not come. Now you know it and may do as you like. I'll lay down my sword, Nicholas."

"Do not."

"Nonetheless." Unbuckling the scabbard, Tom Wentworth laid it beneath the bench. From the houses beyond they heard the sound of children playing at the water's edge and somewhere a young man singing.

Nicholas did not move from where he stood, but he noticed that Tom winced, and leaned slightly to rub his sore calf and foot. After a time, the Yorkshireman said unsteadily, "I said come to me, and she wrote back and told me that she would not. And I was ashamed to have asked such a thing and begged her to tear up my letters. I'm not a good man nor always an honest one, but I hope to do some good things. She loves thee more than she will ever say. Love is not often easily contained and sometimes spilleth where it should not go: still, promises can be kept. I can't help the need of my heart, but beg charity for my actions. Nicholas, it tears my heart to be from thee! Of all men I feel you would never leave me."

"Mayhap I would."

"Then I would merit it."

Two of the painter's apprentices had come out with stained aprons, hearing the voices which had suddenly risen.

Nicholas threw down his cloak and shouted, "Turn!"

Wincing slightly from the pain in the leg, Wentworth turned, and Nicholas struck him across the face twice with the back and then front of his hand. Wentworth staggered and fell to one knee. He brought up his arm, for his nose and mouth were bleeding. The faces of the painter's apprentices standing by the dock were pale, as were the boatmen's, and

Master Van Dyck had himself run out in his apron.

"Your worships, your worships!" cried the boys. "What ho, call the constable . . . take them apart . . . help for my Lord of the North . . ."

Tom gasped, motioning them away with his hand. "Stand off!" he shouted. " 'Tis but a private quarrel, as any man may have with his neighbor!" He wiped his mouth again and tried to rise, whispering, " 'Twere not for my grief, I would not have done such a thing, Nicholas."

"I do not know what wouldst do."

"Does believe that of me . . . towards thee?"

"I do."

"Couldst not save my wife!"

"Have I forgiven myself for it?" He looked down at his knuckles, which were scraped. Then he held out his hand, and the Yorkshireman took it and rose clumsily. There was blood on his lips, and Nicholas gave him his handkerchief.

They stood in silence for a while before the apprentices and the painter and some women who had come to their windows. Tom dabbed at his mouth and would have returned the cloth. "Shall not be troubled by my company longer," he said in a dull voice. "His Majesty is sending me away even further than before. I'm going to Ireland, for he's appointed me Lord Deputy of that land. You were at war there as a lad, or so you told me when you did tell me things, Nicholas. I'll marry again to have someone to see to my children, and hope the girl will excuse that I've no heart to give but only my name and honor. God knoweth when I'll return. I think sometime to die young. I would not die having offended thee."

Faint trumpets sounded over the water, and when they raised their eyes, they saw the King's barge approaching from the west. Tom straightened his cloak almost diffidently, stooping for his sword; in his clumsiness he knocked it to the side, and it would have fallen in the water had not Nick knelt swiftly and grasped the hilt. Their eyes met for one moment. Then Nick turned away and said curtly, "I wish thee well!"

"Sayst only those words?"

"For now they must suffice."

"Then God keep thee, Nicholas."

The barge was waiting: with a slight bow to the physician, Tom Wentworth stepped inside and was borne away in the descending dusk towards the palace. Some weeks later came word that he had departed for Ireland with thirty coaches of six horses each.

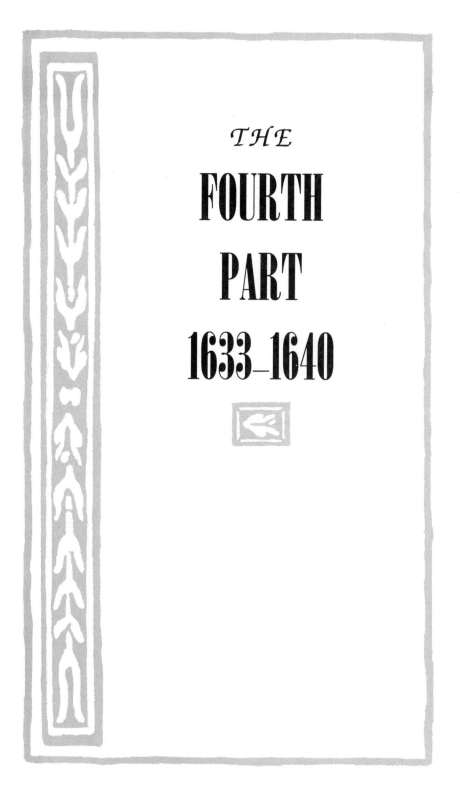

THE

FOURTH
PART
1633–1640

ONE

Lord Deputy of Ireland

T HE QUESTION WAS HOW TO RESTORE PEACE BETWEEN CECILIA AND himself.

He remembered the time in his middle adolescence when he was still with the actors that Will Shagspere had been caught in such a situation of two men and one woman, and how it had torn him. As fantastical as it was, almost any amount of affection was permissible between friend and friend's wife, yet once that boundary was passed into a single act of intimacy, nothing would ever be the same. One moment between them, unexpected . . . a desperate grieving man who wanted to die and a woman who pitied him. Nicholas felt that one moment would leave its mark on him all his life.

Of course, Shagspere had turned the sadness into poetry . . . I am my friend and he is me, and therefore, loving us both she loveth me alone! It seemed but poor poetic compensation for a devastating hurt.

The Yorkshireman haunted his bed: he dreamt himself to be him, and in him loved Cecilia until he was too rough and she turned away with a resentful cry. Sometimes their quarrels brought three-year-old William pattering from his cot to stare at them, the little chin hardly to the bed's edge. They swept him between the covers, chafing his cold feet.

When the child slept again at last, Nicholas murmured, "Dost love Wentworth, Cecily?"

"Yes, but not as thee."

"How dost love me?"

So it continued until she covered her ears with her hands and burst out, "Leave off! By our lady, Nick!"

Angry tears followed, and they tried to keep their voices soft so as not to awaken the child. "One circumstance is not the other: we cannot judge a person by what he does in despair! Would that I had never seen either of you to come between you thus!"

He lay brooding with his little son against his chest, wishing to make it up between them all, and not knowing how to begin it for his pride. And yet, he thought, as he turned wistfully to gaze at the small shoulders of his wife which he felt had once more rejected him, it was true. Part of him was tangled with Tom in a way which might never be undone; they were bound together in a love he could never in his life understand. He would almost have to unravel himself to undo the friendship. He raged against it, woke up shouting, striking his hand on the bed posters, hurling away the pillow. Yet it was inside of him: there was naught he could do.

> But here's the joy; my friend and I are one;
> Sweet flattery! then she loves but me alone.

Once in the morning before Cecilia went off to her law lessons, she bent over him as he sat writing and said, "Shall all that's good between us three be thrown away for one blemish?"

Gazing at the newly ruled paper, he murmured, "I know not."

"Don't you know that I'm sorry?"

"I do."

"Then?"

"Naught."

He tried to forget his stinging jealousy, yet it returned again. It was instinctual, furious, and made him grit his teeth and fall away from his usual good humor. Yet he did not share his anger with his friends. How easy to say from the corner of the mouth, "Wentworth, thou knowst . . ." The tone dipped in sarcasm so that the eyebrows of the listener would rise and the heart beat a little indignantly before news was given. He could not do it for his shame and for his love. Worse, he knew that for some minutes on the wharf, he could have killed his friend. He could have thrown him into the river, leapt after him, and held his head under the water until he lived no more. That terrified him.

Once more he stood apart with arms folded across his chest and gazed at the woman he had married. Had she been a man she could have done anything; he could imagine her black-gowned as the great legislator Coke, who had by mental girth and the knowledge of what was right steered the Parliaments of Elizabeth and James into a rational ship of government. He could see her, with some gentle amusement, hair tied back, her feminine voice ringing sternly to the rafters of Westminster Hall, pleading bills for the rights of man, the honor of the King, the good of England. Yet she had been born a woman and by that one fortune was excluded from so much which she would have done well.

It was not his doing: he had not wished her to walk behind him. Again and again he was startled by the power of her mind. Once when he and Harvey were pondering some impenetrable case, leaning forward from their chairs so that their knees touched, she looked up quietly from her law books and made a suggestion which was so simple and accurate that they could but stare at each other.

No, he did not think that his wife would ever slip into the arms of Wentworth again, but knew she could no more uproot Wentworth from her heart than he could from his. He was angry with his wife, and yet in some way admired her: she knew what lay on one shelf, and what on another. The incident had become a strange and somewhat muted part of their lives: much washed over it, dulling its memory. And yet he could not entirely put it away.

Nicholas was about the court that season, attending the King and his friends more often, hearing the band rehearsing rooms beyond, and passing suites of ambassadors come to make formal presentations from their own monarchies, raising his hat and bowing when the need came to do so. Tom was far away across the Irish Channel. Once he sent bolts of wool for each of the wives of his friends, and then nothing more. Several months passed.

It was one snowy evening when Nicholas was clearing through old medical notes that he came across a recipe for carrot seeds in wine to cure a woman of barrenness and remembered his early friendship with Wentworth. He was unguarded at the moment, having nursed his son through a fever and not slept a full night in some time. He pushed away the notes and began to write.

to the Lord Deputy of Ireland, Thomas Wentworth, from Nicholas Cooke, physician

For so many years it hath seemed that many events of my life had not quite occurred unless we had discussed them, broken them down, and put them in their proper place.

At least let me know how you do.

Though he knew he would not send it, he wrote on for several pages, resharpening the quill and inking his fingers, trimming the lamp.

Nicholas was filled that night with the old wild inner poetry which had haunted him since his youth, and which made him feel when it was upon him that he could put his hand into God's heart and be transformed. Life shimmered about him in indescribable, moving happiness. He felt strongly once more his belief in the ultimate goodness of mankind. Without this belief he would not have the courage to rise from his bed of a morning, would lose all he was. It came upon him so intensely that he was one moment in his comfortable parlor, and the next he could not say where.

He had written for an hour or more when someone began banging on the door from the lane. Nicholas experienced a sense of dull injustice beneath his ribs that he should always be interrupted when two thoughts had begun to find friendship with each other. Reluctantly he rose, and went towards the sound.

"Yes, what is it? I am here. . . ."

In the darkness someone grappled at his shirt; he had an instinctual desire to push him away, though in truth the man did not seem harmful. His shape was large, and he knew it must be the brickmason who had come new to Silver Street. "Parson, I've sinned!" the man muttered drunkenly. "I've beaten my children until they fell to the floor, and drunk away my wages. . . . Forgive me, forgive me . . ."

"God will forgive thee if you sin no more."

"Nay, tell me He hath and will not send me to hellfire!"

"Surely He will not," replied Nicholas with great gentleness: he felt so soft that evening he could be melded into anything. "He will not if you have truly repented. But we have been given so much . . . and we must do much with it. We cannot waste ourselves." He talked on and on about the responsibility of people towards each other, understanding the whole time that the man was bewildered by his words. Saying, "Go in peace," Nicholas gave him some coins for food for his family and then crossed into the church and sat there for a long time with his hands over his face.

He brought the letter to the Mitre to be called for by the Irish coach that Wednesday. The reply came within two weeks.

Parson,

I am most grateful to have news of thee. Ireland's damp and I am sick to my heart missing my own country. I work and work on my plans for Thorough and an infallible government. My heart aches with our quarrel.

Then Nicholas wrote more effusively and at the end scribbled the word *Forgiven* and underlined it thrice; he showed the letter to Cecilia, who added, "with my love as well." The answer came rapidly: "Most grateful thanks, beloved friends!" It had healed. There was always while on this earth the chance to begin again. On Sunday when he elevated the chalice he felt tears burning in his eyes.

Letters began to come weekly again, if not more often. There was no position more difficult in the kingdom than that of Ireland's Lord Deputy. Careers had been wrecked and lives lost in trying to contain that truculent country, with its regular uprisings of nationalists who felt the English King had no right to give away parcels of their land to his fellows and control their economy and culture. The right of the throne to be there was a matter which weighed heavily on the conscience of many of the friends: nevertheless, it had been so as long as anyone could remember. Nicholas also wondered, as did Wentworth's other close supporters, if he were well used in that position. The great vigilant statesman guarded an outpost of the kingdom, while the center of the government remained unfortified. They knew this, though most did not say.

Nicholas read the letters eagerly, passing them back and forth to Cecilia on winter evenings when the housekeeper slept and the fire burned warm and comfortable. In wool dressing gowns they sat, their feet on the same wide stool so that they touched, she with her cheek resting on her hand, every now and then adjusting her spectacles. All of the country was amazed at the swiftness and excellence of the work which the new Lord Deputy brought to Ireland. He had begun to strengthen Dublin's Parliament and to clear the pirates from the channel; he had plans to train an army which might if necessary be used in the service of his Majesty, was studying the better organization of the church, and had commenced the improvement of the wool industry. In disputes with the English landowners, he kept the King's interests foremost.

His household, he wrote them, now exceeded three hundred people: teachers for his children, pages, secretaries, advisers, churchmen, cooks, and old friends, all of whom lived within an enormous house which had not yet been completed. Appalled by the unpaved streets of the city after the medieval elegance of York, he fought homesickness. He reviewed the newly formed troupes wearing black armor and riding a black horse. Someone had said wryly that he ruled Ireland like a king.

TWO

The House in Covent Garden

I N THE TAVERNS AND STREETS OF LONDON THERE WAS ENDLESS TALK OF the growing settlements in the New World, and on the wall of Nicholas's house even a map showing that strange land. His old friend Tom Hariot had been there as navigator and written a book about it. The physician had also read, and lent to his friends, Captain Jon Smith's *Description of New England.* Jamestown, in a low, swampy island, had been settled in 1607 by stock to which Englishmen of every class subscribed. Conditions were so wretched that few men wished to populate it, even with its tobacco crop.

Word of this and the other settlements came in letters; there was now a tattered *Weekly News* in pamphlet form which circulated about the Mitre Tavern. The vast new world was like the pull of the sea. Raleigh had gone, and the explorer Gilbert; Shagspere had been fascinated, as had Francis Bacon, and even the late Dean of St. Paul's, John Donne, had in his wilder youth written a love poem to his mistress invoking those foreign shores:

License my roving hands, and let them go
Before, behind, between, above, below,
O my America, my new-found-land!

They had to go down to the sea to see the ships. The call of other places blew through London. Had not that very tobacco come to be made into medicines and enemas? Had not the sensual Pocahontas in strange, alluring skins of beasts been presented at court some years before? Again, Nicholas regretted what he did not know and might not have and his scanty allotment of one life. All his friends had talked at one time or another of going for the adventure of it. Once in his bachelor days he had cried out to the bookbinder Keyes, "For God's sake, let us go also." Initial enthusiasm flagged, and they shook their heads. In the end it was, as anyone who had been there could tell you, a wild, bitter, savage land. Not a theater, not a pisspot tavern, not a decent bit of conversation, as a friend of Harrington's who had traveled there had reported.

Not that their own country was perfect. There was widespread unemployment, and Nicholas remembered the famine in the lands when he had gone out as a players' boy in the 1590s; he remembered the pinched faces of the children, and their distended bellies. Famine had almost come again a few years before. It was not the way citizens of this country should live, Tom said. He said he would be damned if in his own county landowners should trample on the rights of the common man; he would help form a government where there was enough for all.

The map of the Americas fascinated Nicholas, but so did maps of other places, older ages, other times. Ancient oval maps or oblong rectangular, printed from woodcuts or copper. Maps from the twelfth century with their audacious acceptance of a spherical world, which placed Jerusalem always in the center, for the Bible had said, "God hath set Jerusalem in the midst of the nations and countries." There were neither parallels, meridians, or scale. Paradise was generally in the far east. Harvey had once calculated how long it would take to walk there.

Now there were excellent maps, including those of every part of England by the brilliant John Speed. Nicholas bought these and others in stationer's and cartographer's shops, spread them on the floor, and spent whole evenings holding the candle above them to point out the contours of the lands and the seas to his sleepy son. Here were straits and shoals and uncharted waters. Here, should a canal ever be possible, a passageway would be formed.

"East and west, home is best," said Harvey again to the boy as they crawled over the maps and pushed away the cat, who had come to sit upon them. Again, not that their own country was perfect: there was the dirt, and the poverty, the corruption. There was the crowding within the city walls and men of different opinions bursting out angrily in the monthly ward meetings, and still attempting to live closely. There were the religious issues.

Though Nicholas was a man who held staunchly to the traditional church, he had as much awareness as any other Londoner of the growing number of divergent sects within the city. They were as plentiful as the pigeons in Paul's yard, clucking and pecking each other. Some were his patients, and those he liked. He did not trust them absolutely, but he was willing to live contemporaneously with them; he wished them peace.

Bartlett had walked over that winter afternoon to borrow a book, and the two men had pulled a great many down to the floor before they found the one he sought. When their talk had turned to the sects, Bartlett had said curtly, "Your Archbishop despises them." Nicholas looked up from the large number of volumes still about him. He felt the slight familiar tug within his chest which meant he would be called to be conciliator once more, would be required yet again to pull all the disparate factions of his world together and make them agree. He did it cheerfully, and with steadily increasing belief in himself. Every Sabbath he stood before his congregation and, lifting his hands, said, *"The peace of God, which passeth all understanding, keep your hearts and minds in the knowledge and love of God . . ."* Stoically, he was determined to live those words and share them where he went.

After Bartlett had gone away with the book—he never stayed much these days—Nicholas remained on his knees, his thoughts moving in a scattered way, as he had just before looked at the pages of a heavily illustrated book of maps, randomly flicking through them and retaining a vague impression of the contours of places he did not really know. For what did anyone know but his work, and the feeling of his own banister as he mounted up to bed at night, and the sleepy voice of his own child calling?

He reasoned that life in this world was like this. It was like a pile of leaves in your garden which you neatly raked, and the wind came and blew them, or the rats came into grain storage which you thought was sealed and dirtied it. Sinners were absolved, and crept shamefaced back again, having stumbled anew. Nicholas was an orderly man; though he still left his shirt in a heap on the floor, or pulled on some garment inside out in his haste, his inner life was tidy. He knew what he valued, what he believed, and whom he loved. And he knew that even when you love in this imperfect world the feelings contained in that word would vary and change from day to day, again as leaves blowing. He knew, which left him more uncomfortable, that what you loved could itself change. Christ was unchanging, yet much else was not. Even the crust of the earth, Harrington had pointed out with some triumph at their last gathering, had modified.

Now and then he held things too tightly: even his beloved son, William, squirmed sometimes with resentment from his lap. It was aberrant behavior for him: mostly he gave others the freedom to move as they would. Anything else came from fear from his own early losses. It came from the knowledge deep in his soul that he and all whom he most cherished were mortal.

Outside the window on his lane, children were throwing a ball, and Avery, with his usual reassuring smile, passed Nicholas on the way from the dispensary, touching his shoulder with his light fingers, and went upstairs. Nicholas supposed the sign had been hung that the physician was away, and the bell should be pulled. Shortly he would hear either the scrape of the chair as Avery sat down to the writing of his momentous book on London, or his light bootsteps on the floor, walking back and forth. Avery was a good man: he carried sweetcakes in his pockets, embedded with tobacco bits, for any children he might meet, and daily took on more of the work of the dispensary. Still, there was with him as with Bartlett an inner emptiness, which was perhaps why his footsteps slowed so perceptibly as they mounted up to his own rooms high in the house where he would meet himself alone.

He looked about him, slowly returning to the present. He was in his parlor of his house on Love Lane. The books of maps and medicine were strewn on the floor; his knees ached, a stew was cooking on the hearth, and the day was drawing to a close. The sound of voices in the lane reminded him that a few other priests were coming to visit them for supper.

He had by this time many churchmen about the city who were good friends: canons of St. Paul's, the scholars who hung about Lambeth, men he met at table with Laud or processed with on great occasions. It was to discuss one of these processions that he walked one overcast day over to a chaplain who lived on the grounds of the Tower of London. He stayed too long, for by the time he emerged to the yard, the rain had begun.

It fell tumultuously over the grimy ancient stones of the towers, yards, chapels, and servants' shanty huts which made up the medieval walled fortress. Taking shelter under an arch, he watched a man pull a screaming pig across the yard and a little girl run by with a basket of wet vegetables. He could not make out the top of the White Tower for the downpour.

Several men were hurrying from the chapel of St. Peter ad Vincula, heavily cloaked, tips of swords just showing. They were in animated conversation of some treasury matters and laughing. One brushed against him, turned with a murmured apology, and then seized his arm joyfully. It was Cecilia's brother, Lord Dobson.

"Pricklouse, 'tis thou!" shouted Nicholas over the beating rain on the roofs, embracing the fastidious lord. "I've not seen thee these three months! Speakst of bills and subsidy? Is Parliament called again?"

"Marry, no such matter!" returned his friend. "Six years without it, and his Majesty does well enough with ship money and other means. I'm content enough: my pockets are full." He patted his sides, and watched as his comrades hurried towards the gate without him.

The two men moved further under the portico to watch the rain pour down the towers and over the cobbles. Nicholas said, "In all seriousness, I cannot remember when the science fellowship last met! Keyes hath not a moment, and Harvey may set out in search of more paintings. My mind grows dull."

"We must prevent that, good soul! Look ye, I'll send messages around to gather a week. I've a fine aged drink we must sample. Wentworth's returned, knowst: mayhap he'll come."

"Nay, sayst! When is he back?"

"These few days; I saw him but briefly. There was talk of the King making him Lord Treasurer, but some bishop's been given it instead . . . Juxon. Men know our Tom will be too vigilant. Why, the English gentry now in the north and Ireland both cannot siphon off their portion when he's about!" Dobson took off his hat and shook the rain from it. "Black Tom, as some call him!" he said with a wry smile. "I fear he's falling more and more in men's minds to represent what's wrong with the country."

"And what's wrong with it?"

Dobson frowned. "For us, and most we love . . . nothing. And most men are better off . . . but he makes hard rules for others, and bends them for himself as he likes. He's no saint, Nick."

"No man's that."

"Word is he plans to give a gathering in his new house week next and have everyone of import in the kingdom there, and hopes his Majesty will come as well. May he fail to invite that meddling little Laud of whom he's so fond!" Dobson grimaced as he gazed at the water seeping down the old stones. "That fart of an Archbishop, Nick! Called me and some friends before the ecclesiastical court on a charge of adultery. Admonished me like a schoolboy! I half expected him to take a switch from behind his back ... I had to hold my laughter! I was more amused than angry; others felt differently. The two of them, Nick, Wentworth and his grace! They are certain they know best for the whole country."

He paused. "How long is it since hast seen our Tom, Nick?"

"Nigh three years."

"He's greatly changed; his health is poorly and he's not the same since Arabella died. He needs people to love him, and fewer do. Come, my carriage is at the gates!"

They hurried over the cobbles arm in arm, shouting above the drumming of the rain.

Though Nicholas and Wentworth had written much since their quarrel, they had not met, and it gave Nicholas a curious feeling in his stomach to think that he would soon do so. The strange, dark, acquisitive energy of the Yorkshireman made him hesitate. He had decided to go early to the gathering to avoid the many people sure to be there, but William had come down with a fever. He hurried down the steps to scribble a note saying he could not come at all; then the boy seemed better, and he debated it. So it was well two hours past his expected time that he went round to the mews for his horse and set out.

Torchlight shone from Wentworth's new house and across the many carriages which were before it. As he hurried towards the steps he saw that though some people were leaving, so many coachmen and servants lolled about that it would be a long time before the rooms emptied. Once inside, he had to excuse his way past both men he did not know and those with whom he had a passing acquaintance. Bartlett was drinking wine in the corner and telling loud stories to a pretty woman. Nicholas saw by his eyes that he was no longer sober. "Such a show!" he cried, slapping Nicholas between the shoulders. "There've been four hundred here if I can count, all paying tribute to the Lord Deputy! They say the King's beside himself with delight at Wentworth's achievements."

One after another, he wandered through rooms brilliantly lit by candles and so full of people there was little space to move. Flames glittered in the creases of men's faces, and in their eyes. In yet another room, a supper had been prepared of peacock roasted and sewn again in its feathers, and there was a cathedral and palace carved from ice. All about were members of the court and the law temples, and everyone was talking in the jubilant way people do in the presence of fortune.

A servant in blue livery whom he recognized touched his arm respectfully. "Sir, if you please, my lord's been asking for you. Will you come this way with me?"

In the main hall by the edge of the stair, Thomas Wentworth was standing in a dark doublet with a simple, wide collar of finespun lawn which lay flat on his shoulders. He was laughing over some matter, and held his youngest daughter in his arms. Under the black curled mustache the face was very pale, and when Nicholas came closer, he saw that his friend's hair was turning grey. So many mixed emotions passed through him to see him again that he stopped halfway across the floor. Voices floated through the room, mingled with the low, beautiful one of the Lord Deputy.

"What of the Irish wool trade, my lord?"

"Thanks to God, greatly enhanced."

"Do you hunt, my lord?"

Nicholas looked about, but there was no sign of the King. He tried to make his way to Wentworth, who was too busy conversing with others, and for a time found friends in the corner. He was aware that the hour was growing late and was concerned to be home for his son. Still, he could not bear to go without greeting Wentworth, for it had been three years.

The clock struck ten; quietly the rooms began to empty of lords, churchmen, courtiers, women, and musicians. Kisses were exchanged in the vestibule, last murmurs of state ended. Women were pulling off their satin embroidered shoes for rougher leather ones in which to walk the cobbles. Standing by the door in the cold night, Wentworth bade each guest goodbye. He had taken his smallest daughter up in his arms. When he turned back to the room he saw Nicholas waiting for him.

For a moment they only looked at each other, and then embraced. Wentworth's shoulders, always slightly inclined to stoop, had rounded slightly, and there were silver hairs in his mustache as well. Nicholas pushed his friend away and gazed at him strictly.

"Why dost gaze at me?"

"I've not seen thee in so very long."

"Couldst have journeyed at thy will to Dublin."

"You know I had my work here."

"Where is Cecily?" The last was almost casual.

"Home, for our lad's ill. I'd promised to come, Tom, and didn't want to disappoint thee."

"I've been disappointed enough this night," replied Wentworth sharply. "His Majesty stayed away; perhaps he didn't wish to greet me after the letter he had sent on this afternoon. He's denied the earldom I've requested, though God knows my work for him hath merited it! I shall serve him as well without, though with a less cheerful heart." His mouth hardened.

"Why dost want it so?"

"The authority it would give me . . . and the proof, mayhap, of his trust. I'm sorry thy lad's ill. Anything he can want I will be glad to send him!"

They walked into the supper room and gazed for a time at the slowly melting effigy of the palace in ice. Nicholas said, "Dobson tells me thou art not well thyself, my friend."

" 'Tis true. I suffer from the damp climate; sometimes I can't use my hands. They tell me also I have the stone, but am feared to have it cut . . . I've not the time, in truth. Nicholas, I wish thou wouldst to Ireland with me."

"What would I do there?"

"Be my physician. I'd also have you elected to represent one of the boroughs in the Irish Parliament. I've done the same for friends and my brother. You'd be rich. I have influence now, very much. If you ever want to begin a hospital, I'll help you. A hospital in Dublin, mayhap! Perhaps you should rise in the church. . . ."

"I don't need these things."

"I need to give them to you," was the stark answer. Wentworth stripped off his doublet and draped it over a chair; he sat down wearily and for a moment covered his face with his hands.

Nicholas drew a chair next him. "What I need most is thy well-being, Tom," he said simply. "I need thee safe and to have thy letters. Mayst be Lord Deputy of Ireland, but art also my friend. I wish you a full healthy old age. Tom, list to me. I need little else . . . I may not be fit for other things. I am I think too idealistic for a great part in the world. What would I like? To have thee within a stone's throw again, and talk half the night by the fire. The rest can go hang. Tell me, Tom."

"Come back with me, Nick. I've need of thee."

"I can't go."

"Wherefore . . . art not afraid of Cecily?" He looked up. "Not that!"

"Nay, not that . . . mayhap a little. I've my research here with Harvey, and feel I belong in this city. And I must be myself . . . not merely part of thee, my friend. I know nothing of representing some obscure Irish borough for Parliament. I want to remain here."

A silence fell between them.

Nicholas took an apple and looked at it reflectively. He knew Wentworth. He had known for a long time that his friend would continue to grow as a young oak does into something so expansive that when you look up into the branches, you can no longer see their shape for the sun streaming through them. And he hated to lose this moment alone with him; there was so much to say he did not know where to begin it.

He said, "Tom, thy light's like a fire across forest lands; mine's more contained."

"Yours will in the end last longer."

"I don't know."

"Hast no ambition, Nick?"

"Aye, much, but a different sort than thee. 'Tis as fierce, but differs. I want to find what I think I shall never beneath the glass. Mayhap I dreamed it. Even in this we are much alike, Tom. We want the best for everyone."

"It *is* Cecily, that you won't come."

"Mayhap . . . no 'tis not. Let me feel thy chest . . . unlace thy shirt. Christ's wounds, I shall not hurt thee, Tom! Never didst stiffen thy chest so with me before! I'm thy friend . . . I love thee. Is this where the stone lodges? Harvey can cut as well as any, and would have it in a trice. I would stand by thy side and tell thee things to make thee swear so loudly you'd feel nothing. Sayst, Tom."

"Nay."

"Stubborn fellow."

"Thou art worst."

"Art sick as I have ever seen thee."

"Naught's the matter."

"Dost not trust me?"

"More than most."

"And how much can that be, eh?" the physician answered gently. "How can it be when you won't listen?"

Dropping his low voice, Wentworth murmured, "Scold me not, Nick, for we've been too much apart and there's much I'd share with you. Only go up now and kiss my children good night, for they always ask of thee."

The smallest girl had fallen asleep in a large chair in the vestibule, and gathering her against him, Nicholas mounted the steps. Near the child's white-curtained bed hung the portrait of her late mother the lady Arabella with the lamb in her arms. He looked at it, overwhelmed with feeling. When he had said good night to the others and come down he found Wentworth speaking with his secretaries. The last of the food had been cleared away.

They walked into the empty hall.

Wentworth looked about. He said grimly, "I wonder how many of the men who laughed and drank here tonight would willingly see me fall. They've no vision of government, only wanting what each one desires like children who grab at sweets and knock the pile to the floor in their haste. Ah Nick, I'm so weary. I don't believe I can do another thing this eve." He reached his hand for the banister and leaned against it.

Nicholas took his arm. "Go up to bed now."

"Wherefore? The one I loved's gone, and my new wife's a stranger. I call her Arabella at times, and it pains her. I give everyone pain, I can't help it. I don't want to go to bed. I want a fortune. I want a name that will never die for the good work I've done, and that to pass on to my son. I no longer sleep for wanting these things. There shall be peace and stability in his land. I shall stand over it like the last man who watches from a tower. One state, one faith, one King. If all the country hates me, I shall do it even so with my last breath."

He straightened and said painfully, "I can mount up myself! Give my love to Cecily, willst?"

"I shall."

"Nick."

"Aye, my friend."

"Come to Ireland with me."

"I cannot."

They parted in clumsy silence, and the physician rode home through the now empty square, his lantern held high. Avery was waiting for him to say the boy was better, and together they went upstairs.

Nicholas loved few things more than books, and had by this time several hundred of his own. Seldom had he been able to pass the booksellers in Paul's yard without stopping to examine their newest publications: plays, philosophy, dictionaries of Latin and Italian, books on becoming a gentleman and books on religion.

Yet each time he walked through the gate to the yard, he noticed an increasing number of pamphlets for sale on the dissident religious sects.

Brownists, separatists, Quakers, Puritans, those who condemned everything about the present regime, those who condemned nothing: those
who disapproved of the hierarchy of bishops and kings, those who respected it. Baptists, Anabaptists. There seemed more every day, as mul-
titudinous as the pigeons about the booksellers' stalls.

Epiphany came that Sunday. It was a rich service, and though he lost
his sermon notes he managed to preach from memory and did well.
Returning to the house to hang his cassock carefully on the hook by the
door, he noticed Avery sitting alone at the kitchen table. That scholar had
folded his small hands before him as if deep in thought. "Didst not come
to service!" Nicholas said cheerfully, kneeling by the fire to warm himself.
"Art unwell?"

Without moving, his friend said, "I'm well enough. Nicholas, I can't
bear it. All over the city people are leaving only because they can't
worship as they like, and it's William Laud who's making them go by
closing their meetings. My friends are leaving, my patients." He opened
his arms clumsily. "The man should never have been made Archbishop;
he should have stayed in Oxford with his books!" The hairs on his wrist
trembled, and his wide mouth grimaced with discomfort.

Nicholas looked about for a place to put his prayer book and then sat
silently beside his friend. Much of what had been broken during the
Reformation was now being restored by William Laud, from the oldest
churches in the city to the windows of colored glass that filled Lambeth
Chapel with light. Only last night Nicholas had gone into the church
cellar and pulled from an antique chest a deep red velvet vestment, smelling of centuries. He had worn it during the morning's service. The boys
had sung the music of Tallis, and incense had been wafted to the old
beams of the roof. Candles had glittered on the altar, which was now used
once more, and on the crucifix which had belonged to Sydenham. A little
worm-eaten statue of the Virgin which he had found by the coal hole and
brought up to the sanctuary stood by the door.

Some people did not like it: papacy, they said, Laud is driving the
church back to Rome. Did they not understand? Theirs was an English

church. It was true Laud offended many men. Nicholas had no illusions about the Archbishop's temper, which was now notorious about houses and courts of the city. Sometimes he thought wistfully that the prelate was composed of two men. The first shouted, trembled, slapped the desk with his palm, and grew red in the face when crossed. The other was the one Nicholas truly knew, and perhaps the more important. This was the fussy, round-shouldered priest who prayed seven times a day, who felt himself unworthy and worried for his dreams. ("Last night, Nick, I dreamt Lord Buckingham was alive and came to me. . . ." "The night before, three men did come and quarreled with me exceedingly. One wore great jeweled rings. . . .") If you knew a man well, to his fears and what made him laugh, you could not let others dismiss him with a few words; you couldn't judge him by what irked you alone, but must weigh all he was to you in the balance.

Still, even if the stubborn Archbishop was a great man of God, Nicholas could not help but know that he was a meddlesome statesman. He had quietly hoped for some time that William Laud would abandon his secular posts in the government. Courtiers did not need to hear about his moral strictness, like that of some severe headmaster striding down the corridor towards them. Men worth a fortune did not need to be chastised. Nicholas remembered Dobson's haughty laughter . . . would he take a switch to half the court, Nick!

And now this as well: oh, he had known about it, for everyone did. Men you had nodded to pleasantly in the street were no longer there, their houses empty. The knowledge of it had passed the edge of his thoughts, drifted about a corner, and was gone. Other families came to fill the dwellings: French Huguenots, craftsmen from the Netherlands.

Now Avery moved his mouth crookedly. "My friends are leaving," he repeated as if his throat hurt.

They spoke for a time until William hurried in, clutching the miniature sailing ship which Wentworth had sent him and which he intended to sail with his father in one of the large puddles in Finsbury Fields. As

Nicholas fastened the boy's cloak, Avery said wistfully, "Nick, hast ever been to these other services? I swear they are not so very bad. Wouldst come with me and see them?"

"I would rather not."

"Very well then," replied the scholar. "I've said it, and will say no more. Must do what thou would to thy own conscience, Nicholas, but if I do not come from time to time into the church, it is not for you, but what it represents." Nicholas went off to the boat sailing distracted and disturbed; indeed, his son had to thrice tug on his hand as they walked through the city gates to get his attention.

In the days which followed, Avery came less often down to supper, but his sadness traveled down the stairs and permeated the rectory on Love Lane. Nicholas, as he sat over his work below, could feel the fever underneath his hand, like that coming on of a beloved child.

He had stopped by the booksellers at Paul's the next morning again to look over some of the pamphlets against the established church with their vile caricatures. Tear down this, tear down that, they said. Easier said than done, was his wry response, as he replaced them on the booksellers' tables. Easier to tear down than to build again. A way of faith handed down sixteen hundred years could not simply be laughed at and thrust aside. Why, there were rumors they even talked about throwing away the prayer book which Archbishop Cranmer had compiled in the last century, and which meant everything to him, for those words defined his faith.

Lighten our darkness, we beseech thee, O Lord; and by thy great mercy defend us from all perils and dangers of this night....

The spires which rose into the early twilight shimmered before him, and he went home with a firm determination to hear no more of these divergent sects.

Yet a week later a pleasant supper was interrupted when news came that one of Avery's closest friends, a man who had worked with him with the mentally ill in Bedlam, was leaving the country for America. The scholar had said nothing, but, clearing away his trencher, bade them good night and mounted the steps once more to the garret, where he walked the rest of the evening. Cecilia went up to him, but he begged her not to stay. He wanted, he said, to be alone.

Nicholas sat below in exasperation. By God's love, the man was drawn to outcasts: beggars, whipped felons, lonely old women, the mentally deranged. His sympathies were wide, and particularly for those who suffered. At last he pushed aside the sermon he was writing, bounded up the stairs, and threw open the door to the small attic room. The small scholar had turned and lifted his arm slightly as if in anticipation. "Lord take thee, fellow!" Nicholas muttered uncomfortably. "Have it thy way. Show me these services which you favor—these other ways. Show them to me." They stood looking at each other, almost panting as if they were two adversaries who had met at last.

Nicholas repeated, "Show me."

Avery only nodded, and bowed slightly as he did when leaving the bedside of a gravely ill person.

In the next few days the tall, incredulous priest and the small scholar who walked with his head bent studying the cobbles as if he expected to find wisdom there went through halls and down crypt steps to visit a few different religious meetings about the city. The services were bare of ornament: there were neither vestments nor candles, incense nor crucifixes. Some of the sermons warned of predestination, that terrible creed in which the question of a man's salvation or perdition is decided before his birth. Nicholas pressed his lips together under his mustache.

He listened. Some preachers cried out in praise of the King's health; some scoffed him. All in all he found the worship barren and strange. Then one evening someone told them that a Puritan barrister called William Prynne was speaking at the church of Lawrence Jewry a few streets away and they turned in that direction.

It was a late autumn evening with children tossing a leather ball, and windows open and wash fluttering on the lines. Men were hurrying down the church steps to the meeting hall in the crypt, and Nicholas and Avery followed them, finding places against the wall, for all the seats were gone.

Three somberly dressed men took their places on a bench. Prynne was a hard-featured young man who could not be far from thirty. He began to speak at once. "Brothers," he cried. "Know ye God's mercy to ye? Sinners that ye be! Sinners in a city so corrupt, so corroded, so displeasing to the eyes of God that soon He must turn His face from us forever. How can we begin to weep and repent, to rend our clothing? I have come to preach to you today the sins of men all about you so that you may not fall into error and thus be damned forever! For many of you are already written to be damned before you were born. He has cast ye out, for He knew how ye would be. Unredeemed souls! Once He destroyed the world by water; can He not do it again?"

Nicholas winced. He glanced about at the men, some of whom writhed and cried, "Amen, amen!"

The speaker continued. He ranted, walking up and down the room, about the evils of dancing, singing, and the embraces of men and women. He then went on to call the church a muckpile, a dungheap. "Pray for repentance of the men of this city," he shouted. "Rid the stages of singing boys who mince like harlots in their skirts. Whip the whores from Winchester! Rip the organs from the churches. And hurl the bishops from their rich mansions. God never meant bishops to stand between Himself and the souls of men. Bishops, my brothers! They count their money from whorehouses on their land, and their hearts are rotten and wound about with sin."

By that time anger had risen in Nicholas's throat until it threatened to suffocate him. Pushing past the men and up the steps, he thought, If this is the sort of thing, it all must be suppressed! They are like stupid children, wanting to tear down what's long been built, and having no capacity to build something of equal durability. And what about God's mercy and love? *Love one another as I have loved you. . . .*

He stood with furious tears in his eyes, and Avery came up and said simply, "I'm sorry. . . . You can't think I'm with this man." He squeezed Nicholas's hand and went off alone, disappearing down an alley with his head lowered, his worn shoes slapping the cobbles.

The chapter house of Paul's Cathedral had been built in the early fourteenth century, somewhat after the time that Henry III had forbidden the teaching of law within the Cathedral precincts. It was surrounded by a two-story cloister, and in the days of the old religion monks and priests had met here to discuss excommunications, proclamations, or the thrice-yearly summoning of London citizens to the compulsory folkmoot where the word of church and King would be given.

Nicholas was hurrying from a visit to a Cathedral canon some weeks after his troubling journey with his house guest when he passed that way and saw William Laud writing alone at a desk in the center of the ornate stone chamber. At that moment the highest churchman in the land seemed but an unassuming fellow in plain black cassock and wool cap whom you might find already at his desk in a university library when dawn rose over the towers. A Hebrew scholar, or perhaps a translator of a gospel from the scrappy Greek of the apostles, called koine. Scratch, went the pen, as if to remedy all syntactical errors. Scratch . . .

Nicholas hesitated. In that moment, he felt once again the sense of spiritual closeness with the small, diligent Archbishop which had grown over the years since that first visit to the library at Fulham House. He blinked, thinking in a sudden way, surely I can speak with him! At least these things ought be discussed. He will listen to me if anyone, for he's often said as much.

One of the chapter house windows high above had long been broken, and pigeons had come inside to nest on sills and ridges, their cooing echoing against the round high roof. Some drying leaves had also found their way inside, and blew about the legs of the desk. And with this William Laud looked up and smiled.

"My dear parson!" he cried with pleasure. "Why do you stand there?

Come in! I am working on a list of further churches south of the city which must be renovated. What a work 'tis to mend what's been neglected these hundreds of years . . . what it is to bring beauty there again!"

Nicholas drew a chair close, and then began to speak as they had so many times, as if they just left off some minutes before. The sharp mind of the Archbishop leapt from the restoration of stained-glass windows to proper liturgy, and thence to the sorrows and joys of the royal family. Finally he grew quieter, and folding his hands on his stomach, he looked discreetly at the physician.

"What have you to say?" he asked gently. "Some other affair, I think."

"My lord's grace, it is so. My heart's heavy on some matters, and yet I don't know the right and wrong of them." With much delicacy, he began to speak of the empty houses. He spoke slowly, because what he wished to say was not yet clear to him.

"I am bitterly censored for this," the prelate said when he had finished. "Bitterly censored! Yes, I'd close these meetings and send these men away . . . let them go to the Americas, to the Netherlands, to Geneva! May they go in peace . . . nay, I do not wish to harm them, but only to have them away, for they are dangerous."

His small grey beard quivered. "Many men judge me! Dost think I do not know? Dost not believe I hear their jeers which permeate the curtains of my carriage? 'Tis not the cries of fishermongers, 'Come buy, come buy!' but 'Bad cess to William Canterbury! May fortune look askance at him!' Dost not think I know it? Fools, fools! Do they not understand what I must do, what Our Lord hath directed me to do? Do they think I take the easy path? Would any have done it better than I? Many men think to govern is an easy task, and they have not done it. And now, Cooke—my physician and my friend—do you judge me too?"

The edge of his voice curled into shrillness, and he slapped the desk violently several times. "Does no one understand? Of how much of what is important which concerns me do you think I do not know? All concerns me. What is not known this morning at the hour we have of ten shall be known before the wines are poured for supper with the King."

He had begun to tremble, and pulled himself inside his cassock as if he wished to hide within it. "Lord forgive my temper!" he murmured. "I pray on my knees to be delivered from it, for I move in a courtier's world and have never studied courtliness. For this they find great fault with it! They look not on my heart, but my manners."

Nicholas sought for words. Again he remembered how many times he had physicked this man, touching the tough, muscular small body; he remembered standing beside him during communion handing him the cruets of wine and water. Still he said hopefully, "My lord's grace, can we not differentiate between the sects who'd harm us and those who would not?"

"We do not dare. Do I not know this? Some of these men are good, but the worst would pull the roof about both our heads."

Leaning forward, he began to speak in a slightly hoarse, eager voice. "I shall tell you the reasons for what I do, for everything I do. I speak emotionally, for fools from the court have just been here and angered me. I love this country and its King and its ways, so carefully preserved for so long. Such decisions as are before us cannot be easy. I am as guilty before Our Lord as any man. I know the rash and reprehensible things I have done to create what I believe is a proper vessel to hold the flame of glory of Our Lord forever in this land! I know I shall stand accused of them: I know I shall be punished for them. I know as a man to whom much has been given that all my good works, whatever they may be, shall not excuse me from the wrong I have done. Ah, my friend! Few men have the capacity to understand how closely good and evil are knit within the soul, that whatever faculty for magnification of the lens through which you look to see them, you cannot wholly with even the tiniest instruments take them apart."

His words were hasty, and as he spoke them, he reached out for the priest's sleeve. Nicholas kept his eyes downcast and did not move, for he felt from the small Archbishop a terrible anguish and would have done much to comfort it. Laud spoke in a voice even softer and more compulsive of the poverty of his childhood, of the loneliness of his first years as a priest, which had not lessened. He told of his temptations in the night when he was at last alone, of his desire for women, sometimes for men. He related that he humbly wished in the end to be of service to God, though he feared nothing would ever be enough; that he hoped sometimes that Our Lord might look down from heaven and see the resplendent stained-glass windows in His honor glittering from the red-brick palace of Lambeth. He spoke, his voice dropping to such a whisper that Nicholas could barely hear it, of the nights he did not sleep but remained on his knees too exhausted to cry, his head bent to the floor, his lips whispering his hope for salvation. His head sank forward, the hair silky grey under the black skullcap.

Nicholas understood that no one had ever heard what was told him that day in the chapter house of the Cathedral. Mayhap William Laud would have told another, if another had been in there instead: mayhap he would not. He spoke as a wretched penitent might, kneeling with his hands over his face, pouring forth his heart in hope of absolution.

The Archbishop's hands now lay open on the knees of his cassock. Without raising his head and in a voice depleted with exhaustion, he said, "What sayst now?"

Nicholas's own voice was hardly audible. "My lord's grace, my heart's heavy on it, yet this moment I have just begun to understand. We must not push away all for what a few would do. I say this with all love and humble respect to you, William, my most reverend father in God."

The Archbishop did not raise his head, but his open hands curled slowly together. "At times," he said at last, "I feel myself too old and tired for this work. At times I feel heaviness about me. God knoweth if I am fit for this burden." Then he closed his eyes and cried out, "I have mistook thee, parson. Go from me . . . go! Why have I troubled with you? What use are you to this our church if you will not defend her from her enemies? Thou art unfit to be a priest. Farewell."

"My lord, do you say this to me?"

"I do."

Startled by his cry, the pigeons far above rushed into the air.

Nicholas did not know how he got from the room. He rose and bowed with his hand to his heart; then he did not stop until he had flung himself through the churchyard gate which led to Cheapside, and he ran all the way down to the steps and through the small streets towards his home.

from the lord Wentworth, Lord Deputy of Ireland, to Nicholas Cooke, gentleman and physician, Cripplegate Ward

Beloved Nick,

Marry, coxcomb, thou hast done it well! I understand his grace is so angry with thee that he cannot mention thy name without sputtering. I fear that my plans to have thee made something more in the church will come to naught; still, if he moves to take thee from thy present living, I have enough influence with him to stay his hand. I know his heart's heavy, for thou art dear to him, though he does not allow himself to doubt the wisdom of his actions.

So he hath sent for another physician for his endless woes. Nick, Nick, list to me! Sometimes we must have a little hurt to gain a greater good. Cecily would understand.

Wentworth

Nicholas angrily tore the letter and threw it in the fire. He waited for the hooves down the street, the coldly delivered missive with the ecclesiastical seal, dismissing him. Everything became so dear to him in those days. At times he thought, Let his grace remove me and by Christ's wounds I will preach to the sparrows of the wayside! He had removed priests for their belief: then why not himself? Nicholas was so angry that children moved slightly closer to the doors of houses when he swept down the street, and no one asked him for anything.

He wondered on sleepless nights why he had chosen to be a church-man at all, with the church's narrow ways. Still, he had not chosen to serve God, but God had chosen him. And there he was. And there was the fussy small churchman, laying waste the goodwill of men about him.

Days passed, then weeks: no messenger came. Then strangely calm was he as one who had escaped death, all other dilemmas not worth mentioning in comparison. His heart resumed its regular beat, the ache of his body died away; he needed no longer to douse himself with hellebore waters. He broke the bread and blessed the wine, healed the sick, and once more turned to his studies.

Someone mentioned the name of Prynne, and he spat. Then for days he wanted to write his apology to the Archbishop, shamefaced as it was, and several times he began to pen it. Still he recalled the orderly, more quiet meetings he had attended about the city, the neighbors who were gentle and now had left. To dismiss one was to dismiss all . . . and then he was furious about the way Laud had spoken to him. He tore up the letters, saying, But one is not all. . . .

During those months he fell into some deep thought and tried, as best he could, to put it from him, and yet it left a strange dark place in his heart, like a troublesome dream you cannot quite recall but which moves through your soul at odd moments for a long time after. He woke sometimes crying out, and could not remember why.

Then one morning he left his house at dawn and walked to the river for a ferry. The brick-turreted palace of Lambeth drew closer; the riverman talked of taxes and the price of bread.

The Archbishop was walking slowly from the vestry towards the altar with his Bible and the cruets for wine and water, and for a moment Nicholas hesitated to call out for fear to startle him. Then he came forward quietly, and held out his hands for the vessels.

William Laud's nostrils uplifted in faint haughtiness, and then a look of wistful pleasure came about his mouth under the soft grey mustache. Later after the service was done and they were removing their surplices, Nicholas said bluntly, "I spoke roughly, my lord's grace, but from my heart."

"I could not bear you turn against me, Cooke."

"I could not do that, nor would I! Can you not see? There's so much discontent, I fear trouble . . . I cannot say from whence it will come but I do fear it."

Laud looked at his stole thoughtfully before kissing it, and laying it down upon the table. "What, from a pack of rowdy insurgents!" he said with some scorn. "Is not the power of the King enough to manage them? Praise Our Lord, the last of the raggle-tails will soon be gone from these shores! Wilt come to dine soon, my friend? I have missed thee and that most witty dame, thy good wife."

On a warm evening at dusk some months later, Nicholas hurried down to the docks to meet the boat from Leiden. He had to wait an hour before they located the parcels, but at last they found one bound in burlap and tied with twine, his name almost eradicated by saltwater stains. He rushed as far as Lowin's small dock, sat down outside the house, and opened it.

Galileo's new book, *Discorsi e dimonstrazioni matematiche intorno a due nuove scienze,* or *Dialogues and Demonstrations of Mathematics Concerning Two New Sciences,* had come. Passing his hand over the front page, Nicholas thought of the old mathematician whose sight was failing. House imprisonment had not shaken him, nor had the ills: he was yet working on the librations of the moon.

From inside the house came Lowin's voice marking time as he instructed his apprentices in a formal dance. "Hold their skirts! Peascod, hold up thy skirt! Art a lady, not a baker's boy, pricklouse. . . ." Nicholas sat with the book on his knees. It had been a difficult week, for the Puritan Will Prynne had gone too far at last. He had called the Queen a whore for dancing in her own masques, and the Star Chamber had punished him by clipping his ears. His people had cheered him, and the prison cell in which he was confined was now reputedly decorated with tapestries and silver. Avery despised the man, and yet he felt for him. Nicholas, still angry as he was, could not help but also feel some sadness.

He took his cherished book under his arm and, as darkness fell, walked thoughtfully on towards Finsbury Fields, where Harvey and Keyes were waiting with telescopes. The night was clear and a gentle breeze came from the farmlands. Above them, the dark sky was covered with a thousand stars, each one glittering brighter than the last.

When they returned later through the city gates they found the doors of the Mitre Tavern thrown wide, and half the men from the parish in the street. "There's trouble in Scotland!" one man cried. "The King's set to force the English prayer book there, and Edinburgh is in arms."

THREE

Whitehall

NEWS TRAVELED QUICKLY: BY THE FASTEST HORSEMEN SWITCHING BEASTS frequently on the way, a messenger could come from Scotland to London in four days.

Even under that native Scotsman the late James Stuart, Scotland had been rough to govern, and his son Charles had little idea what to do. He was Whitehall-bred, and did not understand the strong pull towards the Presbyterian Church in that northern country. He did not understand the pride of their self-rule. A man understands only what he surrounds himself with, Dobson had said wryly, and in the case of their gentle sovereign it was horses, art, and his growing family.

His faith was stubborn within him, and so he had created a Book of Common Prayer much like England's own and gave orders that it be used in worship throughout Scotland. That country refused. As the months passed, the news traveled down crookedly, perhaps exaggeratedly, to London and left in its trail a sense of awe within the city streets. Jagged and half drunk staggered the reports, yet the men who met in taverns and in the monthly ward meetings gruffly understood them to be true. Their voices hushed, and they lowered their heads and pawed at the ground like horses knowing they must go forward in time, and yet without direction, and yet unwillingly.

"I will subdue the northern rebels!" rang out the voice of the handsome, small, fastidious King from the inner privy chambers of Whitehall, and the city merchant, sheriff, unemployed soldier, or angry boy sullenly lifted his head and murmured, "Will it be Scotland now? And then in some ways me? What will he have of me?"

It was no longer the days of supplication, the medieval days of war. A strange pride filled the countrymen. Nicholas saw it from his pulpit on Sunday: it was slight, like the fall of certain light across the memorial slabs in the floor, and when you turned your head it was gone. Then from another angle it seemed to say, I will do what I wish! (Jaws hardened.) I am freeborn English . . . who is this Majesty, this holy ordained and sacred King in the inner chambers of Whitehall, who tells me I must gird my loins, open my coffers, and go to war over a book!

Yet it wasn't a book alone: Dobson said it starkly. Oh, it was so far beyond a simple prayer book, or a handful of wax candles or vestments. It was, of course, what things meant, and these things meant popery, or a slavish return to the Roman Church, where you fell to your knees to some prelate who did not know your language and kissed the edges of his dusty cope. On one hand, Londoners might curse and spit and shout, "Subdue the dirty Scot!" On the other, they muttered dubiously: "Leave him alone—'tis the foreign wars all over, and we don't want them. What will taxation bring now? Into what rights wilt put thy ringed hand, Majesty, and skim away the cream from what we've gathered?"

Then they grumbled, bowed heads, drank the cup deeply, grew sentimental, and muttered, "God save him!" Nicholas sometimes left the chancel of his church bewildered, not quite able to explain what he had felt. Still, as Dobson said in the once more frequent science meetings, the problem focused on what the problem never was. By Christmas, his royal

Majesty had spoken with his whole heart to his furious northern province. He hated popery as they did, he claimed, and would do nothing against the law. Yet as they were one state, they must have one way of worship. He urged them to see it.

Winter passed; Scotland yet balked. A National Covenant vowing to resist church reform was signed in Edinburgh by ministers and noblemen, housewives and shopkeepers; apprentices cut their arms and signed with their own blood, and a rebel army of clansmen, professional soldiers, and ordinary citizens began to form. Another season flew, and then one more. By the early months of the year 1639 the citizens of Scotland were rallying an army.

Servants moved quietly in and out of the rooms of Dobson's now sumptuous house on the Strand. Nicholas arrived late, for he'd been attending a man imprisoned for theft. He entered the parlor through the side door without announcement, for even the great dogs knew him well.

The group of friends were standing or seated at the other end of the large room by the fire, over which hung a portrait of the Queen with a rose in her hand. Dobson was reading a handful of papers, crumpling some and dropping them into the flames, while at the same time keeping up a vague conversation. He stood casually, his belly very slightly rotund between the edges of his unbuttoned doublet as when a man is in his own home and comfortable to be there; every now and then he rubbed the edge of his finger over his upper lip. He would stand for a time like that in repose, and then break suddenly away as if he had been weary of it a long time.

Over the pleasant sound of the fire and the soft feet of the servants on the carpet drifted the murmured voices, laughter, and now and then a whole sentence or two. Cups clicked softly when replaced on tables of inlaid wood. Harvey was sprawled low in the chair he always took, his thin legs in slightly wrinkled black wool hose stuck before him and the lank hair brushing his plain collar. The clock, with its naked silver nymphs about the face, slowly ticked the passing minutes.

Timothy Keyes, with his great height and growing bulk, stood with his elbow on the mantel, the large fingers now and then reflectively turning the globe on the table beside him. His tender brown eyes were fastened on Lawrence Avery, who was listening to him reverently, every now and then nodding; the two had become inseparable. Bartlett sat apart, breathing heavily, for he suffered from congestion, and leaning over a heavy volume which he held in his lap; he had removed his hat, and the top of his head was sparse of hair. Harrington walked stoutly between all of them with his cane as if on a specific path, and Nicholas suspected that his mind was far from this place and company, into greater conflicts. "Let us have war and be done with it!" he often said. The others knew that the specific division of opponents and right and wrong alone made life clear to the old soldier. He could not pass the smallest matter in his life without being for or against it.

Nicholas remained with his hand on the door's edge, gazing at them by the fire as their murmurs came across the room.

"... 'tis not the prayer book, but that the King, who's a foreigner, hath come into Scottish houses and told them how they are to live. . . ."

"Doth he not come into English houses and say the same?" This was Harvey.

Harrington pointed his cane at them. "In the perfect days of Good Queen Bess . . ."

Dobson barely looked up from his letters. " 'Twas not perfect then, 'tis not perfect now," he murmured. "Dear heart, there hath never been perfect harmony between crown and country. Thy memories are as dusty as the swords which hang in thy vestibule."

"Art impudent! Were I a younger man I would beat thee," replied the old soldier angrily. "What manner of court can it be with youths like thee about? Aye, there shall be war . . . I cannot say I wish it, myself, or my wife or my sons . . . however . . ." He gazed at them with the wrathful blue eyes of one who does not believe himself and wishes to convince others.

Nicholas came across to them, loosening his cloak and laying his hat on the table near the globes. Dobson, seeing him, thrust the remaining papers under the weight on the desk and corked his ink. "Well, parson," he said. "I grow daily richer. When this northern conflict's done, I intend to build a better house and leave this one to you and Harvey for your hospital. 'Tis time you turned your minds to that. . . ."

The men murmured, and Avery looked about bewildered at them from the deepest thought he was having; he looked like a man just risen from sleep. They made themselves comfortable before the fire while the servants tiptoed about.

"Puritan divines speak in every cellar and in the private halls of many a city company, though the Archbishop forbade it!"

". . . and if the conflict gets worse . . ."

". . . our King will send for Wentworth. There isn't anyone else who can better advise him. He'll break down and call for him."

"And then?"

"We won't know what then. . . ."

Harvey scowled. "As expected," he said, "we talk of turds and farts. Are we the most unprivy council, gentlemen, that we are reduced to this? I say the devil is a statesman and we must exorcise him. To our work, gentlemen, to our work!"

Cecilia also watched the growing unrest in the streets.

She saw it as a street game when boys from different wards begin in baiting each other and then end in blows. Rough soldiers, understanding nothing, had beaten two Brownists some streets away. One man had stood up at the end of service in Mary Aldermanbury and protested aloud against the King's actions. Nicholas had left the church with his hands cold from emotion. But he always held himself in like that.

Alert and without fuss, Cecilia looked about her and understood a great deal. She was by this time well into her middle years, one of those slender women who grow more radiant as the years increase. Her old sharpness had turned into a wistful, acute intelligence. The perpetual nagging misery that she must stay apart from life for having been born a woman had not left her, but was now diverted into seeking other ways to serve. Her knowledge of the law as it was studied in the temples was by this time deep and unsullied for being yet theory alone. She waited as one does to be called. She was not especially interested in making jars of preserves for the winter, in salting meat, or in mending the holes in her son's hose, though she supervised these things. She loved the contours of her life, and having come late to it after much unhappiness, she wished to devote her greatest intelligence to preserving it.

She loved Nicholas in ways for which she had no words, and liked to stand at the dispensary door and watch him with his patients. There was an inexhaustible gentleness in him, and yet in the set of his mouth under the mustache it seemed to say, We must pull down the curtains about us, go this far and no farther. All of heaven for him seemed to center between the jars of herbs and the creaking three steps of the church pulpit. He saw heaven, and the people he loved, so clearly that he saw little else; he wanted to see little else. In this perhaps he slowly acquiesced to growing older. He had built a sturdy little world and without speaking planned to live within it all the rest of his life. He had built it solidly, as a good carpenter, taking care of every small matter of foundation and the joining of beams.

His microscopes gathered dust on the parlor table: he said he had no time. Yet there was no friend or supplicant for whom he would not have come down to the cold kitchen at two of the morning to hold his hand and speak of his troubles and joys, and send him away feeling far better. All he touched he healed, though he would no longer try for what he said could not be done. With a soft laugh he shrugged and said these things belonged to younger men. There was a slight sadness in him that he had given in to the Archbishop: he tried, he often said, to move him in small ways if great were impossible. Humor and time would work, he said. Each day he gained or lost a little, and brooded over it accordingly.

She loved him, and she loved Tom Wentworth as well. She had never ceased to love him.

Wentworth's letters came weekly. She would take them off to sit by herself in the window seat overlooking Love Lane, reading them again and again. He was going to rebuild Christ Church Cathedral in Dublin; he had made a progress through Ireland and was greeted everywhere by praise, which, as he wrote to her, "rather taught me what I should be than told me what I am." He spoke of his spiritual life, how he retired to pray for some time each day. He would not allow the English Privy Council to raise Irish customs. He confiscated land from those who did not use it well, and gave it to those who did. He was creating a fortune; he hoped to make a theater there.

In his personal letters to her, he complained now and then of Nicholas's complaisance. He wrote to her both as a colleague who had the intelligence to share his vision and as a man to a woman who understood him. He poured out his devotion to England, his hope for it, and his frustration at being apart from the King and receiving but inadequate, misleading news of the Scottish situation. War! The King had no money to go to war. Most ship money this year had been refused him, and he had no power to impose it. Wentworth felt those who withheld should be sharply punished. He wrote passionately of the few separatists who spoke so scathingly against the established religion and government. He would have them locked in darkness all their lives, for, as he wrote, it was not to end prelacy they wished, but to let forth the lifeblood of monarchy itself.

She felt that in these letters he reached out his capable hands to both of them: he depended on Nicholas's steadiness of faith, though he railed bitterly that the physician would not be moved, and cried out when Nicholas wrote that he had spoken to the Archbishop against forcing the prayer book on Scotland. "Nicholas! One state, one church, one King!" came Wentworth's heavily underlined response. He felt his old friend was growing thick and stupid, and yet, by Christ, he needed him. Cecilia's mind was supple, and understood. She understood there was more to her own city than the sleepy guard at the gate, and the ale drawer pouring out the same measure of beer and marking it to account on the chalkboard.

"Dear Cecily," he wrote, and she longed for him.

She stood now as she had always stood, even before she knew it, silently balanced between them, extending her hand to each to take it when she stumbled. Wentworth's boldness, his harsh angry ways, his brilliance, called her. She felt it in her breasts and sent her soul across the channel to him. His need of both Nicholas and herself was vital. To allow any act of physical passion again between herself and Wentworth would shatter this and all of them. She became custodian: it seemed sometimes a silly act of virtue, but she knew how necessary it was. That there were the hundred miles of bad roads and rough sea between them she understood, and sometimes thanked God for it. If she touched him with sensuality, it would destroy every other way she touched him, and that she was too wise to allow.

She looked back on their one act of physical intimacy with many emotions. The mixture of audacity and awe with which he came to her, and they both half naked: she with her petticoats pushed up, and he ripping the satin lacing which held her silk hose to her undergarment, his passion so sudden that he bruised her thigh with his mouth. His shirt was across the room, his breeches half down his slender hips. His breath was like that of a man going to war. More startling afterwards had been their tears, his furious and boyish, and her own. She had cried that way when her child was ill. He could be brutal, and yet absolutely pure.

They lay together, both knowing that what he had done was not only in mourning for his wife. They knew they loved each other, and had come to each other as a man walks down a dark hall in a strange house, and sees a form hurrying towards him, and when he reaches it, finds only a mirror and puts out his hand to touch himself. And then, falling into rueful silence, they knew that they were too different: she feminine and furious at the limitations of that, he rooted in his northern ways of what women should be and he should be. They knew as well that what had brought them together and would always keep them together was the physician and priest whom they both loved, and who would have been wounded past his ability to continue if he knew of this. So they held each other in this conundrum, with her petticoats retaining the scent of his lovemaking, her lips bruised from his kisses, and her hand on his slender, naked hip.

"My Lord President of the North," she had called him with a small smile. Now it was "my Lord Deputy of Ireland" . . . sometimes in her long letters she wrote "dear Deputy" or "my most dear L.D. of Ireland" . . . or sometimes "sweet Tom." His heavy packets of drafts of speeches, bills, and political letters which he sent for her comments lay on the window seat.

So there was that memory of them both gathering their clothes, glancing now and then shyly at each other: she tall and small-breasted, he lanky and surprisingly muscular, dark hair roughly spread across his chest, shoulders bent, for he was so tall he always seemed to stoop to listen to others, looking at her hopefully, angrily, as if she could find a way to get them from this complication. Looking shyly at each other, knowing with a terrible sense of loss that what was their first time must also be their last.

Now she sat with her legs crossed under her wide loose dress, hunched over in the window seat which overlooked the lane, writing "my darling Lord of Ireland" . . . questioning him about the political situation, consoling him for his need to be an earl, telling him she had spoken with concern as she felt proper to the Archbishop when last they dined concerning the prayer book situation in Scotland, warning him he must not be too rigid in his views ("you and Charles Stuart do not bend enough"), signing her name at the end with some awe.

"Thy Cecily."

"Dear friend," he wrote.

I shall be about the city by Christmas and visit thee more often, for I will soon come to sit on the Privy Council. Canst believe my fortune? His Majesty has called me to advise him! Queen Henrietta Maria writes me solicitous letters. I believe a space will open for me when I enter the palace. How strange to have some of what I have wanted for so long! And yet it's the way with me to earn one honor, and want another. I wonder what I shall do if I obtain them all.

How will I manage the others on the council? There's Hamilton, with whom I don't agree, and the Earl of Northumberland, who's against the Scottish affair. Then there is the Archbishop, who will stand with me. We can expect help from the Spanish, mayhap, if we protect them against Dutch ships. The city will stand with us, for they need Spanish trade. We will have money from them as well for the wars. May it be quickly concluded, so that we may go on with our country! Then there shall be no greater or secure land ever than this little green island.

T.

Beloved Tom,

I asked you a few letters back if you were happy, and you responded, "I don't know. Does it matter?" That haunts me, for it does matter, it must.

Listen to me, dear my love, if ever you have. I know it is your instinct that if enough support cannot be raised for the Scottish wars, to call Parliament to aid them. I know that landowners and gentry have always resented the power of the throne, and they do so now more bitterly than ever. You are the only man strong enough to protect the King's interests, and you, until now, he has kept away.

The wealthy men of the realm can't do anything unless he calls them together in Parliament. They cannot call themselves. As long as he does not call them, he's safe. Certainly you must not advise it, no matter how badly you need help.

Nick sends his dearest love.

She always hesitated over the letters as if she wished to say more. In the end he would continue to give her what she wanted most, and that was a purpose. She stood with his packet of speeches and bills against her apron, looking over the street. All down the lane the merchants' signs blew softly in the wind, and from the house next door, Mark was playing the krumhorn.

Christmas came, and still they awaited him.

In and out of the houses there were pantomimes and dances, and music. Packets of food were made up wrapped in old paper for the poor of the parish, filled with thick slices of brawn, goosefat, berry and cowslip conserve, suet pudding, rose petal tarts, smoked eel, bottled sack, and figgy pudding. She looked at the angel puppets which William had made when he was younger, and held them up to the light before putting them carefully away in a drawer again. He was now too old for those things.

Nicholas had been called to participate in a Christmas Day Evensong at St. Paul's Cathedral before the King and his court, and sometime before the hour of three, he and Cecilia fastened their cloaks to walk over. William, lanky and shy, followed, talking of the play in Latin which his school had given. Along the way people called to them from their windows. Snow tumbled lazily down the sides of small parish churches, landing on barren branches and tombstones.

Clerks and canons, vergers and choristers, constables and royal guards who would take part in the procession milled about the churchyard. The scaffolding had just been removed around the Cathedral entrance, and a new marble portico rose far above the surrounding brick-and-timber houses. Hundreds of other citizens who had come to attend the service paused to stare at it and comment before hurrying inside past the horses. Nicholas whimsically laid the palm of his hand to the cold marble, and then spoke with one of the vergers to make certain his wife and son had good seats. He was to proceed with three other priests of the diocese as clerical escorts of his grace the Most Reverend Father-in-God William Canterbury.

Voices were muted in the snow. There were friends from other parishes. Choristers from the Chapel Royal scraped their boots on the cobbles. The royal carriage had come, and all in the yard knelt when the King descended. His mustache glistened, and he looked about shyly, smiling as if pleased. By this time hundreds of men who could find no place to sit or stand inside the cavernous Paul's filled the yard. They cried, "God save you, Majesty! A blessed Christmas, Majesty!"

"God keep you," murmured his Majesty, opening his arms slightly. He wore lace-trimmed doeskin gloves and a cape.

As the many men who would march were formed into an orderly line, they heard the first call of organ and trumpet from within. It rang until it disappeared in the dark hollows of the roof. Then the boys began to sing as, gravely and with infinite slowness, they moved towards and through the Cathedral doors, each holding a slender burning candle.

Far before him walked the Lord Mayor in scarlet with his Sword-bearer, the Common Crier and Sergeant at Arms, and the City Marshal. Then followed the two sheriffs, the aldermen, and presidents of the twelve great livery companies; next a number of bishops, canons, archdeacons, and priests and a verger carrying an antique rod. Behind them came the royal guard and the King and the Prince of Wales, gazing solemnly about and holding to his governor's hand. More priests followed. Then last, bearing a cross to indicate that he was shepherd of this flock, his grace William Laud proceeded slowly in his long white rochet and sleeveless scarlet chimere, his grey eyes critically surveying the great shadowy spaces of darkness. Soft came the sweep of shoes and robes and gowns. There seemed no beginning nor end of the long procession, and to Nicholas it appeared that he was part of something that must go on forever.

He looked about. Countless candles glittered, making shapes and shadows of the vast throng. He thought, Here we have the mark of civilization, and by this procession, precedence. Who goes before, and who behind? There would be pride and resentment in those things for days. That amused him, and he was still smiling slightly as he walked not far before the Archbishop through the carved choir screen which separated the chancel from the main section of the Cathedral, and found his place in the stalls.

The high treble of the boys and the more resonant lower voices of alto, tenor, and bass sang out in the appointed psalms. Lessons were read, and the words of the Magnificat and the Nunc Dimittis gave forth their praise as they had done for over a thousand years.

William Laud, Archbishop of Canterbury, rose slowly and with the help of one of the boys mounted the pulpit steps. His sermon, sometimes ringing out and then again faint in the great recesses of space all about them, took as its text the passage from Luke concerning the birth of Christ.

> *And there were in the same country shepherds abiding in the field, keeping watch over their flock by night. And, lo, the angel of the Lord came upon them, and the glory of the Lord shone round about them: and they were sore afraid. . . . And suddenly there was with the angel a multitude of the heavenly host praising God, and saying, Glory to God in the highest, and on earth peace, good will toward men.*

When he finished speaking he laid his delicate hands flat on the pulpit and looked sternly over the crowd, which was almost swallowed up in darkness. The boy came again to help him down. Crossing the chancel, he dropped clumsily to one knee before his sovereign. The congregation sat back, scraping chairs and benches. The tip of a sword now and then clanked against the stone floor. With the snowy sky all light from the windows had almost gone.

Then the trumpets blew once more and a hymn was sung, and the procession began to move out of the Cathedral. Candles glittered. They walked slowly as if held within some ritual more ancient than they could ever recall.

Once in the yard, each man went his own way. The royal coach was waiting for King and son, and William Laud climbed inside. He would be shaking slightly from the exertion of his sermon, and somewhat sweaty. Once when he had come home in bitter cold, Nicholas had ordered him rubbed with warm wine. Now he whispered the instructions to Laud's chaplain, who smiled at him and squeezed his hand.

William Laud leaned out. "My friend, a blessed eve of the day of Our Lord's birth!" he said.

"My lord's grace of Canterbury, the same," Nicholas replied. Then the window cloths were drawn down and some men dropped to their knees as the carriage rolled away.

Priests, choristers, aldermen scattered across the snowy yard in the early darkness of the winter day. The congregation was now leaving as well, wrapped in cloaks, down the little streets which surrounded the yard: Paternoster Lane and Ave Maria Lane, named for the old professions of beadmakers and prayer book scribes who had plied their sacred trades near the Cathedral walls. Several carriages still stood about, and little groups of people had gathered near the booksellers' stalls.

When he turned, he saw Thomas Wentworth running towards him through the snow with his hands extended.

The seventh of January was the day of the presentation of the Russian ambassadorial suite in the banqueting hall of the palace. Nicholas and Cecilia found a place towards the end of the room. It was not, however, the Russians for whom they waited.

The ambassador and his deputies came across the floor to the throne in heavy fur-trimmed clothing and made reverence according to the custom of their country on their knees with heads bowed to the ground. The King rose, put off his own hat, sat down, and covered his head once more to hear the speech wishing him good health. With a slight smile, he leaned forward for the translation. He then rose again and graciously made his reply.

Outside the high windows a band played ceremonial music and now and then an English military march. The King's voice, which was not loud and stammered slightly, was sometimes faint amid the rustling of clothing and murmur of commentary. Nicholas waited with more impatience; it was not for this they had come.

Gifts were brought forth by the ambassador's pages: a silver salt with Venus arising from the waters, a soup tureen with mythological birds and griffins, a portrait of the Czar in a clasped and jeweled oval case. When the ambassador left the country there would be the standard farewell gift of plate from the English sovereign. Twice the Queen leaned over to the King and yawned, and her heavy brocaded dress crinkled. Charles Stuart stood, and they all dropped to one knee.

"My lords," he murmured indifferently. Then he turned his face to the door, through which hurried a young page with large ears. Stopping directly before his sovereign, the boy bowed and called, "Most gracious Majesty, Thomas Wentworth, Lord Lieutenant of Ireland."

"Let him approach us," said the King.

With simplicity the Yorkshireman came forward. His face was for a moment harsh as if he fought some dark, terrible emotion. Then it softened. Nicholas had once seen a young priest ordained who looked that way. Charles Stuart beckoned him, and Wentworth came close and dropped to one knee. The King put forth his hand and a sword was given him, which he laid gently on first one shoulder and then the other of his kneeling servant. "Rise, Thomas Wentworth," he said, "Earl of Strafford." The trumpet blew, and the herald's voice cried it out again.

Cecilia had clenched her hands together against her locket.

The newly created Earl took his place beside his King. There was a not yet completed portrait of him and his secretary which even now leaned against a wall in Van Dyck's studio. The secretary's pen was raised devotedly above the paper to catch the every word of his master, but Strafford did not look at him. The very same expression was in his face now as he stood beside his sovereign in the banqueting hall; he looked out, yet saw nothing and no one but his future. Outside the great vast windows of the banqueting hall the snow continued to fall lightly.

FOUR

Scotland

EVEN WITH THE TROUBLES OVER SCOTLAND AND INFLATION, THE CITY had gone about its business, grumbling, overtaxed, and crowded. Foreigners walked up and down the streets with amazement and wrote home long letters. Mansions had been expanded along the Strand, and a courtier had to wait three months or more to be painted by Master Van Dyck, who now had several assistants. The King's Men counted more shareholders than they had ever had before: five-and-thirty, plus boys and hired men, and ofttimes on a mild afternoon a good seat could not be found at the Globe. All the goods that man could acquire by ship from the Indies through Sweden were sold in the stalls and shops of Cheapside and the Exchange.

Trained bands drilled in Moorfields twice weekly, as they had always done, and the football teams, competing for the same muddy grounds, rushed under the pikes shamefaced to retrieve the inflated pig's bladder, doffing their caps to the captain. A little boy sat in a tree and played

"Come o'er the Bourne, Bessie" on his piping recorder; the company drummer ate bread and cheese. Andrew Heminges was ensign in his company and carried a blue square flag whose rough pole sometimes left splinters in his palms.

Into this city came the newly appointed Earl. He left his house at dawn each day, his linen crinkled with starch, and paused only to look up at his now three little girls and his slender, red-haired son, who had come to the window to watch him go. Then he climbed into his waiting carriage and hurtled over the half-uncobbled road of the Strand towards Whitehall. Nicholas often thought of Tom when his work took him past the palace; he wondered behind which windows his friend might be as he sat long hours on the Privy Council, debating the problems of the nation and the war. Once he waited for him with the early dusk falling about the shabby palace buildings, and they rode home in the carriage.

"Art not well, Tom."

"I am most certainly."

"Thou sayst."

"Nick." He raised the curtains for a moment to look out at the receding palace, then let them drop again. "There's no help for it! We *must* call a Parliament in the spring. There's nothing else we can do to raise the money for the war."

"Knowst what Cecilia thinks on this."

"Ah yes, but she can't know everything!" said the Yorkshireman playfully. He stroked one side of his small mustache and then, concealing his expression, looked away. "Englishmen will put aside their grievances to rid the north counties of the Scot who now threatens us!" he continued in the rapid way he always presented problems. "And even with it, my friend, I'll be back in the city! I have had enough of Ireland to last me for this life and the next! I'll leave my brother to manage it in my place, and serve at the King's side after the war's done. Then we can discuss ... what the devil is it that you do discuss now?"

"The properties of light."

"Indeed! I should like that ... walking to the fields with you! I've been away so long we must have a month of walks to speak of all we've missed. I cannot do it now, but soon. You won't forget all that you have to say to me, eh, Nicholas?" His voice was wistful.

"No, my friend."

Wentworth flung himself back wearily: by the scant swinging carriage light Nicholas could see the crevices etched down the sides of his mouth, and the breath which seemed to go to the edge of his lungs and no further, as if he had neither patience nor strength to take in more.

"Tom," he said, "I've read thy physician's reports. How many times have you fainted that was not writ there? Look ye, fellow! Your body cries out for rest, you've one fever after another. Rheumatism, worse pain from the stone, loss of the use of thy hands from time to time, inability to walk . . . a bloody, painful flux, Tom."

"Enough!" was the sharp reply. "I'll take my place in the Lords this spring and serve my master well, but first I must open the Irish Parliament. Wait for me: I'll return; then you may coddle me. Don't look so stern, Nick: I need thy goodwill."

"Well, thou hast it."

There was a celebration that February in the house in Covent Garden for one of his little girls, who had a birthday. Lining the edge of the great stairs were the presents her father bought for her: boxes of ribbons, a satin kirtle, two rag dolls, and a set of linen sheets in preparation for the day when she would, as a young woman, be betrothed. Through the double doors of the parlor the dancers could see into the library, where the lord Strafford sat with his head resting on his hand, in consultation with two messengers of the king who had come on urgent matters.

from the Lord Lieutenant of Ireland, Thomas Lord Strafford, Dublin, to Master and Mistress Cooke of Cripplegate Ward, the month of March in the year of Our Lord 1640

I have just these three hours returned from opening the Irish Parliament, and have writ as duty bade me, first at great length to his most gracious Majesty and then at some lesser length, with humorous comments (one or two scatological), to our William Laud. Now I can write to you, and have kicked off my shoes to do so and put on my oldest slippers. My girls are even at this moment playing under the table at which I write. I shall complete this and give it with the two other letters to my brother, who will deliver it by his own hand.

News could not be better! The Irish Parliament received me wholeheartedly, addressing me like a Solomon, and mayhap they thought I was, with my great train carried by lads and my own son. My son hath said I looked a fair handsome fellow, and my wife hath kissed me and brought me my dressing gown. What more can one ask? To make short of my report (the good Laud will have a fuller one and tell you more), the speeches went on and on, and they have granted many subsidies for the King. They have also agreed to raise an army for his Majesty by May to employ against the Scot. Clergy and everyone are with me. I thank God humbly on my knees each day that my work hath been for something. It maketh it all seem but little to have it come to this great matter. And now I am coming back to harder work, but with God's mercy I shall do well.

In April the English Parliament convened. Nicholas was walking through the gardens of the Dean of Westminster a few days later when he came across Harvey in intense conversation with some men from the court. He left off at once, and hurried over to his friend. "Very bad news, Nicholas!" he said gravely. "I've sent word to thy house just this hour by one of the choristers. Tom's here, but not well at all. He crossed from Ireland in terrible weather, with a bloody flux, and was ill and feverish by the time he reached Chester. They brought him by litter."

"From Chester?"

"Aye, and he's in his house now, where he cannot stand at all. His fever's so high he hardly knew me. Damn the man."

He hardly saw the elegant house, or the marble floors of the vestibule, or the secretaries and servants who rose in respect as he came through the door. Tom's son hurried down the steps at the sound of his voice, and taking him entreatingly by the fingers, led him up again past the portraits of monarchs and his sisters which lined the stair.

Strafford was lying in his heavy four-poster bed behind white hangings embroidered with scenes of a hunt. He opened dull eyes slightly at Nicholas's touch and tried to smile. "I do badly," he said in a cracked voice. "I don't do well at all. Still, the King came to see me . . . stood across the room there near the wardrobe with my court clothes . . . said, 'My friend, how dost?' " He began to mumble about the seas, and curse, rolling his shoulders as if fighting a bad dream.

"Why didst come from Ireland so ill?"

"Dost think I'd stay away?"

Nicholas shook his head. He began gently to move his hands over his friend's feverish body and to question him. Then he had the braziers filled hot with coals, sent for warm water perfumed with roses, and, wringing a cloth, began to wash the sick man. The Earl obeyed, allowing his limp arms to be lifted. He sighed like a child as he was turned, washed, dried, and dressed in a clean linen shirt. All the time the boy kept the water warm and gazed reverently at the physician.

Strafford murmured, "Now I must get up."

"Canst not. I should have come to Ireland with thee; I should not have left thy side. What ails thee? A hot distemper and much else, and I see by these reports you've had bleeding and purging enough. Shalt have something to ease the fever, but more, something to make thee sleep, for that's what's needed. List to me, Tom! I do not care two pins if Parliament meets without thee."

"Ah . . . I do! The rebellion must be crushed and money raised," groaned the sick man, heaving about as if quilts and pillow would argue with him and he must answer them. "Nick, dost not understand! The Lords have convened for two days and I'm here . . . Christ's blood, I have worked my life for this and I am here!"

"Canst sit?"

"They meet and vote without me!"

"Canst sit?"

"Mayhap . . . no, God's wounds, never mind it! I sat before for some time, ask the lad. I sat fairly."

"And then what occurred?"

"I know not; I am told I fainted."

"Indeed. What sort of pricklouses hast for physicians that they cannot tie thee down to thy bed?"

Tom muttered resentfully, "No one can keep me: 'tis not their faults. Neither could you, knowst well. Must help me dress, Nick. I am getting up now."

"Tom, shalt not."

"What does it matter what happens to me? The Lords meet, and I'm here."

He pushed the blankets aside and tried to take his leg from the bed but fell forward into Nicholas's arms. "I can do nothing for thee," the physician cried, grasping the tall, heavy body. "Tom, what dost? What dost?"

Strafford fell back with a groan; Nicholas doused the candles, locked the door, and sat down beside him. The delicate boy had climbed gently upon the bed and had begun to stroke his father's hair as if it meant all the world to him. Nicholas took his friend's hand and held it until he slept at last, while all the time, below, the messengers from the court walked through the halls.

He did not leave the house, and on the second day Cecilia came, and sitting brusquely beside the bed as well, began to read aloud the day's dispatches on Parliamentary proceedings. Strafford listened carefully, muttering now and then or clenching his fist in anger. Late at night he asked to hear of the friends. He was amused to learn about Dobson's escapades and concerned that Keyes's eldest daughter had been disappointed in love. Nicholas told him also that Bartlett had been elected to Commons for the city, and had now left off physicking and lived wealthily on money inherited by his wife. They gave large gatherings, and many of the more influential men in London began to congregate there, determined to stand for their rights and concede the King nothing unless he met their demands. Tom heard these things grimly and nodded. Washed again, he slept peacefully that night.

Two days later on a spring morning which was so fair that it seemed there had never been one like it before, the Earl of Strafford's carriage arrived before the House of Lords. As he climbed slowly down, leaning upon his son, he looked towards the building with an inexplicable joy. Then his face grew stern, and he went inside.

Apprentices and dockhands had begun to gather about Old Palace Yard. Nicholas did not know how much they knew concerning the matters discussed within the two chambers of old Westminster Palace. He did not know if they were aware of the names of many of the Lords, or if they were familiar with any of the industrious men who had made good fortunes from mines or fenlands or shipyards or coal pits and who now sat in Commons for their shires. The people milled about the yard, resentful for their own reasons, and soon there were quarrels enough for the sheriff's men to be sent frequently to keep the peace.

Each day the crowds grew. They were boys and men and sometimes women: bone thin or heavy-bodied, recently without work or long employed. The Lords arrived by ferry or carriage, hurrying with their attendants through the peddlers and beggars. Half the barristers of the city inns seemed to stand about the doors of Westminster Hall.

During the second week of Parliament, Nicholas and Keyes were walking towards Aldermanbury in the middle of an afternoon when they passed the Mitre Tavern and went in for a glass. Notices of shares to be had in ventures overseas were nailed to the wall, along with others of the execution of a thief and a house to be let on Milk Street for six pounds a year. Few men were about, and the barkeep was picking loose bones from the straw floor rushes. "Ha, Cooke!" he said, standing and adjusting his belly under his apron. "We don't see you these present days! I could close my doors for all you come!"

Keyes sat down to one of the foreign newspapers with a sigh. "Let me have ale, master," he said contentedly.

The barkeep served them, slopping the drink and wiping it with a rag from the table cracks. "Art much busy, master parson, eh?"

"I am."

" 'Tis quiet now, but of an evening one could not hear the trumpet announcing the Resurrection for the chatter! Aye, aye, these are controversial times, and men have much to say concerning them!" He wiped again, adjusted some of the papers which fluttered from the wind under the door, and stationed himself by the bar with his arms crossed, staring at them.

"Aye," he said, as if to himself. "They talk so much I know every word of what happens in Parliament! Most men do. They say Parliament offered Charles Stuart many subsidies but refused to grant any of them until he had settled the many grievances of his eleven years of solitary rule! John Pym, who leads Commons, will uphold men's rights! 'Tis true?"

Nicholas looked up from his paper. "Marry, I think it may be; I know not," he said in a dreamy voice.

The barkeep opened his arms congenially as if to embrace them. "Know not, master parson! But surely thou knowst if any man about this parish does. Art not sworn friends with his lordship Strafford, he who is so fond of kingship?" The corner of his mouth sneered slightly.

Keyes lowered his own paper and looked at the barkeep somewhat bewildered, thrusting back his pale hair and stretching his great legs as if he were not sure he wished to remain so comfortably there.

Nicholas said gently, "What mean you, Harry?"

"Knowst him if any man does."

"Mayhap."

"Ah! But why would the good parson know such a man and eat at his table? It's said he steals from men, dishonors his wife, plans an overthrow of the English government. These words are plainly spoke here each night, and we are, knowst, loyal men of fair intelligence, though I myself have but little Latin."

Nicholas was astonished to find his hands were trembling. "Enough

. . . enough! What fools are ye?" he muttered. The papers on the wall fluttered as he violently opened the door with Keyes at his heels and left, the ale hardly tasted on the table and the foreign journals opened where they left them.

News was shouted from Westminster to the Tower. Charles Stuart, who could get no monies granted from Parliament, had dismissed both houses. They had sat but three weeks.

Sailors and apprentices rushed through the streets shouting and beating drums. Some freed a few of their fellows from the Fleet by breaking in with staves and knives. Rocks were thrown through windows: a housewife near the river was struck in the side of the head and fell down bleeding on the bank, where her children later found her. Cecilia, who had been delivering some papers to Tom's house, hurried home by alleys alone because she could find no carter to take her. It was here and there, put down and breaking out again, she said.

The brawling passed as quickly as it had come, and the streets were once more filled with little girls selling flowers, and processions on the water. Then on a day in May it began again.

Nicholas and Harvey were attending a criminal's autopsy in Barber-Surgeons' Hall when the sound of drums and shouting made the surgeons put down their knives. Shopkeepers along Monkwell Street rushed into the lanes, aprons tied about them, and the cabinetmaker's boy turned with wide face pale and shouted, " 'Tis cried they're rioting in Westminster, sir! The mob hath stormed Lambeth Palace and killed a man there."

And Nicholas answered, "Lambeth Palace! Where's the Archbishop?"

Half the city lined the banks and the other was upon the water; from the spaces between a few derelict, burned houses on the bridge, apprentices leaned over the river, wool caps on short-cut hair, jeering at the ferries below and throwing stones. One ferryman glanced nervously over his shoulder as he glided past, while two large ships bearing wines from Portugal moved serenely among the smaller craft. A woman on the bank was wringing her wash with two dirty children beside her. The two physicians found a ferry at last.

"Whither, gentlemen?" cried the boatman.

"Lambeth, by God!"

Hastily he rowed from the bank, the passengers shading their eyes against the sun to stare up at the boys sitting in the windows of the derelict houses on the bridge, broken bricks in their hands, which they continued to hurl down, their voices fading in and out of the wind. "Papists! Whoremasters!" Several fell close by.

The ferryman rowed to the center of the water, muttering, his elbows as close as possible to his body. Nicholas cried, "What news of William Laud?"

"Nay, I know not!" Standing and cupping his hands to his mouth, Nicholas shouted the question to other ferrymen as they passed, but they shook their heads as well. They were approaching the wharf of the low-lying brick palace on the south side, where they saw two ferries belonging to the King's guard. Along the embankment and looking from the windows of the gate towers were the young soldiers themselves, muskets over their shoulders. The Archbishop's barge was not there.

Nicholas shouted, "I am physician to his lord's grace! Is he within and unharmed?"

One of the captains also cupped his mouth and replied, "Escaped to Whitehall, though mayhap wounded." At Harvey's shout the ferry turned, and made its way towards the great buildings of old Westminster Palace, the halls and courts, and the crowds of hundreds and hundreds who had gathered on the bank. Every merchant and craftsman had come into the streets, and they could barely make their way. The sentry at the Holbein gate touched his hat briefly at the doctors' approach and motioned them through into the yard full of royal mounted guard and palace servants. Some of the women were weeping.

Within the doors several men stood to stop them, and then an usher who knew Nicholas took his arm and hurried them both through the rooms. "They killed a man, a Catholic, didst hear?" he whispered.

"They killed him for sport. For sport, may Our Lord have mercy on his soul...." Laundresses and undermaids, many weeping, stood by the walls wringing their aprons in their hands, huddling in the corners near doors. At the top of the stairs, the great doors to the banqueting hall were open, and a group of ushers, courtiers, and clergy huddled in a circle towards the throne. The physicians pushed their way through with little courtesy.

The Archbishop was half reclining on a folding camp bed which someone had brought in. One young deacon was pulling off the wet boots, and other nervous pages thrust into each other in their hurry to get to and from the room with messages or warmed wine. William Laud's anxious voice cracked as it rose to the ceiling panels. "They've hurt someone, I heard his cries . . . this is terrible, terrible. Had he a family? They had staves and knives and beat him to death. They beat him to death, ah, ah!" Hunching his shoulders, he covered his face with his hands and rocked back and forth.

In a moment Nicholas had taken a blanket from one of the pages, and dropping to his knees, he began to spread it over the legs of the prelate, saying, "My lord's grace." He took Laud's hands and kissed the palms, then gently encircled the wrist with his fingers to count the racing pulse. The Archbishop's hose were wet, and his teeth chattered. Nicholas called sharply, "Lads, run to the kitchens for hot beef broth and a heated brick wrapped in thick cloth."

The Archbishop looked up and about at the faces which surrounded him, repeating the same words again and again. Had the miscreants been taken? Who had told the poor man's wife? "Who did these things?" he demanded, lifting his chin. "Have they a conscience?" The grey eyes flashed and the voice rose of an indignant, bitter old man in cracked, uneven sentences.

" 'Twas the boys," said the Bishop of London gently as one of the pages hurried forward with a silver tankard of beef broth on a tray. " 'Twas the boys, my lord's grace. They want to be governed by no monarch and ministers, to answer to no church, to answer to no one at all. Like their masters they'd make their own laws. They would tell the monarch what he must do, good my lord's grace!"

"But one cannot tell a king what he must do!" the Archbishop cried in a high, excitable, fragile voice. "My lords and masters! A king is ordained by God."

It was a time before he would drink the broth, into which Nicholas had mixed some soothing herbs. In a voice cracking with exhaustion, he murmured, "I am so frightened . . . 'twas like my dreams. God help me that I fear so much."

Voices died away outside the palace walls but for the guards, and ushers came in several times to report that the yard had been cleared and some of the trained bands had come to restore peace. Several ministers of the King had come in, as his Majesty himself was not at home. Nicholas stood, surprised to find his knees trembling.

William Harvey took his elbow. When they found a ferry towards the city once more, they saw that the banks had been cleared of the wild boys and the graceful boats sailed down yet again towards the sea between the swans. Kites and ravens perched on the houses of the bridge and hesitating but a moment, flew up to the beautiful blue sky, glittered in the sun, and were lost from view.

Shortly after, the boy William climbed to Avery's room one evening after coming home from friends.

The quilting was laid neatly across the empty chest, the bookshelves clear but for a few tattered volumes on the city. His manuscript with all its endless corrections and amendments had been left in a box by the wardrobe. Laid on top of it was a letter.

I have gone to Plymouth and will sail to the New World. Embrace our friends for me. Art a good man, Nicholas: you are all good men, as I hope before Our Lord also to be. May we all in His wisdom remain so. My deepest love to thee: kiss Cecily and the boy.

Avery

Keyes could not believe it when told him; he felt for the portrait of the sovereign which he wore always about his neck, turning back to his work in the shop crowded with colored leather, inks, and unbound books. "Avery!" he muttered, wiping his eyes. "That dark, savage place! My youth's gone now. Oh heart's friend, Avery!"

FIVE

The General

EVERYONE ABOUT THE CITY KNEW THAT THE LORD STRAFFORD WAS ONCE again so ill that it was uncertain if he would recover. Sometimes he did not understand where he was, and then wept to find himself a prisoner in his chambers and fought the friends who had come to sit with him with what strength he had. The treaty with Spain was lost, he shouted, and they could only rely on citizens in England and the Irish army and funds to help them in the war, and nothing would be done if he could not go forth. He damned both Lords and Commons with rich, plentiful Yorkshire invective. For a time he was delirious, but when he could even grasp at consciousness, he called for Cecilia and demanded that she read the dispatches which came every few hours from Whitehall.

"You must make my body obey me, Nicholas!" he shouted.

"Fool, I cannot if you do not do what I say!"

"You want to ruin me, yes, that's it. Hast never been for me, hast tried to hold me back . . ."

"Ah Tom, in Our Lord's name!" answered Nicholas. He was greatly disturbed on other matters, for Harrington, who was not a well man, had mustered ten soldiers and left for the north to fight for his country, wearing at his side one of the swords which had hung so long in his vestibule. In addition he spent many hours pacing Avery's empty chamber, going in mourning heavily, as the psalm says. It did not seem like his house without his congenial, intelligent friend walking above. A physician scarcely known to him had come to take over Avery's part of the work, and Nicholas did not quite trust him.

The dispatches from Whitehall were troublesome, and Cecilia would have hidden them but that the Earl always knew when one had come, and spoke scathingly to her to read it. So it was that as he lay there dry with fever and hoarse with another uncontrollable weeping spell he learned that the Earl of Northumberland, who directed the army, was ill and the other generals could not hold the territory. Nicholas understood his friend was possessed with a violent melancholy and wished once more for Avery, who understood these things. News that the King himself had left for the north came on the worst day.

The royal messenger arrived just when the sick man could walk on the arms of friends to the window and back. Now he sat in the window seat overlooking the piazza, passing his hand over his chafed lips. "I am wanted to go to him," he said. "I am to direct the armies. What know I of such things? I am a councillor, no general. Still I will go." He began to heal. He was courteous again, and thoughtful of them. He kissed their hands and begged pardon if in his illness he had said anything to offend them. He asked for their prayers. And when he was scarcely able to walk unaided, he left with an escort of several carriages for the north to join the King.

The city was quiet once more, though there were guards about Whitehall, and small gatherings here and there of the same out-of-work sailors and discontented boys. Three here, four there: nothing that they had not seen. Two apprentices had been executed for their parts in the riots, and, as several men in the Mitre said, they well deserved it. Nicholas, who had gone there to make peace, was of this opinion.

Puritan preaching was once again forbidden, and this time the law was strictly enforced. One night soldiers for the ecclesiastical courts broke into the lower room of the Fishmongers' Hall with their pikes and routed the men gathered, heckling and coercing them to their homes. Three more families moved from the parish. For the first time one of the empty pews in St. Mary Aldermanbury stayed that way. William Laud had frightening dreams, and Nicholas made potions to help him sleep.

Strafford did not write, but reports of him came through Laud and messengers who traveled back and forth. The Earl had thrown himself into his new work with all the passion of his life, yet things were more difficult than he had ever expected. His gruff, harsh manner in whipping the English forces together made him enemies whichever way he turned. Still he could not keep the Scottish forces from crossing the Tweed and occupying Durham and Northumberland. The promised Irish army never arrived. One event tumbled on the other one, and the war faltered, stumbled, and came to a halt.

A council of peers was called in York in September. They urged for a treaty and that Parliament be called to raise the compensation money that the Scots were demanding. The whole of England, they said, ranted and grumbled for this contest to have an end. Almost every peer who met despised the war, and as they could not bring themselves to despise the King, blamed the Earl of Strafford for it all. Nicholas only knew that his friend was ill yet again. Once he packed his things to join him, and then hearing he was better and being badly needed at home, did not go. Still he brooded.

Fall came to London; heat and discontent lingered. It was all over, wherever he looked. Like a crack in a building which is nothing one day and more the next: like a sturdy ancient wall which had to everyone's astonishment begun to crumble. There were letters on church doors against the clergy, writing on the city gates, papers on horseposts and tavern boards. There were angry landowners, muttering men in Old Palace Yard, surly boys. He seemed to hear them through his wall. They sang bitter ballads against Tom; he heard them through the doors. The King had taken the goldsmiths' lot from the Tower in a forced loan to support his war. It could not in the end be the sovereign's fault, but that of his servant, Strafford.

Towards the middle of October when the physician was closing his dispensary for the day, Keyes rode down the lane and came quickly inside, shutting the door behind him. "Nick," he stuttered, "Parliament's called and his Majesty's returned and sent for Tom and swears to his safety."

Nicholas did not sleep at all and at dawn wrote to Yorkshire by the scanty light which came between the roofs of the closely grouped houses of his lane:

to the Earl of Strafford, West Riding, from Nicholas Cooke, physician

My friend,
    I am uneasy for thee; hast too many enemies. Do not come.

       Nick

Six days later an answer was returned:

    Thanks for all your most loving care of me and your prayers, but I cannot answer your request as you would like it. I am to London, with more danger beset, I believe, than ever man went with out of Yorkshire; yet my heart is good and I find nothing cold within me. To the best of my judgment we gain much rather than lose. I trust God will preserve me.

       Strafford

THE

FIFTH
PART
1640–1642

ONE

The Arrest

THE BOY WILLIAM WAS ELEVEN YEARS OLD.

Now and then when in the church sacristy over the years he had taken down the heavy book of records and found his own baptismal date written in his father's hand. It puzzled him that he could not remember the serious occasion with the cool water and himself bedecked with heavy lace garment. He did not understand how there could be a time when he did not recollect things. The only reality was what he knew: the broken cobble on the corner of Huggin Lane before St. Michael's Church where he had once found a silver penny, the clank of the door of the coal brazier in his schoolroom, the sickly soldier's widow who had taught him letters, Alexander, the watchmaker's lad, with whom he had fought once and now loved more than anyone. His father's hands, which blessed the bread and stroked him from childhood illnesses; his mother's low singing voice when he could not sleep:

"Western wind, when wilt thou blow,
The cold rain down may rain.
Christ! that my love were in my arms
And I in my bed again."

His first memory was of clambering to his father's brown wool breeches to stroke his mustache, and the solid feeling of the physician's thighs under his own sharp knees; his second was of riding fast on the shoulders of slender Andrew Heminges over the bridge, turning his face as they jostled along to stare greedily at the vast river which rushed from under the narrow arches ever towards the sea. His Uncle Dobson said the boy should be a barrister and serve the crown; William, however, intended to be a physician and a priest like his father for he assumed if a man was one, he must be the other. He thought of this each morning as the bells woke him and he knelt sleepily on his bed to see from his window once more how the early, cold light which precedes dawn hung over steeples and rooftops as if it would never change. He could see just the edge of the physician's worn, faded sign swaying in the breeze.

Harvey often said he was like his father: the way he compressed his lips when concentrating, and how he walked rapidly, head bent slightly forward, as if weighed with complex thought. Even William's hands were large and had Nicholas's delicacy of touch. The slightly angular nose, however, was from his mother. The boy thought of these things as he gazed at his reflection in glass. The streets stretching out as far as he could see were also part of him: puzzled, he sometimes wondered how all these things could be within him, and yet he could be himself and that alone.

On this cool November evening with its dusty smell of coal smoke lingering about the streets he hurried home from school, threw his books down on the parlor table, and rushed up to his room to kneel on his bed by the open window. It was an evening he had waited for, though perhaps he did not know it. He longed for things and then forgot them again: still when they returned it was with such intensity that he could not admit they had ever been from his mind.

From the kitchen below he could hear the housekeeper laying out a number of pewter mugs and plates for the science society. For a moment other thoughts took him, of friends, of the rising cadence of one of Cicero's orations, of a flat-chested girl with blond braids wound upon her head who he sometimes saw drawing water from the fountain when he was on his way to school. Then he resumed his vigil, gazing down the street, whose drying leaves rustled against the parched wood of the overhanging houses and caressed the tops of shop signs. Autumn! There was a poem he had heard of it, now forgotten, and for a moment his eyes darkened as he tried to bring it to mind.

A single horseman had turned down the lane; the sloped, brimmed, feathered hat obscured the rider's face, but the boy's heart leapt, for he knew the shape of his shoulders. He was coming: the rapid note sent over which the boy had perused many times that morn before he had run off to school had made a promise which was this time kept. William leapt from the bed, thrusting his shirt into his breeches; he wanted to rush down the stairs and throw himself into the horseman's arms, and yet he hesitated. Perhaps the visitor was as busy as always and would have no time to speak with him: then it would be a shame to display how ardently he had waited. Thus he came into the little hall and looked with compressed longing towards the round stair.

Purposeful footsteps came across the floor and then made a creaking sound on the first step. William was for that moment unable to move. With a blur of feeling he saw the lithe, tall figure striding towards him. Giving a full shout, the boy rushed at him, flinging his arms about the black doublet and shouting triumphantly, "Tom!" In a moment the Yorkshireman had lifted him, and he looked closely at the tender, dark eyes before burying his face in confusion in the man's shoulder. His heart fluttered with joy.

"I thought . . . shouldst have no time to come, my lord."

"Would I not come to thee? But art heavy enough for a soldier! Hast grown, peaspod!"

"Hast truly from the wars? Art well?"

"I am from the wars, such as they were, and am middling well," was the thoughtful reply. Then slowly and with some stiffness, the lord Strafford lowered him to the floor and looked about the room as if he could not believe he was there. The arrogance in his face melted as he gazed with some boyishness at the wooden soldiers which had fallen into a heap in the corner of the room. He asked, "What's this battle, sweet heart?"

"Before my cat got into it, 'twas Agincourt."

"Ah! Dost not play out our armies against the Scots?"

The boy answered seriously, "Nay, I don't know the strategies of this present war."

"Nor, lad, did I," replied Strafford dryly, "though by Christ's wounds, I was supposed to!" He rested his arm on the boy's shoulder for a moment and then, sitting on the cot's edge with his hands on his knees, studied him.

William asked, "Wilt stay long this time, Tom?"

"Mayhap. Now tell of thee, lad! Our good Archbishop hath reported shalt be a fine scholar."

They sat closely on the cot and talked of books. The boy remembered all their times together, and how last winter Strafford's son had walked with him and they had spoken of the acquisition of power and the necessity of that to men. He recalled as he sat now with the Earl the reproduction of his portrait which hung in the hall in a dark place, so that you had to hold up a candle to see it clearly. The expression was almost scornful: he always tried to find in that depiction the generous, amusing northern lord who had sent him presents over the years and whom he had known all his life.

"Did thy son not come, Tom?"

"Nay, he bides in York with my wife, his stepmother."

"I'll write him."

"Yes, give the letter and I'll send it with mine own."

They spoke further, and then with the sound of voices and hearty laughter below, William said wistfully, "Hark, Tom, they've come. Hast seen my father?" He bit his lip, as if debating his next confidence, and then, throwing back his head manfully, said in a lower, older voice, "He's much worried for thee."

Nicholas had expected Tom, since a longer letter to him had also been sent over that morn; he had turned the pages slowly, receiving the words of his friend's sudden arrival with a sense of growing heaviness, and could not put them from his mind all that day. Now when he came from the dispensary, unfastening his apron, he was so deep in thought that for a moment when he saw the fellows, he forgot the small meeting and wondered why they had come. There were Keyes and Dobson laughing by the hearth, and Harrington, who had recently returned from the war with many stories, and was now sitting in the coffer chair, heavy hands drumming on his knees, impatient to tell more of them. Dobson had thrown his burgundy feathered hat across the room, where it had landed on the keg of salted herring, and Cecilia was emerging from the cellar with wine.

Though Nicholas greeted them in warm murmurs, he was more aware of the footsteps which came from above and his son's eager voice. Strafford descended buoyantly, one of his long slender hands, which even the Queen had called "les plus beaux mains du monde," grasping the boy's. He was obviously once more in pain from the gout, for he came slowly, his dark clothing adorned only with the blue ribbon of the Order of the Garter. Nicholas studied him closely, and then bit his lip and looked away.

The men pushed forward, teasing, belligerent, and warm to greet him. "God speed thee, my lord," said Keyes stoutly with a smile, taking the Yorkshireman's hand between friendship and respect.

Harvey looked at him critically. "What hast done to thyself, eh, Strafford?" he barked.

"I think I may not be dust yet, Harvey," was the soft response.

"Why here and not at Whitehall?"

"Oh, I shall be there in the morn with his Majesty before I go to the

Lords. Now I've come because you're dear to me, and I don't know myself in the city until I'm here." He looked down for a moment almost angrily. Then his voice brightened. "Sist in Commons now, Bartlett? I wish thee well."

"My lord is kind."

"Givst me not my name, Harry?" was the studied reply, and then he turned away. "What, Cecily, no kiss for the general come home? My wife sends fond greetings, as do the children, and hopes to come soon to see thee!"

They drew about the table with a scraping of benches. Nicholas invoked the blessing and they all began to eat, but though they spoke of several things, each seemed to fade away in moments. The boy William looked about, feeling a creeping, dull anxiety under his ribs which he could not understand. He was seated close to his father, and every now and then raised his youthful eyes to his face, but could read little there. He wished he could be yet upstairs on his cot which overlooked the streets talking to Strafford of northern topography or his son's studies.

Dobson reached for the bread. "So, Strafford!" he said buoyantly. "Comst late to Parliament, and we've made havoc without thee. Passed a bill just yesterday that they can't be dissolved again without their own consent. Bad-tempered lads they are. I went once, and else stayed away with my own work."

At once the talk opened, and everyone began to speak of laws and lawgivers, the petitions from about the country of dissolute clergy, the muttering against the Archbishop, and so forth. It continued in a rising clamor until Keyes himself was shouting to be heard with the cry of "Gentlemen! Gentlemen!"

Harvey put down his mug so hard that the contents splashed and ran down the old boards of the table. "Hath our society come to this?" he said sternly. "Do we examine and wonder over fossils and the best method of telling the longitude of a ship at sea? No . . . of what do we speak more and more? Laws and lords. Bills and petitions, pah! A piss on them! For what purpose in all this world have we come together? I waste my time here: give me leave to go."

"What, will give us up?" Harrington barked. "Shouldst not live a day, a week, without us, thou bag of herbs! When our souls have gone to heaven he will badger the sexton for our poor mortal bodies and dissect each into little fragments of bone and sinew. . . ."

"Go to!" muttered Harvey.

"Aye, coxcomb, 'tis so . . . shalt dissect us all! And what will he look for, this great doctor? I'll tell thee! For what hath made us differ, I to the wars and thou mealworms here safe in thy beds!" He banged his stick thrice on the floor and looked about with a wide, satisfied grin for approval.

Keyes shifted his broad shoulders. "Masters," he muttered, "he hath spoken right. Why must we talk of these other matters? They can't concern us and as always will come to nothing."

Bartlett, who had been silent during this, rose up all of sudden. " 'Will come to nothing!' " he repeated. "No, this time they shall not 'come to nothing.' The city's weary of its sovereign; the city's weary of his borrowing money, of tariffs, of taxes, of the Catholic Queen, of no representation, of the steady loss of its good citizens from the narrow-mindedness of its Archbishop. The city's weary of those who say the King's supreme and no one must cross him, and now Parliament's met you will all soon hear just how weary 'tis. . . ." His large white hands were trembling. "No, enough, enough! You may linger here all night; I, however . . . my lord of Strafford is wise to go about his business, and I must as well." Grasping his handkerchief, he dabbed it against his sweaty lips several times and his brow, and then seized his cloak and hurried from the room.

Dobson rose at once and, excusing himself, ran after him. Keyes and Harrington and Harvey remained, as did Cecilia, and the boy William, who looked still more anxiously into his father's face, stroking the knuckles of his broad hand as if there were power within it to undo the quarrel.

Strafford was silent for a moment. "What sayst thou, Nick?" he asked in his low voice. "For thy silence is louder than many a man's shouting."

"What say I?" answered Nicholas slowly. "So much I cannot put it into words. My heart's so heavy I can hardly move. What do I feel? Much, my friend. The city's full of hatred for thee, and yet comst here." He turned to look away at the hanging ropes of onions. "What say I? Take thy carriage now, and go home. . . . Dost cripple thyself, and I'll not watch it. There's little health left in thee. No, if you persist, Tom, I'll no more of thee. . . ."

He could feel his son murmuring and now stroking his doublet over the chest as if to calm him. Cecilia had folded her arms and stared at him forbiddingly. Abruptly Nicholas rose. "No matter what you all say," he cried, looking about at them, "this is where I stand. We're not as we were, and we cannot pretend to be that way anymore. I'd give all I have to have it back again. I don't understand these times, and I don't understand thee, Strafford. Hast said we are alike: we are not. We are different. . . . I could not do the things you have done: some of them leave me in horror. Yet I love thee and here's the dichotomy . . . more than this love, I want a life of peace. I do not think I ever influenced thee, though as a priest thou hast said now and then I have. . . ."

The Earl of Strafford listened with arms folded and lowered head; his face, under the shadow of his broad-brimmed black velvet hat, could not be seen. He did not move.

Nicholas was trembling. "I cannot bear what hast chosen," he said, his voice curiously light. "Comst here an thou wilt to see my wife and son, but do not seek me. Let us be parted." His voice rose, and he walked up the steps and shut his chamber door.

He woke aching and listless far later than usual the next morning, resentful and full of swollen grief beneath his ribs as if he had been beaten. In the kitchen and parlor, the glasses and plates remained. Cecilia had gone out.

Strangely quiet were the parish streets that grey November day. William, whose school was on holiday, hurried uneasily down from his sleeping chambers to the dispensary and asked if he might go with his father's new apprentice towards Westminster to deliver letters or medicine parcels. The whole city had turned out there yesterday, the boy explained, for he'd heard it in school, and today there would also be the trained bands for inspection by the King. Even Andrew Heminges had put away his playscripts and was carefully rubbing his company flag with bread crumbs to clean it.

Nicholas scarcely heard his son, and after a time realizing the boy's anxiety, sat down with him to ask him of his school and other matters. Of the Lord of Strafford he did not speak; he could not bear it.

Rain pattered on the roof: women drew their shawls over their hair as they went towards the market, and small puddles formed between the street cobbles. Rain darkened the stones of the churchyard and wet the shoulders of his cassock as he walked from church to kitchen door after prayer. He finished his letters, marked the corked bottles and wrapped packets of tonics and herbs with the owner's names and proper dosages, and packed all into a basket.

The boys rushed off cheerfully. By four they had not returned.

It was at that time with the short day beginning to fade into the stones when Nicholas, walking home from Old Fish Street Hill, noticed that a crowd had gathered. It was thickening rapidly all along Cheapside, huddled in doorways, about the conduits, and even into the street so that coachmen trying to make their way leaned over and spat curses on the wool-capped heads of apprentices and boys.

"What news?" he cried to one lad.

"The lord Strafford's coming this way from Westminster!"

"This way? Whither does he go?"

"They've impeached him: he's sent to the Tower. The men of Commons did it, but 'twas the Lords demanded his sword."

"Of what accused?"

"Treason."

The boy threw back his head and laughed, and then was pulled aside by his friends and lost within the crowd. Men and women were pouring from alleys and tenements all along the ancient marketplace. Nicholas began to run in the direction from which the carriage should come, almost as if he had some plans to throw himself before it in the road and make it halt. Instead he found himself wedged against a cart of hay with fifteen or twenty women rushing up from the conduit to his left, skirts splashed with water. "Black Tom's come!" the stoutest cried, hugging her tin bucket. "My husband hath heard at the stationer's! And they've sent him where he deserves, and long ago should he have been taken up."

"Aye!"

"He counsels evil to the King. The Scottish wars must lie upon his head, for he began them, he and the Archbishop, as they have instigated every bad thing in this land."

Several small boys had climbed to the roof above and were lying across the beam on their stomachs. Then one squealed, "Masters, on your lives to the walls, for it's come, it's come . . . there, there!"

Along the cobbles rushed the huge carriage, its windows shuttered fast. Half standing and with gritted teeth and whip in hand was the coachman, driving on the six horses, their nervous heads uplifted, panting between large white teeth. The wheels slewed and skipped, throwing up the dirt of the streets, almost as if the carriage would fling the whole crowd before it. Men's voices rose. A small loose stone was thrown from the crowd at the vehicle, an egg, a bad apple. The cobbles after the rocking conveyance had gone were littered with eggshells and flattened onions.

Nicholas never ceased to run until he had come to his house. He found Andrew in the kitchen. The actor threw his musket and the buttoned jacket of his military uniform grimly across the rectory trestle table and sank in the inglenook chair. "Christ's wounds," he whispered. "My lord Strafford . . . Tom!"

"We must go to my brother," Cecilia said. "He'll know the truth of it all." She carefully put down her market basket and stepped forward. They would have gone at once had they not been concerned for the boys. Nicholas had just gathered his sexton to search for them when William and the apprentice called from the street and rushed breathless into the rooms, explaining that they had taken back streets for the crowds and carriages and sporadic fighting which had broken out in the lanes. They said they had passed Nan Keyes, who told them that the Sergeant Painter Van Dyck had put down his brushes when he heard the news and gone upstairs and shut the door.

William grasped his father's hand and said simply, "Dad, must get Tom from that place at once. Must go and do so, on my faith." He did not release the fingers for some time, tugging on them to show the importance of his words.

Early darkness had fallen. Ordering the housekeeper not to let the boys leave the rectory, Nicholas hurried to the mews for his horse and, taking Cecilia up before him, turned towards the Strand. The November night was cool and damp, and even the stone city markers smelled like the sea. Here and there in the houses down lanes and behind churches, candles glittered faintly behind small leaded panes. When they approached Dobson's house they saw a groom with a lantern waiting for them outside the walls. The lad was weeping.

They found Dobson in the library before the heavy book presses of scientific and classical texts; he had been drinking from a bottle of sack, and his handsome face closed at the sight of them. As his sister ran across the room to him, he flung up his hands slightly. "Tell me thou had naught to do with these matters!" she demanded. "Michael, on thy life, didst know of them?"

His voice unfocused for the sack and half turning away his face, he muttered resentfully, "I didn't know for certain! I . . . heard rumors, but I never thought they'd dare." He felt for his neck lace, and put it straight as if presenting himself. "Cecily, I'm not overly fond of Tom's ways and have made no secret of it. . . . I should call him Strafford, for God knoweth he now pays for that title and all other favors given!" Motioning them to sit, he threw himself into a chair, twisting one of his rings on his handsome fingers. "Commons hath proclaimed him a traitor," he said starkly, "and the Lords can do nothing but exclude and confine him as befits a gentleman and a lord until he's been properly tried." He hesitated and then added in a thick voice, "Bartlett voted against him."

"Bartlett?"

"There hath been no love between them, sister!"

Cecilia turned from him and began to pace the rugs between desk and table. "Very well then." She continued in a way sometimes sharp and sometimes confused, "We have one traitor among us. That's done. Now we must do something this moment. We cannot leave Tom there one night." Back and forth she walked, her face angular by the firelight, eyes fluttering as when she was deeply troubled.

Nicholas began to break wood and throw it into the fire. "Cecily," he said carefully, "the King hath promised his safety. Naught can be proved against him, for he's innocent; they can but hold him a time and let him go."

"Still, he must from that place before the morning."

Dobson had twisted his rings off, and then putting them in his pocket, stood. "It may take some more hours than this!" he said. "Many men of both houses are against him. He's ruled harshly these eleven years and made many enemies in the north and in Ireland who were there today."

Her dark eyes flashing, she demanded, "Wouldst have voted for this impeachment?"

"Nay," he said with some shame, and then, with a gesture of disgust, he picked up a goblet of some wine and hurled the contents into the fire. Cecilia had sunk into a chair, and he glanced about as if to find something to give her; he moved to ring for the servant, thought better of it, and passed his hand nervously over his handsome mustache.

She had begun to weep. "Cecily," he murmured.

Covering her face with her hands and rocking back and forth slightly, she gasped, "What canst know of me, either of you? What canst know of me? With these hands I would beat down the walls of the Tower if I could! Whatever I might do in this world I've been denied . . . Nicholas, knowst this and he knew. He knew. But it matters not, for I still can do nothing. Oh sweet Lord, I can do nothing to help him!"

Bewildered by her passion, Dobson repeated, "Our help may not be needed. Naught will be proven, for naught can be proven. He hath ever been a loyal servant of the King."

At the sound of footsteps from the wharf, Cecilia pushed both the men away and leapt up to open the window towards the Thames. The cold sea air of the November river blew the lace of her collar and the leaves of the late fall flowers in the vase. Voices came from the steps and the servant of the lord Harrington came into the room. Bowing several times and clutching his cap, he sputtered that his lordship had sent him first to Aldermanbury and then here to seek them, and that he requested the three to come without delay. He was so old that he could scarce get the message right.

Dozens of horses and grooms were already gathered before the brick house on Great St. Thomas Apostle Street. The old knight, his thick white hair flowing loosely in a sudden mad gesture towards reclaiming some former leadership, hurried forward to greet them. In the vestibule they passed many cloaks hastily thrown over chairs and the same portrait of Charles on the fading, blue-flocked wallpaper which had not been moved in sixteen years. By it were suspended on carefully arranged brackets Harrington's collection of swords and rapiers, some of which he yet used in fencing practice.

A number of prominent men from about the city were already gathered, some from the Lords and a few from Commons, as well as courtiers, barristers, merchants, and churchmen. The rooms were cold with the constant opening of the door, and the fire huddled against the grate whenever the wind met it. Aged servants carried bowls of hot spiced ale to the tables. A fist was slammed against a thigh, a curse rose above the voices up the stair. Men ate and drank greedily, not knowing that they did so.

"He went quietly, almost courteously."

"He couldn't have expected it."

"Some say he did and came anyway."

Harrington held up his broad hand, and the murmur of voices fell away. "My friends," he said, lingering on the words. "The accusations to my lord Strafford are each one more mendacious than the last. He hath raised the Irish army to subdue England! Nay, he raised it to come to England's aid. Why, I myself could defend this baseless accusation! God save our King, gentlemen!" He glittered, chest expanding, enjoying this moment. Nicholas, appalled, turned away.

More hot ale and pipes were brought round, and soon the pungent smoke filled the room. Oil lamps glistened on the edges of the portraits of the royal family. Harrington went about shaking hands and embracing friends. Then from a corner Harvey, who had come in some time before, said quietly, "Apprentices have made bonfires on the fields outside the walls. Mark also if thou wilt on the way home candles in windows. They celebrate approval of his lordship's fall, and servants here have told me some candleless windows have been smashed with rocks."

Turning to the old knight, Cecilia cried, "Look there, my lord, candles in thy windows! Out with them . . . even if the glass is smashed. What does it matter but that we stand beside him?"

The old man stared at her aghast. "They were but to light the way of these good men, my dame!" he muttered, flushing and ashamed; he suddenly seemed weak, and had no more words. He could only stare as she ran to the windows and blew out the flames, or snatched at them with her bare hands.

Nicholas came to her with her cloak, slipped it tenderly about her shoulders, and took her from the door. From streets away they heard laughter, and all down the lanes the smell of bonfires lingered in the cold air.

He knew when he awoke that the woman beside him had irrevocably changed. Something steady and hot burned within her narrow rib cage and in every minute altered her. She dressed without a word, and hurrying down the steps, went directly to the study table. From there she began to write letters to many of the members of both houses of Parliament and as many foreign ambassadors to convince them of the innocence and loyalty of the lord Strafford and urge their help in his immediate release.

They heard nothing from Tom himself, but news came from one of the warden's staff that they must not be concerned. In turn, they wrote his family in West Riding and urged them to have patience. Still nothing was as it had been about the rectory. William came home from school one day having had a fight with whom he would not say, and would not return. Close friends came each night, and did not leave under long after the midnight bells had sounded.

Early on a December morning, word came that members of the House of Commons had ferried across the Thames to Lambeth Palace the afternoon before and placed William Laud under arrest as well, taking him also to the Tower. When Nicholas hurried through the gatehouse of Lambeth, he found servants huddled in the kitchen and pantry, many of them weeping. For a time he searched the familiar grounds past stable, buttery, orchard, and fig trees for the Archbishop's chaplain. Finally he discovered a page in the crypt who told him that the old holy man had gone quietly and his chaplain, Malverne, had left on his heels for Parliament to see what could be done.

Taking Nicholas up the steps to the dressing room, the boy showed him three trunks of things he had just finished packing to be sent along to the Tower, including cassocks, vests, and sleeping shirts, plain caps and nightcaps, and a fur-lined robe against the cold. "The one he took with him isn't his warmest," he blurted. "I'm told it's bitter cold there when the wind blows from the river. He hath his diary with him and his prayer book, the one he wrote himself, and when they took him all the people came from the neighborhood and blessed him and said, 'God save your grace and may you soon come back to us!' They can't keep him long, master, think ye? For there's naught can be truly said against him. He prays seven times a day and honors the King."

Then, dropping his voice, the boy added, "Parson, there's something else I'd show thee!"

The library with its thousands of books rising to the ceilings lay in the soft light of early winter. There was the desk, with its unfinished letter and the quill pen, laid across a paper with the nib now dry. Nicholas corked the open ink. Then he looked across the polished floorboards and drew in his breath. The painting of William Laud which had been completed but a few years before lay facedown on the rug. "It fell," said the boy in a small voice. "He came in and saw it there."

"Was there a wind?"

"Nay, none . . . and look, the rope which held it's not broken or frayed, nor is the hook pulled from the wall. He said it was an omen. He was much frighted. Knowst how he is on these matters. Will you go to him, sir?"

"I will."

As he hurried past the buildings to the gatehouse, one of the kitchen women came running over the cobbles with a pair of knitted hose which she begged him to take to his grace. Nicholas tucked them in his satchel of medicines next to the Greek Testament he had noticed in the chapel and thought the Archbishop might want as well. Then he ferried across the waters once more towards Tower Wharf.

The entrance of the venerable fortress was well guarded by several young soldiers. Approaching them, he demanded, "I am physician to the Archbishop and must see him."

"No one may see him."

"He hath need of my care."

"Your forgiveness, sir, but no one may enter."

"At least say if he is well!"

"Well enough, we are told."

"You must let me through."

"I am sorry, but everyone is denied."

"Then, wilt send these things from his house servants with their respect and duty? And say that they are eager to greet him and kiss his hand once more."

The tallest shifted the worn straps of his leather helmet and replied in a bored way, "We will, master physician." Nicholas bit his lip. He would have liked to slap the man to his knees and cry out, "Art so ill taught to allow no veneration in thy voice when thou speakst of him!" Anger would be wasted there: it needed hoarding, to be used judiciously. He stood for a long time on Tower Hill looking towards the rooms where the Archbishop was held, murmuring "God save your grace, William Canterbury, and may you come back soon!"

TWO

The Trial

FRIENDSHIPS WORE RAGGED THAT WINTER, GAVE OUT IN THE SEAMS unexpectedly. All about, men took offense where none was given. A dull murmur of rage seemed to come from the back alleys and the stones. Crowds assembled. They milled about Old Palace Yard near Westminster even in the snow: little fires sprang up, around which gathered old sailors, vagabonds, dock workers, and the city apprentices who would or would not be beaten by their masters for loitering there.

Men stood about Paul's churchyard, arguing. Men argued in the taverns. Through the doors of the Mitre the shouting came so loud that it echoed down the lanes. Nicholas thrust open the doors and looked about, and then went on his way. He felt he could not bear it. The Archbishop's chaplain, Luke Malverne, sometimes came to spend an hour with him. He reported that the people of London had brought a petition to abolish bishops to Parliament with fifteen thousand signatures.

Christmastide came and passed, and February found the city poor, short of coal and wheat. People hesitated to spend: merchants' wares gathered dust. Ice hung from the overhanging houses. Parliament deliberated and waited: it argued petitions, it gave speeches, it muttered, and grumbled, and considered. And then in March it called the trial of Thomas Wentworth, Lord Strafford, in Westminster Hall.

Dawn had not yet broken, but a small crowd had already gathered to find a place on the public benches for the proceedings. Cecilia wore an enormous hooded cloak which so enveloped her tall, slender body that she might have been taken for a boy. Her dark eyes gazed about at the shabby soldiers who hung near the door. She stared contemptuously at their dirty hands, rusty, dented swords, and coats worn at the elbow as they spat and talked from the sides of their mouths. A living was what they wanted: the man on trial today had somehow prevented it.

By a horsepost stood a frail fellow, carrying a pole on which hung copies of the penny songs and newssheets. All about were small groups of apprentices, staves over their shoulders. Timothy Keyes, who had joined them, leaned his large body over hers and whispered closely in his innocent way, "I would his Majesty had let Scotland alone! Then he would not have needed the money and called this Parliament. Yet who am I to say? I am a craftsman, though I live hard by the courts!"

The crowd gathered until it swelled out to the lanes and alleys and mews on all sides of the yard, and the soldiers moved brusquely among them shouting for order. With a great creak of hinge and wood, the doors of Westminster Hall were opened, and they were pushed through with the others so violently that they almost fell to their knees. Barristers and apprentices, housewives and serving men shoved and shouted as the soldiers from the trained bands came stoutly to demand their courtesy. Nicholas scanned the faces of the guards. Andrew Heminges was not among them.

From the tightly crammed third tier of benches in which they had found places, he tilted back his head to look about. Bleachers had been erected of twenty rows or more rising steeply on either side of the hall. Below in two lines the Lords would convene with their stewards to attend them. A dais with a box for the accused so that he might face his judges stood to one end of the long space, with room for his staff behind him. Lord Arundel, who long had disliked Strafford, was Lord Steward for the trial. Commons, who by custom sat uncapped in the presence of the Lords, were placed behind the prisoner in rising rows. Across he saw Dobson, and near him Harrington, who was shouting at his servant. Many he recognized, many he did not. The great sweep of them made him almost dizzy.

At last the side doors opened and with guards before and behind, the prisoner, in a dark cloak and hood, was brought in. A hush fell about the hall. Nicholas leaned forward. The prisoner . . . could he be called such? Such a name was unrecognizable. At the moment he could recall nothing but how Strafford threw back his head and laughed when amused.

Unable to sleep last night, he had looked through the thick packets of Tom's letters over the years, until now certain paragraphs played like an old tune in his mind, with bits remembered and bits forgot.

> The God I know is merciful and saves us with His grace. This grace is at times given through the meeting of people, and thus I am somehow certain that our lives will be intertwined. Therefore may I say that I know thou wouldst fill thy arms with others as I do, and yet holdst back from fear—of what? Of loss? Loss will come, finding us even in a small room. Yet it doth not matter. I know this alone: that what we want as much as our lives we will surely, surely be granted the grace to obtain!

Strafford had taken off his hooded cloak. Under it he wore heavy robes against the cold and a close-fitting black fur-lined cap like an abbot's which gave him the air of a weary penitent. His only ornament was the insignia of the Garter on its blue ribbon. Nicholas leaned forward to watch him, and drew in his breath when he turned. Christ's wounds, the man had no more color than something kept in a dark hole year after year. Nicholas had sent him ointment against rheumatism, purges, syrups against congestion and cough; he had packed bottles in straw and taken them himself to the gate. The man was sick, and older; every vestige of youth was gone. Still, he stood proudly, and when he spoke his voice was clear.

More fragments of the letters filled his mind.

Is it fitting for a man to say to another, I know thy grief? By Christ's love I believe in friendship as one thing most divinely given. . . . Promise me in all thy life whatever comes thou wilt not cease to do what's fitting for thee: thy research, thy studies. And I shall go forward always to do my best, which is my vow, wherever it leadeth me.

Nicholas straightened. He said to himself, Well, lad! We shall soon have thee from this place and back in thy lands. Ah, quickly, quickly! To be carried in a litter to do the King's bidding and then be brought here like this . . . Tom, this cannot be right, by all that is holy. I love thee, Tom, in ways I shall never understand. Canst hear me, fellow?

His eyes burned with tears. Cecilia leaned forward with her hands clenched on her knee. Keyes had thrust his arm about her slight shoulders, but she seemed not to notice him.

All rose as best they could, for the King had come in.

He wore dark clothing and the Garter insignia, and his long melancholy face glanced about in disdain. A curtain had been hung to conceal him from the common gaze, and with one sharp gesture he tore it down. Then he sank resentfully into the red-upholstered chair. The ten-year-old Prince of Wales stood on the steps by his side and gazed curiously about the hall. Once he would have spoken, and his father hushed him.

The Lords hunched forward, muttering now and then to their pages or ushers. Lord Arundel stood, and his light voice rose out. "My lord of Strafford!" he called. "You will kneel, my lord, to hear the charges of treason set against you."

A murmur went through the hall. The Yorkshireman was motionless for a moment, and then turned towards his secretaries and barristers as if to understand what had been said. Then, resting his hands on the railing before him, he lowered himself painfully to his knees. Cecilia dug her fingernails into her palms; she had almost ceased to breathe.

The clerk of Parliament read out the accusations, with Mr. Pym and Arundel following with their own.

"My lord of Strafford, you have assumed regal powers to subvert the laws of England.

"You have misappropriated the revenue."

The accusations were long. Winds crept through the windows and rattled the hammerbeam roof; once a hardened tennis ball which had sequestered itself in one of the joints of the beams from some game played generations before fell to the floor and rolled under the defendant's box. Someone laughed unexpectedly. On either side, men munched meat and onions: cold, curling onion skin fell to their boots, and blew away when someone opened the door. They munched as they would at the bear baiting, and wiped their hands on their breeches. They blew their nostrils between their fingers.

Cecilia turned her face: her sharp delicate nose made a shadow against the edge of the hood. Nicholas felt for her hand.

"My lord of Strafford, you have encouraged papists in the overthrow of our country.

"You have brought in an army to subdue England.

"You have threatened Londoners to give you funds. You have advised the King to debase the coinage. You have betrayed on more than one occasion the English to the Scots."

The King leaned forward steadily, his lips parted, and the little Prince, by this time weary of the proceedings, sat on the throne step with the hair-stuffed ball which he had rescued and soundlessly rolled it between his feet. All the time the grey late winter sun moved across the sky, faintly permeating the windows, and the torches dipped and hissed, so that it was one place warm with them and another bitter cold. Cecilia had taken a small bound book from her packet, and holding it on her knee, she began to draw the man before her on the defendant's stand. Her dark eyes burned.

The light faded outside the windows, until it was nothing more than a memory and the torches alone cast shadow here and light there, and the lord Strafford seemed to bend his head lower and lower with weariness. Still the answers came clearly. Cecilia's pen had ceased, for they sat almost in darkness. When the session was closed and they came to escort the lord Strafford away, he looked up towards where they sat and smiled as if to say, Have courage! It will be well!

Stumbling slightly from having sat so long and from the cold, they were urged by the crowd through the door and found themselves standing in Old Palace Yard with night just come. There was no sign of the ballad seller; some of his papers, however, had been trampled and strewn across the yard.

Nicholas kissed his wife's hand. "How doth my love?" he said.

She stood with the wind bending the edges of her hood. She seemed something purified, like a bleached shell long lain at the foot of a cliff, or an old saint's statue left long in a forgotten woodland chapel. Hardly daring to touch her, he brought the edge of his hand up to her cheek.

"All shall be well," she said. They moved through the dispersing crowd, bid Keyes goodbye, and found a rocking boat to take them home.

Week after week the trial of Lord Strafford continued. Nicholas found himself unable to work; he turned his practice over to Harvey and went every day to Westminster Hall with Cecilia by his side.

He knew the faces of the men about the yard, the ushers, the servants and coachmen, and those of the houses who opposed and who upheld his friend. John Pym, the leading speaker from Commons for the prosecution, was a blunt, heavyset fellow who had long stood for the cause of conservative reform. With other members, he repeatedly brought forth the twenty-eight articles of the impeachment, only to have each carefully refuted and disproved by Strafford and his counsel. Again and again, Strafford stood and spoke, the long hands grasping the rail before him. He had never intended to overthrow the kingdom. He had raised the army to march against rebellious Scotland, never to subdue England. He had taken no bribes.

His judges continued to accuse him. Under their many words, their intention was as clear: they wanted to snuff out his power. If they could eliminate the King's best minister, they could then scrub clean the perquisites of royalty and have their way with ship money and the allocations for war and the disposition of the English armies. Nicholas understood that the trial was about many things, and few of them were as stated. There were centuries of resentment; there was resentment from long before any of them had been born.

The low voice of the lord Strafford rang out. "My lords, these accusations do I deny with all my heart. My lords, these things are not true, and you know it. You men who stand before me know they are not true."

He continued to refute everything, and all the while Cecilia sat motionless but for the hand which continued to draw what she saw before her: the benches of gentry and landowners, the guards, the sovereign whose face was obscured by his slope-brimmed hat, and the man who stood on the stand day after day defending himself. At times he remained seated because he could not stand and spoke that way. At times he seemed too ill to continue.

At home Cecilia pinned her drawings to the wall: there was the rapid sketch of the King, and the Prince of Wales at his feet. There were the Lords and Commons, the men of the city who had come to watch, the ushers, the servants who filled the coal braziers, the women in the yard. All was in light and shadow, for what she could and could not see. And in the center there was Tom in his close-fitting wool cap. They brought more medicines and a dish of meat pasties to the Tower guards and stood below the rooms where they knew him to be, and looked up joyfully towards his window. The whole city knew that the Earl of Strafford would not be defeated.

Spring began to creep up the steps of Westminster Hall. In the cool and yet brief daily sun, women in the back streets past the abbey hung sheets to dry. Cold and grey rushed the river down towards the sea: the end of winter was in sight.

Thomas Wentworth, Lord Strafford, spoke that day as he had never spoken before. For two hours he laid forth his innocence and his life of service and his love for his country. Only when he mentioned the name of his dead wife Arabella did he begin to weep. Cecilia sat motionless; she had ceased to draw. There was not a sound in the house, for the man they now knew had surely won his freedom by his eloquence.

Word came early the next morning in a hasty note from Lord Harrington. Parliament had decided to use the last weapon it possessed to take down the lord Strafford, by bringing an act of attainder against him. They had been unable to bring him down through impeachment; by an act of attainder, a majority of the Lords and Commons could vote that he was a danger to the safety of the kingdom and thus must be put to death.

The houses were barred to all but members that day.

Andrew stopped by the rectory to say that though he felt faint he had a difficult part to play that evening at Blackfriars, and he asked the physician to come. At six Nicholas took his packet and walked over with a heavy heart.

Up and down the carved theater galleries sat the ladies, their fair flesh glowing in the warmth of the coal braziers and the many brackets of candles. Boys moved among them with closed jugs of hot spiced ale and porcelain cups, and the sweet melodic music of the turn of the last century rose from viols earnestly played by the company musicians. Still, all was strangely subdued, as if someone held a secret he would not share. Parliament still sat, for not a member was here. He wondered how many other men did not know or care what play was given, for their thoughts were also two miles away in Old Palace Yard.

The prologue entered and the comedy began. A few people laughed at the quips, and from his seat he could see that Andrew was not well and might not last until the evening was done. Again Nicholas turned to the doors below to see if anyone had come in. Leaning forward, he opened his watch and then shook it next to his ear. The spring had wound down, and the hands did not go.

When the interlude came the peddler boys once more climbed the galleries with cakes and ale for sale, and pleased voices rose up with a whisper of words and laughter. The musicians had begun to play old "Wolsey's Wild" when the doors below opened and several members of the Lords came in. A hush fell over the theater as they took their places. Among them was Dobson, his fair brown mustache curled up at the edges. As he mounted the balconies with friends, someone said to him, "Stone dead hath no fellow," and laughed.

One woman cried out, "What news?"

"Commons have voted for the act of attainder by a wide majority. Lords vote tomorrow."

The musicians laid aside their bows, and from the doors within the proscenium arch the actors slowly came to the stage. Nicholas pushed his way through the gallery until he had reached Dobson's side. He did not understand what he saw on his friend's face. "You will defend him, Michael," he said.

"Dare not look at me like a preacher!" was his harsh whisper. "I want no sermons." The other men who had come in with Dobson looked at Nicholas with some amusement and shook their heads. Then Nicholas seized his friend's arms and cried, "Michael, for Our Lord's mercy! Wilt defend him?"

The handsome courtier flushed; he looked as if he had been drinking. "The devil with all of you!" he hissed. "I'm pulled this way and that . . . I am sick of the lot of you." He tried to pull himself free, and angrily felt with his hand for his sword hilt.

A cry rose from the audience, and when Nicholas looked down at the stage he saw that Andrew had stepped to the edge and cried out, "God save the King! God save his best servant!" Then he fainted. Several of the men were kneeling over him when Nicholas reached him, and the audience had begun to depart.

All night long they did not sleep.

Cecilia walked up and down the room, the boards by the bed creaking as she passed them, her arms folded over her dressing gown. Dobson had disappeared after the play, and when Nicholas had gone to his house, he found him not within. William, who had woken with nightmares again, was now in a deep sleep.

Somewhat past dawn they heard carriage wheels and ran down the lane to climb into a shabby coach which Harvey had borrowed for the day. Wheels splashing through the puddles of Cheapside, they descended towards the Fleet River and over the bridge towards Westminster, where the remains of the old palace rose up to the grey sky.

Across Old Palace Yard, young soldiers from the bands stood guarding the door of Westminster Hall. Rain fell down their hats and jackets, darkening the barrels of their muskets and soaking the surface of the thick leather pouches in which they kept their gunpowder. To the side were the carriages of the men who sat so early within, and edging ever and ever closer to the door under cloaks and shawls came the people: draymen, housewives, carpenter's boys, merchants, stationers, wax chandlers, barristers, ward constables, water carriers, school lads and their masters, cobblers and cottage weavers and old soldiers. By ten in the morning the crowd had swollen until it seemed no more could come. When at last the Lords emerged, they could barely pass through the assembly. A great cry rose and the city trained bands, forcing back the sailors and boys and shrieking women, using their fifteen-foot pikes as barricades, shouted, "In Christ's name . . . back, back!"

"Hath the Lords passed the bill?"

"They have and voted death. It wanteth now only the King's signature."

Tears were running down Harrington's face when he reached them. When Nicholas turned he saw Dobson fighting his way towards them with a stave to part the crowd. He almost fell against them and then murmured with head lowered in a voice so weary that it could scarce be heard, "I have voted to save him; less than a dozen of us did, and most stayed away. My future is lost, but I have done it for my friend." He embraced them, his chest heaving. Harvey gently stroked his shoulder.

"The King will never sign," said Cecilia. "They cannot do this without his agreement, and he will never sign the bill."

They went that night to Whitehall because they could not stay away.

The citizens of London had gathered before the palace, torchlight illuminating their faces. They stood about the white marble banqueting hall. Behind it lay more stone buildings weighing into the streets with the soot of centuries, and crooked stone and wood houses wedged in between with their laundresses and buttery shops, meat salters and embroideries, bootmakers and weavers. The lovely gardens, both public and privy, with the greenwood slumbering beneath the crusty winter bark, and sprouts stirring into life beneath the earth. The suites of rooms belonging to the ushers and stewards and masters, the doors opening into halls and then more doors until you came to the carpeted privy chambers. And there he was secreted, delicate and ordained by God, the sovereign Charles Stuart. He would remove his watch and lay it on the stand and then raise his arms for his nightshirt to be slipped over his boyish chest. He would kneel in prayer, hands over his long face, and once more commend himself to God. And all outside in the dark the crowd grew.

The friends gathered when day came in Dobson's old house on the Strand. All the furnishings had been moved away from the rooms, for he had just moved his family to his magnificent new mansion, leaving this as he had once promised for a teaching hospital and the science society. The library was now empty of its books, and eight rope string cots with straw mattresses waited for the sick. Surgical tools lay on a table, and chamber pots were piled in a corner. The possessions which the fellowship had gathered over the years had been taken to the parlor.

There Dobson paced up and down between the microscopes, instruments, and one large map of the world upon the wall. With some incoherence he told them that he had gone last night to Bartlett's house and struck him to his knees. Then he said, "Now we shall sit and plan as never we have done before. Whatever happens, we shall save him."

"Wilt ask us to sit?" Keyes murmured. "On my life, I could not."

"We must be prepared for everything. If the King signs—he won't, but if he does—there are plots to rescue Strafford. There was one a few days ago with some poets, but it failed . . . botched, stupidity!" He threw open a map on the table, and they gathered around to look at the placement of the buildings and gates of the Tower. "See this route here . . . if they make to execute him, the procession to the block will be interrupted at this point. We'll take him from the crowd no matter what it costs us. There's enough men loyal to him, by Christ."

In a voice dry of feeling, he continued, "There's ships at Tower Wharf to take him to safety; Mainwaring his secretary hath arranged it. There's that. Then there's money: more money than would buy a man a dukedom has been offered the warden for his release. His friends and I have given everything. There are these things and others we can try, but they will not be necessary." He looked about, and then they gathered together over the map, their voices rising now and then through to the empty library with its naked cots. Other friends came as well, until there were no more chairs. Cecilia sat on the floor with her arms clasping her knees and her head against Nicholas's leg.

Towards midnight, Keyes's apprentice rode from the Westminster shop with the news that crowds yet gathered before Whitehall Palace, more every hour shouting insults and threats at the window so that the guards were all alerted that the palace might be stormed. Inside the King sat with his advisers, and no word had come.

In the late afternoon of the following day, Nicholas received a letter from the lord Strafford bidding him come. He alone would be admitted by the warden. His hands trembled as he dressed himself in his cassock and clergyman's hat, and promised Cecilia that he would take her love.

The bells of St. Mary le Bow had already tolled the hour of six, and such apprentices as were working had laid down their tools. Shops were closing their shutters. As he came closer to the Tower, he saw the ravens circling above it in the sky. Admitted past the guard, he walked by the little huts and the sentries' children carrying coal buckets and turned up the steps, his hand touching the old stones.

The lord Strafford was standing by the window. He had taken off his cap, and the thick, now slightly grey hair sprang forth unbrushed as if he had just arisen from a sleepless night. When he saw Nicholas, his harsh face did not smile, but some light came to the dark eyes.

"Why marry, parson!" he murmured hoarsely. "Methought thou wast too angry with me to visit. . . . Last time we met face to face, those were thy words. For a man of God, hast a temper now and then."

"Now and then," answered Nicholas. "For what cause have I given thee any manner of physicking, ointments, enemas, purges, tonics, and pages of advice writ small to find thee here? My patience groweth small: I shall soon give o'er my work with thee."

"Speakst in truth, Nick?"

"What thinkst thou? God knoweth I love thee as few men upon this earth, my lord Strafford. God knoweth. I have no more words upon seeing thee again."

Strafford stepped forward and fell heavily, rather than stepped, against his friend. His chest shook with the struggle to control himself. "How doth Cecily? And my lord's grace, the Archbishop?"

"Hast not seen him?"

"Not once: we are not permitted." Scorn passed over the crevices of his face. "I've seen little but these walls and my secretaries, and then the daily ride by ferry to Westminster with the crowds jeering. They thought me in need of some counseling, mayhap, and granted my wish to see thee. They suspected mayhap my heart was heavy." Smiling wryly, he lowered himself to a chair, and Nicholas knelt before him.

He said, "Tell me everything, Tom!"

"Of what, this place? The rest thou knowst. Sometimes I wake and dream I'm in my own estates, and my man's calling for the hunt to begin and I ride out with the wind in my face and my tenants calling, 'God bless ye, lordship!' Had I stayed there . . . had I gone home. Even now, God knoweth . . ."

He pulled away a little and sat with hunched, heavy shoulders. "I've been looking over the accounts of my estate. Men think me wealthy. I was at one time. This past year and more I've given all I had and could raise elsewhere to support the King's army and his needs. I've no longer dowry for my daughters, nor has my son an inheritance." He shrugged. "I gave my fortune freely and would do it again, many times over. Sit, Nicholas, for I have matters of which to speak to you that are more deep than any we have spoken of before."

Taking a chair, Nicholas leaned forward, so that his head was but a short way from that of the prisoner. "If ever in your life you were friend to me," Strafford said quietly, "must be so today . . . no, more than that's wanted. I need thy counsel, parson, for I perhaps may die."

"Tom, what sayst?" Nicholas cried. "The King hath not signed the bill!"

"No, he hath not. I know his heart, Nicholas, and 'tis a good one, though he's not the strongest man. He does not know how to be or to be made great; he would have been a fine churchman or country squire. Nevertheless, he is as he is and I am as I am, and so in our strange ways we came together."

Reaching out, the Yorkshireman grasped both of his friend's hands. "Twenty thousand men," he murmured. "Twenty thousand men have signed a petition against my life. 'Tis a strange thing to think so great a number could wish me dead when many times that number I've wished well. They gather below the palace windows and the little Queen huddles with her ladies and her priests. They swear if they don't have my life, they'll have the life of the King. What then? We'll both die, and with it all I've lived and worked for. What can a man do when his work is demolished? How can he then go forward, and what purpose will he find in it?" Shaking his head, he added, "I ask thy prayers for courage . . . but not the sort thou thinkst for me. Of that I have had, and more than enough. No, in that I am not lacking . . . 'tis another kind I need, my friend. A sort I had not expected. Will you hear my confession now?"

"Thy confession?"

"Aye."

Deliberately Strafford dropped to his knees, and covered his face with his fingers. "Put thy hands on my shoulder," he said.

"Thou hast it."

"Here 'tis, with as much honesty and shame as I can muster. I've loved very much. May the rest be forgiven me. I have circumvented the laws I upheld in many small ways to build my estate; I have done it for my children. If I have wanted honors and titles, it was from my weakness. These are sins. . . . I have been unjustly harsh with some enemies, but I have never taken a man's life but for the thieving soldiers in the war. I have tried not to take a man's honor, though I know I have done it now and then. As Christ is in His heaven, let Him look down upon me and hear my words! I kneel before Him humbly as ever I did, and beg His mercy." His words were so murmured that they sometimes slipped away into inaudibility; he spoke of everything from his childhood to the present. At last he fell into a whisper again.

"If I have ever wronged you, pardon me; that one matter in particular," he concluded and fell silent.

Nicholas had listened carefully, closing his eyes against tears. With his hands still on Strafford's shoulders, he heard the dark, stunned voice murmur the act of contrition. Then the priest laid his hands on his friend's hair and spoke the words of forgiveness of the Lord which he had been ordained to do, making the sign of the cross on Strafford's forehead. He kissed him then slowly on the cheek, and lifted him. The weight of him seemed to sink again to the floor, and Nicholas almost fell forward with him until he regained his balance.

With some help, Strafford lowered himself once more into the chair, and looked mournfully and angrily towards the window.

Nicholas said huskily, "Thy leg troubles thee?"

"That and all my body. Never mind, it will be healed soon."

"Tom, shalt not die."

"I've writ a letter to the King. I've told him that I know the minds of men are more and more incensed against me though he and I and they . . . they as well . . . know I am guilty of no treason! I've told him there's strife in me in the offering of this . . ." He fought the breaking of his voice, and then continued, looking not at his friend but still away towards the window and the light. "I've relieved him of the burdens of his conscience,

Nicholas. I have asked him to sign the bill condemning me to have my head struck from my shoulders."

Nicholas stood up. "Christ's wounds, Tom!" he cried in a terrible voice. "Has gone from thy senses? Wouldst ask him to agree to thy death? By Christ, I will have naught to do with this!"

"Read it and understand. God's wounds, Nick, thou at least must understand!"

Nicholas threw himself back into his chair, and with his fingers of one hand to his lips looked over the letter he had been given. "Sir, my consent shall more acquit you herein to God than all the world can do besides; to a willing man there is no injury done, and as by God's grace I forgive all the world, with calmness and meekness of infinite contentment to my dislodging soul; so Sir, to you, I can give the life of this world with all the cheerfulness imaginable. . . . God long preserve your Majesty. Your Majesty's most faithful and humble subject and servant Strafford."

By the time he came to the end of it his heart pounded so that he felt faint. Throwing the letter to the table with a cry, he took his friend by the arms as if uncertain whether to embrace or shake him, and then brought his arm across his own mouth. "Writest as well as ever! Still, what madness is this?" he mumbled hoarsely through the dark cloth of his sleeve. "What madness?"

"None: I have been awake last night thinking on it."

"Canst not send it."

"His Majesty must sign the paper: there's no other way. What—give it here, Nicholas! Darst not tear it on thy life! Hast brought me once to my knees only because I allowed it, else thou couldst not have done it. As weak as I am, if thou tearst that, shalt have more to fear than any man hath ever in this country from Tom Wentworth!"

"In God's holy name, Tom!"

"And hear this as well!" he shouted. "Hear this as well, and tell it to thy friends, the motley lot of them! If Charles Stuart signs, I'll not be rescued . . . dost hear me? You shall stand like fools with your arms if you come for me, for I'll not go with you."

Strafford drew in his breath. After the outburst his voice became slowly more calm, and he began to walk about the room like a gentleman at leisure in his own chambers. "List to me: I say it again. The mob will storm the palace and kill him in their anger, and then what will we have? Wouldst have me lose the very thing I have given my life to protect? By Christ, I will die protecting it. My life's no great matter compared to this."

"To you mayhap," Nicholas answered bitterly. "To you 'tis nothing, but what of those who love thee, thy household and wife, thy children. Cecily, Christ save us, what will she say? Will she live through this? Still, God prohibit we should keep thy paltry soul within thy body! Christ forbid our bitter grief should influence thee!" He began to weep and stumbled from his chair against the wall, as if surprised to find it there. He wept in gasps, his palm against the stone.

"Nick, Nick," Strafford said astonished and ceasing to walk. "My sweet friend! I go into the arms of God, where there is no dispute. And then they will leave off their rioting and go home, and the country will be safe. Dost resent my going? Wouldst suggest this world's the better part after preaching a year of Sundays on the other one? Shame, parson!"

"Dost teach me my work?"

"It needs be taught thee," was the stern reply. "For I do believe me thou hast forgot it seeing me here. Answer me, parson! Dost believe as thou hast preached? Dost believe I shall go into Christ's arms?"

"I do."

"Then let me go and bless me."

"Mayhap the King ... won't sign. Tom, *he cannot!*"

Strafford turned to face him. "I know not," he said softly. "I dare to hope that he will refuse. I want to live; he surely must know it. But if he feels it best, I make the offer freely with all that I have ever been and more." Slowly he walked towards his friend and held out the paper. "I trust thee," he said. "Take this letter to Whitehall for me. I'll at least know that you believed the reason for all I've done. And then God deliver you safely out of this wicked world according to the innocence that is in you."

For a long time Nicholas was silent; then he nodded. "I will," he said quietly.

"There's also a letter to my son: see he receives it if I . . . Radclyffe will see that the girls have some dowry, and mayhap my name one day restored. And his grace William Laud . . . do what you can to save him if he comes near danger."

"It shall be done."

Tom turned to gaze out the window once more. "There's sunlight on the water!" he murmured. "The best time of day." He opened his arms to embrace his friend again. "Mayhap he will not sign," he said wistfully. "Then there'll be hell to pay, but we'll manage as we've always done. Kiss Cecily for me."

Nicholas walked down the old steps and to the wharf, where he stepped into a boat and was borne west towards Whitehall. That night, between the hours of eleven and twelve, word came to Aldermanbury that the sovereign Charles Stuart, after many hours with the council of his churchmen and ministers, had taken his pen and in the greatest grief put his signature to the bill delivering his servant the Earl of Strafford to his death.

All night long, people walked through the cobbled streets towards the Tower. They had not woken him, for he never slept at all, but watched the flicker of their torches through the closed shutters of his house near the city gate, and heard the muttering and laughing through his wall. At five in the morn he could wait no longer, but dressed rapidly, buckled on his sword, and threw open his doors. Cecilia lay in a drugged sleep; he had given her laudanum to calm her hysteria after he could no longer hold her bruised arms and prevent her running out the door to the Tower and beating on the stones with her bare hands.

What good would it have done?

William lay sobbing in his chamber; he wanted to accompany his father, but Nicholas sternly refused him.

Still came the shadows of men in Sunday clothes and women in best lace caps, hurrying arm in arm towards the river and Tower through the overhanging, half-timbered houses down Aldermanbury Street.

Drawing up his hood, he fell in beside them.

Above them the stars were beginning to fade, and as they came closer to Tower Hill he noticed the faint rosy light of day rising beyond the ancient buildings as it had each morning since the beginning of time. More and more did the crowd jostle, though lanterns were slowly extinguished.

Thus they came to Tower Hill.

A hundred thousand men had come to see the lord Strafford die. They had walked from every ward in the city and many of the surrounding villages, carrying their dinners wrapped in cloth; they pressed against each other until the women cried out and the men threatened and the children began to weep.

The sun had risen almost to over the heads of the crowd when they brought him from the Tower. He walked more like a general at the head of an army than a man to his death. They heard nothing of his final words, which commended his love to the King. Nicholas saw him place his hands in those of his chaplain. "My body is theirs," he had written, "but my soul is God's."

They took him away after in a cart, and the crowd slowly departed, grumbling and half satisfied. It was raining slightly as Nicholas walked across the trampled, muddy grounds to the now empty scaffold and stood looking at it for a long time.

Someone was coming up the hill, running and stopping to catch her breath, half trailing a long great cloak. Thus Cecilia came towards him through the rain, staggering slightly, struggling against the drugged sleep and still hoping to prevent what had already been done. Holding on to each other, they went home. It was then his rage escaped him, and he smashed plates and cups. He would have broken the King's portrait over his knee, but his son, who was frightened, stopped him.

THREE

The Church

FOR SOME WEEKS AFTER HIS LOSS, NICHOLAS ROSE EACH MORNING
exhausted with shock and went to bed before dark had fully come.
Then he'd awake, and stare into the bed hangings.

Throughout the hot summer, Parliament sat, though its numbers
shrank as men escaped the city for their cooler shires. Both houses then
voted for Parliament to choose the King's ministers, which his Majesty
abruptly declined, then leaving for Scotland to raise support for his
royalist cause there. Nicholas remained indifferent. More religious sects
had sprung up in the city than could be numbered, and small riots broke
out daily here and there. When the second session of Parliament opened
the third week in October, the trained bands were called out to protect it.
There were rumors of plots against Lords and Commons by Catholics
and royalists.

Fall had come.

The first approach of that season which he loved best always brought to mind suppers with friends in small wainscoted rooms, warm ale, and early twilight. This was the season of books, and the sound of old leaves in the garden, the longer nights, the smell of ancient wood fires over the city. It was the season when Tom would come and say, Let's walk in the fields! Once the physician thought he heard his shout, and running to the door, threw it open and gazed down the lane. Then he wept bitterly.

Cecilia did not sleep: below he heard her walking back and forth, nor would she take the wine with laudanum drops which he prescribed for her. None of the men considered meeting, for it ended only in quarrels. Keyes wore only black in his mourning, and Harvey shut himself behind his doors. No work progressed in the teaching hospital. The boy William was worried that something should take his father away. The actors were quiet.

Andrew no longer went with buttons polished and sword at hip to carry his company's flag in Finsbury Fields. He had always assumed that the companies were organized to serve first the King and then the city; he no longer believed they were that way, and so he left. He also began to wear a small portrait of Charles Stuart over his heart; to the back were pasted a few strands of the lord Strafford's hair.

Dobson did not return to Parliament, but had shipped that summer to the East Indies, hoping to negotiate for silks to replenish the fortune he had rashly depleted. There he would find another love, whose skin was as dark as coffee beans, but they did not know that, and his sallow wife settled herself once more to wait for him. Sir Anthony Van Dyck, Sergeant Painter to the King, had given up his soul after a brief illness, and Keyes's wife set up her own studio at home, and began to reproduce portraits of the royal family on commission.

Nicholas was at first too stunned to pray: he performed the services required of him, read old sermons on the Sabbath, and in general moved through that part of his work as if it were a job of which he had grown weary. Then when his heart was too heavy he would go into the church with a shirt which Tom had absentmindedly left many years before when staying the night, and laying it across his knees, begin to ask God's help to heal himself. He understood that Tom would have wanted him to go forward in his work. Gradually he found his tears came more easily, and with it his desire to go forth among men. Still, he did not understand how he had been given such a friend to have him taken away again.

On a white, windy November day, Charles Stuart returned to the city from his time away in the north. Trumpets and viols sounded and the trained bands stood at attention all along the way. Anthems of loyalty and welcome were sung in the Cathedral; rows and rows of liverymen from the twelve great companies dropped to their knees as he rode by. Snow had begun to fall, delicately outlining the branches of trees and resting on the high stones of church steeples. Smoke from chimneys curled into the sky as they moved through the churchyard, banners from the guilds and the military bands barely stirring in the wet, snowy air and the high piping voices of the choristers and boy actors singing, "God save the King! May the King live forever!"

Through Ludgate they went over the grey cold waters of the Fleet, turning west on the Strand with the last copper rays of the sun descending in the distance behind the courts of Westminster. In front of the palace, the pikemen whipped through their thirty positions and the musketeers fired ceremoniously over the heads of the crowd into the last of the day.

Again the boys sang. The King and his family withdrew to the banqueting hall, and from there the great windows were thrown open, and he stood above them with his fine warm brown hair blowing under his feathered hat, and the tiny Queen beside him, her arm through his. Nicholas, who was on his way back from attending a neighbor of Tim Keyes, saw it diffidently. He did not raise his hat, but the cheering crowd was too great for anyone to notice it.

Christmastide snow lay down the lane and on the window ledges, the chimneys, and the rectory on Love Lane. Evenings a few friends gathered.

Outside in the lane the wassailers sang to flute and viol and danced in the old country way.

Yet scarcely had the snow covered the marks of the wheels of the royal carriage from the King's entrance into his city when a reluctance rose once more from both houses to answer with favor any request of their sovereign. Charles Stuart had asked the Lords to raise him an army of ten thousand volunteers to bring the Scots under control. They had refused, may it please your most gracious Majesty! The mobs of boys and soldiers and the rough men of the docks had so taunted the bishops who wanted to take their places in the Lords that they had to turn back for safety, and when they demanded that any bills passed during their enforced absence be expunged, twelve were imprisoned within the Tower. The Archbishop of York was assaulted. There it lay.

February came. The bells struck ten outside the Aldermanbury rectory, and still that night Nicholas could not sleep but remained with his writing on his knee by the kitchen fire. A covered bowl of dough had been left to rise on the table, and when he raised his head, he could see drying garlands of holly and ivy which they had hung from the stair for Christmastide, and never bothered to take down again. He had been writing to a friend in the country concerning Archbishop Laud, who was yet imprisoned.

Now he heard his neighbors walking down the street and fitting the key to their door across the lane. Shortly after came the bell of the night watch. Rising and opening the door, he called out, "Mark, all's well?"

"Not a mouse stirs. Where be thy sexton? He hath not burned the candle late, as is his wont."

"To the west country to see his sister."

"Keepst late hours!"

"I have just thought me to go to bed."

"A good night then."

"And to thee."

Closing the door and covering the fire, he began to mount the rounded stair. Though it was now dark below, he could still sense the worn red velvet cushions of window seat and coffer chair, the scrubbed trenchers and the pewter mugs upon the shelf. Floors creaked, bed creaked, then a sigh.

He was almost to the top when he heard, quite distinctly, the sound of glass splintering. No sound there was quite like it: once William had slammed the garret window shut and the glass rattled to the bricks in the garden below, and just last week he himself had knocked one of his precious brown jars from the shelf. Motionless, he listened as the sound came again, and then several times more. Grasping the stout stick which he kept behind the door, he moved quietly to the lane.

To the left, St. Mary Aldermanbury rose with its tower of six bells and medieval stonework. Above the arched entrance were the gargoyles whose faces were long worn away and a stone Christ, one hand raised to heaven. Crossing the graveyard, Nicholas pushed open the creaking door and looked about.

The white altar cloth shone faintly, as did the two pewter candlesticks, baptismal font, and pulpit. The moon had been rising for some time, and glistened as it often did through the high stained-glass windows. As he stood there, part of one gave a crack and fell to the stone. Then he understood. The antique windows which he had loved since a boy had been shattered.

With a cry he ran from the door, staring wildly down the silent lane. Every way he looked the streets were empty. In rage he took his stick and smashed it against the thick stone graveyard walls; then he flung himself down on the low wall and covered his face with his hands. Nay, he thought, it cannot be true! Once more he stared up at ragged edges of glass clinging yet to the leading. In his mind he willed it back again, and in his mind it was restored. Hurrying back inside the church, he struck a flint to light the lantern which John always left by the door. Duller now lay the glass, scattered across the memorial slabs and the white linen communion cloth.

More was to come as he looked about.

The Florentine crucifix which had been left to him by William Syden-

ham had also been shattered against the stone wall, and a little statue of
the Virgin had been hacked in pieces. On the floor was his prayer book,
the cover ripped away. Falling to his knees with a cry, he gathered it to
him.

As hurrying footsteps crossed the churchyard, he reached for the broken stave. "Nick, art within?" called the voice. " 'Tis Andrew. I heard
men run down past my house and came out; my man Hanks is with me."
Then he hesitated. "Lord save us!" he cried. "What's been done here? Ah,
the bastards! They have . . . Nick, didst see them?"

"Nay."

"I'll rouse my brothers; we'll find them!"

Candles still burned in the Wood Street kitchen, and soon there were
five or six men with staves and swords rushing along the streets. Yet from
every alley and lane came only darkness, the shape of a swinging sign.
There was no one about; even the watch had gone. For more than an hour
they looked, then they returned to the church. Dropping to his knees to
gather the sections of the smashed cross, Nicholas cried, "Who could
have done it?"

"Christ knoweth, parson!" the actor replied. "Soldiers lacking work,
brickmaker's apprentices, mayhap some men from the bands. There's
been some trouble about, vandalism here and there. I could never have
expected it here. . . . Art greatly loved, Nick."

Nicholas had stood. "We must have prayers here," he said in the firm
quiet voice which he used when on the edge of great anger, and holding
himself in. "We will consecrate bread and wine, and have holy communion to push away what's been done here."

In the little vesting chamber behind the altar he pulled on the deep red
brocaded chasuble and brought the stole to his lips before draping it
around his shoulders. Andrew found hardened bread in a covered dish,
and the cruet of wine and water in a cupboard. From a higher shelf he
lifted down the chalice and paten and a clean linen embroidered cloth for
the altar, and a little dish for Nicholas to wash his hands in before
breaking the bread that the priest might cleanse himself in innocency, as
the psalm said, and be made whiter than snow.

Glass glimmered faintly across the stone floor as they entered the chancel. Nicholas turned to the altar; bowing, he raised his hands and began.

"Almighty God, unto whom all hearts are open, all desires known, and from whom no secrets are hid: Cleanse the thoughts of our hearts by the inspiration of thy Holy Spirit, that we may perfectly love thee...."

He consecrated the bread and wine, drank and ate of it, and gave some to each of the men, who had knelt with palms uplifted. Glass fragments clung to the knees of their breeches when they stood. Afterwards they sat about talking until the dawn came, and then carefully swept the church.

The birth of Andrew's youngest child began violently towards the end of that day. The babe seemed to cling to the womb, and when Nicholas inserted his fingers towards the straining uterus he touched her hand. She came two months before her time: he did not think he had ever seen anything so tiny or beautiful. At first she did not breathe: he turned her across his knee and tapped her back. Then he covered her mouth with his and gave her his own breath. They called her Margaret.

Downstairs in the Heminges kitchen, lanterns and fires burned, and the neighbors came, many friends, and the ward constable; some came for the mother, and others, who had heard about the vandalism in St. Mary Aldermanbury, came for him. They came to and from the birth chamber, which smelled of new life and blood.

Nicholas was ill for days, feverish and angry and ranting, and once woke with a shout and leapt from his bed to find a stick to beat the men who had desecrated his church, and struck his head on the doorway forgetting that he must stoop to pass through it. How Harvey got him back to bed he did not know, but through all this he remembered the sweet high pure cooing of the child Margaret, which came to him in his dreams, seeming to say, I have come from the angels! Her voice mingled with the words of the service. He had given her his breath, and therefore loved her deeply. Love and hatred mingled for him.

The vestry mounted the rectory steps, gathering about his bed hangings, hats in hands. They shuffled and glanced at each other, these several merchants and tradesmen who had worshiped with him every week for many years. With heads hanging they muttered that there was more anger about the city than he could know concerning churches such as his which used the traditional service and prayer book. Several families were going elsewhere to worship. Nicholas could only nod dumbly. He had seen little these past months. The priest had been too occupied with grief over his friend to feel the discontented stirring within his own nave.

Stay apart, do not become caught in disputes . . . these were his old bishop's words. Now he shrugged this old advice impatiently from him. Dispute he would if he must. He would fight harder now. He would hold his splintering parish closer so that by the strength of his love it would be made whole again.

Had the ward constable heard the vandals or had he not? Whom could he trust? It was happening, of course, here and there, they told him: priests had been beaten, and thrown from their houses. A bishop had been attacked as well. Many who came to see him said in passionate, quiet voices, Well, it's done, but there it ceases. Naught shall harm thee, Cooke! Naught shall harm thee or thine. Stones and glass are naught. The church door was unlocked, there were angry men and boys with staves and hatchets, and that is all of it.

That was all.

He was still unwell when he mounted the steps to the pulpit two Sundays later and looked out over the small church and the men and women he knew so well. Some he had married, many he had counseled; there was not one of whom he did not know some private grief or joy. Cecily sat with her head bent slightly, her hands folded in her lap. All this dark week and the one before he had felt her love and strength. William had slipped his arm in hers, and even the small boys of the choir had ceased to swing their legs to listen to him.

His voice rang out to the memorial stones. As far as was humanly possible, he said, there should be peace among men. That which had been wounded must be healed. They must heal not only what was broken here but what had broken between men. The church was dim, for the windows had temporarily been covered with canvas and boards. He could not make out all the faces by the flickering lanterns, but when the singing began he knew some people were missing. After the service, Tim Keyes approached him shyly with his prayer book, rebound. Nicholas was deeply grateful.

Nine months had passed since Strafford had died, and not once in that time had Nicholas mentioned the King. He brooded darkly, and wished to once more gather things neatly about him. When Harvey asked him directly of his feelings, he had replied, "I have such angry dreams I don't know what to do."

Then his friend replied wryly, "Now speakst like most any other London man. If they'd known it, they'd gladly glue thy church back together, friend!" He looked around at the microscopes and boxes of lenses on the parlor table. "As dusty as much of my own things! Cooke, dost no longer study magnification?"

Nicholas shook his head. After Harvey had gone he realized how long it had been since he touched them. The truth was he had lost all interest in looking for things which were not possible. Carefully he gathered up microscopes, lenses, and notes and put them in a box in the cupboard so that their presence should cease to be a reproach to him.

When he walked out some weeks later, he found barricades had been erected on Cheapside and stout black cannons on wheeled carts parked by the snowy walls surrounding Paul's. All goodwill between crown and Parliament had broken down. The crowd was unruly once more; small bands of men gathered nightly in Old Palace Yard and shattered the windows of the shopkeepers. Charles Stuart claimed Parliament incited them. He ordered the city bands to fire on the mob if there was further rioting, and took his coach to Westminster followed by four hundred armed troops to arrest the five leading members of Commons on a charge of subverting fundamental laws. The men fled to the city and the safety of the Grocers' Hall. Armaments, hastily thrown up, remained. Soldiers stood by the barricades which no one thought to breach.

Some afternoons following, the physician was brought from his dispensary by the hooting of boys. They cried that the King had left London for Hampton Palace, and was not expected to return in peace. On the walls of Paul's churchyard someone had writ words in ink on one of the stones. "No King," it said, "no bishops, no priests."

Summer came, hot and stifling within the city walls. Everyone knew by this time that the sovereign had begun to draw together military supplies and soldiers, and that some of the Parliamentarians who disliked him had also gone to their shires to raise men for their side. There was some famine about the country, and the price of wheat in London was very high, which added to the general anger. Boys were pulled from their work to stand watch at Temple Bar. The bickering of the religious sects, the violent disputes in Westminster Palace, the falling off of trade, the vandalism of shops and stalls continued. Tim Keyes twice repaired his windows, and once much of his fine leather was taken before he ran down with his journeyman to beat the marauders from the street.

Michael Dobson spoke about it when he came home from India. "Darst not say the news, Nick, for I know it already," he said wryly as they closed the door of the tavern booth. "My steward told me before they had finished docking: those who support the King are now declared traitors and their property is to be forfeited to the state. This present method of governing's thrice worse in injustice than the one it proposes to supplant."

"Wilt join the King, Michael?"

"Nay, but many men I know who were indecisive are now going. Property confiscated! 'Twas a bad move. And thee?"

"I preach to half a church with a terrible sense of uneasiness. Priests are being put from their parishes all over the country. It shall happen, mayhap, to me as well."

Dobson laid his ringed hands on the table as if they were all he had.

"They'll force the King to fight; they'll drive him to it. He'll raise his standard and there will be war."

The College of Physicians met to vote upon the officers, and when the returns were in, all present functionaries including Nicholas had been dismissed and a new coterie, all loyal to Parliament and its burgeoning new laws, took their places. Shamefaced, they requested that Nicholas also surrender his present work as medical supervisor.

Astonished, he cried out, "I've ever been a good physician! If I'm no use to you now, devil take you all!"

"Dost say that as parson?" one asked.

"I say it as a gentleman," was the sharp reply.

"What saith Master Harvey?"

Harvey, who had sat beside him, opened his mouth and let loose a flood of vindictive, bitter words. Then he closed his lips, thrust his arm in Nicholas's, and walked out. "I should have pulled down my breeches and shown them my arse," he said between his teeth as they strolled towards Paul's churchyard. "Wouldst have done likewise, fellow?" Then he broke into such laughter that he had to bend over and slap his knees.

Shortly thereafter, Harvey received word he was to come to his sovereign as tutor to the royal children. Grimly he packed his bags and rode north to join the camp.

FOUR

Letters

October 1642

to the physician in ordinary to his Majesty, William Harvey, at Christ Church, Oxford, from Cooke, priest of Cripplegate, London

Harvey,

We have received the news here of the King's battle and victory at Edgehill under Prince Rupert his nephew by soldiers, travelers, and the Dutch papers. Parliament, of course, hath published another version recounting that their armies alone held the day. I am sick at the thought of the fighting and am relieved that you have armed yourself only with some scant knowledge of physicking and a habit of caustic letter writing. Christ's wounds, I miss thee, but I believe negotiations will soon win the day and we shall have masques again at Whitehall, if not by Twelfth Night, then soon after.

There hath been sad news here, for Harrington hath been felled by a seizure. The left side of his mouth is twisted upwards and he speaks with difficulty. For all he irked me, my heart is heavy. Cecilia goes daily to see him, which I should never have expected. I shall write more of her presently when I have leisure for thought.

The city is in a sorry state. Paul's yard is taken over by the pamphleteers against bishops and royalty. One cannot find a decent book of poetry or any of the sciences. We heard Bartlett is now sheriff and close to those in Parliament. I cannot go to the Mitre for a glass but that they take verbal arms against me, so few men remain in this part of the city who believe the King hath been wronged. There are so many quarrels among men this twelve months, it is God's mercy that the right side of a man's body doth not rise and quarrel with the left.

My congregation is every week smaller, which I try to bear with good cheer, wondering if by this Our Lord meaneth to test me. My patients are less than half of what they were. Many of them have left the city upon the threatened confiscation of their property, and others turn from me for my beliefs, as they assume to know what these are. When shall we wander about the royal parks and come away with a pregnant doe to study? Walk betwixt musket fire, sweet my friend.

> Ever,
> Nick

He brought the letter to the Staple Inn, from which the couriers left twice daily for the King's army. Already the coach was piled with couriers' things: boxes of fine kid gloves, some lengths of blue satin cloth, a small library of classical literature. Three musicians he had known for years were traveling out as well, their lute and viol cases strapped carefully to their horses. 'Tis no holiday, he said to himself as he walked away, his stride somewhat slower.

There was more he had not mentioned in the letter, for all public theaters had been closed in the city. Parliamentary soldiers had come in the middle of a rehearsal at the Globe and ordered the actors to leave at once. Doors were nailed shut and notices posted about the streets.

Trunks of costumes and properties were removed to be stored in parlors and attics.

Nicholas ferried over one day with Lowin to remove a few more of the smaller boxes of props and playscripts which they had forgotten in their haste. The neighborhood was quiet, for the bear gardens had also been boarded up, as were the cockpits, and most of the doxies who plied their wares near the Bishop's palace in Lambeth had been driven from the city. Leaves had blown down and lay gathered wetly against the barred doors of the Globe. The men let themselves in by removing the hinges of a window and once inside walked about the stage, raising their faces to the vast empty galleries and the thatched roof. Impulsively Nicholas knelt and touched the boards.

Lowin sat on one of the small stools they used to place on the stage edge for the gentry and looked about wistfully. "When I was boy to the actors," he ruminated, his wide hands on his knees, " 'twas my work to raise the flag each day we performed, and I shall raise it again! For I tell the men, don't sell off the costumes! Live quietly on what you have saved! We will play again before we know."

"How do the others, John?"

"A few plan private theatricals, for those Parliament can't stop. Three or four hope to take a company to Italy. Several talk about going to fight for the King. I would go with them this moment, Nick! Pack an extra shirt in my satchel and my prayer book, and go off to serve his most sacred majesty, but my health's not good. I breathe with difficulty. If this lasts long, Nell and I will open an inn." He paused as a flock of pigeons flew over the straw roof of the theater. " 'Tis Andrew who troubles me," he said.

They talked about it as they made their way to the Thames. When the soldiers had come to close the theater, Andrew had argued with them until they pushed him aside, and he had fallen, bruising his leg. Now he did not seem to know what to do with himself; he told all who would listen that actors were the conscience of the city, for they stood in every man's cloak and knew each man's inner sorrows. In the past months he had become increasingly morose, and could be seen sometimes walking slowly towards the water and standing there looking at the ferries as if he wished to hail one and had no place to take it. Now and then he muttered that he had failed his father, and betrayed the trust left to him. That it had come hard on the desecration of his church was too much.

On a brisk November day when the leaves littered all the lanes and gardens, the serving man Hanks hurried over to the rectory to see the parson. His master had gone off to join the King in the wars, he stammered. Andrew Heminges was now a soldier.

Cecilia was also changing.

She had seemed to her husband at times during the months of Strafford's long trial to be like the boy who carries the banner, running forward before the troupes towards the battle, so fleet of foot and proud of bearing that she could not be stopped by anything on this earth. Her dark eyes had burned, and he was at times almost afraid to approach her. Again he asked himself, What have I married? For as much as you thought you knew a person before you took those vows, you would find much unexpected after. Then after the execution she would sit for hours by the window; she sometimes did not wash her hair or change her chemises for weeks. She ceased to come to church, making one excuse after another, and when he said his prayers in the bedchamber at night, her silence seemed to condemn him. All things which had interested her so much fell away. Again, he was pushed to the wall in admitting that he did not understand her.

The desecration of the church, and subsequently the beginning of the war and the closing of the theaters, awakened her again. It was as if each thing shook her until, stunned, she opened her eyes as one does from the deep sleep of sickness and looked about. He had had enough, and wanted once more, as he had done many times in his life before, to close his doors and retreat to his books; he had even put away his microscopes. She, however, remained alert. The dark eyes swept over her world with contempt, and her peculiar, individualistic intelligence began to respond ... How shall I manage this? What will I do?

As he sat writing one morning, she pulled a chair beside him, curled cross-legged within it as she used to do, and looked at him for a long time. "Nicholas," she said, "we must do what we can to help the King's cause."

Without raising his head he murmured sternly, "And why should we do that?"

"Because he is the cornerstone of the arch of the country; there's no cornerstone now, as Tom would say."

He raised his head and looked at her. She sparkled in the old way, and he felt, which he had not for some time, the stirring of desire for her. It was as if he said, Dear Lord . . . here is life! So he put down his pen and asked more gently, "What wilt do, cony?"

"I'll raise money for his armies. I'll ask all I trust in the city to give gold, plate, jewelry, whatever they have. There may be a negotiated peace soon, my sweet, but if there's not, he must have help."

"I don't want you to do this."

"Ah," she said, jumping up with a smile. "I will anyway." She stretched, and again he felt desire rising . . . something in him trembled. Sunlight was coming through the windows on the boards of the floor, and the early winter day with the trees bare and dark on the lane seemed suddenly exquisitely beautiful. His thought swelled with longing and at the beauty, and at his friend who would not see it anymore. He would have crossed to her, but he changed his mind and sat down again, though he could no longer remember what he was writing.

He did not truly believe her until he came home one day and found a small basket of gold and jewelry on the bed. Astonished, he looked through it. Harrington had also lent his house for the work. At first he looked askance at the tall, slight Cecilia hurrying up his steps with gold tucked under her skirt. Then he joined her, for he would not allow himself to be beaten. In the end, he almost fell in love with her. He went about in his carriage and visited friends and demanded their support; together they traveled out into the country for weeks at a time to visit estates of friends, and came home with gold and jewels under a board in the seat of the coach.

They packed plate into straw in wood boxes and jewelry into hollowed books or sewn in seams to be smuggled out in carts or worn against the body by travelers towards Oxford. The King had now set up his camp in that ancient university town; they heard reports weekly in papers brought in the baskets of peddler women that a little court was forming there. The Queen herself had taken her own jewelry to France to sell.

Harrington continued to make tiresome speeches in his slurred voice that if he were well, he could better direct the war. "I have given my sons," he would rant. "I'll give everything else I own from my old christening robes to the plate . . . from which . . . I eat. We shall see if the bastards will raise army and cannons to fight against their lawful sovereign. We shall show them he can raise a greater number of men and more arms and horses. We shall give him the means to fight until they fall . . . to their . . . knees. . . ." In the middle of his work he would begin to weep, remembering Strafford in the kindest words as a saint. Cecilia would smile wryly, and answer, "Yes, father," which was her new name for him. Because of this, he assumed she agreed with him in every matter and proclaimed her a good woman, the best he had known.

One night when Nicholas had just gone to bed, he looked up to see her standing before him with her gown half unlaced. With a smile she said, "Surely dost not sleep! Take out thy accounting books, cony, for we must decide what we can give as well."

Ruefully he pulled on his dressing gown and allowed her to lead him to the study table, place a mug of warm spiced ale before him, and light the candles. Outside the leaves blew and rattled about, and below their streets, the river was freezing over. She carried down the box of money and valuables, papers of property and sums deposited with the goldsmiths. "Now," she said with a smile, opening it before him, and crossing her legs under the loose gown in her chair.

"I love thee," he said wistfully.

"Aye, but what amount can we give?"

"Cony!"

His pen scratched at the paper; he drank, then rested his head on his hand again, looked up at her, smiled, and planned. They had given away a great deal that year to friends: to Keyes to repair the vandalism of his shop, to the actors who had no income, to servants of Strafford and Laud who could find no work. He himself had now one third of his former patients and no living from the church.

Lifting the pen from his figures, he said with a sigh, "Suppose we are poor, my sweet."

"I shall love thee as much."

He felt himself grim, grizzled, and dazed for want of sleep and concern about Andrew away at war, and his son's increasing silences, and the endless bills and closures on his rights and those of friends. In the end they took a quantity of gold and sewed it in cloth, and she brought it next day to Harrington's house. He was not sure why he had done it.

He was alone in the house some days later when the men came.

The river had frozen indeed, and he had come from the death of an old woman whom he loved. The house was so cold that he saw his patients by the kitchen fire. He missed Cecilia, who was gone from the city again; they had begun to make love once more, and he wanted it very much. When the knock came he thought by the sharpness of it that it was an irate patient, and then reconsidered; such a man would have come to the dispensary and not to the street door.

They were men of middle years who stood there in dark, plain clothing, and at first he did not understand who they were, and thought they wanted a subscription to some charity. "Hast the wrong house, mayhap, gentlemen," he said mildly.

The smallest, who wore spectacles, looked at the paper he carried, and said, "Art Cooke of Cripplegate Ward?"

"I am."

"We are here to shut thy church: art no longer priest. It is forbidden for thee to perform sacraments and preach there or anyplace else under penalty of treason."

His hand felt for the door lintel, and his voice grew deep and grave as it did when faced with serious things: loss, death, something inevitable which must come. Even when they crossed the frozen ground of the churchyard, he had the desire to call after them that they had the wrong place. Men had always assured him he was loved and respected, and that this could never happen to him. He was the physician who had stayed through the plagues; he was the man who condemned no one.

He should have stayed away, but when they began to hammer the boards across the doors of his church he had to come out. The doors were old, and shivered as the nails were driven into them. If they had beaten him, it would have hurt less. Then it was done, and they went off. For some time he sat in the churchyard overlooking the worn statue of Christ above the door, and then raised his eyes to the pigeons of the Tower who flew freely in and out of the windows. It was a very white winter sky, with the sun only faint round light as a candle seen through oil paper, and the earth was hard under his feet. His soul seemed to huddle in a very small space under his ribs as if it hoped it would not be bothered there.

He tried to think reasonably. Other priests had gone away, been locked out or replaced: dear old friends with whom he had spent many a pleasant evening. He could, of course, have expected no less.

William found him there when he returned from school. He heard what had happened, looked at the church with tears in his eyes, and tried to recall the words from the psalm that his father was a priest forever. Nicholas only nodded. It was his way to be absolutely still when muddling over a problem he could not yet solve, training long enforced by his work. Now he sat quietly by his son, patting his hand, explaining what was occurring in the country and when and why they could expect it to cease. Darkness came early, and being very cold, they both went inside the house.

Something ended for him then. The yearning for what he had lost overwhelmed all else. He would awake on Sundays and stand in the churchyard, looking at the church which had been for so many years under his care. He would gaze down at his broad hands, which had been consecrated to his vocation. The cassock hung behind the door, as did his four-cornered clergyman's hat, for he dared not wear it in the streets. Some men turned their backs as he passed, but some looked at him with compassion. A few swore quietly that they were by his side and they must but bide a better time. He only knew that what God had given him to do had been taken by men, and those who knew nothing of it.

He dreamt one night he was walking by St. Paul's in a terrible storm of rain and thunder where the water ran down the gutters, rushing downhill towards the river. In the corner of Paternoster Lane a beggar crouched. He said nothing, but Nicholas knew at once how cold and hungry he must be. At first he passed the man, for he was eager to be home, but then turned again and said, "Walk with me and I'll find thee something hot to drink."

The vagrant rose, and Nicholas put his hand under his arm to steady him. They began to walk, but God only knew where their feet led them, for the distance between Paul's and the physician's own corner was not far, and yet they walked for hours and hours. He could sense the beggar's weariness, and was ashamed that he could not remember his way home. They were perhaps in the slums behind Westminster, yet nothing was as he recollected it, and there was no possibility of having gone from the city without passing through the gates.

Nicholas knew that had he not stopped for the man, he would now be home, and he said with slight irritation, "Hast a light?" At once the beggar took from under his cloak a tin lantern such as poor servants carry, but with the sound of enough oil to last awhile and already cheerfully lit. They had come to Blackfriars, and the physician could sense the beggar's failing and said to him, "Here's the old house of my friend Tom, who'll give us shelter! Come then, for I also am wet to my soul!"

Through the rain they went into the small central hall under the picture of the monarch. But when he returned from the kitchens with wood for the fire and ale to heat upon it, he saw that the man he had carried home was no beggar but his sovereign. He wore the plain clothes of a printer's boy, and his hair was plastered down with rain. Nicholas cried at once in rage, "Dost come to me? Dost dare ask aught of me?" And then he woke.

It was in the end more his need to serve as priest that made up his mind also to go to the war than his loyalty to the crown. The crown he revered, but the man who wore it he despised. These things were so complex he did not tell them to anyone. Cecilia understood it without speaking. It was also agreed between them that she would remain and continue her work. He was not happy with it, but he agreed, because he knew this was yet another time he could not move her.

Friends gathered one night, and there on the kitchen table below the hanging kettles and pots they celebrated communion. Footsteps of the watch came and passed, his nightstick tapping first the tombstones and then the low stone wall which surrounded the church.

"Ah that I could go as well, lads!" Lowin said, his hands on his breeches. "My breath cometh short, I'm dizzy and must sit! I'll open an inn, and naught but the best shall ever be served thee should you come. God speed thee, parson."

"And thee, John Lowin."

He packed his things for early departure, and went upstairs to bed with his wife.

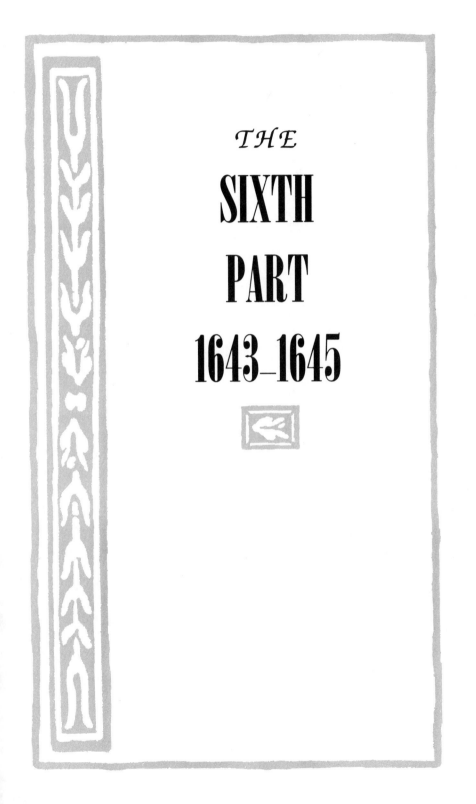

THE

SIXTH
PART
1643–1645

ONE

The Gatehouse of Oxford

ALL HIS JOURNEY NORTH UNDER THE WINTER TREES HE HAD REMEMBERED the little town of Oxford as he had first seen it traveling with William Laud years before: a celibate world of young boys and gruff lecturers, gorgeous chapels and dark libraries where underfed scholars huddled by the light of dawn. Now his first sight, as he came through the gate, was of three mounted cavaliers, plumes in velvet hats, thick curls down shoulders, laughing over some matter. As he rode into the town he was curious to see satin banners floating from the college gates, while ladies leaned their plump arms on the ledges of the windows of Merton College and gazed down. Music of lute and virginal floated from taverns as he made his way through the streets full of soldiers and merchants towards Christ Church College.

Harvey was waiting for him at the top of a students' stair, and flung open the door to reveal his little room poked in a corner. "What kept thee so long?" he barked. "Hast recollected to bring my coffee beans? I'm half dead of mental inertia! If I cannot come to the meetings, at least they hath had the decency to come to me!"

This room was as cluttered as the great doctor's had been in London with books and notes, surgical tools, and many sketches of the growing fetus tacked here and there to the wall. Nicholas put down his bag. "Dost tutor the royal children?"

"Ugh, I do! Never mind them, think of the sewage! The water's bad, men sicken, and no one wants to do anything about it . . . why bother, they say! We'll all pack up in a few weeks and be home."

Seizing his friend by the arm, Harvey threw open the lattice to the cold, still winter air of the quadrangle. "Behold the court! Or shall we say, behold hundreds of rooms of courtliness compressed into a much smaller space." His mouth twitched critically. "His Majesty is lodged behind those windows over the gatehouse and is in blessed fine health for all his troubles; he exercises on horseback below. Aye, I see thy opinion of him's not changed! St. John's College houses his nephew, Prince Rupert, and men who are hoping to negotiate for peace. Other men of influence have the rooms of masters and presidents in the various colleges, and the less important folk such as tailors, bootmakers, actors, and musicians are stowed where they can find a hole. Physicians and priests are given privies such as this. The soldiers are in the fields in tents and shacks." He took Nicholas's hand, made a curtsey, and turning him clumsily, said in a high-pitched voice, "There is at times even dancing . . . wilt thou, sweet?"

Nicholas shouted, "Christ's wounds, I have missed thee!"

After supper they walked arm in arm. Torches burned up and down the streets, and from a tavern there came the sound of soldiers quarreling over dice. Harvey pointed out a painter's studio and another where a dancing master gave daily lessons. " 'Tis the very court!" Harvey said. "But for lack of space and money 'tis the same."

In Christ Church Hall, candles glittered against the polished wood paneling of the walls and the faces of young soldiers. From the end of the room they were pulling in small trunks, flinging each open, and kneeling to unpack silver patens, goblets, and chalices from the layers of velvet and straw. A few priests had also come with boxes.

"The colleges have given their treasure for the King's cause," Harvey said. Nicholas watched it with folded arms. He thought of his wife hurrying through the streets with gold hidden in her bodice, and that this night she would not be by his side. From the window came the sound of a boy lutenist and his faintly raspy, adolescent singing. " 'Tis not expected to last," Harvey said, taking his arm. "No one wants war . . . we shall be home by springtime, Cooke." The corner of his mouth twitched, and he passed his hand over it to hide it.

In the morning Nicholas once more pulled on his black ankle-length cassock and four-cornered hat, which he had not worn in some time, and sought the chapel. No one stopped him, and two other churchmen greeted him warmly. Scarcely had he returned from prayer, however, when Harvey demanded they begin at once to do something about the water and the sewage. No one was much concerned, as he had said, for they expected the negotiations with Parliament to succeed weekly.

Still, by the time spring was beginning to come to the college fields filling them with wildflowers, nothing had been settled.

My dearest Cecily!

I must confess that I ache for thy touch, and last night put out my arm to embrace thee and struck instead the wall. My right hand is yet somewhat swollen.

It does pass my mind whether the mice have made nests of the altar cloth inside our church. Odd the things one thinks of, as if such small things should matter! Perhaps we struggle back to where we were, or at least attempt to, saying, "these things don't matter." Aye, they matter, but not so much as this greater one—that I am able to say prayers each morning in the chapel and a fair number of people come. I have also baptized a child.

Harvey is a good soul, but our chamber is so close that last night he trod upon my shaving kit and smashed the little mirror. Still, some physicians are three to a room.

Nick

She came unexpectedly in the early spring for a visit with William before her on the horse, and Nicholas ran towards them with a great shout, and almost pulled them to the ground in his delight. All day long he walked about with her on one arm and his son on the other. He showed them the chapels with their stained-glass windows and the dining halls. They toured the masters' gardens to the buttery shops where the students ate, and made their way up dark, steep stairs to bookshops tucked in little holes of rooms. He and Cecilia borrowed a private room for the week, and William stayed with Harvey, whom he adored.

He was now thirteen years old, a nervous, intelligent boy whose voice was just beginning to break. During the days he hung over his father's shoulder, lank hair falling into his face, mouth swollen and rueful. "Well, lad," said Nicholas.

The reply was stout. "I think I should stay."

The physician, who had been folding packets of herbs and marking them, turned to look tenderly at his son. "And why shouldst, prithee?"

The boy began to stroll about the small room, now and then overlooking the quadrangle or addressing his remarks to the ceiling. "I'm needed here," he said, thrusting his voice as low as possible. "I could be a messenger, or help thee. I could be a page or a soldier."

Nicholas listened gently. " 'Tis best thou go home with thy mother and watch after her, wag. Within two years when these troubles are forgot, shalt be here as student."

The boy's head shot back. "I want to stay with thee." His dark eyes pleaded, and then he angrily looked away. Nicholas sighed.

He knew when the boy left that he was discontented. "I'll tend to the garden," his wife said as she kissed him. "You shall be home before the quinces come."

Midsummer came, and no assurance of peace.

He found a mathematics scholar in a room high in one of the colleges and spent much time with him. Letters came for him weekly, and at night he often sat up late to answer them. "Wilt douse the flame, fellow?" grumbled Harvey. "Scratch goeth thy pen like a soul from hell!" Chagrined, Nicholas went quietly out to the stairs, where he sat with letters to him spread upon the board on his knee, deciding what answer to make.

to the physician and priest Cooke, Oxford College, from Luke Malverne, chaplain to his grace the Archbishop of Canterbury

Dear friend,

I send you warm greetings from our prelate William Laud, who is now beginning his third year in the Tower. They have confiscated his property so that his household is dispersed with no work. They bring him down to chapel for service every morning, and there they preach on his wickedness while he sits quietly listening. He says nothing, but it breaks my heart.

The simplest virtue, that we should love one another and, as far as possible, live in peace and harmony with all men, hath become an impossibility. Would the apostles themselves have quarreled had they lived longer? Is this inherent in our natures?

The Puritan barrister William Prynne hath ridden in majesty into the city to take his place in the Commons and further bring his grace down. He bears that as well.

He hath several times spoken of you. Be assured you have our loves.

A second letter came, so precious that it took his breath away. It had been addressed to him in Cripplegate, and Cecilia had forwarded it within a packet, much crumpled, sealing wax cracked and redolent of something incomprehensibly far away.

to the physician and priest Cooke, from his sworn friend Avery at the Plymouth Corporation

This is the third letter I have sent you, and have had no response, so either mine hath been lost in the going or thine in the coming.

I write from my hope and disappointment. Each year I wished to have more to tell you, and little has happened. I live in a colony of some eighty souls. I find their rules for a moral life to be suffocatingly strict. We are surrounded by savages; when you have such you understand how the very worst of Englishmen are not so bad at all. I live by farming and hunting and am physician when I am called to be. We have few medicines here, and I have enclosed a list should you be so kind as to provide them.

The news of Tom's death reached us, of course, and I wept over it. I would come home, but have no money and know not what to come to. What hath happened to the life we knew?

It went on for several pages, which Nicholas read many times, and then found Harvey and read them to him as well. He wrote back a letter as long, enclosing a packet of herbs and other medicines which he bought from one of the Oxford apothecaries. He addressed it to the Plymouth Corporation, finding it strange to write the name of that place, which he had never done before. It was odd to know someone who had been to that dark land, and remained there . . . it seemed bitter against his lips. Heartily did he resent the thousands of miles of heavy water between them.

Fall came. Cattle were now penned in the Christ Church quadrangle, and the smell of hay and animal flesh mounted to the frosted window of the small chamber and mingled with that of Harvey's coffee. Cecilia arrived once more with William, who had grown now almost to her height: he was as delicate as a sunflower, and not knowing what to do with his body, was forever knocking into things. When Nicholas took him to physic a soldier who had been wounded in a brawl over a whore, the boy was sick. He walked with him to the meadows by the river in the early mornings so that he could watch the cavalry exercising, their long curls flowing to their collars and the first frost rising from the earth between the bare trees. William was lost in envy, and on returning, he quarreled with his father.

"I don't know what to do with him!" said Cecilia later. "Some of his friends are trying to persuade him to leave school and join the armies."

Nicholas went to search for his son, and found him at last in the now empty field, violently cutting the air with a heavy stick as a sword. He sat down with him for a long time on the low stone wall, and the boy wept. When he and his mother went home, Nicholas buried his loneliness for his family in his work.

A few actors from the disbanded King's Men arrived. They lived in small rooms, and were never paid, and wore only threadbare costumes which they had not bothered to sell. They told him that some of their old colleagues in London were working surreptitiously at the Red Bull, a small theater in the Clerkenwell district known for its lewd comedies. They said that bishops had been deprived of their income and Lambeth Palace was now headquarters for the Parliamentarian soldiers. John and Nell Lowin had closed their house by the wharf and opened an inn. The leader of Commons, John Pym, was ill of cancer and near death. Parliament would then be without leadership, or inherit a still harsher one, making things worse than ever.

Nicholas shook his head; he felt things were quite bad enough. Dysentery had sprung up in the city, and he was in no mood for plays.

Sometimes when hurrying along the streets of Oxford in his dark cassock and four-cornered hat, he would see the King and Queen walking hand in hand. Men would fall to their knees in the dust until the sovereign gave them leave to rise; his smile was reserved and grateful. Nicholas withdrew into the shadow of a doorway until Charles Stuart had passed.

Then sometime past Christmas, the thing that he had dreaded occurred, for Harvey burst into their room, threw Nicholas's good coat at him, and said, "Come! We're called to the King!"

"I will not come."

"Art crazed? Dress!"

The double bed of the royal chamber above the gate was hung with white embroidered satin. Two gentlemen of the bedchamber stood close with arms folded over their chests, and there was a priedieu with the open Bible upon it. Upon the clothes rack hung fresh lace and an embroidered white shirt, and near it were riding boots and coat. A faint scent of smoky warmth filled the small room, for the curling irons were heating on a brazier by the fire. Charles Stuart was seated on an upholstered chair with his foot upon a stool; his shirt was unlaced, and a book lay open upon his knee. He was pale and seemed tired.

In a perfunctory way the physicians fell to their knees. "By your leave, Majesty . . ."

"Rise, sirs, and health to ye. Master Harvey, an thou wilt."

Nicholas watched as William Harvey bowed again and then approached the sovereign. His own heart beat loudly: he felt resentment, anger, grief, he knew not what. Good and evil were closely intertwined in the heart of man, William Laud had said . . . as much were love and hate.

He only murmured, "By your leave, sire." He stood in the corner of the sleeping chamber with its white bed hangings. The hairdresser would have come forward, but the King wearily shook his head. Harvey took Nicholas's arm upon leaving, and when they were half across the yard, the former priest of Mary Aldermanbury stopped and covered his face with his hands. "I could not have touched him!" he said in a harsh whisper.

Each morning prayers were read out in Christ Church Cathedral, the young boy singers giving out the psalms and hymns from their stalls. Always Charles Stuart came and knelt quietly, staring ahead of himself. Nicholas, from his place in the chancel, began to see him more clearly than anyone else: the delicate nose, the long face which never smiled, the righteous look about the mouth. He came always with several close friends. Evenings he came as well. After a time Nicholas, in his surplice, seemed to sense that there was no one else there but the two of them.

His heart beat in rage.

On Sunday mornings he gathered about the altar with the other priests to take the host and wine, and then to give it to the congregation, who came forward to kneel at the rail. It was something he had done weekly since he had been ordained many years before. And on the Sunday following his visit to the royal chambers, when he turned with the chalice in his hand, he saw that Charles Stuart had come forward and knelt to receive. Already another priest had dropped the consecrated bread into the sovereign's hands, and still he knelt for the wine.

For a moment Nicholas could not move. He was aware of the candles, and the wrinkled velvets of the court, and the perfume of the women and incense lingering over the small chapel. There were but a few steps between himself and the kneeling sovereign. Even the very air seemed to stand still.

Slowly he went forward, the chalice held in both hands and yet close against the deep burgundy cope which covered his chest. He could feel the pounding of his heart increase. Charles Stuart had removed his hat, and his head was bowed so that the face could not be seen. He seemed delicate: even his fingers were small. Nicholas stood there with the chalice of consecrated wine against his ribs. He had but one instinct, which was to take the full contents of the vessel and hurl it into the face of the man who knelt before him.

The sovereign moved slightly and then raised his face. At the moment he was as unguarded as a boy awakened from sleep. His puzzled eyes alone asked the question of the delay, and he raised one hand to take the chalice base. For a moment Nicholas prayed very hard, and then took a deep breath. Then he tilted the chalice carefully and said, *"The Blood of our Lord Jesus Christ, which was shed for thee, preserve thy body and soul unto everlasting life. Drink this in remembrance..."* and watched the lips of the King as he drank.

He remembered nothing of the next moments, but that he somehow put down the chalice, bowed to the altar, and hurried from the chapel to the vestry. Closing the door behind him, he leaned upon the table full of Bibles and patens and chalices and sobbed as if his heart would break.

That night men ran with torches through the streets, shouting that the battalions must assemble before the city gates at dawn, for they were going to fight.

There had been the battle of Adwalton Moor in Bradford, near Yorkshire, where the royalist armies had won and taken West Riding, Wentworth's shire, defeating Fairfax's men. Now the armies were expected to meet in Wiltshire, some forty miles from Oxford. Nicholas, Harvey, and six other men (some very young and two elderly) and one surgeon rode out in carts with the medical supplies.

While waiting they sat in a field by the carts of bandages and medical supplies, which had been stored near a large barn commandeered for the wounded. Behind for acres and acres was the army camp.

Towards the day's end they began to walk through the woods, which were full of small flowers, with the carts following them over the wretched path towards where the battle had been. No one could say who had won. There were bees in a wild hive up in the trees, and a little boy who'd gone fishing looked at them with terrified eyes.

At the edge of the field was a body here and there, and then as they walked further they were beyond number, and sometimes they did not know to which side they belonged. The physicians' boots were soon sticky with mud, and there was the smell of hot blood everywhere like a room after childbirth, and the insidious buzzing of flies. Several captains accompanied them, leaning over to poke this man with a stick or gently turn a heavy heap of clothing over with a boot toe to identify it. "Know this one, men?"

"Nay, not of mine."

"Wait! 'Twas of Harry's division from the Cambridgeshire recruits."

"Where's Harry?"

"I don't know."

"Leave him then for later: wounded first."

"Look at that pile! The King knows this one . . . he sat for the Lords until he broke off and came here, but I can't recall his name."

The air smelled of rain and burned flesh. Leather helmets choked dead necks, pike lances were split in half, horses lay with legs sprawled and eyes covered with insects, for the day was warm. The earth was uneven with the dead as back and forth went the teams of old men and boys carrying the litters of the wounded, who groaned, or sobbed, or called for their sweethearts. Nicholas found scapulars of both Charles and Lord Essex, the leader of the opposing army. He found small books of poetry or meditations, and coins, and a soprano recorder. Some men lay with their chests or faces in fragments, sharp white bone of rib or jaw laid open; others were a tangle of intestine, kidney, liver, and lung.

Then they were in the barn and Harvey said, "This leg's gangrenous and must be amputated," and they did so, Nicholas holding down the boy with others and the lad drunk with sack and screaming. He dreaded to find Andrew Heminges among the dead. The actor, however, was still serving in the divisions of the army farther north, and from recent letters, was unharmed.

On the last trip to the field in the dying light, a little stumpy man came towards them waving his hands and shouting. "What have they done? My field, my field . . . why don't they go home with their laws?" He stood shouting, "Go home to your wives! Go home! This field is mine!"

The side of Harvey's mouth twitched; he swore.

Across the grass, morris men were dancing beneath a tree, great white handkerchiefs in both hands, coming forward to bow and turn about each other, now forming a circle and gravely moving first in one direction and then the other. Faintly through the orchard came the tinkle of their bells. They were very young, and when they laughed their new bass voices edged to breaking.

The next day Nicholas walked again over the field to the farmhouse, where he stood looking about for the dancers. They were not there; only one small tin bell glittered dully on the grass with its bit of red ribbon. He wondered if he had imagined them, and he fell into his tent that night grim and unwashed.

Some weeks later a letter came from Keyes saying that Cecilia had been set upon by Parliamentary soldiers crossing Cheapside, dragged into an alley, and assaulted. Nicholas left for home at once.

TWO

London

E GALLOPED THROUGH THE CITY GATES AND THE BARRICADES. ONLY when he rode past Paul's churchyard did he rein in his horse for a moment, and bite his lip to keep from crying aloud. The great outdoor pulpit had been pulled to the ground; stones and timbers still lay in a heap and pigeons were pecking about them. The bookstalls remained, but none of the sellers were friends, for those had gone to join the king. A few nodded briefly to him, and he spurred his horse until he came to Love Lane, and leapt down with his key clasped within his hand.

The house door, however, was unlocked and open.

In the parlor most of the books had been pulled from the shelves and kicked across the room; pillows were flung this way and that, curtains torn from their rods. In the kitchen, ale and flour barrels had been emptied, as had been the spice jars, and the ropes which had swung from the beams and held onions and herbs and dried meat were stripped clean. Throwing down his cloak, Nicholas rushed up the stairs.

Boards had been ripped from the sleeping-chamber floor, as if some-one had sought something. Stunned, he walked down the steps again to his dispensary. There he found jars of balms and medicines smashed, their contents scattered across the floor. William's wild grey cat, who came and went as he pleased, had eaten of some of it and lay dead. Nicholas raised his eyes to the cupboard. But for a few sheets of paper, it was empty. His writings on kidneys, lungs, and stomach were gone, as well as his first charting of Mars and the transit of Venus, which had been bound in red endpapers. They had been crumpled, thrust into the hearth and set afire to warm the hands of some man he would never know. Some man had crouched by his fire and warmed his hands on his life's work.

Then as he cried in rage both at the stupidity of the destruction and his impotence, Timothy Keyes hurried shyly through the open door, his large heavy body soft and placating. He wore his apron. At once Nicholas shouted, "In Christ's name, friend, I have thy letter. Where are my wife and son?"

"Be at peace, parson! I took them to good Lowin's at his inn on the Old Kent Road. Thy lad went with much reluctance."

"Are they well? And she . . ."

"Unharmed. Here, she hath writ thee." Nicholas seized the letter and, muttering his thanks, sat down before the ashes of the fire to read.

> Sweet heart, first you must know that I have not been hurt and can't bear to be made a fuss of! The risks had become too great to continue my work; still, a soldier must risk, and I am no less. The men had nothing of me; I would have killed them.

He looked up at his friend, who had knelt to gather some broken cup fragments. "Did she know of the destruction here?"

"No, they left three days before." Nicholas nodded gravely and con-tinued reading.

> You won't find us at the inn, however. I think it is best to proceed at once to France. I can hear you draw your breath and begin at once to

shake your head, saying, "Oh Cecily!" Sweet heart, many men loyal to the crown have now gone there to seek help, and the Queen herself is in Paris to raise support. My brother has decided to settle there for a time, and you know I've many friends and will be able to continue the work which I feel I must do raising money for the royal armies.

There is also William, who is so angry at both of us that he cannot join the King that I think it best I take him across the channel. My love, do not fret for me. All will be well, and we hope to be home soon.

Many neighbors who were fond of him stopped by that night; complaining bitterly over the destruction of the house, which had been done secretly, they swept and tidied, and brought clean sheets for the bed and coal for the fire. Nicholas fell into a deep, grieving sleep. His sexton reappeared at dawn, from where he would not tell, and began to work in the garden as if he had never been away. Nicholas hung his sign of physician once more, but though he sat much of the morning in the dispensary, only one woman came to consult him.

One of the actors came later that afternoon and told him that soldiers were pulling down the Globe. Nicholas took his cloak and they walked across the bridge to the south side until he came to the playhouse. Boards were torn from each other: splinters gaped, nails glinted. Behind the stage the tiring rooms and storage rooms had been ripped apart. The upper galleries were heaps of boards and cushions, but the lowest one remained to form the polygonal shape. In the center of this where the stage had jutted into the orchestra, soldiers had made a fire from the last boxes of playbooks and prompter's copies.

He wondered wistfully if any of Shagspere's scripts had been there, mayhap from the amended edition the writer had made of *Hamlet* when the theaters had closed during the 1603 plague. He had sat by the window of his room and the quill had scratched; the sun had fallen across his balding head and down the wrinkled leather sleeve of his jerkin to the neat, nervous fingers. He had bitten his nether lip and wouldn't have light brought until it was too dark to see, and then he had leapt up and stood looking over the Thames, one hand hooked in his sword belt and the other on the window frame. On the top of one page which lay on his desk had been a faint spattering of ink where he'd pulled the quill too rapidly from the well before tapping the excess.

Protect the actors, Heminges had bade him.

Turning from the theater in the light, cold rain, Nicholas walked a long time between the houses of Southwark past the marshes and the empty brothels before he saw the Archbishop's palace, red brick and low-lying, along the water. Horses stood about the yard, and in the high fresh grasses outside the chapel lay dull shards of stained glass. The windows which William Laud had so meticulously restored were shattered, and rain was falling through the jagged bits of remaining glass. Nicholas turned away. When he ferried across the river he discovered that the altar of Westminster Abbey had also been pulled down, as well as the old cross in Cheapside. Then he could bear no more, and went home and shut his door.

Harvey returned to the city some days later, banging over the threshold of the rectory in his old way, thrusting back his lank, greying hair. The little body seemed dryer, thinner, and compacted with resentment. They made themselves comfortable before the fire, and between sentences he poked his pipe, or turned to spit violently into the ashes of the hearth. "I couldn't bear to be away longer!" he grunted. "Enough, I said! I want a good Cheapside meal, a walk along Lothbury. And what do I find when I have come? London's changed completely. It's a closed, sullen, suspicious place . . . apprentices standing about ready to beat a man for blowing his nose! Yet that's not enough—I have suffered like thee. They came when I was away and burned my writings, Nicholas! My new work, burnt. . . ." The corner of his mouth twitched several times.

"What hast lost?"

"Most everything, but for what I published."

"Ah, Christ's blood!" said the physician, reaching forward to squeeze his friend's knee in the wrinkled wool hose. Then he sank back shyly, respecting the sorrow before him by his silence.

Harvey muttered, " 'Twas the greatest rape . . . ever to endure."

"God help us."

"The question is, will He? Is Our Lord on our side or theirs? Or hast He as much difficulty choosing as many of the men do? You see, most of us were in the middle, and now we're hurled to either side. . . . It's killing some of them. It's breaking their bloody hearts, my friend! Men I have known, old fellows. Is this just or wise? Never mind. I must also tell thee I stopped by Harrington's on Great St. Thomas Apostle Street and found he'd had another stroke. He didn't know me, Nicholas . . . poor fellow! Our numbers are once more diminished and our potential to understand all knowledge gravely undermined by it, at least for these present days. . . . Here, I've brought coffee beans! Can set the pot to boil? Good fellow!"

As they sat sipping the bitter drink, Harvey smiled crookedly and commented, "Well, fine bachelor, so thy wife's gone to Paris! Many people go there or to the wars. Who'd stay here? Christ's nails, not I! Where's the life, the joy, the singing of our city? Where's the processions, the choirs, the mummery? I shall go presently: when wilt thou?"

"Never."

Harvey put down his mug. "For what reason wilt linger?" he muttered with a dark frown. "Dost think many men will come to us for physicking? God knoweth who wrecked our houses and what else they'll do next. We have served the crown and are not popular: a physician friend hath been shot, and other men beaten."

"When is this 'presently' in which thou wilt go, Harvey?"

"Soon."

"Nay, wilt stay I do believe me."

Nicholas had begun to walk about the kitchen; he took a cheese and, holding it against his chest, cut two wedges from it. "I've walked and walked these streets until I'm too sick to sleep," he said. "And I ache for my wife and my son . . . dost think I like to be from them? Still, this is my city. Our old friend, Bartlett . . . hast heard of him? He hath power and approves of destruction of beauty, or popery as they call it."

He put down the cheese and threw himself into the chair opposite Harvey again. "Look you, William!" he said. "I wanted to love everyone. I said, respect the rights of all . . . mayhap I was a fool, but I still must say this. Why? I cannot do otherwise and live within my body. My church may be locked, but I'll remain. I'm no less priest than I was before."

He added, "There are men preparing a petition to retain the prayer book, and I am thinking to write it. And then there's . . ." He suddenly fought to steady his voice. Every night since he had returned, his dreams had turned towards the river to the ancient Tower, where in a small room with plain bed and austere prayer table, letters, some books, and yet some hope, waited the fussy, devout little man who had been consecrated Archbishop and was even now no less than that.

Harvey, narrowing his eyes, studied him. "Ach, William Laud!" he spat with some disgust. "I can well read thy mind, Cooke. That meddling old nuisance who with his intolerance hath dragged down so much! Oh, we are all irremovably intertwined. The priest in thee, the damn priest who goeth forth with prayer book in hand when something else is needed . . . yes, that's it, I suppose. Will stay here in this dirty, wretched city . . ."

". . . which thou lovest."

"I abhor the very dung between the cobbles! And what dost propose to do concerning this wretched old man whom almost all have forsaken, eh? What dost think thou canst do, thou enema-giver? What wilt bring upon thyself? Nay, I cannot bear to think on it!"

Nicholas brooded a time by the fire after his friend had left. Harvey did not understand, of course, and he wanted his friends always to understand perfectly. Something had formed in him as he had entered the city gates, and in the past few weeks of walking about. He could not abandon what had been broken: to do so would be to abandon himself. He must do what he could to heal it.

The Archbishop's chaplain, Malverne, had told him the Puritan lawyer Prynne had come and taken away not only all the papers which his grace had prepared for his own defense, but his private prayer journal: would he know what passed between the Archbishop and God? What greater indignity could be given?

Nicholas's dark brown eyes grew soft with this resolution. Much of what had been scattered in despair within himself returned with gathered strength. He felt it in his chest. He knew there were times in a man's life when he felt that everything he had known and all he had lived led to this moment. It gathered under his ribs until it could not be displaced. All his life passed before him: all loves, and failures, children, and conversations and knowledge and joy. It had all led him here. They should not bring down the old man as long as he had strength to protest.

He walked east that night and stood looking up at the Tower. By this time all thought had left him, and he was perfectly still.

When he woke the next day he began to go about the city, gathering the names of those men who would help him in a petition to keep the prayer book, and to release the Archbishop. Several hours a day he sat at the very table at which Cecilia had written her pleas summoning help for the lord Strafford, and composed letters to all the men of influence whom he had ever served.

Many mornings before the sun had risen he made his way along the two miles of houses, taverns, and law temples towards the City of Westminster and the houses of Parliament. The yard was always filled with vagabonds and petitioners, and citizens already lined up for places to hear the day's proceedings. Parliamentary guards walked about, shouting and poking them with the butt ends of muskets; those who waited cursed back. By the time the faint golden sun began to rise over the houses to the east, there were more citizens wanting places than space. Some held heated bricks or little iron boxes filled with coals to warm them. Parliament sat even on Christmas morn, not wishing to regard it as a feast day. He was scandalized, but kept his peace. He realized he must keep his peace about many things if he were to achieve his end. Then he regarded them dreamily, because they did not know what he was determined to do; nor did they know that this thing for him would in some way make up for what he felt he had failed at before.

After a time he had two hundred signatures; it was very little, but he was proud of them. On the day the trial of William Laud began in Westminster Hall, Nicholas came early to find a place in the galleries. There, below him on the stand, stood the little man in his red cap. The physician leaned forward. The accusations were so much nonsense: the Archbishop had subverted the fundamental laws of the kingdom, had held secret communication with the court of Rome, had promoted books and sermons against Parliament. Nicholas had heard much of this before. What stunned him deeply was how much he loved this man: he had not always agreed with him, and yet it did not matter.

The petition, which he had assembled with the help of Cecilia's books of law, he had written himself. He would have liked to have asked for her help, but hesitated to let her know what he was doing. There was some strain in their frequent letters: she did not want him to remain in the city and he would not on his life go. Once more he edited his careful words, wistful that he was not a barrister: the clear honest thought of the physician and the spiritual strength of the priest were not what was needed here. He chafed.

Still he was the priest of St. Mary Aldermanbury. Even the barred doors and the silent bell could not change that. And he would stay by his church, and his Archbishop and the city he had known, until the very last. There was a sense of heightened exhilaration, or almost sensual excitement. He hardly slept. He lay awake listening to the bells tolling the hours and the footsteps of the watch. He wanted to run down the steps and throw open the door, boyishly shouting, "I will do this thing." He panted like a runner before the race. He felt nothing could stop him.

When he understood that no more signatures could be had, he managed to seek out an old friend of Dobson's who reluctantly agreed to present the petition at the Westminster trial. He knew the man, for he had also dined with Laud in the old days, and had been one of the eleven only who had refused to sign the bill condemning Strafford.

By this time, fall had come and the russet and deep gold leaves had drifted down from the heavy trees to every lane and alley of the city. On the day when they had agreed to the presentation, Nicholas walked with the petition in his coat over the wet fallen leaves of the streets towards Old Palace Yard as a bridegroom to the wedding. His steps were light; girls turned to smile at him. He had not felt so happy in a long time, though he had spent several lonely weeks. Keyes had moved from the city some weeks before, and Harvey was so angry at what he called a wasteful expenditure of energy that he would not speak to Nicholas.

He strode, almost singing. It was as if the barricades were not there, nor the sullen young soldiers, who were bored and wished themselves back at their crafts, nor the theaters shut and his friends disbanded. He whistled. As the rising sun drifted through the russet and gold leaves and glittered on the cobbles, he could see himself rushing up the steps of the Tower, hurling open the door, and stretching his hand out to the surprised small Archbishop, crying, "Come, you are free . . . much is restored. . . ."

Once and again he crossed Old Palace Yard and fell into a place in the long line which had already formed. Above the stones of the ancient buildings and the beautiful trees the sky was clear and blue; the day would be fine. He craned his neck to look around. It was yet early; the members were just donning their woolen gowns to endure the hours of coolness and damp within this vast building. Still he continued to watch for the lord Fairfield, Dobson's friend, who had promised to meet him there.

"A fine morning, Nat!" one of the soldiers said.

The first carriage arrived; a beggar sprang through the crowd to open the door. Then they began to come more rapidly, while at the wharf below ferries docked and men emerged with their clerks to walk up towards Westminster Hall.

Someone said, "Canterbury's not come today; he's poorly!" and others laughed. The ballad sellers had begun to sing in quavery voices.

"Some say he was in hope
To bring England to the Pope,

But now he is in danger of a rope,
Farewell, old Canterbury!
Alas, poor Canterbury!"

A few men threw coins, and then another seller whipped off his cap, bowed to the crowd, and sang out from the sheet he held:

"Though Wentworth's beheaded.
Should any repine?
There's others may come
To the block besides he.
Keep thy head on thy shoulders,
And I will keep mine.
For what is all this to you or to me?

"Then merrily and cheerily
Let's drink off our beer,
Let who as will run for it,
We will stay here."

"Ah, that's an old song!" someone spat. "Give us new poetry!"

By now the men were mounting steadily from the wharf and the carriages turning one after another to the yard. The doors of the hall opened and all of them were blown inside with bits of this and scraps of that, pamphlets, ballads, announcements, newsletters, poetry, petitions. They were crammed into benches high up on either side, rows from the members but in clear view of the house. The petition was now crinkled next to Nicholas's shirt and near his heart, and still the lord who was to present it had not come.

Debates began: the phrase "prayer book" arose several times, and the argument to make it a treasonable offense to use it, and then the name of the Archbishop several times and laughter. Beneath him was merely a collection of dark hats and cloaks. He could not hear well.

After some time he saw the man before him turn, and then his neighbor touched him and shoved a paper in his hand. He read it by the dim window light. Dobson's friend was not coming; he begged his pardon. He loved the ways of the old church but would be imprisoned for presenting the bill. He had already lost much by voting for Strafford's life; this would utterly impoverish him.

Nicholas was stunned. He stood to walk out, not knowing quite where, but instead turned to the great sweep of men within the hall. They were laughing over some matter, and suddenly all he was rose within his chest and he cried out, "Cease! Listen . . . my lords and masters, I beg you!"

The voices below died away as his full, ringing voice echoed back from the deep windows. "My lords and all good Englishmen who here are gathered . . ." It was strange: he almost watched himself as he did this unaccustomed thing, as if between his sitting and rising he had split somehow into two men.

Surprised silence fell upon Westminster Hall.

Swiftly Nicholas climbed and stood upon the bench. The faces below had turned up, only somewhat shaded by the dark hats, and at the moment he saw nothing but goodwill in them. "Beloved friends," he shouted. "This paper was to be presented to you this day. Here 'tis for anyone to see it, signed by two hundred honest men. But the words it contains are not as important as these I am going to say to you. I spoke in this paper of retaining the prayer book and freeing his grace William Laud . . . nay, nay, list to me! What I have to say is greater than these things! I have seen the war: I do not speculate upon it, my friends. Nothing is more precious than the peace of our land. We cannot throw away what we have built as a civilization these hundred years!"

The words poured from him as if he were drunk, and he thrust his hands forward wildly. "I have loved this city and this country," he cried. "And I say this cannot continue, it cannot. We must cease. . . ." He had not meant to say so much: he meant to be logical, arguing calmly as the best of the barristers. "Release our prelate!" he cried. "As I live, he's a worthy man and even now prays for his enemies! Restore the King, and once more let us meet together. . . ."

The soldiers were mounting the benches towards him. In a moment one had him by the arm, and he was pulled and handed over the crowd to the cries of anger about him. He shouted, "Do not throw away all we have known . . ." but they had him from the hall by that time, and were hurling him across the yard. He fell facedown in a puddle of filthy cold water.

They were laughing.

Slowly he got to his knees, and though he understood at once that his leg had been injured, tried not to limp too badly as he made his way to the smaller streets which would lead him to the Strand. It was only by leaning on a heavy stick he had found that he got to the city gates, and he had to rest several times against houses and sit by fountains. He went stubbornly, furiously, and in pain towards the house on Great St. Thomas Apostle Street. No one answered when he knocked at the door of his old friend until a scullery girl came timidly from the back and murmured that the old man and his wife had left the city.

So deep a sense of shame and disappointment did he feel in himself that he could hardly bear his own company. The old impulsivity of his youth had overtaken him. He looked back on his months of work, flushing with humiliation. As if a few hundred signatures would mean anything, as if any reasonable man would risk his future by delivering such a thing!

He found his house cold and empty, for John had begun to drink again and would disappear for days, and the housekeeper had long left his service. Shivering uncontrollably, he made up the fire, stripped to wash the stinking mud from his body, and wrapped himself like an old man in wool sleeping shirt and gown. Like an old man . . . exactly that. Had someone said those words about him as he was thrown . . . old man? He flushed as if he had been struck.

He wondered if all the good he had ever tried to do had turned wrong. Had he thought too much of his priestliness? He considered in his worst moments that evening if his outburst had hurt the man he was trying to help. Who had he helped, truly, in his life? Cecilia wrote that she and William did well, but missed him very much. He wondered with some wistfulness if she were not simply kind: he wondered if anything was as he thought it was. He had bruised his leg muscles badly, torn something perhaps, and come away with a shivering ague and mockery ringing in his ears. He did not dare pass the mirror by the door, for the disdain he felt for the man reflected in it.

When he had warmed himself enough with hot ale and wool coverings that he could think again, he fell into a deep brooding resentment as if he contemplated a life which had been so wrongly constructed that it could never be made right again. Walking into the parlor, he saw the piles of letters he had been writing, and gathering them distastefully to himself, thought to thrust them into the fire. He could not quite bear to let them go, though, and remembered the cupboard under the stair. As he tucked them there he felt a box towards the back, pulled it out, and found his microscopes and papers on his studies of magnified objects, and instructions and thoughts on the grinding and combination and polishing of lenses, and focal lengths and lighting and such.

This was his true work, Harvey had often told him, and even Wentworth had said it. Yet it was insipid, nothing. A man he cared for deeply was in danger, and he could not bear to think of him and could do nothing to help him, so he turned to this. He always had sought refuge in his work and studies at times of incomprehensible troubles, and he did so now.

When his leg was better he found a Puritan family who were now grinding lenses in Old Fish Street. His ability to see things far was not as good as it had been, but he made out small objects as well as ever. And this became the greatest passion he could remember, for he worked at it almost every hour until it seemed there was no world but the one he was determined to find beneath the lens.

He found it on a damp late November day.

A new earthen pot full of rainwater stood outside the door, and on a whim he took a little of it and curiously carried it to the microscope, to which he had just fitted a new combination of lenses, and lit the candles.

It was a dark day, and the sky above the grey stones and thatched roofs of the city was shifting and sullen.

A neighbor's daughter was singing from the lane.

His eyes ached as he tried to focus upon it. Then he saw that what was beneath the glass was alive. There were creatures of inconceivable minuteness, more than ever he could count and yet of every possible shape. Some seemed to be made of globules without anything to hold them together. Most of the bodies were round, having long delicate tails and little horns. Whether it was minutes or hours he remained there he did not know. At last he sank into the coffer chair, letting his head drop back.

His mind sought for words which could be bent into the beginning of expressing it. Cautiously he reached out and rubbed the edge of the worn table, frowning as he stared afterwards at his fingers. He held his palm up to the damp ash-and-rain-smelling air and afterwards looked at it for a time. He remembered vaguely walking by Shagspere's side when he was sixteen and the writer had lost his son, muttering, "Something smaller than we can see mayhap strickens us . . . but where?" Was this it indeed? And if it was, what would he make of it?

He thrust himself forward, pulled the folder of loose foolscap to him, and began to scratch rapidly with his pen. "Thursday the 29 of November 1644. I have seen living matter of infinitesimal size. This is a world so small that it has not been heeded, and yet . . . "

He threw down his pen. He had seen it, and already he was beginning to understand the living forms within the rainwater, the immensity of it, the immensity of the value. Yet again, what immediate use could it be? Should he stomp up the steps of the College of Physicians and interrupt the fellows with his wild claims? Considering his present state of affairs, they would not wish to see his face.

Then a week later, he tried yet another experiment. Curious as to the white matter between his teeth, he took a little on a cloth, mixed it with the rainwater again, and saw an even smaller world. These creatures were even more varied. Some were long and delicate, others circular or oval: some swarmed, some twisted and dipped.

The small creatures haunted him: he saw them everywhere. When his neighbor's daughter scraped her hand the next day, he looked as hard as he could at the raw bruise before he salved it, bringing it gently to his lips at last to taste what he could not see. She said, "What do you look for, parson?"

He answered, "Something I can't see."

"Saints do that," she said confidently, "and those that foretell the future."

He went back and looked again, and again. He changed lenses, focal lengths, lost the vision, distorted it, blurred it, changed again and found it better. What were these things? He did not sleep, not at all, and might not have spoken to another living soul in his compulsion had not Harvey sent a boy to him. Dobson's house on the Strand, which was to have been the hospital, was being confiscated by Parliament at last, and they had to pack away the remaining possessions of the science society if they did not wish to lose them.

Nicholas ran almost all the way and came charging up the steps splattered with mud, microscope in a soft bag under his arm. Bursting into the emptied library, he cried, "I have seen . . ." and told him.

Harvey began to weep. He sobbed with his hands over his eyes, stumbling into things because he could not see where he was going, trying to get out of somewhere. "It's only that I'm most glad, my old friend," he gasped.

So they began to spend hours once more in rusty half-sentences, their heads encircled with pipe smoke, ideas and fancies rising and drifting away again. The world of microscopy became private, inner; solitude was sweet and their only defense. In between, he wrote long tender letters to his wife and son. Again he did not wish to pass the mirror by the kitchen door, wherein he knew he would see his failure.

Newspapers were smuggled in from Oxford. The war went badly, for the King had lost much of his army and copies of his correspondence. To use the prayer book was now a treasonable act. Then on a late cold evening Luke Malverne came to tell him that the Archbishop's fate had been voted on by both houses, and that the old man was to die.

THREE

Again by the Thames in Winter

OME PEOPLE WERE TO BE ADMITTED TO SEE THE ARCHBISHOP: A FAVOR
perhaps. Nicholas waited without sleeping to find if he should be
one of them, and when the message came, walked up and down
his house, too distracted to pray. He wanted to give to William Canterbury all his strength. He felt there would never be words deep enough
to say to him in the short time they would have.

He found him standing by the window of the Tower room, wearing a
close-fitting black knit cap and a heavy black fur-lined robe, for the small
coal brazier did not reach the corners of the room this bitter, still January
day. The room was small and plain, containing some opened trunks of
clothing and papers neatly arranged, as if he had been packing for a
journey. The Archbishop did not look up at first, as if he were trying to
recall where he had laid something. Still when the physician whispered,
"God bless thee, my lord's grace!" he raised his face and smiled.

"Nicholas Cooke," he said.

Nicholas dropped to his knees speechless, and kissed William Canterbury's hands. He knew by the look the old man gave him that he had heard about the incident in Westminster Hall, and with his head still lowered, he flushed.

They spoke of small matters and then drew two chairs to the table. William Laud leaned his arms on the table. "Life is such a vast matter and containeth so much," he said reflectively. "I was thinking just this hour how poor I was as a lad. I had not a single book, and then one day my father brought home two he had found in the rain somewhere, and those I read and read."

"Which were these, my lord's grace?"

"The first was sermons, terrible ones in foul Latin! I have ever tried to do better. The second one . . . a bestiary if I do recall, and quite torn, but from that came my love of cats and creatures." Wistfully he looked around. "Few people have been allowed to come to me. Ah, Nicholas! My chaplain hath again requested me to flee . . . now even if it could be done, why should I do it? I'm past seventy years of age. Flying would be a shame. No, I'm resolved to bear what a good and wise Providence hath appointed for me. I'm an old man and very tired."

Then he said, "Tell me of thyself, my friend." And Nicholas told him of finding the box beneath the stair and that he had taken up his work again. "You must put nothing aside which you value," the Archbishop said strictly. "Nothing worth doing can be easy. This I know, this I have always known. Now, dear parson, there are a few more words I would say which are as important as any left to me."

His nostrils flared slightly for a moment in the old haughty way as when he felt himself misunderstood. "Tom Wentworth once told me in greatest confidence," he said, "that he had greatly offended you one time. He was sick to his heart to think you'd never more be friends, and then one day came a letter with the word *forgiven* underlined thrice. Can you not also forgive our King for signing the paper condemning him? He could not have done otherwise!"

"I do not know, my lord's grace."

"If not for his sake, then thine own? After my . . . when the time comes, there must be healing. If we do not do this, who will?"

Nicholas said nothing, but slowly nodded.

Laud touched his arm contently. "Knowst, all I wanted truly was to be a priest and serve Our Lord . . . the rest came from it. Mayhap for this moment with thee I was again, dear parson, what first and last I was meant to be."

The guards came to announce that the visit must end. Nicholas dropped to his knees again and kissed Laud's hand. Rain was falling over the Tower as he left.

Knocking woke him at midnight. At once he swung his legs to the side of the bed and felt for his shoes. The windows were frosted with cold and the wind whistled around the edges of old thatching and loose tile. He dressed warmly in vest, cloak, and hat. Lastly he tucked his forbidden prayer book within his jerkin and the little vial of holy oil within his pocket, and hurried down the steps of his house.

Two clergymen stood there, hoods about their faces, and without a word they all turned towards Gresham and then east to the church of All Hallows, Barking. By the door was a cart and within it, wrapped several times in burlap, lay the earthly remains of William Canterbury. They opened the door and pulled it within. One of the men had brought candles, and now lit two to stand on either side of the body. They tilted slightly with the cart slats, wax running to the rough wood.

Luke Malverne came forth from the shadows. From his jacket he drew a silky prayer stole and draped it slowly over the burlap. Nicholas felt for the cold, lifeless face under the wrapping. Uncapping the oil, he anointed the eyes and lips. Then opening the prayer book, the men began the service for the burial of the dead.

"I am the resurrection and the life (saith the Lord): he that believeth in me, yea though he were dead, yet shall he live. And whosoever liveth and believeth in me, shall never die."

The men stood with hands clasped for a time. Then they lifted the remains of their Archbishop and carried them through a smaller door to the grave which had been dug even in this bitter weather outside the wall.

"I heard a voice from heaven, saying unto me, Write, From henceforth blessed are the dead which die in the Lord. Even so saith the Spirit, That they rest from their labors."

They cast earth upon the body as they could, and paid the shuffling sexton, who muttered that they should be away. It was treasonous, as well they knew, to do what they had done.

Snow had begun to fall over the city of London as Nicholas walked away from the church by the Tower walls. It glittered on the cobbles as he held high his lantern, casting a dull light upon his footprints, which seemed to follow him which way he went. He was absolutely alone, and still the footprints followed as if they wished to catch up with him and tell him it had all been a mistake and William Canterbury yet lived.

You were right, my lord's grace, he thought. These men came to power, and look what they have done. And I judged you harshly, as if I in my vanity could have done better.

He turned down to the river towards Lowin's empty house. As he walked the steep path once more, there came voices as if from the stones. *Aye*, they said. *Dost ask me if I know the war? Christ's nails, I know it! Damn bastards trampled the young wheat and wet it with their blood. Cavaliers flittering on horseback, long curls quivering, feathers in hats, trampled my corn. Then came the Parliamentary troops, and between them they pressed my children's bread back into the ground from whence it had come. Complained to the sheriff, the parish constable, the bishop. Bishop too frightened to come from his house, saw him looking through the window. Yes, parson, I know the war.*

Your pardon, sir, another whispered. *Someone's fighting something, but I don't know what. Heard about it last Sabbath, but they say it's been going on for a while. James our King (I do forget easily, but believe 'tis James Stuart) fighting the dirty French, I think. I don't know anything about bishops: I never saw one. It's a damn pity the French have to come on our soil and bother us.*

Another voice: *You tell the King for me, sir, not to fear. Kings are divine: anointed with oil, made sacred. God will save the King.*

Voices carried on the snow, melted into the icy river and grey and tumbling, falling downwards to whatever else lies beneath the water and caught between the pilings of the bridge, to the sea. *Ravage,* they said. *Take hold of any side of the country you can and pull until it rips apart, and that's yours. Pull it until the oaks uproot, and the stones buckle loose from the castles and roll down the valleys. Burn churches, colleges, theaters, libraries, taverns: drown ships and topple bridges.* The cries rose and then died away under the rushing of the cold water, and then all was silent under the falling snow.

There was only his own faint muttering again and again: Goodbye, William Canterbury!

He did not know how long he remained by his old friend's house. He made a fire and sat by the river. He could not tell where the sky let off and the river began, and what on the horizon had been made by God and what by man. All grey and turning and falling, and shivering cold.

Closing his eyes, he thought of standing before the altar, consecrating the bread and wine: blessing it, and the crumbs falling to the clean cloth, his hands enclosing the cool silver chalice and the depths of the sacred wine within as deep as heaven. He felt it enter his throat and belly in an astonishing openness. Then in his mind he turned, and the people of the congregation were gone, yet there was a light such as he had never seen before. It was not the light of candles nor of the sun, nor did it increase, but was simply there. He opened his hands and walked towards it, his feet no longer touching the ground. And as he went he felt the light enter him until all he was began to dissolve. Then there was only the light, a sigh, and nothing.

He had become the light: the Lord had taken him in his grief and lifted him to another place. He walked between worlds, one hand steadying himself in heaven and the other trailing the branches of the bare trees of the earth.

Dawn came, but so imperceptibly that it changed almost nothing: white snow continued to fall on the cold rushing river. It lay on the roofs and steeples of the south bank and barely could he find his way home, so ill and cold was he.

FOUR

The Garden

H E REMEMBERED LITTLE ABOUT THE TIME WHICH FOLLOWED, BUT THAT word came of Malverne's departure for France. Not once did the bell ring. He lay upon his bed in absolute exhaustion. Sometimes he called aloud to see if anyone would answer, hearing the echo of his voice through the hall and down the stairs.

Thus passed three nights.

On the fourth he woke somewhere past midnight with a sense of peace so profound that he did not wish to move. There was no wind to push against the beams and signboards of the streets, nor did the watch call. He lay for a time under the soft, warm feather quilt. Minutes passed, mayhap hours. He did not know when he became aware that someone was below in the churchyard.

Sitting up, he reached for his dressing gown. The room was piercingly cold, but he was warm: even his face, which had been pressed into the pillows, was flushed with warmth. He put his feet into his slippers and stood. Only the vaguest shadows could be seen in the hall: the white glimmer of the candle in its holder, and a descending darkness where the stairs turned in their worn way to the parlor.

One step down and then another, his hand on the wall to guide him until the steps were no more and he stood facing the windows of the parlor which overlooked Love Lane. He had not put up the shutters, and the small glass panes glistened faintly.

Nicholas felt his way to the kitchen with its familiar fragrance of wood fire and dried herbs, recollecting the hours last night before he had gone up to bed. He had read a little of Erasmus, and begun a long letter to Cecilia. He had watched the fire go out. He had not, however, bolted the door which led from churchyard to kitchen.

Then he understood that there were strangers waiting for him amid the gravestones. He should go out to them or they come in to him; it did not matter which, for they should meet. He did not know them, and they had, if anything, but an indifferent knowledge of what sort of man he was. Whoever waited would not take the time to know.

Closely he had walked with death over these many years, sometimes beside him and sometimes behind. He had closed the eyes of those whom death had taken, almost feeling the flutter of the warm soul rising between his fingers. Nicholas's heart began the measured beat that was his old actor's way before a difficult moment on the stage: it was not faster, but more intense, as if counting until the entrance. Carefully he returned to the foot of the stairs and reached up his fingers to the dust of the upper shelf of the cupboard where years before he had placed his sword. For a minute he held it in both hands, testing its weight. He had not swung broadsword or rapier upon the boards in thirty years, yet as he stood there the memory returned to him. His muscles had not forgotten.

They stood outside the door.

He understood that they would kill him. Strangely, it did not matter. Very much had been allotted to him, and in time all men must die, as Shagspere used to say. "There is special providence in the fall of a sparrow. If it be now, 'tis not to come; if it be not to come, it will be now; if it be not now, yet it will come. The readiness is all."

He was not afraid. He should fight, lest the souls who had taught him look down from heaven and be ashamed. He had no wish to take any man's life; he did not want that sin upon his soul. Still, though he was no longer young and they outnumbered him, they should not have him for cheap. Then came the astonished thought that though all men must die, he had not expected it would come to him. Arrogant mayhap, but there stood the truth.

Lord have mercy on my soul, he said. Thy will be done. Then he opened the door and went into the graveyard. The cold of the earth slid up his bare legs under sleeping shirt and dressing gown. Before him stood the church, the great trees to the right and the long low wall, and the stones to the dead.

One man came from behind the church and some more from behind the trees. He was seized, but the moment he felt someone's arms hold him, he kicked loose and shouted. In the dark they grappled, and one had his arm about the physician's throat to choke him. The stave came about his back and shoulders: whichever way he turned it fell. He did not know he would fight so violently, and he cut at least one and drove his blade into another. A dagger flashed, silver and sharp. The pain in his chest was dazzling and then he knew nothing.

He thought his soul began to make its way through the bare trees towards heaven; then something in his body called, and it returned within his bruised ribs and huddled there. The stone was cold beneath him, his chest was on fire and his gown wet. Two men lifted him, and he sagged; pulled between heaven and earth, he was jerked and troubled towards some warmth. Fire crackled. Hands touched his face; someone was binding his chest. Then he passed from consciousness for a long time until, waking somewhat later, he found himself on a bedding of rugs on the floor before his own kitchen fire with several people about him. The first face was Harvey's; the others neighbors', and still there was one more, a face which swam in and out of his mind.

He was in his own bed then, and drowsy with whatever had been given him against the pain. He lay behind the half-drawn bed curtains, between dreams and wakefulness. There was the wardrobe, the shadows of his cassocks on the wooden pegs. From the kitchen below he heard the murmur of voices, and slept again.

The door creaked: he moved his lips to inquire who it might be, was too sleepy, and knew nothing more for some minutes. Then he became aware that a candle had been placed in the sconce which glittered faintly against the painting of Shagspere and the heap of books on the shelf. History books, the classical world and early England. His lips were cracked. "Harvey," he croaked.

No one answered, and he knew himself alone.

Again came comforting voices from below, and the smell of beef broth drifted up the steps. He tried to raise himself to one elbow, and gasped with sudden pain. Furious at his lack of strength, he sank back again and croaked out as best he could, "Art friends this time, I sense it . . . come!"

Light footsteps sounded in the hall, the door creaked again, and in the faint light a woman stood there. The next he knew she was sitting beside him, and her hand when she took his was warm. It seemed natural to him, in the dullness of his pain and drugged sleep, that his wife should be sitting there, though he was too weary to wonder how it could be. He was not capable at that moment of feeling many things, and only knew that he was content in the way he had been on cold winter nights when he came in shivering from a midnight call and she opened her arms to warm him. He lay back on the pillows and smiled up at her, and after a time she bent her head and kissed his mouth.

"Art in pain?"

"Aye, some."

"Art glad I've come?"

"Must ask? Where's the lad?"

"In Paris; my brother brought me."

"Cecily, the old man's dead."

"Sweet love, I am truly truly sorry. You loved him very much, as did I, funny, bad-tempered old fellow as he was!"

Voices drifted from below. His ran his tongue over his lips and frowned slightly as he listened. "Christ's blood!" he whispered, hoarse and incredulous. "Cecily, is it Bartlett below? Henry Bartlett?"

"Aye, he's come."

He again tried to rise. "I shall go down and make him go! I shall beat him as he deserves!"

"Nicholas, listen to me! He came in the night with his men and fought off the others. He said he knew they'd come for you, and he had the house watched. Now he says you must leave, or they'll come back again and he may not be here to stop it." She began to weep, wiping her sleeve over her eyes.

He watched her with such tenderness that the other emotions fell from him. "Oh my love," he said wistfully. "I'm growing old. What can that mean? Incapacitated or soon to be so . . . there goes the old priest, the old doctor! But the worse is I've failed. Peace on earth, live in harmony with your neighbor . . . these were not simply words to me." Then because she could not stop weeping, he carefully raised his arm and drew her down against his shoulder. The candle flickered against the walls. "Cecily," he murmured gently. "Cecily."

It was many days before he was well enough to travel. People came to wish them a safe journey, while outside in the garden and churchyard two young soldiers walked. Bartlett had gone away and not returned. Harvey remained, sleeping in the attic until the last evening.

Just before dawn, Nicholas made his way cautiously down the steps to the parlor. He took lenses and microscopes, papers and writings from the desk and packed them into small boxes and satchels. These would travel with him. He took keepsakes from his prayer desk, and the small portrait of Wentworth as well.

In the garden the first sunlight was glimmering on the top of the western brick wall, catching the leafless branches of the quince tree. John was bundling twigs by the shed. He was filled suddenly with such grief that he sat down on the small bench and covered his face with his hands. My God, this city and this place . . . this beautiful place. No, he could not go . . . they would have to go without him. He would arm himself and continue here as he had been. He would hang out his physician's sign, and take another apprentice.

Then it passed, and he looked up. The sun was rising slowly, touching stone spires and tile roofs, gutter and post. It was all so dear to him, more than he had ever known and more than he could ever say. Still, he knew then that he must go, for the work he must do now was elsewhere. Yet more than anything, he understood that however long he was away, he would return. He would walk from Cripplegate down the old streets, past the taverns. He would unlock his church, and chase the swallows from the roof beams and the mice from behind the pulpit. He would hang up his sign before the dispensary door. And then he would return here to the garden, where the quinces would be ripe and the smell of sweet rosemary, thyme, and sun-warmed brick would be waiting for him.

Dobson was gravely holding the horses before the house. The small party mounted and turned towards the city gates and the ferry which would take them to Gravesend, and then over the channel to France.

Epilogue: France, 1648

T HE WAR BETWEEN COUNTRY AND KING CONTINUED FOR SOME TIME:
weekly came the smuggled reports of battles, losses, and despair.
They called it civil war: it remained to them an uncivil thing,
dirty and infinitely wrong. The cavaliers in exile grew shabby; their hair
fell from curl, their lace wore into holes. Some gave up, some died. The
Queen had sold everything. They lived in poverty. The King was taken
prisoner somewhere in sight and sound of the sea and awaited trial.

In the first months of his exile, Nicholas dreamt strange, distorted,
terrible dreams every night, from which he woke sweaty and crying aloud.
In half of them or more, Tom Wentworth came to him. One day he took
a piece of paper and quill and wrote, "Dear Tom . . . " Stunned, he gazed
down at the emptiness of the sheet. Sometimes in his walks he found
himself speaking to the Yorkshireman. He thought of him so tenderly
that he did not recall his roughness.

He wondered sometimes if it were a good thing to love so much as he had done: he had tried to keep away from it, to shut himself in a little room. Yet he knew now that even if he had failed for a time, he would somewhere find the strength to bring his world to the way it had been before. Friendship, faith, and learning: nothing was dearer. For these he would stand as long as God gave him life.

Historical Notes

Of the interpretation of history in a fictional form:

Few periods of history can be more complicated to present in depth than that of England's seventeenth century, whose turbulent conflicts eventually tore apart the country and brought about the death of the gentle King. Charles Stuart had not the character for his office, but upheld it to the end because he felt God had divinely ordained him. It was not a unique belief, but at this time in history it was roughly challenged. Not only the monarchy but an entire way of life was destroyed for some years: science, the arts, and religious expression suffered badly.

Yet this, of course, is a novel not so much about Charles Stuart and his greater followers, but about one man who was scientist, doctor, husband, father, and priest, and how first the great richness and then the disintegration of this world affected him. He knew the value of it and what it would cost to lose it. Certainly of all the societies mankind has known, Elizabethan/Stuart England was among the most glorious. Amid the joy and turbulence of this age, I have set this story of friendship.

An enormous simplification of the politics of the period was necessary to encompass them within these pages; the rights and wrongs of the fall of the government and on whom the responsibility rests are yet being hotly debated. There has been some minor alteration of time and events for the sake of dramatic continuity, but I have kept to the general spirit of the era and its conflicts.

Of historical characters:

James Stuart, reigned 1603–1625, was the son of the unfortunate Mary Queen of Scots, beheaded by her cousin Queen Elizabeth. He came to the throne upon Elizabeth's death. "A good King," he wrote, "acknowledgeth himself ordained for his people, received from God a burden of government, whereof he must be countable." A crafty, intelligent man, he commissioned the great translation of the Bible which bears his name.

Charles Stuart, reigned 1625–1649, was a small, fastidious, deeply religious man who loved art and horses and was a dedicated husband and father. Originally destined for a life in the church, he became heir to the throne when his older brother died. His belief in the divine right of kings would bring about his downfall.

Henrietta Maria, 1609–1669, was the daughter of Henry IV of France and Marie de' Medici and came to England at the age of fifteen to marry Charles Stuart. At first a difficult marriage, it grew to be an extremely happy one. She fought unceasingly for her husband's rights, and died many years after him.

Thomas Wentworth, Lord Strafford, 1593–1641, was the eldest son of an old Yorkshire landowner and became head of his family at the age of nineteen upon the death of his father. Ambitious, brilliant, loyal, a devoted husband and friend though a harsh administrator, he rose under the King against the growing animosity of landowners and nobles. Having become a symbol of the power of the crown, he was struck down and executed in 1641. Charles Stuart never forgave himself for allowing it to be done.

Though he was condemned by his enemies, those close to him cherished him deeply. His friend George Radclyffe wrote, "I lost in his death a treasure which no earthly thing can countervail; such a friend as never man within the compass of my knowledge had; so excellent a friend, and so much mine." Lord Strafford's last letter to the King from prison, quoted in part in this novel, is an actual historical document.

Sir Francis Bacon, 1561–1626, Lord Chancellor and scientist, is best known today for his exquisite essays and his insistence in scientific experimentation.

George Villiers, Lord Buckingham, 1592–1628, was raised from little but his good looks by King James, who was in love with him, to the position of his chief counselor. However, James's son Charles also esteemed Buckingham as a friend above all others, entrusting him with wars and monopolies to the great resentment of many men. He was assassinated by an unemployed soldier with a tenpenny knife.

William Laud, 1573–1645, was born in Reading, the son of a clothier, and for many years was a dedicated scholar and teacher in Oxford. A religious man, he rose under Charles Stuart to direct not only the church but much of the government. Some say it was his intolerance which made the country fall. He was put to death by Parliament at the age of seventy-two and is still considered by many Anglicans to have died a martyr for his church.

William Prynne, 1600–1669, barrister of Lincoln's Inn, wrote bitter, seditious pamphlets against the crown that brought him repeated punishment. He later served Parliament as prosecutor and helped bring down William Laud.

William Harvey, 1578–1657, physician, was educated in Cambridge and Padua and later discovered the circulation of the blood. According to the biographer Aubrey, Harvey read a book under a hedge during the battle of Edgehill and was "wont to say that man was but a great, mischievous Baboon." Many of his research papers were destroyed during the Civil War.

John Heminges, ?–1630, the informal dean of the London stage, was a close friend of Shakespeare's. Originally a grocer, he banded together with a few other men to form a troupe which eventually under the patronage of James Stuart became the King's Men. He and his wife, Rebecca, had thirteen children, and he asked to be buried next to her when he died in 1630. With his friend Condell he collected Shakespeare's plays into a folio; without this, many of them would be lost to us today.

John Lowin, 1576–1653, actor, famous for his Falstaff and Henry VIII, was one of the men who took over the management of the King's Men when John Heminges died. By the time the Civil War broke out he was in too poor health to fight, but opened a tavern, which did not do well; he died in poverty.

Anthony Van Dyck, 1599–1641, artist from Antwerp, was appointed in 1632 as "Principal Painter in ordinary to their Majesties." He kept several mistresses, was excellently paid, and became an equal of and friend to many of his patrons.

Of the remaining historical figures, actors *James Taylor* and *Henry Condell* were members of the King's Men; *William Juxon,* priest, became Archbishop of Canterbury during the Restoration; *Ben Jonson,* playwright, was a true seventeenth-century character whose wit and outsized personality remain with us to this day. I have called *Will Shagspere* by this alternative Elizabethan spelling to allow his depiction as a person and not a literary deity. *John Pym* can be studied in depth in any English seventeenth-century history, as can the man who eventually swept away royalism and created the Commonwealth, *Oliver Cromwell.*

Many readers who have read the first volume of this trilogy have assumed that *Nicholas Cooke* is a historical figure. Alas he is not, though he is derived from many men of the period. To be a churchman and writer, scientist and physician, merchant and soldier was not beyond the capacity of many gifted sons of the seventeenth century. The characters of *Kate, Andrew Heminges, Henry Bartlett, Lawrence Avery, Timothy Keyes,* and the lords *Dobson* and *Harrington* are fictional, though based heavily on my studies of men and women of the period. Many an educated seventeenth-century lady would devote her life to the royalist cause; from these remarkable women I have derived *Cecilia.* Her discerning sketches of the trial of Lord Strafford I have taken from those of the Flemish artist Wenceslas Hollar, which have come down to us.

Of the English church between the Reformation and the Civil War:

When England broke away from Rome in the period 1529–1550, much was destroyed, including stained-glass windows, statues, vestments; often the reredos was torn down and altar smashed, a plain table substituting for communion. Archbishop Laud restored a great deal of the beauty in the 1630s. In this period of history, church and state were one; most enlightened men of the times would have not considered it could, or should, be otherwise. During the Civil War, much more church property was willfully destroyed as being idolatrous and "popish."

The St. Paul's which Nicholas knew was larger than the present structure and, when its steeple was intact, somewhat higher. The traditional garb for a priest, mandated by canonical law in 1603, was a long buttoned coat, a neck ruff, and a four-cornered hat. I have called the coat a cassock, as it would be called today.

Prayer book quotations are from the 1559 Book of Common Prayer, with the exception of the words spoken on the death of Arabella, which, though they may be much older, do not appear until the 1928 edition.

Of the monarchy and Parliament:

Since the field of Runnymede in 1215, when the nobles forced John Lackland to sign Magna Carta, giving them some rights of constitutional restraints on royal power, there had been an uneasy tussle between crown and principal citizens. When Henry Tudor dissolved the monasteries and other church institutions in the mid-sixteenth century, he and his successors gave much of the church's property to the nobles in return for loyalty. By the advent of Charles in 1625, these men had become too powerful and strong-minded to be easily controlled.

Of medicine and the scientific life of the period:

The first half of the seventeenth century included Harvey's discovery of the circulation of the blood and his work on fetal development. Microscopy was still considered little more than a gentlemen's amusement, and the difficulties of distorted glass and insufficient magnification were abysmal. Antonie van Leeuwenhoek would discover protozoa under the lens in 1675 and bacteria in 1683; Nicholas preempts the particulars of these discoveries in this novel by a little less than forty years.

Though the Royal Society of Science did not officially commence until 1660, many men in London and Oxford met informally from the late sixteenth century through the Puritan period to discuss all facets of what was then called natural science. An actual teaching hospital was not established in London until the mid-eighteenth century, although there was speculation upon it as early as the time of this book. Such hospitals as there were in Stuart London were primitive and intended principally for the homeless and felons. Seldom was more than one physician attached to each. Bedlam, a colloquialism for Bethlehem, did little more than restrain the mentally ill.

As there were in the sixteenth and seventeenth centuries few serious men of science in Europe, it was natural that they seek each other out. Letters are still extant between Johannes Kepler, Thomas Hariot, and Galileo. A serious scholar of science would journey if he could to other countries to meet another man of the same infatuation.

Of the theater:

When William Shakespeare died in 1616, the King's Men were already the most prosperous company in London. His colleague John Heminges remained titular head of all the actors until his death, whereupon John Lowin and Taylor took over this work. The theaters were closed in 1642 and the Globe torn down one year later, somewhat earlier than it appears in this book.

Of the language used in the novel:

I have used an adaptive language, to keep some of the feeling of Stuart English. However, I do not hear the spoken language of the period to be nearly as slangy and free in profanity as that of the period of Good Queen Bess but twenty to forty years earlier. (Compare the dialogue of playwrights after 1625 with those of the 1590s.) Charles Stuart's formality filtered down through all the classes.

Of the London Nicholas knew:

It is still possible to find much of the world of early Stuart London in the present-day city. Not least is the new Globe Theater with its worthy ghosts, rising again as of this writing on the banks of the Thames almost three hundred and fifty years after it was torn down by the Puritans. If you remain on the south side of the river and walk west, you will come to Lambeth Palace, which should if possible also be seen by riverboat as any seventeenth-century man would have approached it. The gatehouse is the very one Nicholas passed under on his visitors to see William Laud. The picture of that controversial Archbishop of Canterbury by Van Dyck which fell to the floor and presaged Laud's own fall has been hung once more on the wall.

Across the river and slightly to the west, you will find the remains of the old palace of Westminster: the abbey, and the hall which saw the trials of Strafford and Laud. The original Parliamentary chambers were destroyed by fire in the nineteenth century. Walking north, you come to the banqueting hall, now the only remaining section of the two-thousand-room Whitehall Palace; there masques and great dinners were given and the slight, curly-haired, gracious King met foreign ambassadors. Turning east on the Strand, you will note where the great houses once stood by the names of the streets and squares; down Fleet Street, called for the river now diverted underground, you enter into what was the old gated city.

Parts of the walls are still preserved. The remains of a somewhat later St. Mary Aldermanbury can be found near a monument to the actors Heminges and Condell opposite the Guild Hall. But for the Staple Inn on Fleet Street, you will not find the overhanging half-timbered houses, for they were swept away first by the Great Fire of 1666 and then, in this century, by the bombs of war. Our present St. Paul's, as I have said, is smaller than the one Nicholas knew.

You can, however, walk freely about the Tower of London, where Thomas Wentworth and William Laud were imprisoned, and then wander over to All Hallows Church, Barking, where Laud's body was brought for burial by his faithful friends. And then if you wish you can turn your footsteps down to the Thames and stand for a time watching that great river, which has seen so much history as it flowed these hundreds of years under London Bridge and to the sea.

Acknowledgments

Research for *The Physician of London* was conducted in London and New York City.

In London, I am most grateful to the Lambeth Palace Library, where I was admitted to study the journals and letters of William Laud. I would like to thank the late Sam Wanamaker, whose restoration of the Globe Theater on the banks of the Thames greatly inspired me; also, the staffs of the Guild Hall, London Museum, St. Paul's Cathedral, and every small church within the old city walls whose boundaries I walked again and again both in person and in my imagination in the creation of this novel.

In New York I am grateful for the collections of the New York Public Library, the Rare Book Room of the Academy of Medicine, the St. Mark's Library of the General Theological Seminary, and the lovely little library of the English-Speaking Union. I would like to give particular acknowledgment to the works of Dr. A. L. Rowse, whose writings on the Elizabethans opened a whole world to me in my adolescence, and Dame C. V. Wedgwood, who first made me love the complicated character of Thomas Wentworth, Lord

Strafford. I would also like to acknowledge A. Wolf's marvelous study on the science and technology of the seventeenth century. Without these and the hundreds of other excellent historical works used in my research, this book would not have been possible.

I would like to thank my rector, the Reverend Dr. John Andrew of St. Thomas Church New York, for the heritage of faith which he has shared with me; the Reverend Dr. Duane Arnold, for his evocative historical lectures and his advice about the politics of seventeenth-century church and state; the Reverend Roberts E. Ehrgott, for his advice on particular period church matters; and the Reverend Stuart Kenworthy and the Reverend Ivan Weiser for their friendship and interest. I would also like to thank Professor Thomas Pendleton, coeditor of the *Shakespeare Newsletter,* for his advice on the King's Men after the death of Shakespeare.

Much acknowledgment is due to my writing group for their constant loving support and suggestions and the many long conversations when I needed them: Elsa Rael, Casey Kelly, Katherine Kirkpatrick, Judith Lindbergh, and Ruth Henderson; and likewise to our much-beloved mentor, Madeleine L'Engle. Also to Russell O'Neal Clay, Isabelle Holland, Bruce Bawer, Chris Davenport, Ellen Beschler, Susan Waide, Sol Rael, John Neiswanger, Linda Lanza, Peggy Harrington, Dr. Saul Farber, Judith Ackerman, Renee Cafiero, and the McGaughey/Whitehead families, and in most tender memory to Carol Saltus, Phelicia Wingfield, Jimmy DeVries, and Edwin Manchester. To the staff, clergy, and parishioners at St. Thomas Church New York, and the St. Thomas Choir of Men and Boys, whose beautiful singing of seventeenth-century music much inspired me; to my friends at the Cathedral of St. John the Divine and the Sisters of the Community of the Holy Spirit for their dear support of my work. To my editor Mary Cunnane for her wise shepherding of this book and wonderful humor, her assistant Nicole Wan, and all the rest of the staff at W. W. Norton. To my colleagues at Manpower Demonstration Research Corporation, who so graciously adjusted to my needs for free time when writing a complex second novel while launching a first, particularly Patt Pontevolpe, Judy Griessman, and Michael Wilde. To many others who have helped in so many ways and whose names are too numerous to include here, and to any whom I may have inadvertently forgotten. And of course to my family: my father, James Mathieu, and stepmother, Viraja; my sisters, Jennie and Gabrielle; my daughter-in-law Jessica and my sons, Jesse and James.

As of this writing, Shakespeare's Globe Theater is rising again after 350 years on the banks of the Thames. Much help is needed in this enterprise, and interested readers are encouraged to write to Friends of Shakespeare's Globe, PO Box No. 70, London, SE1 9EN, for information.